TALES OF THE LOST

Kravae: Betrayal of a Mage
A Planar Lost Story

The Blackened Yonder
Planar Lost: Book One

The Ember Reach
Planar Lost: Book Two

The Faceless Man
Planar Lost: Book Three

The Vile God
Planar Lost: Book Four

THE BLACKENED YONDER

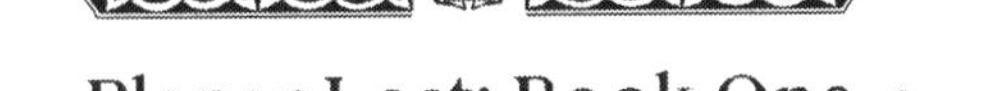

Planar Lost: Book One

THE BLACKENED YONDER

CONTENT NOTE
The following work depicts violence which may be disturbing to some readers.

Published by The Lost Press

Library of Congress Control Number: 2020914917

ISBN: 978-1-7363677-0-4 (eBook | Standard Edition)
ISBN: 978-1-7363677-1-1 (Print | Standard Edition)
ISBN: 978-1-7363677-2-8 (Print | Special Edition)

Edited by Mark Antiporda
Interior design by Bodie Dykstra
Standard Edition cover art and chapter sigil by Diletta De Santis
Special Edition cover art by Daniele Serra
Standard Edition cover layout by GermanCreative
Special Edition cover layout by OliviaProDesign
Title page, maps, and calendar by Veronika Wunderer
Map and flag concepts by J. Gibson

First Edition

Printed in the United States of America

Connect with J. Gibson
Website: www.jgibsonwrites.com
Social Media: @PlanarLost

Subscribe to the newsletter at the link above to keep up with releases, discounts, reviews, news, and more.

★★★★★
Remember to leave a review wherever this book is sold!

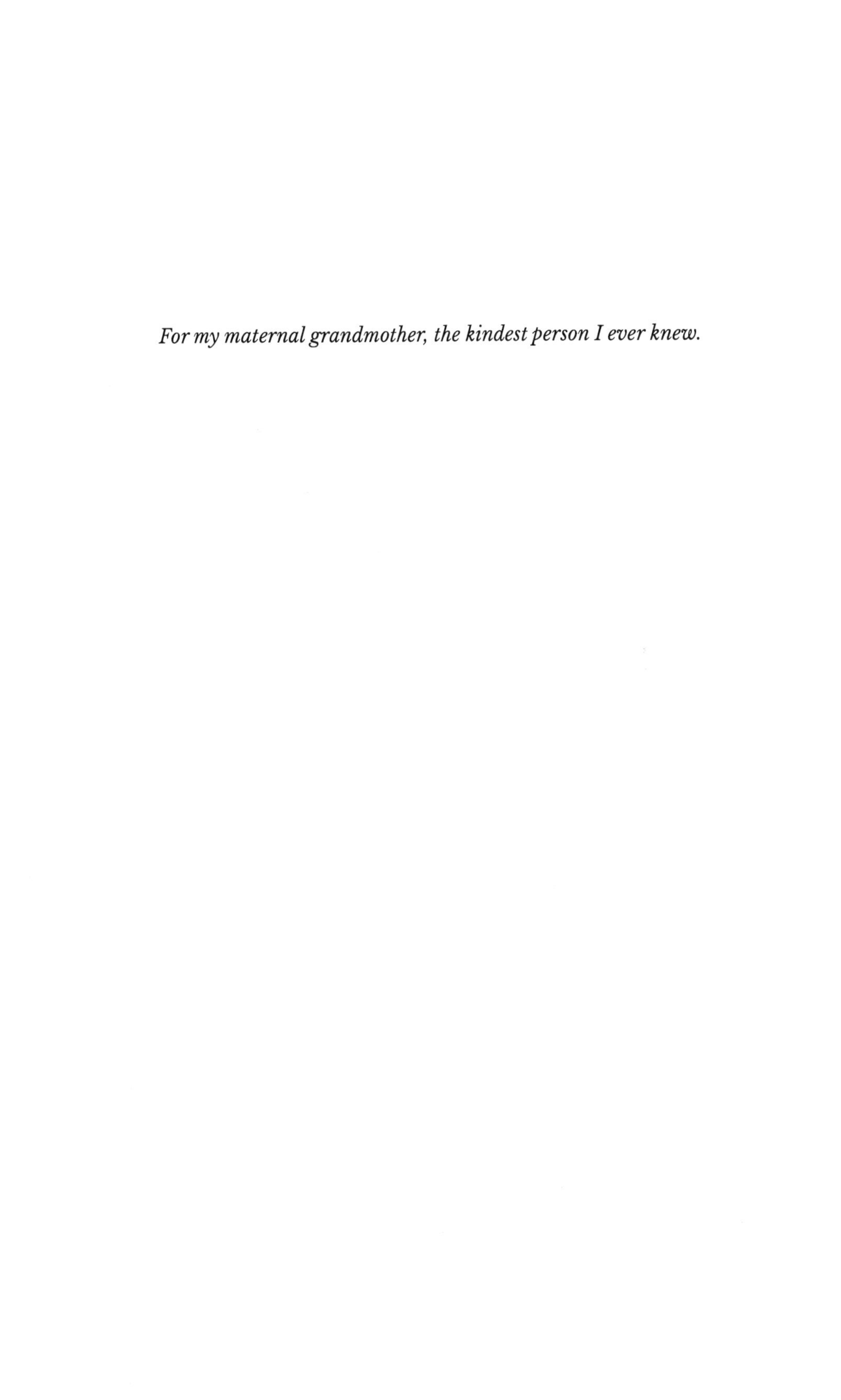

For my maternal grandmother, the kindest person I ever knew.

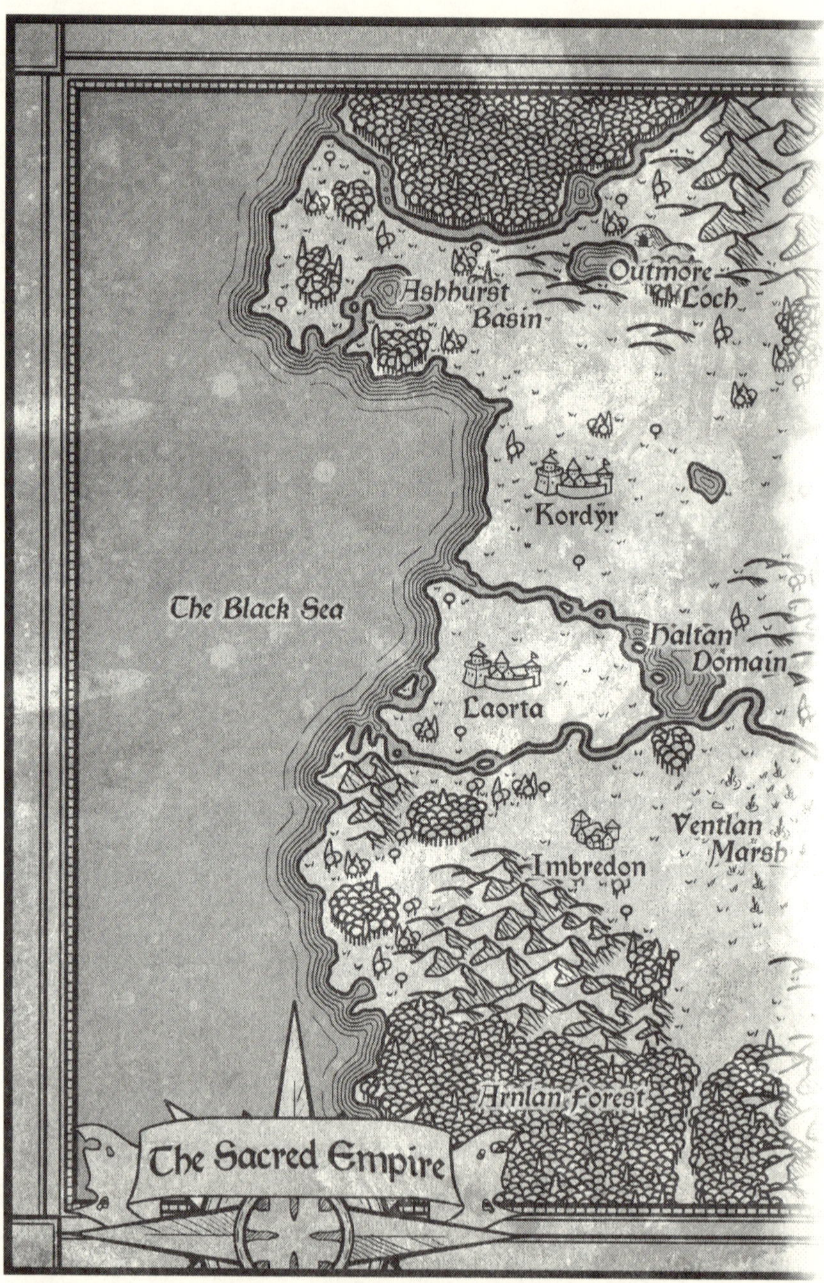
Ashhurst
Basin
Outmore
Loch
Kordyr
The Black Sea
Haltan
Domain
Laorta
Ventlan
Marsh
Imbredon
Arnlan Forest
The Sacred Empire

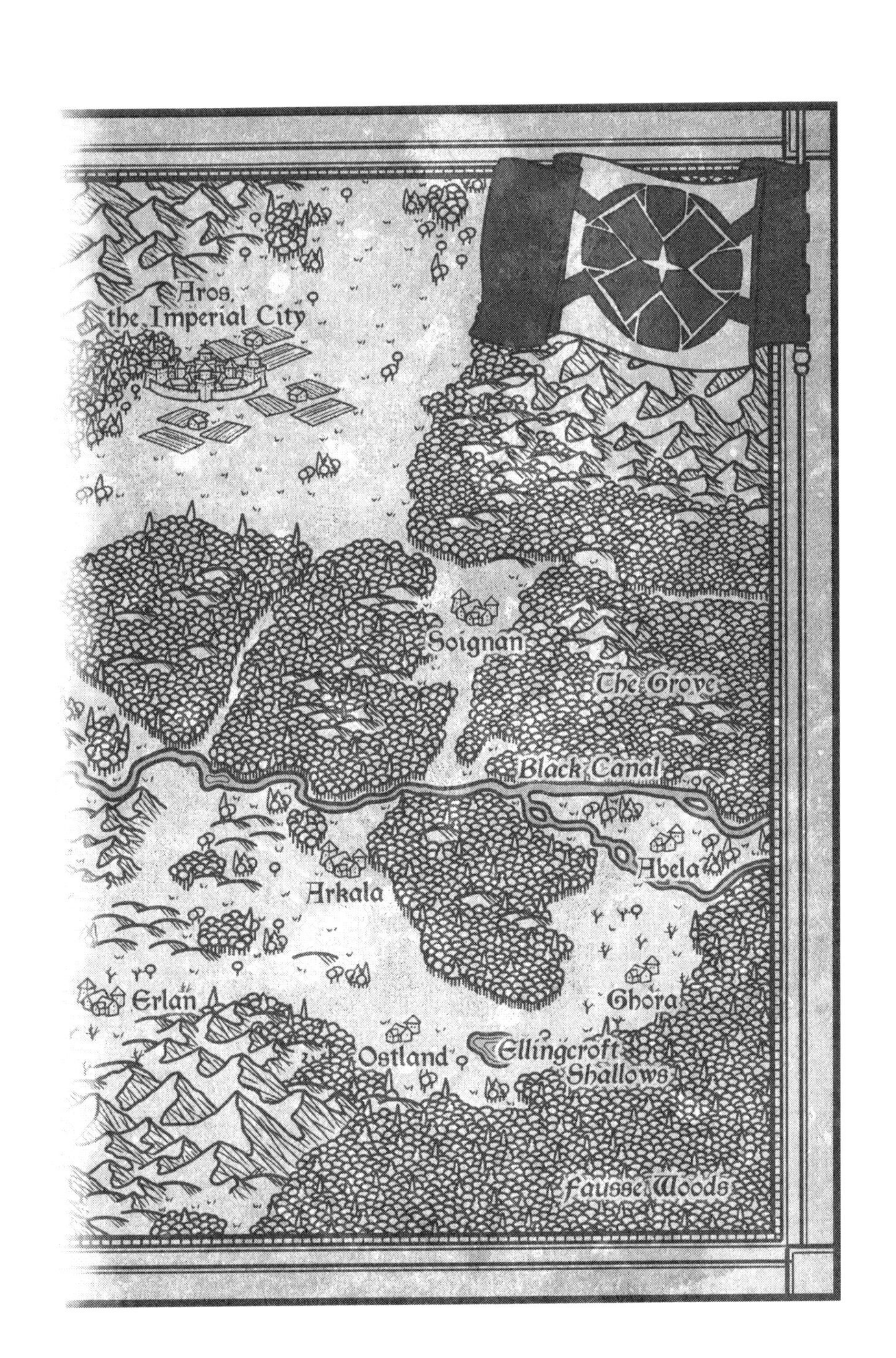
Aros,
the Imperial City
Soignan
The Grove
Black Canal
Abela
Arkala
Erlan
Ghora
Ostland
Ellingcroft
Shallows
Fausse Woods

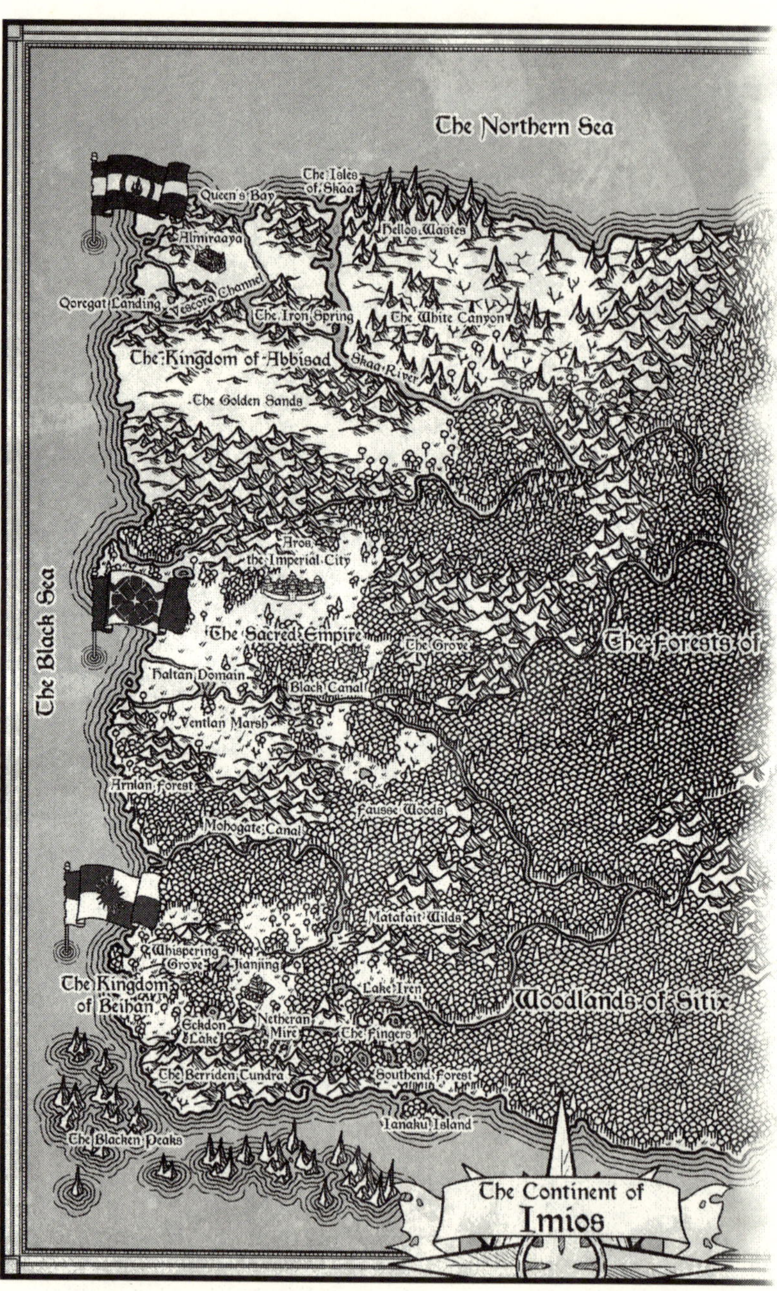
The Northern Sea
The Isles of Skaa
Queen's Bay
Helios Wastes
Almiraaya
Vescora Channel
Qoregat Landing
The Iron Spring
The White Canyon
The Kingdom of Abbisad
Skaa River
The Golden Sands
Aros, the Imperial City
The Black Sea
The Sacred Empire
The Grove
The Forests of
Haltan Domain
Black Canal
Ventlan Marsh
Arnlan Forest
Fausse Woods
Mohogate Canal
Matafait Wilds
Whispering Grove
Jianjing
The Kingdom of Beihan
Lake Iren
Woodlands of Sitix
Eckdon Lake
Netheran Mire
The Fingers
The Berriden Tundra
Southend Forest
Ianaku Island
The Blacken Peaks
The Continent of
Imios

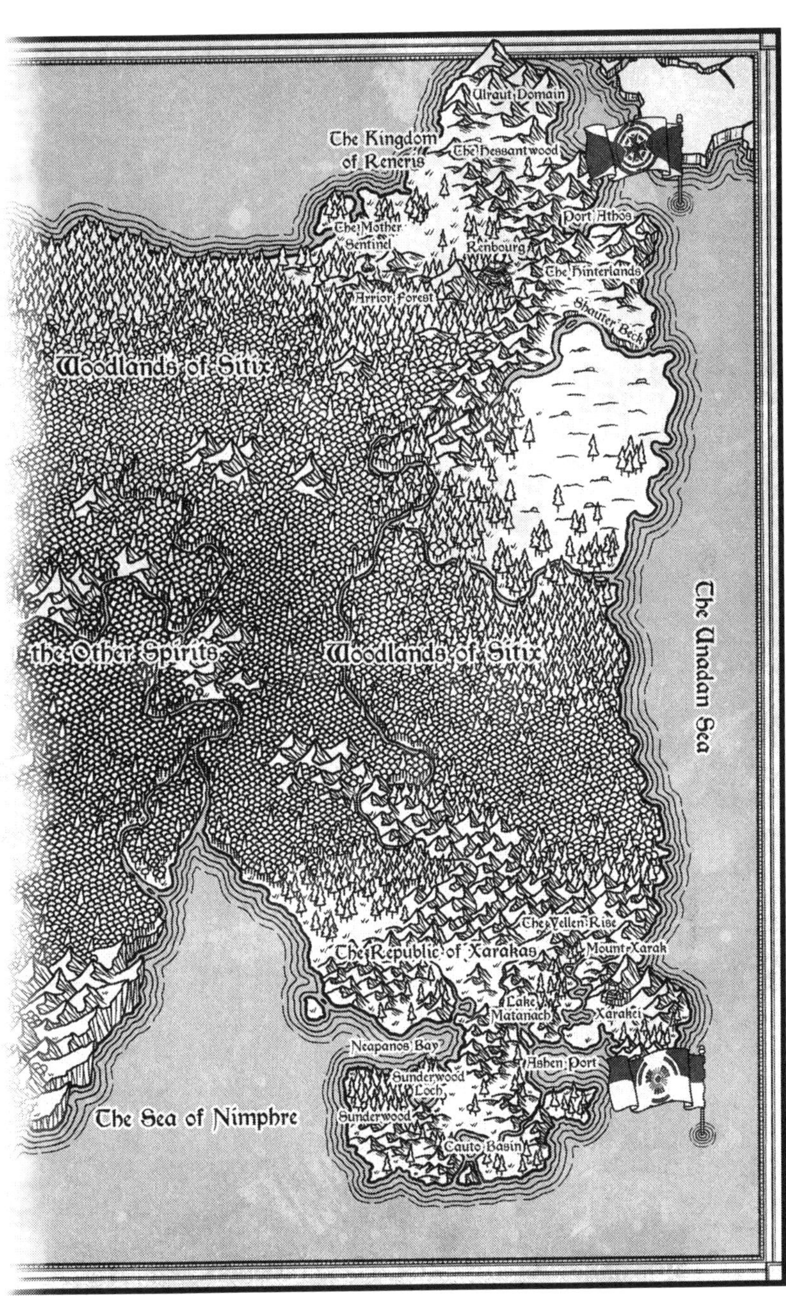
Ulraut Domain
The Kingdom of Reneris
The Hessantwood
Port Athos
The Mother Sentinel
Renbourg
The Hinterlands
Arrior Forest
Shauter Beck
Woodlands of Sitix
the Other Spirits
Woodlands of Sitix
The Unadan Sea
The Vellen Rise
The Republic of Xarakas
Mount Xarak
Lake Matanach
Xarakei
Neapanos Bay
Ashen Port
Sunderwood Loch
Sunderwood
The Sea of Nimphre
Cauto Basin

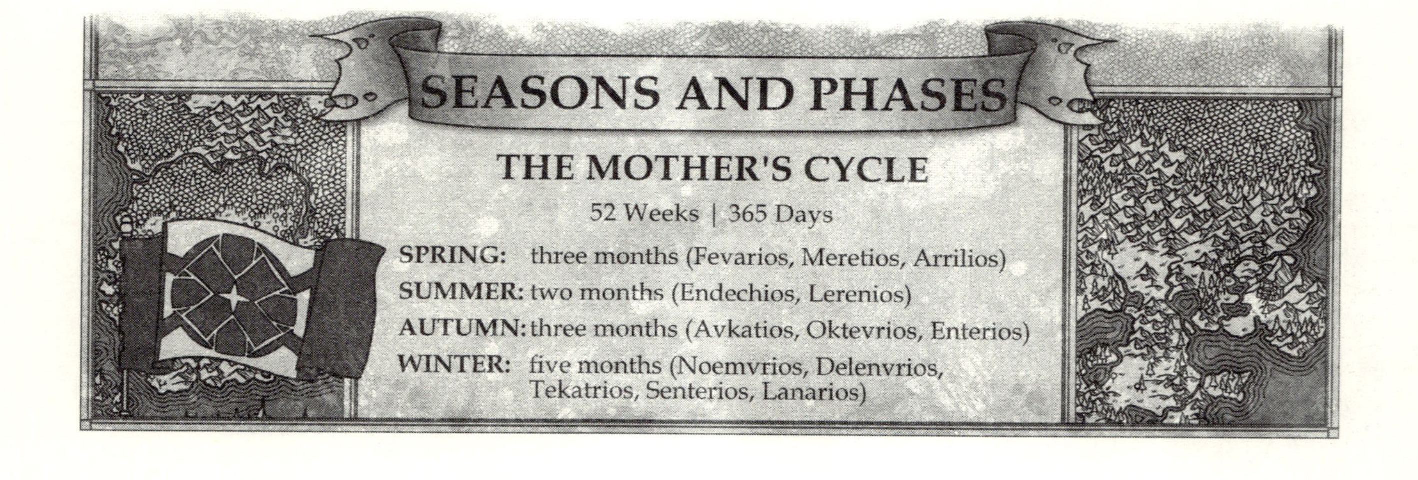

SEASONS AND PHASES

THE MOTHER'S CYCLE

52 Weeks | 365 Days

SPRING: three months (Fevarios, Meretios, Arrilios)
SUMMER: two months (Endechios, Lerenios)
AUTUMN: three months (Avkatios, Oktevrios, Enterios)
WINTER: five months (Noemvrios, Delenvrios, Tekatrios, Senterios, Lanarios)

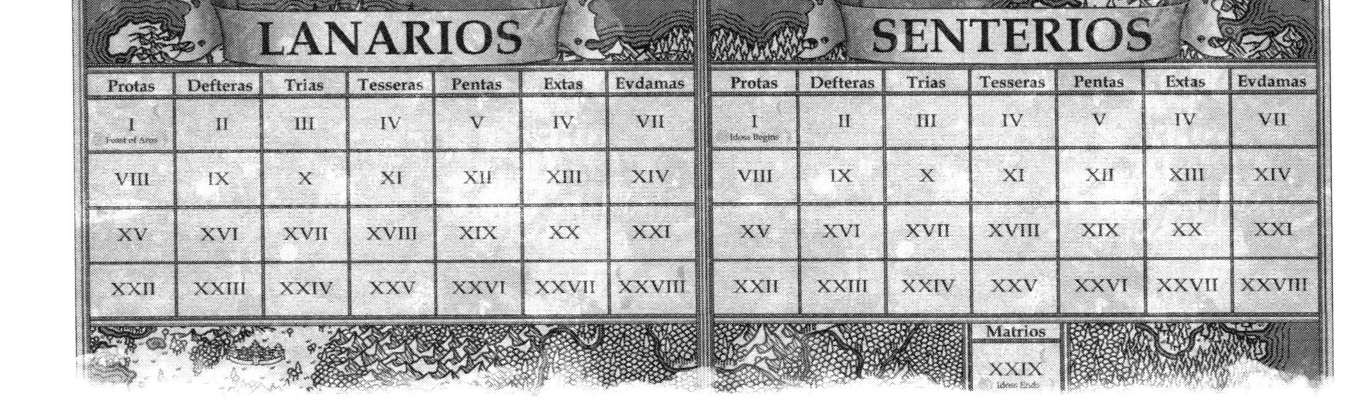

LANARIOS

Protas	Defteras	Trias	Tesseras	Pentas	Extas	Evdamas
I Feast of Aros	II	III	IV	V	IV	VII
VIII	IX	X	XI	XII	XIII	XIV
XV	XVI	XVII	XVIII	XIX	XX	XXI
XXII	XXIII	XXIV	XXV	XXVI	XXVII	XXVIII

SENTERIOS

Protas	Defteras	Trias	Tesseras	Pentas	Extas	Evdamas
I Idoss Begins	II	III	IV	V	IV	VII
VIII	IX	X	XI	XII	XIII	XIV
XV	XVI	XVII	XVIII	XIX	XX	XXI
XXII	XXIII	XXIV	XXV	XXVI	XXVII	XXVIII

Matrios
XXIX Idoss Ends

CHAPTER I: DEALINGS

Athenne

She prayed. Her eyes rolled skyward in search of heeding, and she opened herself, as she had learned in her youth, to the All-Mother, Queen of the Celestia. She sought direction in line with the burden of their hour. As one of many sacred daughters under the stars, she made a single, solemn promise, and asked for their safety and success. When she finished, she breathed deep and bottled it, the task at hand returning to her mind.

After this day, I'll be a terrorist. The Church will hunt me down.

Athenne knelt before the incense altar of a Matrian sanctuary, at the head of a fire-gutted church. "Why do you think they left this place?" she said over her shoulder to Uldyr. Beyond the odor of smoldering incense crept a scent of stale earth and aged animal filth, the outside encroaching on crumbling human edifice. At times, she longed for the whole world to smell this way; for nature to overtake women and men in their dreadful stone houses and opulent temples, to dash away the artifice and return the plane to its inborn glory.

Exhalations frosting the air, Athenne's hands fell to her sides.

The censer at her front and the candle next to her, whose slight tongue of flame fluttered against unrelenting shadow, lent the church its meager warmth, too little to keep her fingers from going numb. Light from the four moons, bisected by the three rings of the sky, peeked through sparse, rolling clouds past windows and fissures in the structure's walls and ceiling.

Her gaze traveled up the glass mosaic at the peak of the steps behind the altar and choral platform. *The All-Mother, Gohheia, depicted with such detail. None have witnessed Her as flesh, so whose visage is this?*

"Perhaps, too far out," Uldyr answered after some delay. "Why do you still pray?"

She rose to her feet. The candle in her hand lifted to illuminate her face. "I believe in the All-Mother. The priests, bishops, and magisters of Her Church cannot change that."

Uldyr stood a head or more above her, broad of shoulder and back, with wrists the size of her neck. She had never asked his years, but reckoned him to be in his early thirties. Despite his youthfulness otherwise, he had a rough face, battered from ages of journeying, fighting, and hard living. His long hair had the color of a forest wolf's coat, and the hue of dull slate tinted his irises. He had a sense of humor, but rarely smiled.

Athenne never asked about that, either.

As she walked along the pews, her black robes stirred grime in whirling bursts. Shattered stone, layers of dirt, and spider's web coated the surfaces around them. "Are the others to arrive soon?" She sat at the end of a row behind Uldyr, balancing her candle atop the bench ahead of her and brushing her palms together. Floating motes of flickering dust winked at her in the gloomy haze of her fire.

"Soon, by the light of the sky." Uldyr turned toward her, resting his hand on the pommel of his shortsword. He had always favored a sharp blade and the protection of a leather-faced gambeson or mail to magic. Shifts in Matrian policy and Imperial culture had strangled the Aether, the arts of every aspect, and rendered most combative spells inoperable. His preference had proved prudent.

"Are you afraid?"

"Nervous," she said. "Not afraid."

"Don't underrate this." Uldyr's face darkened. "I've been with the Saints for ages, participated in attacks on the Church, taken innocent lives in the name of our cause." His voice softened. "It wears on you."

Why is he telling me this now?

She squirmed in her seat, a block of ice against her clothes, as the drop of ache in his voice sank through her. Doubt lingered in her mind, uncertainty about the mission of the Saints and those involved. Even so, she could not betray it this night. "I care about the freedom of magic and its study. I'm here for that purpose."

Before he could reply, the doors of the church opened. Chilled wind rippled through the room, swam around its four corners and back out. In the entryway stood a woman, an elf by her pointed ears and coquelicot eyes, a shade resembling the pedals of wild corn poppies. She wore a sleeveless dress of pink and white and silver chains, rings, and bangles. Her steps carried her forth as though she floated atop a calm pond, graceful and even.

Aitrix Kravae.

Athenne got up, steady as a newborn calf, her chest tight. She glanced at Uldyr, who seemed unmoved, a boulder embedded in a dim setting of forgotten architecture.

No surprise.

These were his comrades in a long struggle.

Behind the elf were two others, a woman and a man in fur-trimmed black and brown leathers, riding breeches, and muddy boots. She had expected a greater showing for such an important event.

The elf's eyes danced over Athenne. "You've brought a friend." Her flat tone masked her disposition.

"She'll be a powerful asset in this venture. She is a strong and learned materialist who believes the Aether should flow uninhibited." Uldyr gestured toward Athenne, as if beckoning her to introduce herself.

Aitrix's expression remained unchanged. "Your name?"

"Athenne Zedd. I'm from Reneris, where Uldyr and I met." Her heart galloped. "Orilon, actually."

"A tough city, or so I've heard."

She attempted to compose herself. "Yes, Mys—Kravae?" Athenne didn't want to shame Uldyr on her first meeting with the Saints, especially not with Kravae herself possibly in attendance.

"That's the rumor," Aitrix quipped. She smiled, to Athenne's relief. "If Uldyr trusts you, then so do I. Give me no reason to doubt you, and I'll show you boundless faith. I'll never ask more of you than I believe you capable."

"Uldyr has told me as much."

"That said, I must warn you." Aitrix's smile faded. "If you ever betray this order, consider your life forfeit. Once you pledge your allegiance to us, you are one of us. Hereafter, should you elect to conclude your membership, you consent to having your memory of the Saints erased—in totality."

Erased? Uldyr had told her nothing of this stipulation. He stared at her from the side and she returned his gaze. *Surely, he meant to tell me. It must have slipped his mind.*

Losing her recollection of the Saints would mean that if she left, they would take the majority of her memories of Uldyr. Most of their discussions had focused on the Saints, from this meeting to a vague future of the organization. She and Uldyr would become almost as strangers.

"Uldyr informed me. I am committed to the mission of the Saints." She lied, at least about Uldyr. This knowledge compelled her to remain. *How often can there be deserters?*

"Then we shall proceed," Aitrix said. "For the benefit of our uninitiated, the gentleman to my left is Eclih Phredran. The lady to my right is Bhathric Ezeis. Eclih is a mentalist, Bhathric is a materialist, Matrian wards notwithstanding. They are two of our best, and have assisted me in a number of endeavors."

"A pleasure." Eclih bowed. He looked more elven than human by the lean, sharp length of his features, but his green eyes and rounded ears laid bare his humanity.

Bhathric flashed a grin, her arms folded behind her. "Well met." She had a steady poise and confidence. An assertive brightness layered her timbre like flowers over a field.

"Eclih and Bhathric came to the Saints after they were shunned in the overlands," Uldyr told Athenne. "They deemed Eclih a wizard for his psychic gifts, and Bhathric, a witch, for her interest in necromancy. Fortunately, the Saints welcome practitioners of every talent and inclination."

"Small words from small, frightened minds attempting to contain what they can't comprehend," Aitrix said.

Eclih glanced over his allies and grinned. "This is the spirit of our calling. It's no secret that ordination isn't necessary for magecraft, so why must we involve the gods? Why does the Church condemn and shun those with unique abilities if their own god bestowed them?"

"Any deviation of conviction, they view as an existential threat," Bhathric added, in a natural flow of sentiment. "It's why they suppress schismatic factions and prohibit the reading of so-called subversive texts. It's why they hired Forgebrand daggerhands to murder me."

Disbelief rattled Athenne. Never had she heard anyone utter such contempt for the Church or accuse members of the Clergy of such heinous misdeeds. She found it difficult to accept. "The Church hired mercenaries, who themselves break their laws, to kill a mage for practicing necromancy?"

"I never *practiced* necromancy." Redness blazed in Bhathric's cheeks. "My crime was taking an interest in the *study* of necromancy. A curator in the Imperial City reported me for requesting a copy of *The Obsidian Manual*."

"Breiman Umbra decreed the text heretical a week prior, as every work by Abbessa Alamanor," Eclih said. "Many were ignorant of it. They made no declaration to the public."

"Not long after, they uncovered my identity and whereabouts. If not for a terror that woke me hours earlier, the daggerhand they sent would've killed me—in my sleep, no less." Bhathric stepped forward. "The Clergy covet power above all else. Consider the danger their restrictions pose. If they can make curiosity itself a crime, what else can they outlaw?" Her speech became a rasp. "What gives them the right?"

"I'd no idea they'd gone so far." Athenne looked at Uldyr and then toward the ground, her face and ears hot. She suspected there must be more to the story, but she would not press the issue.

"Do you understand?" The tension in the sanctuary ebbed at Aitrix's voice. "Magic across the Empire is at the mercy of individuals who veil their greed in false virtue. We cannot allow it to continue. The Aether must flow, unfettered by the fear and avarice of fools who long to subdue it rather than understand it." Her words snapped like a whip toward the end. "If you have any reservations, *leave now.*"

The pressure in the room swelled once more. A hostile silence descended on Athenne and bound her at the chest. "I—" She fought to sound assured. "I dedicate myself to the cause, to all of you. I long for the liberty of magic as you do." *I have not cast freely since Reneris, but can I trust these people?*

Uldyr placed his hand on her shoulder. "Though I've known Athenne a mere few months and have much to learn of her, I believe that she is faithful to the cause of the Saints, that she is worthy of becoming one of us." He looked over to her as if to encourage her, his grey eyes displaying a genuine fidelity.

Aitrix's haunting off-red gaze, like blood diluted in water, meandered between Uldyr and Athenne. "Let us get to the aim of this assembly." She signaled to Eclih with her hand and he came around her.

"This venture is our most ambitious to date." He moved to the prayer altar at the head of the sanctuary and turned to face them. "We are going to destroy the Iron Court."

Athenne's eyes widened. Such an attack would deal a significant blow to the Matrian Church and its morale. *Impressions of the Church are in decline*, Uldyr had said during their journey. *In part due to the propaganda of the Knights of Faith, fallen paladins in service of the mental god Vekshia.* If the Saints aimed to disrupt the Church's control over magic, this would be one method by which to do it.

Yet to endanger so many innocent lives, and to destroy such a consecrated space, seemed unconscionable, even for their ends. Not all members of the Clergy were a part of the Church's constraints on magic, and as best she knew as a foreigner, the Emperor had served the Sacred Empire well.

Aitrix walked to Eclih's side. "We must send a message that they cannot conceal."

"Do we assume that all members of the Church are complicit in the restriction of magic?" Athenne protested, meek but mustering a sliver of nerve. "What of the innocents? Wouldn't indiscriminate slaughter lay the reputation of our cause at the mercy of Matrian propaganda?"

"How do you propose we differentiate the guilty from the innocent?" Aitrix's observation bore into Athenne. It made her feel small. "Suppose we submit to your magnanimous discretion. How do we decide who agrees with the edicts of Breiman Umbra and who does not? Shall we walk into the Imperial Palace or the Grand Priory and interview every bishop, priest, and deacon, their children and machines? Shall we keep a detailed tally of the ayes and nays and sketches of the lot? Enlighten us of your grand design."

Athenne looked at everyone around her. Eclih and Bhathric, analyzing. Uldyr, stone-faced, grey gaze set upon the floor, forsaken by its former heartening glint. Aitrix, whose shadow seemed more like a smothering of light than its absence. She had no rebuttal, for their leader spoke the truth. *There must be no compromises if we are to realize our goal.* The deaths of innocents, including children, would forever stain her spirit. All of their spirits.

"Our aim is not the murder of innocents, as you alluded," Aitrix continued, as if reading her thoughts. "We are at war with the most powerful body on the face of the Earth. In times of war, casualties are inevitable. Many more will die if the use of magic remains confined to the hands of the few at the expense of the many. Umbra has deemed us terrorists because a world at liberty fills his coward's heart with fear. You must be willing to die for this cause, or as I stated, trouble us no longer."

"You claimed moments ago that you align yourself to us without reservation," Bhathric followed.

You cannot renege without cost. "I am with you." Athenne's hands prickled, as the feeling returning from a limb she'd slept on. Numbness, the tingling of growing sensation. Except a sense of emotion stirred, not of touch.

With all their sights on her, and with this affirmation, she had become another fletching on the arrow, guiding its way. These people, including Uldyr, had done terrible things. Their steadfast solidarity in the face of a certain mountain of corpses, bloated with death, charred, gushing red, broken, exposed their disaffection. In their view, in the eyes of Aitrix Kravae, their objectives hoisted to the absolute, beyond any concept of the value of every mortal life, or of fairness to the individual and justice.

If this was Gohheia's answer to her prayers, Athenne wished instead that there had been no reply.

CHAPTER II: UNDEATH

Garron

A chill swept over the village of Erlan that night, peculiar and alive.

At a small round table in a small stone hovel, Father Garron Latimer sat, sipping tea from a small tin cup. His blue eyes, lit in the pale light of the Earth's moons, affixed on the sky through a cracked window, caked in dust. Outside, winds whipped past, blowing the trees and grass, battering the house's thatched rooftop and rough grey exterior. Scattered clouds drifted overhead.

This hovel resembled most in the village, its thick stone walls outfitted with a window at the front and a wooden entrance door, too heavy for fewer than three people to mount. Inside, candles and an open hearth illuminated plank flooring, a single room with a bed atop a handcrafted oak frame, crude stools, tables, chairs, a chest. During severe winters, those who kept modest animals often brought them inside, to the detriment of their sanitation.

Most nights, the smells of worldly living and aromas of lesser beasts suffused the air. This evening, however, there drifted a hint of decay, a pungency as in a house of the dying. Rotted flesh, like pounds of fouled meat nearby, offensive to the senses. In a village of so few, such a stench aroused curiosity.

A foreboding crept up his neck, frigid and prickling, pins of ice. His breath became visible, puffing in white mists before his face. He clutched the lunar tear beads at his wrist.

"Father." The voice of Aefethla, his charge that night. Her words tremored. "I'm so cold."

He made his way to her bedside, knelt, and placed a hand on her forearm. Crusted at the edges, her green eyes had gone pink as a sunset sky. Her lips split like parched earth, and a paleness around her mouth set it apart from her flushed cheeks and chin. A marker of thirst.

Aefethla coughed, then inhaled, her lungs wheezing and gurgling. The cooling weeks had laid her low.

Despite Garron's labors, death marched steady in pursuit. The air held it in sight, touch, taste. Death spread through Aefethla's visage as weeds in a garden, rooting and chilling her outward from deep in the flesh, strangling her speech and ailing her motions. Garron had read these signs many times. Nonetheless, he would spend his greatest effort to save her. The Mother's children were precious in life, even when that life fought to be free.

He held the water pouch at his waist, removed the cap, and pressed the spout to her mouth. She sucked down the liquid in gulps. "Easy," he said, tilting the container away and brushing her tangled brown hair aside.

Aefethla ceased drinking and nodded.

"Rest." He plugged the pouch and stood. "I'll fetch firewood and return to tend the hearth." He pulled her bed's blanket up over her shoulders.

She shook her head again, weaker this time, and shut her eyes.

Garron made his way to the hovel's front door and opened it with restrained effort, its hinges corroded and begrimed. Vicious air from outside rushed in, gushing past him like water through a boat's leak. Shuddering, he stepped out and closed the door.

He headed for the firewood shed near the edge of the village. The shared storage arose after a vengeful frost ages prior had killed members of the community who lacked kindling and heat. Never again, he had vowed, would winter's song lure his flock from their beds, so long as he stood as guardian.

Yet this night, whether one would remain gnawed at his mind.

Aefethla.

May she live when I return.

Darkness hid the forest path to the shed. The glow of the moons through overhanging branches and twigs provided his only vision. His steps seemed loud against a soundless night, save the irregular rush of a breeze.

He paused and surveyed the area around him. *A still evening, this is.* Brown and barren tree limbs crept upward above him in twisting, interwoven patterns. Icy fangs angled downward in shapes with curls and patterns of perforation, unlike any icicles he had ever seen.

In the air, neither a tune of cricket nor bird, nor a toad's croak or cicada's shriek; not a swinging branch from a creature's leap or a broken stick at its step. Ice, without snow or rain.

An angry howl tore across the timberland, slicing through folds of cloth and hide and sending him in aching quakes. The day before had been warm. *Too warm for this sort of night.*

Then came a cry in the distance, dispersing the dense

emptiness around him, yet not even this roused life deeper in the woods. Next, shouting and screams. Face ruddy, Garron ran, as hurried as he could in a priest's garb, no longer thinking of the kindling he had intended to gather.

He carried himself with the quickness of one driven by unspoken duty. Honor bound him in the service of Gohheia to protect Her daughters and sons here, and he would. His steps had taken him far. Despite the cold, sweat streamed down his forehead and stung at his eyes. He wiped a marching line of perspiration away with his sleeve. "I must hurry," he said to himself between labored breaths.

As he broke through the trees, he came upon a man's body in a pool of blood, stomach and chest opened and shredded down to scraped bone, muscle, and organ. The air dragged the stench of the corpse to his nostrils. Dead, and already soured. Too soured, too soon, and brutalized beyond recognition. At the ends of the man's limbs, ragged stumps; hands and feet, ripped away, but nowhere in sight.

No mere animal could have done this.

He masked his nose with his arm. His eyes danced across the faces of village homes and the gaps among them, his insides painted in frantic hues of yellow and red. No figures made their presence known.

The sky, once sparse, had gone dark with thunderheads, black as soot and churning. Bolts of lightning crackled. Waves of thunder bellowed in their wake. Another chorus of screams arose, a few at first. These crescendoed into a cacophony of harrowing wails. As swift as they had come, the cries ended. Beyond these sounds, a dull murmur of groans and strained hissing, like a far-off pit of snakes.

Garron moved in long-legged strides. "Mother, protect me," he whispered, heading toward the source of the commotion. The ground blurred beneath him, and the air bit at his skin, growing colder the further he flew. Soon, ice had formed around his face in clear crystals at the tips of his peppered beard and hair. It mattered little, for he could not relent until he uncovered the catalyst of this distress.

Someone killed his flock. Not his flock alone, but the Mother's. His Mother, their Mother. The Mother of all mothers. The murder of Her children rendered one beyond absolution. Gohheia's greatest regret. Those who let it happen, who stood by, attendant the slaughter of Her children, were second-most.

Isolated and aware, Garron sprinted, like a wolf on the hunt, but feeling hunted.

"Father!" came a voice to his right.

He halted and turned, in the small market now.

A girl of the village called out.

Alina.

He knew their names, having lived there for over ten ages. She came to him, blonde hair disheveled, brown eyes inflamed, bedcloths torn and spattered in dusky red.

Blood, all over her. "What is it?" He took her in his arms. Her body shook with such a fierceness that not even his embrace fixed her. His hands quivered, too, but not for the same purpose. A brooding, consuming rage skulked through him. His chest sank with anger, making it hard to breathe.

He contained his fury for the girl's sake.

"Father!" she cried. "They kill us all! Please, please help!"

He buried her face against him to comfort her, and to muffle her squalls. *Her tears may draw them.* He draped his robes around her shoulders to warm her. Her skin chilled his palms, so cold it burned.

"Who is, Alina? Where are they?"

"Monsters! A woman. A monster. Horned. Grey skin." She struggled to speak through heaves. "Everyone's gone!" Her sobs reverberated off the walls of the surrounding buildings.

Garron knelt and met her face to face.

"Where is Emmelina?" she asked. "Can I go to her?"

Officer Emmelina. Her dwelling resided across the village, and the furor he heard sounded nearer. *If she hasn't stumbled upon it yet, I'll likely run through it before I find her.*

"I've not seen her, but I'm gone to look."

"I—is she dead?"

"Nay. Flee." He changed the subject. "Escape to the forest, to the wood shed by the well, down the eastern track. You know it." He took her face in his hands, his thumbs wiping the tears which hadn't frozen at her cheeks. "The chill bites, but it won't be long. I'll come for you when this is over. Until then, hide beneath the logs, and do not come out until you hear my voice."

The girl's eyes were puffy from crying, the circles beneath them accentuated.

He removed the water pouch from his side and passed it to her, placing a hand on her cheek again. "The magic of the Mother charms this carrier. It will protect you. Drink as you like, for it never empties when needed. Be not afraid. Gohheia is with you, and watches over you." He did his best to reassure her. In truth, certainty eluded him. *I may not survive this night.* If he did not live, she would freeze to death.

He had to survive, for her.

For all of them.

She fled, leaving him alone once more in the blackness and the hazy shimmer of the moons, his body encumbered by the weight of his task. Then manifested that awful sound anew. So many screams, deep and high, varied in unrestrained terror. They were as the calls of a hundred melted into a single horrific roar, the noise of struggling survival and impending demise.

Garron returned to his race over the village, past stone hovels, wooden stables, leaning fences, bloated and cracked and warped from the sun and rain. He found emptiness and abandonment, except traces of the village's residents in the forms of cloth from tunics and gowns and blood in sprays. Some of the houses appeared to have burned, as if long ago they had been set ablaze and had their flames extinguished.

Impossible, for he had taken a stroll upon this street two hours earlier.

He turned a corner at the end of a road. As he did, a voice entered his mind, slithering and hissing like a serpent through the air. "*Father*," it whispered in a woman's pitch, loud, as if risen from his own lips.

Stiff and uncoordinated by the frost, he lost his footing, crashing down to his hands and knees.

Jarred, he groaned, fighting to regain his senses.

The grunts and rumbles of quarreling met his ears.

One tone stood out.

"Father Latimer!" someone called, accompanying the shuffle of feet traveling nearer.

Rising to one knee, he lifted his head.

Emmelina.

A familiar face and companion in authority brought him a jolt of relief, but fleeting. As they convened there without another spirit to witness, something sinister lay beyond. Something which brought the grey sky, the unforgiving cold, and death. Savage, merciless death.

He pushed himself to his feet, countenance twisting at the pain in his knees, hips, and back. The ground had become ice, inhospitable to his eldered frame in its descent. To his gratitude, Emmelina lived. He had expected to discover her slain. Her youthfulness afforded her a greater ability to deal with unsavory sorts and situations.

A snowflake floated down in front of his face, catching his eye. "What comes?"

They peered up. Beneath dark, swirling clouds, the sky had flooded with a great salt sea. Snowfall, below a net of lightning, ridden by claps of thunder. Flickers of white cascaded from every direction until they fell in veils. Faint through the flurry and overcast sky, the light of the moons continued to reach, casting a luminous aura. Any other time, he would've appreciated such an ethereal vision as this.

"Undeath, Father."

"Undeath?"

"The dark magic of the Patron of the Undead has come about us. Those dead rise, ravenous, wild. Most of the village is slaughtered, or worse." Terror filled her face and eyes. Fright laced her voice. Her hands trembled.

Garron had never witnessed Emmelina so disquieted. In all their ages together, he had known her as a pillar of strength, a seasoned warrior, a hale woman who had bested many a strong opponent.

A sheet of snow had formed on the ground, so shallow it barely left a tread. Reflections in the ice magnified each flash of lightning high beyond. No normal weather surrounded them, but a sign of malevolent forces. Emmelina spoke the truth. The servants of a dark god lay siege to a mortal village, to Gohheia's children. Had he not lives in need of saving, he would have collapsed and wept.

"We—we must—" His speech trailed off. "Anyone who lives, Emmelina. If there is anyone." He swallowed. Sand and fire set his throat ablaze and his nostrils burned. He feared his insides might freeze over as he drew in the air around them, cold and dry.

Emmelina approached him, her gaze downcast. "Anyone who lives, Father." She placed a hand on his neck. "If we die here, it has been an honor."

He smiled, thin-lipped, tears welling in his sight. The drops ran down his cheeks and hardened, the ice stopping short of his eyes. "And to you."

The pair were off, shifting closer to the chorus of cries, rising in frequency and volume at every yard. Death and sulfur consumed the air. The village road became the remnants of a path. This route grew rugged and steepened as they descended the valley to the overgrown western edge, the deepest point of the Vale.

A tree wall composed the decline, leaning and swaying, their naked branches shading the ground. The grass shifted from a coarse yellow to a scorched black, ripped and uprooted by overturned oaks and cedars, and melded with accumulating snow which soaked up ash and turned a watery grey. A light bled through the open scars between the darkness of the trees, playing like fire.

Another scream punctured the air, nearby this time.

Garron and Emmelina lowered themselves down the last few feet of hillside and made their way toward the newest calamity. Though the night's chill grew with every step, he dripped with sweat which continued to form into crystals on his skin, hairs upright over his arms and the back of his neck. The abnormal frigidness froze liquid against his flesh with atypical quickness, but did not kill him.

As they moved through the brush, another girl—teen-yeared—appeared at their flank. What sounded like a low growl escaped her lips, loud in the eerie calm that followed, as if the world had gone silent at her command.

"Please," she said. "Can you help me?"

Snow fell harder.

"Speak your name." Garron had never seen this girl.

Emmelina placed a hand at the hilt of her sword.

The girl tugged with a feigned nervousness at the lower hem of her threadbare rags. Her eyes flashed an amusement. She smiled, a grin of faint, reserved malice. A cursed smile.

He gripped the lunar tears at his wrist, fingers aching against the strand. "Emmelina," he said.

"Please, these creatures." The girl's voice sounded airy and small. "Wait," she paused and let her eyes drift between them without aim, "it's already here."

Garron revolved as Emmelina shouted, the glint of her blade catching his eye in the shimmer of the moons. A woman attacked them, unnoticed until she neared, soaked in blood, flesh torn, hair matted and tangled, nightcloths shabby and ripped at the torso and legs.

Though the cold delayed her, Emmelina evaded the ambush and countered with a horizontal sting of her sword across the woman's chest. The gash drove deep and the woman bled fast, a tainted blood, thick and exuding like honey. Catching a high surface root, Emmelina lost her balance and stumbled backward into a tree. She managed a defensive guard before the woman lunged, snarling and sputtering, ferocious as a starved beast.

"Father!" Emmelina faltered against her assailant's leverage.

The woman warped and screeched with a violence. As if jointed in three places, her legs shuddered and bent, toes tearing at the soil beneath them until the nails lifted from the surface of her skin. Her back arched and produced with it a wretched crackle from what sounded like shattered ribs.

Garron's hands rose, his lunar tears wrapped around his fingers in a diamond pattern. Before he began his incantation, the girl stepped in front of him.

"Those lunar tears shall not protect you," she said, her voice a mixture of a child's pitch and that of a deeper power. The dulcet, menacing resonance of the woman he had heard in his head. "You'll be dead before the words."

He tried to speak, but no sound escaped his lips. Arms lowered, he stepped away. The world around him rolled and his thoughts clouded. Feeling in his legs evacuated.

Behind the girl, the battle went on. Burdened with the cold, Emmelina had lost her sword. The dead woman had gained the upper hand, now mounted over the paladin, gnashing her teeth and spewing saliva. Emmelina held the rabid woman at bay by the throat and wrist. Uneven, grimy nails sunk into Emmelina's exposed neck, between her jaw and mail. She howled as blood ran from the wound, dripping and staining the snow.

Emmelina struck the woman in the face, then turned and took her blade in hand. Dazed by the blow, the woman rolled to her side, a leg still over Emmelina's body. The paladin drove her sword into the woman's neck, the tip gliding through her throat, into the base of her mouth.

This attack made the already-incensed woman berserk. She shrieked and thrashed, releasing vicious, wrathful noises. The world around them filled with a clamor and blood and horror. Moments later, the woman's movements ceased. She fell lifeless against the ground, her head propped at the base of a tree.

Emmelina writhed to her feet, blood trailing from her hairline to her chin. Staggering, she dropped to one knee, perhaps more injured than she appeared on the surface. "Garron," she gasped, "that girl is corrupt—a foul magic works here." Her words became a growl. "*We must kill her!*"

Garron snapped from his haze as the girl concentrated on Emmelina. The voice snuck into his head once more. A woman. That thing. *Speak my name, Father. Speak it and be free.*

Emmelina pushed herself to her feet, using her blade for balance, her hands on the pommel. The tip sank into the soil, but the frost had made it hard enough to sustain her weight.

"I cannot do this alone, Garron." Her body swayed. Were Emmelina anywhere else in the world, she would surely fall to the ground, curl up, and shut her eyes. Here, she would find no respite.

"You would murder a child?" the girl said, reproachful, a false note in her inflection.

"Silence, beast," Emmelina snapped. "This sordid shell does not fool me. Show us your true nature. I want to look into your eyes when I kill you!"

"Ill-mannered." The girl turned toward him and frowned. "She cannot go, Garron Latimer."

A wind moaned through the trees and across the hills, washing over the three in mocking waves. Emmelina's hair fluttered and fell, Garron's robes rose and settled, but the girl did not move. Neither a hair on her head nor a thread of her garments reacted. With the gust came the acrid smell of burning, dying flesh, humanity in embers, and smoldering stone and wood. Garron retched.

That thing, that voice, brought to his mind a quaking swarm like buzzing locusts, its words unintelligible. He grabbed his head, ambled backward, eyes clenched. The dissonance became deafening. Like the dying of a torch, the white world around him blackened. His weight no longer beneath him, he stared up into the stormy sky, seeking in desperation for light. A numbness captured his body from his feet to his head. He could not move.

"Father!" he heard someone say, their appeal muffled, as though filtered through water.

His heavy lids fluttered and the noise consuming him subsided, replaced with a high ringing. A scream came next. Familiar, yet beyond recognition.

Above him slid a figure, guised in shadow at first. As it came into focus, he saw it. Black of hair and horned. Grey of skin with empty eyes. A woman. A creature. The corners of her mouth curled up, revealing rows of jagged teeth. She fell closer, as if drifting through the air with the snow. The voice in his thoughts cleared as the space between them narrowed; penetrating, invading, forcing him outward, hissing in a thousand tongues at once.

Vor . . . Kaal.

CHAPTER III: RED

Athenne

That morning, Athenne rode with Uldyr, the meeting of the previous night in her head. The details of the Saints' machinations would keep with her until the day of execution. Their plan, Aitrix had proclaimed, would permit every woman, man, and child to shake off the bonds of Matrian control. Athenne believed that Aitrix had meant what she said, and that she cared about the freedom of magic. *After all, it benefits her directly.*

Despite Aitrix's self-assuredness and magnetism, a sort of affable authority, these low schemes rose to odds with Athenne's heart. Outside, she seemed well. Inside, she blackened with grief.

The forest sprawled at each side of the road. Ash and holly dominated its canopy. Light descended through openings in limbs and branches and washed over a sloping, slanting range of shrubs, herbs, and saplings. Curving creepers hung from every tree, and coiling, climbing plants grasped at their bases. An array of flowers clung to any space they found, brightening the russet lower level.

Wild sounds breathed life into the woodlands; prowling and

foraging animals, singing birds, larger creatures in the distance. She longed for an existence of such simplicity, a life that had once been hers.

Her horse whickered, and Athenne settled her with a touch. Shah was dependable, sturdy, the right size for Athenne to ride comfortably. During her travels, Athenne had acquired Shah from a grazier more in need of coin than another animal to feed. *A sickness has her*, the woman had said, smoothing Shah's white blaze with her palm.

Athenne had spent months nursing her back to health, taking her out for light runs and brushing her grey coat until it shone again. They cantered through the woods, down mountain paths, across cool, rushing streams. When Shah regained her size and strength, they had bounded even fallen trees with ease.

Uldyr's steed, Athos, had a black coat, interspersed with white hairs that gave him a blue tinge. Broad at the shoulders and hips, he moved with strength and power, similar to his rider. Uldyr claimed Athos prone to biting, but Athenne had never witnessed that tendency herself.

At last, they arrived at Uldyr's house, still south of the village of Ghora, near the border between the Sacred Empire and the kingdom of Beihan further south. A mesh of grey plaster and stone occupied the spaces between an exterior frame of painted timber bands and beams. Crossed with iron bars, a window and wooden door adorned its front. Cherry tomatoes, onions, and other mixed crops claimed a garden at its side. The average commoner's hovel paled in comparison.

Athenne stopped at the fore, inspecting the construction. "How did you come about this place?"

"Built it myself," Uldyr told her with a playful pointedness, as if the answer should have been obvious. He dismounted and tied Athos's reins in a loose hitch around a post at the house's corner. "You can tether yours here." He gestured to a pole next to the one he had used.

"Where'd you get the materials?"

"Took from the hills and the gorge to the east."

She followed him as he opened the door and stepped inside. "How long did it take?" At one end of the interior, a living chamber, sat a dining table covered in candles and jars of grains, oils, dried fruits, and meats, pickled in a brine and pink with blood. On the other side of the room stood a writing desk with two chairs. His bed resided in the attached quarter straight ahead.

"Two ages. Lived northeast in the Fausse Woods in the meantime. This far out, no one notices."

She eased into a chair at his writing table, sore from riding. "Impressive dedication."

He raised his hands, as if to say, *of course*.

They talked for a while of things they had not discussed in all their months, when they had lived so long in the moment, and for the next. Uldyr spoke of his life before the Saints. He talked of working on the ocean, fishing for crab in the cold Sea of Nimphre to the south, past the sweeping forests and Beihan.

"I injured a man in the throes of a tempest," he had said, with the tone of a confession.

"An accident?"

"Aye." He rubbed his mouth. "I soon became an outcast among the crew."

"It wasn't your fault, Uldyr."

"Nay, it was right," he said. "Not long after the exclusion, my employ on that ship ended."

She did not press for details, and Uldyr did not offer many more, except that he could not look the man in the face when he returned from the sick berth the next day.

"For a time, I worked any job I found. I considered taking up with the Black Feathers or Forgebrand. I labored for graziers and farmers, tending their livestock and crops." He paused for a sip of his toxic homebrew, as if to wash the memory from his mouth. "I hated myself and the reality I'd made."

"That's when you joined the Saints?"

"Aitrix Kravae, for all her faults, saved my life. She lifted me from despair, delivered me to my courage. I'm the man I am this day because she found me."

Athenne's eyes lowered to the floor.

"I know you don't agree with all that we bring," he said. "But what we do, it's for the good."

She looked at him and nodded in hopes of moving on.

As their drink set in, Uldyr talked of a love he once held.

"She was seventeen-yeared in those days. I was eighteen." He described her as a woman of enveloping handsomeness and razor wit. "She had a scourging mouth," he had regaled, but one he'd let lambaste him again with gladness. Never cruel, her face always alit with joy. "If ever Gohheia had a daughter," he added, "it was she."

For the first time, tears welled in his eyes, abrupt and unwelcome. He shifted subjects to shoo them away, and asked her about herself.

Athenne spoke of her study of materialism, theology, combat philosophy, her girlhood in Reneris, at the northeast corner of the continent. The magnificent capital, Renbourg, initially, and later, the subdued Orilon to its west. There, after her mother had passed, Athenne came into her womanhood, and she and Uldyr met, by chance or fate of fortune.

"I ran, jumped, played, traversed valley, stream, and crevice, freed myself in the world," she said. "I spent days and nights in the southwest Hinterlands, blinded by sunlight as it beamed against frosted winter fields." She laughed through her nose. "The woods were old, inviting, untouched, humble, radiant. Birch and larch and breeds I couldn't name conquered the overhangs. Branches groaned against shafts of dripping ice."

Uldyr's mouth curled up at the left corner. "You've a bard's recollection, Athenne."

"I kept rabbits for a time," she continued, "until a wild dog ate their feet through their cage. I had it suspended over wooden horses to put them at shoulder level. I spent three hours sharpening a stick with my mother's whittling knife, intent on hunting the beast down and having my revenge. My war march commenced, and mother stopped me."

"'*Only you would sharpen a stick to kill the thing instead of using the knife*,' she chided. '*Now my blade is dull*.'" Athenne's eyes watered at the thought of her mother's voice. "That evening, we buried my rabbits together. Mother gave them a candlelight vigil and told me they'd returned to the Overrealm to rest with Gohheia." She waved her fingers in the air. "It makes little sense in a scriptural context, but it helped assuage my woes."

As Uldyr listened, expression attentive, Athenne had lost herself in delineating the calm comforts of dreams from ages long past, notwithstanding the harrowing happenings of her hares.

A loud bang came at the window.

Her heart leapt into her mouth and tore her back to the present. "What was that?" she said.

Uldyr ran his fingers through his whiskers and scratched his chin. "The wind."

Then came another thump, sharp and deliberate, enough to rattle the wall this time.

Uldyr jumped from his chair, leather-gloved fingers at the grip of his sword, still strapped to his waist. He threw open the door and went outside. Athenne trailed and brought the door flush behind them. The day had warmed from the night, and the trees cast timid shadows. Their horses were aflutter; shying, whinnying, querulous.

A man stood in the middle of the yard, before the woods of hazel, crystalline lake at his rear, amidst the flowing sward, waving emerald in the wind. He had an angled and slim face, with a thin, straight nose and smooth, unflared nostrils. A smile strung across his jaw like a strand of pearls.

"Are you Uldyr Friala?"

"Who calls?" Uldyr answered, gravel in his throat. He turned to Athenne. "Stay back."

She stepped toward the wall of the house.

Uldyr's attention reverted to their guest.

"Aliester Haldis, the Red." The man unsheathed his blades, attached to his wrists by martingales, in a same-side draw. First came a rapier, then a schiavona, the latter the more substantial of the two, a blade with a superior edge. "Supreme sword this far south of the Golden Sands." He appeared to size Uldyr up. "You fit, all right. I worried I might be after the wrong person."

Uldyr towered over the man who called himself the Red. Through layers of cloth and armor, his size laid bare. The self-professed mercenary wore fine linens of garnet, a slashed jerkin in black with sable trim, and a baldric and belt, hardly defensive at all, sacrificing protection for speed and agility.

Before Uldyr had time to react, the man had driven toward him at a run, unusually swift, closing the distance of three or so meters. Shifting on his feet, Uldyr turned to draw, but too late. A blade lashed out for his face.

Nearly divorced an ear or cheek, or both, Uldyr's front foot followed his back foot in reverse, features tilting to the left, placing distance between them.

The man brought both weapons to a guard, shoulders squared, arms raised, then parting. He seemed to be waiting for Uldyr to respond. "I haven't all day," he said with an unconcerned musicality. "Come now."

Athenne recognized the daggerhand's style; an Abbisan dancer. She had studied the form and its techniques in her lessons on combat philosophy, more theoretical than practical.

They reengaged, their struggle almost a blur. The man swiveled as they met in a sword bind and caught Uldyr across the chin with a blow of his hilt. Uldyr's head snapped back. He stumbled to the right, nearly lost hold of his blade, recovered, and retreated. Thin silver lashed out for Uldyr in furious thrusts. Uldyr caught the swords with his own and forced them off, then swiped at the mercenary's neck and missed.

Moving lighter on his feet, the daggerhand made six strokes for every three of Uldyr's. Even so, with another advance, Uldyr almost clipped the man across the throat again.

The mercenary backed off.

Uldyr's stupor encumbers him.

Athenne had read of many battles in her youth. She had witnessed a number of sparring matches, some with wooden training swords, others with sticks or edgeless blades. This bout surpassed those displays. Here, two men, strangers, gave their greatest effort to kill one another.

In the frenzy, steel rang against steel and the pair dodged, parried, and lunged. They were more skilled than the individuals she had watched play at fighting. The man fought with elegance and aggression. Uldyr's advances were brutish and forceful, yet not without refinement.

The one who called himself the Red looked increasingly eager to finish the duel, and confident that he could. They separated and converged, growled and sweltered in exertion. Uldyr nearly gashed the daggerhand across the face with the tip of his sword. A few close-misses later, one found first blood. The quicker of the two.

Uldyr groaned.

The man's lips curdled into a smile as the length of his schiavona penetrated Uldyr's armor and bit flesh. His rapier came thereafter, but Uldyr grabbed it with his gloved right hand at the half-sword and trapped the blade.

With the mercenary's apparent strong side occupied and his other immobile, Uldyr pivoted. His own left arm jolted down and back, his edge aimed at the extended forearm that had shot out to pierce him, perhaps overextended with zeal and hung up in his padded jacket and tunic.

The man released his schiavona with a curse, and Uldyr lost

hold of the rapier. Attached to the mercenary's wrist, the Abbisan blade swung in suspension. As agony blossomed in his fresh wound, the daggerhand staggered with a hint of urgency to distance himself. His face betrayed surprise, as though he had underestimated his opponent.

"That your best?" Uldyr's words filtered through taut lips. "Dual-wielding longer swords." His left side dripped with blood, coating his trousers and gambeson. He looked to Athenne.

Their eyes met and parted.

Awarding his assailant little time to recover, Uldyr refocused and charged. He rained cuts overhand, his left foot powering forward. His sword came down in repeated strikes, in the spirit of a war hammer, making use of his superior stature and strength. Some blows were steady, others were faint and poorly directed.

Uldyr's injury hampered his ability to fight, but fitness maintained him, encouraged his assault.

The man retreated further. Uldyr's sword had destroyed the tendon in his arm and grated into bone. White and pink dotted the bloody crevice, and grey skin stretched in ribbons at its edges, the loose, pulled flesh of shredded meat. The mercenary met Uldyr's force with impressive guile for his wounded state, deflecting the commanding energy driven against him, and managed to set more space between them.

"You're more than I thought," the man jibed through tortured breaths as he jerked his mangled arm with a grimace, the schiavona trailing by its martingale, which he finally severed. His jaw tightened and bulged.

Uldyr's advance halted, head tilted forth the slightest. He winced at the laceration in his ribs. His left hand held his blade before him, tip pointed upward, guarding the shoulder of his sword arm.

Uldyr must end this soon. His strength will not hold.

As if reading Uldyr's state, and acknowledging his own, the daggerhand waited. His right arm had suffered considerable damage, and his formerly smug countenance wore a scowl of haggard frustration, his eyes as wounds beneath his creased brow, wild with a quiet rage. The rapier he wielded remained to guard, its end weaving slight spirals in the air. He spoke once more, his words grated from between clenched teeth. "It's your move." Even with his disadvantage, the daggerhand's bravado lingered. "Should I cut you up more?"

Uldyr chuckled and wiped the flat of his edge across the front of his gambeson. "You're down an arm. I don't need my side to kill you." His face hardened, eyes flared and blazing. "Tell me, what's your purpose here?" Uldyr appeared weaker by the second as shades of scarlet and carmine washed his side. "Why have you come for us?" Even the sturdiest man could withstand but so much.

"For you"—the mercenary pointed his rapier at Athenne—"not her." Blood from his arm muddied the soil at his feet in copper and brown. His body wavered. They each did. She hoped Uldyr would not be the first to falter.

I have to act.

"Enough." She interposed herself between them.

"Athenne," Uldyr objected.

She ignored Uldyr's dissent. "I am a materialist. As you are, I could incant before you'd reach me." Her brow furrowed. "Relent or perish. The choice is yours."

The man's rapier endured in the air. His thin lips bent into a wan grin. From the wearied expression in his eyes, he did not seem likely to test her bluff. What she said could be true, by the All-Mother's grace. *If he advances, the Mother will protect us.* She had to believe it, to garner the favor to cast.

A flicker crossed the daggerhand's face, as if by the light of a flame in his head. "Nay," he started, "you'll incant nothing." He approached, dragging the tip of his blade through the soil, drawing a line. "Have you forgotten, Renerin?" His tongue clicked against his teeth. "All magic is restricted—offensive, defensive, healing. Even this far from Aros, it'd be by the grace of the gods if you mustered a spark." He raised his rapier. "You were not my intended, but I'll cut you down the same."

Before she could retort, or the man could take another step or spew another threat, he let out a cry and lurched backward. His rapier fell to a swing and jerked as his hand clutched his neck, eyes wide. From his throat sprang a throwing knife, and around it rushed a fountain. He collapsed, face to the sky.

Uldyr had unleashed the blade, hidden in his wears.

Athenne turned toward him, stunned but relieved.

"I grew fatigued of the bard's melody," he jested with a grey smile. His incorrigible resilience, free of its need, escaped and let him fall to one knee.

"Uldyr!" Athenne rushed to his side, tearing fabric from her robes and applying pressure to his wound. The cloth soaked through. She placed her other palm at his face. Fever lit his skin. "We must get you inside."

He shook his head, glowering, as if that simple motion injured him. "Check his belongings. This was no random attack, not this far south, not that skilled a fighter. Someone's out for me."

CHAPTER IV: KEEPER

Garron

"We are joined this day with an incident recounting, a dedicated document, conveyed to Bishop Maxima Ayleth by Father Garron Latimer, regarding events said to have transpired under his guardianship at the Vale of Erlan. Am I correct?" Archbishop Sangrey's eyes shimmered a dutiful hazel, and obsidian bejeweled her ash-blonde hair, drawn at the crown by a black ribbon.

"Aye, Your Reverency," Garron replied.

Garron stood in the well of the council chamber, before seven of the nine archbishops who composed the Ennead, ruling body of the Matrian Church, and true power of the Sacred Empire. At the center of this group sat Breiman Umbra, the first man ever appointed Vicar of Gohheia; a face of the Church, a conveyor of its edicts, by tradition, little more than a formal title. Yet hushed condemnations within the Church had claimed that Archbishop Umbra had maneuvered to expand the title's influence during his tenure.

Of no less importance, the six women at Umbra's shoulders were his fellow members. Each sat on thrones of marble amidst statues, and wore black and grey robes, embroidered and lavish, in keeping with the custom of honoring the glory of Gohheia on Earth as in the Celestia. Like many of the Clergy, Garron had met the nine of the Ennead during the Idoss festivals held annually at the capital. The Fest of the All-Mother marked the sole time in which the Church permitted members of the priesthood to leave their ward villages and return to Aros.

The Grand Priory had always made Garron feel small, and this chamber was no exception. Its embowed ceilings hung massively overhead, dancing in the glow of burning tapers which draped between crimson banners bearing the sigil of the Empire, the Overcross. His eyes scanned above the walls of similarly-crimson curtains and stained-glass windows to view the sculptures of figures past, which seemed to gaze down in judgment.

Archbishop Sangrey flipped the paper in her hand over. "Archbishops Dred and Hart will not be in attendance." Camille Sangrey spent most of her time micromanaging the affairs of the many in the Clergy beneath and even equal to her station. It had assuredly added years to his life, current events aside, when Garron retired from her primary service after he made his priesthood and received ordainment as guardian of Erlan.

"You are charged, though only as an investigative rather than punitive matter for the moment, with the act of dereliction of guardianship, of which you have confessed," she said. "That is, the Church has found that you abandoned your station in Erlan, thereby severing your sacred vows of priesthood to maintain the village until the end of your life. Do you concur with these facts as herein defined?"

"I do."

"You have argued in your admission that you did so because what you experienced on the night of your departure rose to a greater urgency than your duty as warden. Am I correct in defining this statement?"

"Aye, Your Reverency."

Sangrey tapped the edges of the parchment in her hands against the table, then laid the front page face down. "The council is considering that your service to the Church has been unremitting for over forty ages, since you were a boy of late teenage. Further, we are taking into account that your work in protecting Erlan with the aid of Field Officer Emmelina Avelane of Kordyr has been well-regarded for the last decade. Do you affirm these facts as I have conveyed them to you?"

"Aye, Your Reverency," Garron said once more.

The day he had turned himself in—pale, shaken, carved and bruised, raw at the feet and hands—he had relinquished Emmelina's service license to the Matrian Evidentiary Office. The attendant deacon had to clean the badge to read its rank insignia and name. Garron could not bring himself to wipe away Emmelina's dried blood.

"For the record, Officer Avelane served well as the paladin of Erlan, did she not?"

"She did, Your Reverency."

"Do you know her location at the start of the attack?"

"I presume she had been asleep in the guard's bothy before the commotion outside woke her and she found me. We did not discuss the matter at the time. Other concerns pressed."

"You noted in this report that Officer Avelane initially served as a chevalier in the military, but requested a transfer to the inquisitors. From there, the Silver Knights assigned her to the Vale, as the then-field officer had intended to retire. You stated also that those of her graduating Knight's Circle called her by the honorific, Emmelina the Courageous, for her bravery."

"Protector of the innocent, defender of the weak, willing to die for the sake of honor and justice—a true adherent to the code of the Order of One," Garron followed. "I wanted to ensure truth and fullness in her remembrance." The air that slipped past his lips shook like water displaced by the force of a hand.

"Father Latimer," Archbishop Holle Mallum chimed in from the far end of the table, "we know you are neither a coward nor a man who would desert his post without just cause." The common body, and many of the government, regarded Mallum as the most virtuous of the Ennead, despite that she often defied the Clergy's dress code by wearing colorful costumes in place of her issued robes.

Garron relaxed as she spoke.

"You have a longstanding history of adherence to the three pillars of the Mother's Truth, and to your oaths." She extended a reassuring smile, her eyes, the color of cocoa beans, crinkling in the frame of her light brown hair. This day, she wore bright blue and white. "We have all read your testimony summary from Bishop Ayleth. I feel confident in saying that we found it difficult to fathom. In light of the details, which are certain to find an ear in the common body soon, as is the way of rumor, we need you to tell us, with as much description as you can bear, exactly what occurred following your loss of consciousness during your encounter in the western descent."

Garron inhaled, absorbing the dark fragrance of the coals

smoldering in the braziers that surrounded the four marble pillars at his back; a faint, dirty odor. "With the Mother's guidance," he said, his eyes low. The mere thought of those memories caused his hands to quiver, festering as an untreated wound.

The Church's Scribe Officiate, an elf by the look of her, sat in the corner, quill and parchment in hand, recording the assembly's proceedings. She stopped and peered up as silence rolled through the room.

That night.

Hecos had hung low in the sky, near half down, a marker of deep evening. To affirm the hour, her celestial sisters, Senas, Enon, and Minaris, encircled and claimed the hue of midnight blue.

Time had passed, though how much, he could not be certain. His head throbbed. In the distance, he heard the howl of wolves or coyotes, he could not be sure.

Garron brought pins of cold air into his lungs. *Do I live?* He did not know. He drew in once more. His chest expanded. The ache in his stomach abated to a numb pulsation and he no longer felt fastened to the earth like stone.

Am I wounded? His head must be intact, for consciousness had returned. He shuddered and bent upward. Did he cry out in pain? He was ignorant of it if he had.

Nothing stirred. No movement, no sound.

He surveyed his surroundings.

Dead air swam in every direction.

The pounding in his head shattered his skull as the crashing of the surf, dragging him to sea and returning him to shore to twist in anguish. His reality offered less charity. Nearly broken, he sat alone in a woodland clearing.

Alone, save one.

Managing to rise to his feet, he stumbled over to the tree line. As he approached, he recalled another that had lay close by. A reanimated woman of the village, the one who had assailed Emmelina. The village woman had vanished, a faded stain of viscera her lone remnants.

As though in a dream, Garron gazed upon her ruined form. *Dear Emmelina, valiant to the last.* Like hay, her hair had turned coarse and brittle. Her eyes had sunk in, and her face, speckled in grey and black, had already fouled. Around her mouth, green and purple kisses of decay. From her ears, dried blood.

"She had already putrefied when you awoke?" Archbishop Sangrey interrupted.

Archbishop Umbra's dark gaze focused on Garron. "Consistent with the summary testimony delineated in Bishop Ayleth's record." Dry of manner, as always.

"Any mortal skilled in necromancy could've accomplished such in Father Latimer's period of unconsciousness," said another voice to Umbra's side. Serafina Mortem. Perpetually frowning, one could hardly tell she lived until she uttered a word.

"Not in such time," Archbishop Aramanth Delacroix interjected from the next-to-last seat at the rightmost end of the table. If anyone could be certain, she would. Aramanth Delacroix, one of the fiercest mages to ever live, master of the Aetherian arts of metaphysics and materialism, perhaps surpassed in exclusion by the Imperial Archmagister. "A mortal necromancer may find favor in his might from the God of the Dead, but our borderland wards ought to have restricted such foreign magic sufficient that even a powerful necromancer would have been rendered next to impotent. Perhaps in many hours or days, such a feat could be accomplished."

During Archbishop Delacroix's time as a bishop, women and men in their envy whispered the slur *witch* at her back. A dangerous charge, and untrue. The aftershock of her ascent had expelled these malcontents. Later, the ousted agitators spread rumors of her private love with Archbishop Sangrey, to which neither had admitted, that he knew.

"What Father Latimer has described in his testimony and now seems to have been a period of an hour or less," Delacroix went on. "Am I correct, Father?"

"I estimated such by the depth of the snowfall."

"'Tis not possible we deal with a mortal culprit. I ought to know, for I imbued the wards myself." Scarlet lips, often bent with an untroubled grin, offset Delacroix's porcelain, chiseled features. Two long braids of flaxen at her shoulders, beginning above the ears and joining at the center of her nape, balanced her warm umber eyes. Her characteristic half-smile did not accompany her face this evening.

"We've asked Father Latimer to narrate to us the events," Umbra reminded the room. "We'll be here a fortnight if we do not let him speak."

"Indeed," Delacroix said.

Mortem nodded.

Umbra rolled his left hand. "Proceed, Father."

"It," Garron began again, "was not a natural death."

When a body dies by normal cause, it deteriorates in a slow process. The figure becomes bloated and sore and scabbed, declines over an extended period. Upon Emmelina had been the stink of rot, but a different sort, and too pungent that shortly. Her body had hollowed and aged. In a typical decomposition, the innards decay and swell to their escape until they wither. Hers had liquefied, as though a spider had caught her in its web and drank her clean.

A shell remained.

Garron lowered himself. On bent haunches, he placed one hand to her hair, the other to her cheek. His eyes closed and his head fell back. Shoulders slumped, he wept. A cold hovered in the air, but not the frost from before, that insidious chill. The tears that streamed down his face did not freeze at his cheeks. "Emmelina!" he pleaded to the sky, to the Mother. He wept harder, his body shaking with each sob.

His head jerked as he shook, his mind swimming in misery. The song of his lament, the only sound around him. A rush of sensation in a sea of vicious nothingness. Devoid of reprieve, a hostile dream. Over ten ages he had served this place, and she had perished while he lay helpless, worthless, on the ground.

As he rose and tottered, full with grief, he found no blood on him. Had he escaped unscathed? His memory played against him. He turned to draw in details long in the distance. No life stirred anywhere, not even a trickle of flame. Emptiness called. He walked, plagued by a headache and sickness.

"I must," he said, or begged. He remembered something; two things. Important. The girl in the storage shed, Alina, and the one in his care, Aefethla. "Please, Mother," he may have whispered, "let them live."

He had staggered back up the path, the decline, and the road, the distance he had traversed earlier, drifting past ruined hovels with naught a spirit to guide him, greet him, or relieve him of his burden. In his uninvited sleep, the world had iced further. Snow covered rooftops and frost crept down stone in ribbons and sheets. He saw no animals, bodies, or blood in the mounds of white. Even the wind had forsaken them.

Outside Aefethla's hovel, he stopped. The journey there had been lengthy, but he did not remember it. His palm met the cool, rough exterior of the door. Not long ago, he sat within, tending to her, stoking the fire of her hearth, preparing her evening's meal, reciting to her the sacred words of the Mother's *Blest Writ*. As he wavered at the fore of her dwelling, he tasted fear at the back of his mouth. The thought nearly overcame him, to look upon her sunken features, pale lips; eyes dull, listless, voided.

I must. The door rested ajar. His hand swung it open with unsettling ease, hinges grating. He stepped inside with his gaze locked to the floor, allowing his sight to trail timidly up toward her bed. The room had become as a cavern. Within his chest had welled a tension that made it arduous to breathe, as if a weight pressed against it. He shook from the chill, and the terror.

Through the pool of darkness before him, nothing formed. Aefethla had disappeared from her bed, as if she had never been there. Perhaps she hadn't. He had lost faith in his senses.

"*Vor-Kaal*." The phrase rang out from Sangrey's lips into the chamber. "Keeper of Death," she added. "You understand the weight of this claim, Father?"

"Aye, Your Reverency." Her words returned him from his vivid recollections to the assembly. "'Tis the name the voice whispered into my mind." His fingertips tingled, as though warming from a frost.

"If it were as you described," Archbishop Mortem said, "and if the wards are as efficient as we hope, we must assume the words you report hearing were true. *True*, that is, in that you *heard* them." She sounded incredulous. "Whether the source of those words *spake truth* is another matter."

"In your testimony, you described the creature, the woman, as horned, black horns, with grey skin and white eyes," said Archbishop Aris Crane, her dark skin aglow in the light of the hall.

"As it appeared to me."

"As Vor-Kaal is described in Scripture," Umbra rasped.

Garron expected that one of the Ennead would point out that most members of the Clergy could describe the appearance of Vor-Kaal, and the other Incarnations and First Gods above them. However, none did.

Delacroix leaned forward. "'Twould not be unprecedented. Ankhev once stood in this city. The Incarnations Ruhlter, Ulraut, Taerem, and Lasson make themselves known in the world."

"Largely in tales," Mortem said. "Nonetheless, 'tis so."

"Before we proceed with that line of discussion." Archbishop Mallum quieted her associates. "What of the girl, Father? Alina, you mentioned."

Alina.

East, he had walked, overwrought and exhausted. The pathways now hidden under snow, he made his way toward the wood shed, to where he had instructed Alina to flee. He came to the storage and threw its door open. Alina had made it, and died, and soured. She had not melted into the air as the others of the village, as if left so that he would find her, and see, and never forget.

Kneeling once more, his hands numbed against snow and

cold ground. His fingers drew into fists, squeezing ice and turning it to water. He wanted to collapse and die there with her, but he must escape. If he survived to the capital, to Aros, he could warn the Ennead and others, and he must do so in person to verify the seriousness of his allegations. Many more would die if he did not, and in horrific fashion. Children, women, men, devoured by this ghastly undeath. By sacred duty, in service of Gohheia, he could not perish.

"I ventured west again. As if gifted by the Mother, there stood a saddled steed beyond the village edge. I mounted and rode as I could. I recognized but that I must." Garron's voice wavered. "The creature had been run near to death when I arrived at the city gate. It never yielded, as though driven by my purpose, or fed of the finest Hallion. I lost consciousness on the way, slept as it ran, but remained at its back. Nothing pursued me, as if the world had risen into the sky and faded." He put a hand to his chin and smoothed his shaggy beard. "I wondered whether I were still there in the village, dreaming, dead—if it were real at all."

He had lost substantial weight during his ride. There had been no food. He quenched his thirst in long swallows by the water pouch at his waist, retrieved from Alina's body. His robes hung loosely about his form, as a curtain from a window or secondhand rags. He found himself weak, certain his muscles had atrophied. His face felt gaunt beneath his fingers, matching the thinness of his wrists.

The endless drum of hoofbeats on frozen ground remained fresh in his mind. So constant, it snuck into his sleep and dreams. He may never bear a horse's stride again. Much of the trip from Erlan to the northern Empire was a blur to him. Days had bled together. The vision of Alina's body in that cold, dark woodshed lingered, from first sight to that moment. It would stay with him until his final breath.

I shall not forget her, so long as I live.

"'Twas by the All-Mother's grace you survived the way and the frost, Father." This time, a different one of the Ennead spoke, Archbishop Zaria Tornaeu, if Garron's memory served. Her voice conveyed compassion.

Garron nodded to her. "I believe it so."

"I think we have heard enough." By Umbra's tone, the words were more a declaration than a suggestion.

"Retire to your chamber, Father, and we shall deliberate," Mallum followed. "Someone will be with you forthwith to render our verdict."

Sangrey raised a hand from beside the Vicar. "Until then, remain within the grounds of the Priory." She paused to allow him to respond, he assumed. He shook his head in accord. "You are not a prisoner, but for your safety, we shall have no choice but to return you should you leave in the interim."

Garron bowed. "Aye, Your Reverencies." The same words he had uttered in repeat throughout the inquisition, if it were such; a standard formality when addressing the Ennead. He turned and exited. With all he had endured, a reprieve from examination marked a welcome change.

A winding flight of stairs led up to his assigned space, ascending from a hallway to the side of the central vestibule, a grand entryway to a grander main hall. Torches made visible the stone passage he climbed, scattered with paintings of archbishops and others past, and narrow, stained-glass windows that filtered through colored light. Hung from the walls near the vaulted ceiling were tapestries, similar to those in the Ennead's council room, free of wrinkles and brushed on their faces. Machines and attendant deacons maintained the Priory to near spotlessness.

When he came to his chamber, a joined bedroom and washroom, a deacon awaited outside the door and offered him a bath. "A kindness of Archbishop Mallum," the deacon said. His first in weeks.

With care, he had lowered himself into the hot water, cloudy with oils. Eyes closed, he drew in a deep breath of the air around him, spiced by scented candles and warmed by a hearth in the sleeping quarter.

The deacon scrubbed his filthy, calloused feet and scarred back and arms with a stone of pumice, stripping away dead skin. At times, the stone grazed uncomfortably against his ribs and shoulder blades, barely encased beneath thin muscle, fat, and flesh. She scraped the dirt from under his nails and trimmed them. For all her work, he thanked her and asked her to part and enjoy her evening, wishing not to take advantage of her services. She obliged with a smile and tilt at the waist, disappearing and leaving him in solitude.

When the water had cooled and his fingertips had pruned, he removed himself from the tub and dried off using a towel sat out for him on a stool. He stepped into his sleeping space. Undercloths and robes waited to replace his former attire. These robes were different in size, custom-tailored to match his withered figure with a measure of dignity. *How did they prepare this already?* He had forgotten what life had been like in the capital.

He lay on the bed, a feather mattress; a foreign thing, much nicer than anything he had slept on in the south in all the ages he'd been there. The villages were not so common of higher accommodations, and the villagers were unaccustomed to them. In the richest nation on Earth, one might expect better for the lesser folk. Yet they did live decently for their troubles, in large part due to the Church. *No matter what dissenting factions claim, the Church does well for its people, from the farmer to the student and machinist.*

Much time had passed since his encounter. But even in this unsoiled, sanctified place, the most so of any in the world, warded with the strongest of magic, crafted by the likes of Aramanth Delacroix, Camille Sangrey, and the Archmagister and her chosen aids, he remained in a state of unease. His mind preserved a sense of perturbation, as one might feel after a candle has burned out and left them in the dark. Something that he could not seal away had uncovered itself within him.

A knock came upon his door.

"You may enter."

The door opened, its old hinges silent and freshly-oiled. Delacroix stepped inside and closed the door behind her, walking wordlessly over to an oak chair with a wrapped leather seat and back at the side of the room. She brought it to his bedside and sat down, crossing her legs, and offered him a cordial grin, her hands folded in her lap. In her left palm, she held lunar tear beads.

"Father," she said, her voice silken, and her words, unhurried and light. "You look better." She had an ever-refined manner about her, whether in public or private.

Weary, he looked over at her and sat up. He would have risen to his feet, but found his strength had escaped him. She appeared to recognize his lethargy, gesturing that he could remain seated.

"Archbishop Delacroix, 'tis an honor. I expected a deacon may deliver my sentence to me." Even his voice sounded frail.

"You are not to be reprimanded, Father. Where would be the justice in that? You had nothing for which to remain in the Vale. We have confirmed it. The village is quiet as a tomb. Martials recovered the body of Alina, and we shall bury her with proper rites. The inquiry was but a formality, for all the impressing."

"Archbishop." Relief rolled over him. The back of his head tingled and the weight at his chest that had staggered his breathing all day fled. "I was certain Archbishop Sangrey and the Vicar would find me guilty." A shame persisted. "I did not abandon my station out of malice or indifference, though I failed—"

"The tragedy visited upon Erlan remains a mystery. Nevertheless, only a fool would have dared to challenge it. Archbishops Umbra and Sangrey were sympathetic to your plight, as were we each. Nothing you might have bested alone could have decimated a village with nary a trace in a single night. Our business is virtue and burden, not the needless loss of life. We do not desire you dead for dying's sake. You are a good man. Do not question your goodness for the misfortunes visited upon you."

To his left, a window leaked hazy yellow light through its shutters onto the surface of his bed. "What is to happen now?" He gazed down at his legs, slender shapes beneath a thick woolen blanket of black.

"We've received reports of other disruptions in the underlands since the massacre of Erlan. A company of the Martials will investigate and deal with any present malefactors." She paused, extending the lunar tears she clutched to him. "You will remain here. In your own admission, a wicked force has touched your mind. We must be certain that it will plague you no longer before we permit you leave, lest you inflict it on others or cause harm to yourself."

He took the beads from her. His hand appeared aged and rough over her delicate, youthful fingers, even more so by their emaciated state, his knuckles wide and the spaces between them shrunken. These beads were not his. His had been dull and distressed. This strand differed even from his original issue when they were new. *What became of my beads?* He had no recollection of informing the Ennead he had misplaced his string.

Considering their abilities, however, he need not have done so for them to be cognizant of his deprivation.

"Sleep, Garron." Delacroix discarded formal titles. She stood and turned for the door of his bedchamber. "No harm will come to you, so long as I am in this city." With that, she left.

His worry did not dissipate with her words, but he calmed. Much remained elusive to him, and to them. What took place in the south, and how many people may be dying as he rested in his gentle feather bed?

He lay down again. His eyelids were heavy and fluttered to a close. The warmth of his room and the sustenance afforded him since he first arrived had somewhat restored him after the tribulations of his journey, but he felt lesser now. Unsettled, sluggish. His thoughts remained unclear and aggrieved, no matter the comforting words or space. The bodies haunted him, Alina's and Emmelina's distorted, curdled features, as did the timbre of that invasive voice. He would never be as he were.

He did not know whether he could go on.

CHAPTER V: MANEUVERS

Athenne

"So, the Ennead still conspires to murder us." Bhathric paced the room, having arrived moments prior with Eclih in tow. She wore a dark midriff coat over a fitted tunic, grey trousers, and well-kept leather boots. On occasion, she rolled a lock of black hair between her fingers. "They must be aware of our movements."

Uldyr shivered, his body glazed in a thin layer of sweat. Athenne dabbed at his wounds with an ointment. She lacked the knowledge of healing to treat his worst injuries. Her hand rested on his shoulder when she finished applying the medicine, and the other wiped at his brow with a wet cloth, sweeping away dried blood. The light of the sun and candles illuminated the common area of his home.

"Aliester Haldis, the Red, he called himself. Probably Forgebrand. Abbisan dancer. Never met him that I remember," Uldyr said in an enervated tone. "We can't assume the Ennead were his employer just because they work with daggerhands. Could be any number out to stop us. Perhaps it's someone after me, alone."

"Nevertheless." Eclih balanced on his heels against a wooden support beam, arms folded at his chest. "We must be vigilant. Someone knows something. They targeted Uldyr because of it. You've been with the Saints for some time, working, traveling." He looked at Uldyr. "If they want you, they want us."

Athenne adjusted in her seat, as if to remind them of her presence before she spoke. She hated interrupting. "The daggerhand claimed he wasn't after me, yet I've been with you for months. Would they not desire us dead, alike, if it were their aim to strike down the Saints?"

"You were with Uldyr," Bhathric corrected. "Mayhap their client doesn't know of you."

Eclih rested the index and middle fingers of his right hand against his lips, his expression pensive, eyes staring to the floor. "Aye," he said at last. He stepped away from the beam and slipped his hands into the pockets of his breeches. "We best assume they watch us, but not always. Often enough to be of concern, but not to distract us."

"Should we not return to Aitrix and inform her?" Athenne's hand lingered on Uldyr's shoulder. "Is she not in danger?" His tremors remained, and a fever swelled beneath the flesh.

Did a taint from the blade infect his wound?

"She can handle herself." Uldyr inhaled sharply and shifted with strained effort on his cot. Dark blood crusted and dampened the bandages over the injuries Athenne had treated earlier. She had failed to stanch the bleeding. "Even with the Ennead's restriction of the Aether, her gifts exceed anyone's capacity to contain them. Forgebrand's best couldn't harm her."

He is not well. Labored breathing, skin flushed, words ragged.

Bhathric stopped by the window, gazing out toward the front garden, to the body of the mercenary lying motionless in the grass and weeds. "This one's dead, anyway. We can't afford to lose the time for him. I'm certain Aitrix would instruct us to push forward."

Uldyr could die. Abbisan dancers and mercenaries each coated their blades in toxins, including feces and exotic poisons and venoms harvested from plants and animals. A festering infection caused by such weapons would make for a slow and gruesome death. If the daggerhand had befouled his edges, Uldyr's wounds would refuse to mend. He would fade with each hour and day, if he had days.

Athenne's hands tingled with a jittery unease. A heavy fluttering gripped her chest. Before they had even carried out their deed, peril lurked, nipped at their heels.

Will someone accost us again?

She ran fingers through her hair to brush it away from her eyes and braced her chin on her palm with her elbow on one knee. The others talked among themselves while she reflected. *What if Uldyr had perished in that fight? If he had died, so would have I.* Could a mercenary have afforded to spare her? *Why would the Mother save you, lend you special favor?* She played a dangerous game in this quest to free the Aether with neither a clear path to victory nor any idea of what true success would be.

Her companions discussed their plans. At their gathering, Aitrix had told them of her belief that the constraints on the Aether were a product of a particular warding magic, likely crafted by Archbishop Aramanth Delacroix and the magisters of the Church. Delacroix, revered as one of the most brilliant living mages in all of Imios, rivaled the legendary Aetherian scholarship of the Archmage Besogos himself. Though many thought the ability to access the Aether to be innate, and unpredictably bequeathed beyond calculated means of power and essence, the learning of incantations required extensive study and instruction, at which Delacroix had excelled. She could perform spells so intricate that but a few mages on Earth comprehended them. Fewer had the ability to cast them.

Delacroix's academic knowledge shadowed Aitrix's like a mountain over a hill, but fear of the latter stemmed from her raw power, the deep well of her magical essence. Where the apparent wards limited most in Imperial territory to rudimentary craft, or bereft of magic, Aitrix remained able to execute even higher combative spells. As Uldyr had stated, few could challenge Aitrix Kravae, let alone trounce her.

Before their departure, Aitrix and Eclih had performed a scrying incantation, the former lending power to the latter, dubbed a wizard in the overlands for his unique ability to scry at an exceptional distance. Together, the two of them had uncovered that a central ward restricted the Aether from a chamber deep beneath the Grand Priory in Aros, by virtue of the fact that the space had resisted their scrying most. They further unveiled that boundary wards carried this central ward's restrictive effect to the edges of the Empire's territories.

It would be the duty of Athenne's cohort to make their way into the Grand Priory and disable the source ward. Once they destroyed this ward and liberated the Aether, other agents of the Saints were to disable the boundary wards that might harbor remnants of the spell, too dangerous to attempt while the main ward that powered them still lived. Infiltrating the Priory would be the chief hurdle to surmount.

Aitrix had further tasked Eclih and Bhathric with scheming the second phase of their assault: the annihilation of the Iron Court at the center of the Imperial Palace, home of the Imperial Sovereign.

Athenne found her greatest reservations in this facet of their mission. She had worked to make peace with the fact that attacking the Grand Priory would require the slaughter of innocent members of the Church. *But to destroy the most hallowed space in the world, to obliterate a place where Ankhev the White, the highest celestial servant of Gohheia, once stood?* The notion filled her with unrelenting dread.

Could salvation in death still be hers after this? *Is this wrong?* Had the Church wandered astray? *Is it the Mother, Herself, against whom we wage war?* That would surely resign her to an eternity of anguish in Eophianon.

Eclih and Bhathric continued to deliberate, their words a droning noise in the background. Athenne looked at Uldyr as if they sat alone in the room, drifting between the physical space around her and her thoughts. He rested, sickly, enfeebled, his eyes shut. She had never observed him so. He had always been a towering figure, hard as iron, tough as steel. She could scarcely stand it one moment, but in the next, a numbness seized her. Her cerulean eyes peered without aim, empty, seeing without watching.

As she wandered in her mental haze, a passage from the *Blest Writ*, that sacred Matrian text, came to her:

The All-Mother rewards in death those who live by the three pillars—altruism, order, and progress—with eternal rest in Nihil, the Nothing.

Those among the wicked who defy the Mother's will and want must remain for all time in Eophianon, the Blackened Yonder, home of Korvaras, Patron of the Undead. There, condemned spirits relive their worldly torments, up to their deaths, in a ceaseless cycle.

Most accepted this perspective on the afterlife, including Athenne, who had grown up with and learned it as the Truth, but there were exceptions. Asdamosian cultists believed that the spirits of the dead passed through the Asdamos Rift and entered into his realm, the Abyss, to become a share of the Aether. Some druids of Sitix held that mortals perished and converted into a part of the living Earth; the energy in the storms, the nutrition of animals and plants, the power behind the winds. Worshipers of Korvaras contended that they would become as Acolytes in his plane, the land of the unforgiven, after death.

What should I believe? The damned whispered no secrets, and those put to rest in Nihil took a final vow of silence. Would remaining a part of this enterprise confine her to a meaningless, perpetual horror? Perhaps the late hour had passed, and had always been so since the days of her youth, and her sordid mistake.

That terrible error, so long ago, in the time of her young life, ever at her mind's periphery. When she had climbed the rocks of the riverbanks across the Renerin Hinterlands. When she had scaled the trees and watched from above, longing to glimpse a hessant in the northern woodlands, beyond the Eastern Mountains.

Those gorgeous creatures, half like a deer fawn and half like a mortal. Too beautiful for such an unpleasant world. Hunters pursued them for their hides, the thick coats around their hips, though rarely captured or killed them. Natural healers and limited psychics, the stories claimed, hessants exceeded the abilities of the most powerful human and elven materialists and mentalists.

Athenne's youthful folly had caused her such strife, turmoil, self-doubt. She couldn't talk of it. Fear, anger, and guilt gripped her and prevented her from thinking deeply of it. In the aftermath of her misdeed, she had run and wept, then sat at the edge of a stream, arms wrapped around bent legs, face buried in her knees; afraid to move or go home, scared that wickedness had etched itself on her face, visible in her gaze through the pinholes of her pupils.

Finally, after all her waiting and watching and hoping, a hessant had come to her, less common in the Hinterlands than the Hessantwood. A fonna, as natural philosophers called their females. It stood against the frosted backdrop, glowing, fur sparkling with tiny beads of ice. Its large, unblinking eyes affixed on her.

Hessants were intelligent and verbal. Athenne yearned for her to speak, to hear what so few had. Yet the fonna said nothing, and vanished into the forest. The fonna knew, saw into her mind and through her.

Athenne had felt unworthy since. Meandering and lowly, without purpose. Ages had passed, and that pain, once constant and piercing, persisted as a dull, smothering ache.

Bhathric interrupted her ruminations, tortuous and glum. "Athenne, are you up to it?"

"Hm?" Athenne replied, jolted back to the present.

"Lost in her mind." A tone of concern underlaid Eclih's jest.

Well lost, indeed. She felt isolated, even surrounded by friends, if they were such.

Co-conspirators.

Fellow malefactors.

Soon-to-be-murderers.

Bhathric's eyes crinkled with a sympathetic, deliberate half-grin. "Aitrix has asked us to task you with getting to the source ward in the Grand Priory. It's our duty to accompany you to the Imperial City to aid in secondary endeavors." She paused, as if gauging Athenne's reaction. "Are you up to it?"

"I must be. I am here, am I not?"

Eclih moved to Bhathric's side. "Let us not interrogate Mys Athenne further. Either she's loyal, or she isn't. We'll find out one way or another." He gave a playful wink.

Bhathric drew from her coat a strand of beads. "Lunar tears. The Priory wards deny anyone not carrying a set access to the grounds. Evidently, they don't want members of the common body wandering about."

Athenne took the beads and rolled them between her fingers. This string had a silver charm on it.

These must have come from a deacon.

"We took a number from deacons some time ago," Bhathric said, as a coincidence or reading her expression. "They were not easily acquired and we aren't likely to come across many further strands, so don't lose them."

Athenne looked up. "These permit casting, do they not?"

"They allow members of the Clergy to cast, but we have not had the same success. Aitrix conjectured that access to the grounds is a generalized magic, while casting is tied to the assigned holder's essence signature."

Eclih walked to the door. "Shall we?"

"Give me a parting word with Uldyr," Athenne said as Uldyr

stirred to her left. "He cannot accompany us in this condition." She turned her head to meet his gaze.

"Of course." Eclih opened the door and stepped outside.

Bhathric trailed him and closed the door behind her.

Uldyr smiled, his lips joined.

A forced grin, but kind.

A kindness to her.

"Don't die on me." Her voice withered at the end.

Uldyr's smile faded. "Go on. I'll be here when you return."

Chains of sorrow ensnared her countenance and dragged it downward. *No matter what comes of this, no matter how my relationships with Bhathric, Eclih, and Aitrix progress, Uldyr is my true friend. My last friend.*

Evening beckoned as she and her associates trotted up the winding road on horseback. The tops of the trees clipped the light of the sun, projecting a wall of shadow across the field at their backs, where small creatures skittered and flowers bloomed, died, and rotted. Athenne maintained a pace behind the others to keep herself from the brunt of their conversation. She longed to be as a mute for the night, for her monthly cycle had returned, and fatigue beset her. Twinges sparked in her abdomen, and a heavy ache radiated through her knees to her thighs. Perspiration glistened on her forehead from the pain, which vacillated between pressures and spasms.

Ash, oak, and pine encircled them as they came into the thicket of the Fausse Woods. This forest bore the name of a powerful mentalist, Rivana Fausse, who had once lived in a hovel at the eastern side of the range. The near-dwellers had dubbed her the White Lotus Witch for the flowers she pinned in her hair, and cast aspersions on her for her unusual psychic abilities. It had been a hundred ages since her last reported appearance, though tales cautioned that she may still reside in the woodlands.

Hateful nonsense.

The slurs of witch and warlock worked to shame women and men with odd abilities, primarily psychics; a means of decrying what conventional magi struggled to understand. What they could not control and contain with ease. What they feared. *This is the great frailty of the Matrian Church, their efforts to subjugate the atypical.*

Sounds from animals that feasted on ground-level vegetation produced the lone sign of life around them. The density of the tree crowns darkened the colors of the woods, depressed their disinterested hues.

This foreign land unnerved Athenne. The icy splendor of the northeastern Hinterlands of Reneris stretched as a mountain without end compared to this low place. Despite her less favorable memories, she longed to return there. It had been a simpler time, and happier.

Her lower aching flared anew. She pressed a hand to her stomach, massaging.

"Are you ailing?" Bhathric asked Athenne over her shoulder, probably in note of her face, suspended now in a grimace that she could not pacify.

Athenne exhaled. "My red mother rakes and stabs." She had done her best to hide it during their journey, as she had in her time prior with Uldyr, going off on her own when the opportunity arose to change sanitary towels. Bhathric had not expressed similar signs of suffering. "How do you manage?"

"I thought as well." Bhathric pointed to her abdomen. "Suppression ring. Put in ages ago."

Of course. "I've heard the procedure is perilous."

"The lower navel is a treacherous place to pierce and cast upon so, but I had a capable doctor and suffering beforehand alike yours. Though I might describe the ordeal more as my insides being wrung out."

Athenne gripped her knee. "Who did you see? I'll consider." *If we survive this mission.*

If this doesn't kill me.

"A Laortian doctor, at least when I visited." Bhathric turned around. "Fausta Haltan."

A Haltan heiress? Talk of the Haltan family's wealth reached even to Reneris.

"You may need to find another, should you remain with us," Bhathric continued. "Aitrix previously had a disagreeable association with her. It mattered little by the time I joined. My family had already disowned me."

"Forgive my interruption, but we ought to establish camp." Eclih looked back to Bhathric and Athenne. "Roaming by night shall not avail us, and I'm sure we all tire."

"It is your prerogative, Athenne, but you need not conceal such things." Bhathric halted her horse at Eclih's suggestion. "I wish only that you feel relaxed and open to be as you are. Eclih is a man of understanding."

Eclih stopped as well. "I endeavor to be." He offered an unassuming smile.

Athenne shook her head, though she doubted she could relax. Even when agony did not tear through her, sleep had never come with ease. As a girl and as a young woman, she found herself twisting and turning in darkness most nights. That evening, she would be another restless spirit among the trees.

They had descended from their horses as night fell and the sun sank behind the hills. The air around them dampened and cooled. They unfurled sleeping mats of gathered and bound plant materials and forged a fire pit between them. Creaking trees, shivering bushes, and dense brush hugged in at their sides. In the distance, coyotes howled, and closer, crickets chirped and frogs croaked.

"From where do you hail, Athenne?" Eclih's voice seemed loud atop the evening music.

"Reneris." she answered, forgiving that he had already forgotten her introduction from when they first met. *I suppose I should make some effort to converse.* "You're both Imperial-born?"

Bhathric rolled a lock of hair between two fingers. "I am from Kordyr, and Eclih comes from Laorta."

"What did you do there?"

"Eclih was something of a vagabond at his peak," said Bhathric with an impish grin.

"A thief of the street," he corrected, his tone amused. "Bhathric was a bard. Her fingers pluck the strings of a lute as the feet of a dancer dignify the stage, and her voice is a gift of the Celestia." He looked over to Bhathric, with a glitter in his eye, ever-present when fixed on her. "She even played at the Hall of Marquis."

"From Ruhlter's tongue." Bhathric covered her face with her arms. "I am not that skilled."

"The gods themselves shudder with jealousy, Athenne."

"Eclih!" Bhathric slapped him playfully across the shoulder and he chuckled.

Athenne gave a faint smile. "I hope to hear you play sometime, Bhathric. I'm certain you're a marvel."

As their conversation lulled, Eclih fell asleep. Bhathric sat adjacent to him, across from Athenne on the other side of the pit. Athenne lay, gazing into the flames. The fire's heat warmed her front, while the shadows chilled her back. In defiance of the calm night, peace eluded her.

"May I come to you, Athenne?" Over the divide, the flame crackled, flickering on the faces of the trees. Bhathric's grey eyes shone in the light, as if the fire itself lived inside them. A glow accentuated and washed her slender, sharp features, eerie against the darkness behind her.

Athenne nodded, and Bhathric rose and came forth. She sat down beside Athenne on the frosted ground, her legs crossed beneath her, only her profile visible in the orange glow.

A few moments passed.

"What troubles you?"

Athenne shifted on her mat. "How do you mean?"

"Your face betrays you."

Another bout of silence cloaked them.

Athenne's lips parted, but she relucted to speak, choosing her words with caution. She did not wish to share. "I don't desire to burden you." She closed her eyes and breathed deep. Her lungs burned with the chill.

"We may die, Athenne. Me, you, Uldyr, Eclih, even Aitrix. We may each perish. If we die at the hands of the Church, our burials will not be ceremonious. Fortune shines if they do not toss us together in a pit and burn us living. Shall I know so little of you, if we march to our ends?"

"I don't want to kill anyone," Athenne blurted out, almost with scorn. She regretted uttering the words.

After several seconds, Bhathric looked at her and gave a hushed chuckle through sealed lips. "Then you won't." A consolatory kindness thickened her tone. "Leave the killing to us. You won't sully your hands with it. We are more than mere collaborators. We are your friends—"

"—*I* am your friend."

Could she trust Bhathric, Eclih, Aitrix? Unless she were willing to defect that night, to flee without looking back, she would have to place her faith in them. *It's probably already too late.*

"I hope, one day, you may confide in me, *before* we expire," Bhathric said in jest.

Athenne heard a grin in Bhathric's words and smiled, her first modicum of joy in some time.

Standing and moving behind her, Bhathric positioned such that their backs were together.

They lay stationary, the noises of the forest swirling around them, the stars shimmering overhead through the branches and leaves. Eclih murmured and wallowed in his sleep. Bhathric's breathing grew rhythmic as rest came to her. Drowsiness would not greet Athenne for hours.

I should quench the flames before I drift.

Eventually, her eyelids drooped. The threat of the cold, and comfort, kept her from snuffing their fire out. A wind whipped the blaze to and fro. As temperatures fell, the cold bit at her toes and her exposed ear. She felt grateful that Bhathric had joined her, for the night would have chilled Athenne without her there.

Does she lie?

A sense of camaraderie with Bhathric swelled inside her.

Athenne wanted her words to be true.

CHAPTER VI: ANGUISH

Garron

It had been many ages since Garron had made himself a feature in Aros, the heart of the Empire. It had been even longer since he had fraternized with fellow members of the Clergy at such length. He found the Priory crawling with deacons like ants in their colony, nothing new. Young women, in prime share, but more young men than in his youth. This must have been the work of Archbishop Mallum. She had a softness for the menkind not possessed by ardent traditionalists in the upper echelons of the Church, who had surely opposed Breiman Umbra's most curious ascent.

Garron seemed a figure of small fame at present. Nearly everyone he encountered knew him and his story. Some were amazed or intrigued, others pitied him or kept their quiet distance. He blamed none, no matter their reaction. Even when he had been there himself, he struggled to comprehend it.

A near constant smell of meats roasting and breads baking from the Priory kitchens saturated the air, throughout the far reaches of the living quarters to the assembly chambers. Machines, the creatures of spark and bolt, now handled most

Priory meals. In a few weeks, strength and mobility had returned to him, and proportion too. He had needed new robes not long after his first fresh set.

He ate of stew, thick with butter and cream broths; boiled and salted lamb, beef, chicken, or shredded swine, swimming among roasted potatoes, carrots, and peas. Each dish tasted seasoned and cooked to perfection, the uniformity and consistency known of machines. Delicacies. Enough to fill anyone's stomach.

Since the inquiry, he had seen none of the members of the Ennead, not even Delacroix. He grew restless in the Priory, confined to it for many days. Descending to the Priory's hall of knowledge, he tried to distract himself with Rennera Bhojith's *Lady of Sorrow*, a fictional account of a woman's life during the Century's War. Yet he could hardly concentrate on the text as the horrors of Erlan danced about his mind. He could neither evade them nor shoo them away. By evening, he had sat the book back on its shelf and returned to his chamber.

His beard had become as a weedy garden, speckled with black, white, and grey hairs, more of the last two with every week, thick and hanging in splintered ends to his collarbone. He thought often of trimming it, but a razor remained elusive, in chief because he kept forgetting to request one. By social dictate, Imperial women and men soaped themselves and shaved with warm water. They scraped away the hair beneath their arms, the hair of their legs, the hair around and between, except the face for men and the head for either, unless they willed it.

He sank for around an hour in his bed, staring at the vaulted ceiling above him and the shadows flickering across the room in various shapes. Weary of his chamber's smooth stone walls, polished floor, mosaic window, of the fire in the hearth, of the shining marble tub, he fled to the hall and its dim light. Rain lashed in sheets outside. The walls of this passage must have been thinner, for the world exposed itself only beyond the interior of his room. *Or they've warded my chamber and magic obscures the noise.*

Machines passed him as he meandered the capitol, dusting surfaces with their angled feather tools, scrubbing floors with spinning brushes emitting slight hums and whirs. The machines did not acknowledge him except in simple gesticulated pleasantries. There were machines in the south, but rarely in the villages. They were more common to the cities and the wealthy in private service or the more substantial public markets. There had been far fewer of them in the capitol buildings in his youth.

The halls of the Grand Priory had always been clean, but never this impeccable. Now the floors and walls kept a regular luster, and the draperies and rugs went unblemished.

Each day when he left his bedchamber, he returned to new sheets, smelling sweet like flowers, and a sparkling bathing tub and washbasin and privy. His senses marveled.

As he walked a hall he had not seen in some time, admiring portraits he had not viewed in such a duration that he saw them with newborn eyes, the patter of feet approached him from the rear.

"Mysr Latimer." A young woman spoke, in her early twenties, by his estimation. Of course, she would be. "Pardon," she corrected herself. "*Father* Latimer."

He chuckled and waved a hand at her. "Worry not, Sister." He hoped to sound comforting. "So few are we priests in the capital, 'tis expected." The look of her plain grey garb signified her station as a deacon. Perhaps a greener entry, for she carried charmless beads at her wrist.

She pushed back a lock of bright red hair. "I wanted to say, if I happened upon you, that we pray for you every evening in the residence halls during the nightly ritual. We mourn for you and the fallen of Erlan." Her eyes were a dark hazel, like patches of sunbaked grass in deep summer, and sorrowful. Sorrowful for him, but warm too.

Garron gave a faint smile through his unkempt beard. "The All-Mother extends Her grace to each of us."

"Aye, Father." The deacon tittered and departed.

He observed as she disappeared down the corridor, extending him one last glance before she rounded the corner. Shortly after, he redirected his attention to the portrait in front of him and read of the name.

"Adelheid Valiana," he whispered. The first Matriarch, appointed by the Andesite in Age 3. In her grave by Age 54, after nearly fifty-one ages of diligent, faithful service. Long ago replaced, the Andesite and the Matriarch, along with the Autarch, had been the three powers of the first Imperial government, the Covenant.

Adelheid oversaw numerous religious rites and invented Idoss, the foremost celebration of the Empire, held during the final month of the cycle, Senterios; a lavish show of prosperity and grandeur associated with commemorating essential Imperial ideals; liberty, the lauding of Gohheia, individual autonomy.

During the fest, government officials signed annual political documents before the people of the city and gave declarations of intent. Contests of skill, singing, dancing, and cleverness commenced. There would be mass prayer, public and private intoxication, nudity, displays of art, impressive feasts, parades, music, elaborate theatrical performances. People from across the Empire, and other kingdoms, came each festival to participate. The dictates of the Church permitted priests such as Garron a return to the capital only at this time, conceivably to remind them of the object of their deference. So rare were priests in Aros, often posted to villages and far cities, that deacons commonly did not know how to address one. Thus, he did not fault the sister for mistaking his title.

What would the first Matriarch think of Aros in the Modern Era? Would she be proud of their work, find honor in their edicts? How would she address the massacre of Erlan? Adelheid had been renowned as an exceptional mage, particularly in the art of metaphysics, the rarest aspect, but hardly utilized her skills as Matriarch, a ceremonial position. Chronicles told that the Archmage Besogos had consulted her when devising spells still popular hundreds of ages later. Besogos, though, being half-elven, had lived hundreds of ages himself.

To carry on such a time before the Nothing, a gift or a curse?

Garron spent the next two hours walking the halls. He stopped at the end of a corridor high in the Priory, one of the few thus far within the whole of the structure that had a clear window, free of art or metallic salts. He admired the courtyard below, opened with many cloisters. The garden of the yard contained a number of themed beds: dyeing, fumigating, strewing, cosmetic, medicinal, culinary. He wasn't certain to whom the garden belonged within the Church, or if it belonged to anyone.

In the garden grew lemon balm, chives, and mint, among

other herbs. Trimmed hedges, crape myrtle flowers, maple trees, and white fringe trees ornamented the grounds, elaborate in alignment and immaculate in keep. His current station allowed him a fine vantage point.

As night fell, the rain left the stone walkways below wet and shimmering. It battered the window, and in the distance, lightning crackled across the sky, spreading out like veins and igniting the world underneath in melancholy shades of blue for a moment. Watery moons and reflective rings dripped thinly through the clouds.

"Father," came a soft voice, behind him.

A figure drew his eye from its corner. A woman. He turned. Blonde hair framed a sculpted face, slim and symmetrical. Dead amber eyes watched him with uncanny stillness from delicate sockets. He did not recall having seen the young woman prior. She wore a gown of black velvet with a necklace of rubies that fastened tight at the throat. *Not a deacon.* The Church did not permit the sisters such finery.

"May I help you?"

"What ails you?" A monotonous smoothness layered her intonation, like a serpent gliding across motionless water. Her face glowed white in the moonlight that shone through the window at his back. The room warmed as the light spread.

He observed the stranger with a wariness, lungs convulsing. Did he appear ailed? With all that he had seen as of late, he must remain guarded. "Do I know you?"

"I am called Arulan, Father. Lady Arulan, if it pleases."

"Lady Arulan?" he answered with a careful delay. "Have you but the one name?"

"But the one."

An unnaturalness hung about her, not in anything she did or said, in particular, but in the slightest of her movements. Her face stiffened and expressed in unison. When he asked her name, the corner of her mouth twitched, as though eschewing a smile. A faint amusement played across her eyes.

My mind sees specters in every corner.

"Tell me, do you long to leave this place?" she said.

The question caught him by surprise. He knitted his brow, hesitant to engage her.

What is this?

"Mys, I'm afraid I don't—"

The woman reached out and touched him at the neck. Her motion blurred. He heard a scream. It sounded as if it were outside of him, yet his throat rumbled. His skin burned at her contact, as though she were fire made flesh, and a blackness came over his vision. He fell, descending into a boundless pit, devoid of light or noise. The heat spread until it consumed him, and a coldness followed. He could not move. His body numbed with the chill. If he saw, nothing met his sight.

A droning racket pierced his mind; a dull, familiar squeal, quiet at first, then growing louder. It swelled until he could hardly stand the pressure. He had no hands with which to cover his ears, or ears to find. He had no mouth with which to scream. *The Beast.* She had found him. She had infiltrated the Priory and come to finish their business, to take his tattered spirit for her own.

The voice had returned.

His eyes opened in a daze, caked at their corners as if from a long slumber. Peering up to the night sky, cool droplets of rain sprinkled across his face. He moved to a sit, unsteady and struggling to take on the dual pursuits of restraining an urge to vomit and making sense of his surroundings. His eyes scanned the area at his sides, a road. *Am I dreaming? Dead?* Once more, a surrealness in which his senses were deceitful had thrust itself upon him. Or not. He could not know. One certainty existed, however: the power of this creature, this *Beast,* as he had called her, or *it,* exceeded their imaginations.

Across the street stood a house excluded from the neighborhoods, a stone hovel with a freshly-sodded roof. The rest of the common homes, lined in rows and blocks, were distant and dark in the pale moonlight. Trees and overgrown vegetation littered the area around him. Though his exact location remained elusive, he suspected he may be near Outmore Loch, well beyond the walls of Aros. How had he arrived here, so far from the Priory?

By the window of the dwelling passed a woman, or what he believed to be a woman, if she were real. What might have been an oil lamp lit her living quarter. The source burned too bright and constant for candles. Her home seemed illuminated solely to give him sight of her.

He pushed himself up, the inside of his skull pulsating. The joints of his body ached, his muscles tense and sore, as if overexerted. He tottered, yet kept his balance. His robes had torn at the edges and frayed at the seams. A rush of murky wind brought the scent of sulfur to him, drowning out the smells of the city and outer commune. *I am between the countryside and the residential districts beyond the city's walls. I must be.*

Another aroma came to him. The noxious stench of tainted flesh, filthy blood, and death. He could barely stomach it and covered his nose. The woman passed the window again. He felt a fresh compulsion. He was an eldered man, isolated, still recovering. She was a young woman. But even in his haggard state, he could overcome her.

Why?

Why did he think it?

She passed the window once more.

No, no.

I mustn't.

I cannot.

"*Go forth, Father,*" a tone buzzed, as a hot breath crawling up his neck. He turned to find its origin. Alina stood beside him, her features sunken, wasted, as she had been in the cold, dark woodshed.

No! his mind screamed. *It isn't her!* He did not speak it.

"It won't be difficult," the imitation Alina said, louder.

He stepped one pace away.

"Take her for your first," the girl continued, moving nearer. "No one knows you are here."

"Enough!" He swiped at the air, his arms and hands quivering to the fingertips. "You are not Alina! I saw her dead myself. The capital has her body."

She gave a crooked smile, baring yellowed fangs. Then she cackled. The sound echoed among the houses and trees, and came from inside him. His mind filled with it. "She is weak, Garron. Weaker than you, such as you are."

The words escaped her lips and rose from within him in union; disorienting, overwhelming. He continued to back away and almost lost his balance as his heel scraped over a stone that jutted up from the road.

"Take her, Garron!" she ordered. "*Take her!*"

"No!" His throat grew raw with the cold. He fought with every ounce of his strength to anchor himself in place, until his body burned with the strain. Laughter arose as a cacophony, as a hundred voices in chorus, shrieking in his head. He found himself at the woman's door, hand on its surface. *Please, Mother, stop me. Free me of this creature. Strike me down before I take another step.*

That night began the end. It welled up from within, from the call of his spirit. Waves of heat pulsated through him and made him sweat. Cold air collided with his moist skin and chilled him. The world faded in and out. He heard no noise around him for a moment, then the sounds flooded back. His life had become a dream melted into waking. The hissing swarm in his head persisted as the only constant. So many words, tormenting and scraping, crying and laughing, growling and screeching. The most powerful, that cursed creature's voice.

Take her, it demanded. *Take her!*

With a careful push, he opened the woman's door, its hinges quiet. A small oil lamp on a desk in the corner lit the room. A damp cluster of decayed leaves covered the wooden floor near the entrance. The rest looked recently swept and tidied. The woman was nowhere in sight.

Why isn't the door sealed?

Why, must I?

He stood in the fore of her home and gazed about the space. A modest hearth warmed the air, made it hazy and sweet. Dust and smoke wafted in the streams of light pouring through the window. With a few inaudible steps, he moved to the oil lamp and turned its wick knob until its flame faded out. Shadows crept up from the corners. This was certain to alert the woman, he reckoned, and it did. Measured footfalls approached from another room.

Leave, he begged inside. *Turn away! Do not come!*

Take her, Father, began the voices again. *Take her!*

The woman stepped through the doorway of the common quarter and screamed at the sight of him. Garron lost himself at the noise. She turned to run, retreated to her bedchamber. Garron followed. She pivoted as he lunged and caught him with a dagger, but his size dwarfed hers, even in this state, and he took her by the wrists. They fell to the ground together and he positioned himself over her. She lost the blade and fought, clawing at his hands until she drew blood. She screamed and he screamed back, ribbons of saliva dripping from his mouth onto her face.

Take her, Father! Take her!

The squalling in his head expanded, louder and louder, a muddled clamor. He heard nothing else. It blocked out the woman's pleas and cries for help. A pool of blood spread next to her. She must have stabbed him in the side with her dagger, but he didn't feel it. He yearned to ruin her, empty of all things beyond that drive. They thrashed about one another like rabid dogs. She bit into his right hand and he struck her with his left, freeing her to claw him at the neck. She kicked and ripped and he grabbed her by the throat and squeezed, letting her tear at his forearms as she willed. Blood and hair and cloth spattered the floor around them.

She gurgled and sputtered and her pale face and brown eyes reddened, the veins around her forehead and jaw bulging, her legs flailing against his. Her lips moved, attempted to speak, but the pressure on her throat prevented it. He slammed her head into the floor a few times in violent fits and jerks, dazing her. Her eyes rolled after the third strike and she spat up thick spittle, pink with blood, but she did not capitulate.

A grey hand came down next to his victim's face, claws at the ends of long, spindly fingers scraping across the floor. Another had appeared in the room. The woman from the Vale. That wretched horned monster. Her empty eyes flickered and she grinned with rows of sharp crooked teeth, the same as Alina's, when she had pretended to be Alina. He did not recoil in horror, but instead squeezed the woman's neck harder.

"*Kill her.*" The creature gnashed at him. "*Kill her!*"

The woman under Garron did not react to the Beast, though it hovered at her side on all fours.

Is the creature real? Is this real? His fingers tautened, digging into the woman's throat as her grip on his wrists lightened, nails unsunk like small knives from his aged, leathered hide. He bled down the hands from the wounds she had made. She had gouged him deep and well.

A chill swept through the center of his back and chest. *No, no, no!* Shouting in his mind. He resisted the voice, the compulsion, the mutterings; he defied his ensorcellment. With his full might, he loosened his fingers. The Beast had gone in an instant, in the time between. He tore himself off of the woman and fell, shoving away with frenzied feet until his back slammed into the chamber wall. The wood groaned at the force.

"Forgive—forgive me," he rasped.

The woman wheezed and coughed, breathing jagged and labored. She wept between sharp inhalations, rolling onto her hip and shoulder. Her neck had already purpled from his grip. Much longer and he would have stolen the life from her. She had been close to losing consciousness.

Smeared with blood and sweat, her long chestnut hair had unbound and swept around her face, stuck at the eyes and lips. She bled from the nose and mouth from their struggle.

A mindless rage and fear coursed through him. Before the woman had time to regain her senses and retaliate or run for help, he fled. He flew from the house, raced down the dark stone streets. *How much farther? How much farther?* The whispers had ceased as soon as he had let go of her, but too late, for the damage had rooted deep and taken hold. His breath puffed from his mouth in white streamers and his sores throbbed and stung as his numbness subsided. The temperature had declined. How long had he been there, been gone?

Terror kept him running and shame brought him agony. He pressed a hand to his side as he ran on unbalanced and tender feet, aged legs weak and burning, realizing again that he bled. She had cut him. He had to stall the flow, or die. He might accept the latter. He wanted to fall to the ground and let the life seep out of him. Instead, he kept moving.

He came upon a river and collapsed to his hands and knees. The wind snapped at him from every direction, bit into his neck and ears. He hoped the cold might carry him off, release him from this shell. Why he had kept going, he could not confess. He did not deserve to live and be free.

Through his cries, he listened to the rushing water in front of and below him, spreading off into the darkness between walls of forest. "I'll drown myself," he said into the open air. "I do not deserve to live." He clenched his teeth together and dug his fingers into the ground. "Mother!" he bellowed, a gruff, hopeless wail. He fell to his side on the riverbank, frozen and unforgiving. "Why! Why do you not protect me!" he sobbed with hysteria, pulling in desperation at the neck of his robes until his knuckles turned white.

"Garron Latimer," came a voice.

"Father Garron Latimer." A woman spoke.

Gohheia?

Is this the end?

"'Tis he," another woman, he thought, replied. "His appearance matches the description."

"What's happened to you, Father?" the first said.

"Never mind that. Let's return him to the Priory. Archbishop Delacroix wants to see him. 'Tis not for us to ask," answered the second. "He's out of his head."

He recognized the women through blurred vision. Their attire, that is. Matching, ornate plate armor wrapped them, silver and glistening in the muted light. They were Martial inquisitors; religious police sent to retrieve him for the Ennead, no doubt, or to arrest him for his crime. It mattered little which.

Take her.

The voice had gone, but he could not shake it.

Take her.

He tried to yell, to get up and run and fling himself into the river before they seized him, to end the pain. His body would not move. The grey world around him spun. Thin and thick clouds of off-white swam overhead, combusted by the Earth's moons. Those distant celestial figures, idle among countless, careless stars.

He drifted away.

CHAPTER VII: GHORA

Athenne

They continued their journey northwest, their leather satchels filled with aetherlight-infused powder bombs, concealed from weather and sight by hooded cloaks in dyes of grey and black. They rode in single file down a tapered path between endless leaning trees in copses and sparse rows. The trees at first were green, then rose in shades of orange and brown, then were barren. Empty branches sprawled upward and unfolded and dripped with the misting rain that fell. Darkness crept about them as a storm approached.

For a time, there had been the scent of clean earth and wilds; butterflies flittered, fox squirrels chittered, birds sang and flew. The further north they ventured, the stiller the world became, and the cooler, and the murkier. The wind died down, and only the sprinkle and white fog of the air remained, hovering on the road amidst wood trunks. Life seemed empty in this bareness. It emphasized the insignificance of their quest and themselves in the face of the great, expansive underrealm. So many of their fleeting moments, mortals spent watching the world pass by, eyeing the ground, moving from one place to another without a thought.

Athenne had alleviated her boredom from the trip by burying her mind in a maze of darting ruminations, most pointless beyond the escape they provided. Eclih and Bhathric did not always try to force her to socialize. When they did, she feigned interest and want of them as best she could. This endeavor must not, could not, be joyous. In a few weeks, they would be within the walls of Aros, slipped through as vermin crawling in crevices to flee exposure.

A cool wind revealed itself again and exhaled across her face and dry lips. The breeze blew her cloak such that she became aware of its heaviness and uncomfortable, rubbing dampness. Its seams and stray threads scratched at her shoulders and wrists and neck. Filth clung to her skin like epoxy resin between panels of glass. The stink of dirt and living wrapped every inch of her. She despised the greased tangling of her hair and the incessant labor of grooming it back and rebinding it.

"I tire, but we ought to keep going. We rose late, for Bhathric's handsomeness takes much rest." Eclih shot Bhathric an amused glance and a sly smile.

Bhathric snorted and swept her hair from her forehead with her right hand, at war with the same problem as Athenne. "If I fall to the road, I'll sleep where I land. We're as the beasts in these backwoods."

"Ever the lady, our dear Athenne," Eclih called over his shoulder to her position at the end of their line. "Nary an ill word unto anyone, even in jest."

"Nary an ugly word for Mys *Bhathric*," Athenne said. "Lest I offend the Mother for insolence against Her loveliest daughter." Her words would ring as an undeniable truth to anyone with sound eyes.

The union of Bhathric and Eclih defied social convention. Imperial women and men rarely spent so much time together, or kept to one another with such faith. Then again, they weren't the staunchest Imperials to start with.

Women and men in Reneris, on the other hand, often made mutual pledges of exclusiveness, so Athenne went undisturbed by their prolonged coupling. Had she been Imperial-born and bred, she might have pitied Bhathric for their arrangement, detested Eclih's forthright approach to her, derided them as nesters.

"You flatter me. Though, you're not afflicted with a frightening likeness yourself." Bhathric winked at her.

"Ah, I see." Eclih chuckled. "You do conspire at my back."

Bhathric laughed. "I am compelled."

Athenne returned a smirk. She didn't want to seem so perennially morose. She wished to jest and grin, to know them better. They evidently desired to understand and befriend her. Yet the means to maintain a joyful disposition stretched beyond her grasp, for the looming of odious deeds poisoned the task ahead.

She brooded as well in Uldyr's absence, and could not discard the thought of him. Their reciprocated admiration, their months before this, these played in her daydreams, and her sleeping ones too. His intelligence and experience had captivated her. Kind, powerful, and as much as anyone had ever been, heroic, at least in her estimation. She smiled any time he entered her mind. More importantly, she believed that no matter the outcome of their venture, he would be there, waiting for her at the end.

When this battle with the Church had concluded, she and Uldyr would return to their roaming of the countryside and cities. They might even venture back to Reneris one day, to the city of Orilon or the Hinterlands. The latter would be a challenge for her, but if she faced her former life with him, she might well overcome it.

She wanted to transcend it, to be more than another spirit broken by phantoms of the past. He would expend his greatest effort to help her do so, even if she could not prevail. Even if she failed again and again, or regressed and succumbed, he would lift her to her feet anew.

They had been apart for so long. How long, she couldn't say anymore. An age ago felt less than a day, and each day seemed an age. She was as a wandering waif, and he stood as her sole support. If he died in solitude at his home from the wounds inflicted by the daggerhand, no amount of condolences in the world could mend her.

When they were together, she often followed him with her eyes. She felt empty without that, never knowing where to look. The first few days of their departure had been the toughest, but she retained the sorrow. In the moment, she never felt any urge to weep. Just numb, or unfulfilled, or alone. Even with Bhathric there, she felt out of place.

She had grown used to it, the dull misery; so dull she could hardly call it misery anymore.

They went down a slope and crossed a stream which severed the road, then up the next incline. Up and down, they rode from hill to hill. Another hour passed and her rear, groin, and thighs ached for a rest, but she did not complain aloud. After a number of miles more, the pathway slowed its rolling. It wound like a liberated spool of thread and then lay straight to a deep decline. No signs of travelers or higher habitation presented.

A bizarre stillness thickened the air. Before, the wind spun and twirled, rustling leaves and sighing in the brushwood and fronds. Now the leaves kept quiet, save their crunching beneath shoed hooves.

A few miles further on, they met a narrow passage between rocky hillsides which climbed as high as she could see. Unrest draped over her as a heavy blanket. They were outsiders descending into a dark and vacant landscape of haunted forest and gloomy mounds. Finally, they exited the opposite end of the passage.

There ought to be more life than this.

A force, menacing and hostile, befell this common route of travel. On occasion, she caught glimpses of shadows and light flickering between the trees. The world remained hushed.

Their small party divided the road right at its center, a stone's toss from either side. Uneven ground shifted her in her saddle. The trees drew in closer, ensnared, suffocated. She yearned to be free of this dismal place.

"Don't you think it odd?" Bhathric asked, ostensibly to anyone. "Neither a sign of spirit nor creature."

"It is dull." Eclih sighed. "If luck favored, we'd be assailed by a roving troupe of bandits." He jested to comfort them.

A foulness worked here, beyond the touch of winter and night on the world and sky. Animals native to the forests did not flee unless something foreign invaded their domain. She knew that Eclih could sense it as well as she, for ages on the road had worn him and sharpened his wit.

The stillness sent a shiver up Athenne's spine. Hairs at her nape prickled and cowered.

A community emerged at the end of the road; a sullen pool

of thatched rooftops and crude stone walls. From the contraptions scattered about the buildings, she inferred that it had been a farming village. Had been, that was, because life had emptied from the region. Not even the remnants of life remained.

Abnormally defined, a hard line of snow divided the ground between the woodlands and the first hovel. Clouds hung dense in the sky and blotted out the stars, moons, and rings. A foreboding air refused to leave them. The hooves of their horses and their breathing rose and fell in singular seclusion.

Bhathric's steed startled and reared back. "Easy," she muttered, controlling it at the reins. Nothing moved in sight that ought to spook a horse. Dead grass and shadow surrounded the village beyond the icy ring, stretching out from the buildings to the black forest.

The trees here had gnarled and diseased, layered in snow, soot, and grey lichen. A char like old paint coated the houses and the ground beneath them. Behind each trot, Shah left muddied prints of slush and ash.

With a whispered incantation, Bhathric cast a spell of illumination which swept outward as a flash of light, giving them vision of the area for a moment before it dissipated.

"Ghora, I believe this is." Eclih kept his voice low. "A farming village."

Athenne had been right, though it hadn't been difficult to deduce from the lay of the land.

Eclih halted and they stopped after him.

"Where are the villagers?" Bhathric scanned the range at their sides, desolate and drab.

"I'm loath to evince obvious proofs, but something has

happened." Eclih faced them on his mount. An earnest concern carved across his countenance. "We best not linger."

"You've no interest in investigating?" Bhathric objected. "A village, scorched in a ring of snow, its people vanished, and you've not an inkling of desire to know why?"

"How do buildings burn without burning?" Athenne shifted her weight on Shah as she gazed from hovel to hovel, studying. "These dwellings are covered in ash, yet their rooftops are unburnt. Their wooden doors stand. Burned, but without ruin." She looked back at Eclih and Bhathric. "What sort of magic produces soot without flame and leaves thick sulfur in the air? Summons such peculiar snowfall, within Imperial wards, no less?"

Bhathric stared at Eclih with a defiance in her eyes, her eyebrows raised. "All the more reason we ought to examine the buildings. Mayhap there are survivors."

"Can you two feel this chill? There is something here," he replied, or warned. "Whatever has done this, we've neither the time nor the resources to waste. We must carry on. The others will be waiting for our signal."

A home not scorched like the rest stood over the far side of the road on a grassy hillock. This building distinguished itself from the many round, stone-walled hovels with reed or sodded overheads by its wooden roof and square, half-timbered construction. That, and it spread out twice as large as any other home in view.

The village priest's cottage.

An oak tree like a tower shadowed it from above, too close. The house's door sat agape and a feeble light sputtered within. Rather than acknowledge Eclih's protest, Athenne made off toward the building.

"Athenne!" he yelled.

She did not look back.

As Athenne came to the main door, she dismounted. Bhathric and Eclih approached, still atop their horses. With unhurried steps and senses peaked, she pressed the door open. It shuddered to a start, as if it had not moved in some time. Ice and snow crackled to life and rained down around her from the door frame and wall.

A candle lit one side of the living quarter, as she had suspected from afar. It had burned to a stub, nearing the mouth of its holder's socket. Across the floor, grain spilled out from a torn fiber sack. A hasp fashioned of bronzed iron around a centimeter thick stuck out from the interior of the door, broken in half, as if by forced entry. Her left foot fell through the threshold, to the groaning of lumber.

Bhathric called next. "Athenne." Her pitch rose a shade from its usual sound. "Be careful."

Inside, she found a dining table littered with gardening tools, a chair, a hearth caked in ash, and in the corner, stacked firewood. The air smelled musty, unlived. She did not speak, but listened, and intruded further. Bhathric and Eclih did not follow, and no sound but the creaking of the boards beneath her steps roused. She approached the entrance of the cottage's sleeping quarter. To the right of the door hung a silver mosaic adumbration of the Mother Sentinel, the largest statue in the world, erected near the city of Orilon in Reneris.

The artist had depicted her with her eyes shut and her arms outstretched at either side, an inaccurate pose. In reality, the statue's hands were before the face in a prayer seal and her eyes were open. Though, Renerins of Orilon often said that the Sentinel watched with her eyes closed. *A rough city*, Aitrix had called it. Still, the statue represented the All-Mother, overlooking Her children in all Her glory.

Athenne's hand pushed the bedchamber door inward. She peered within to a near-empty room containing a chest, a bed, and a side table, too short for the bed's frame. At the foot of the bed were a woman's undercloths, heaped in a pile. The priest, or someone, had been there not long before. How long, she could not surmise. No sign of a struggle beyond the shattered latch on the main door manifested.

She emerged from the cottage, surprised that Bhathric, at least, had not tailed her. In hindsight, inspecting alone had been foolish, but she needed know and see for herself. *I must not always be timid.*

"Anyone?" Bhathric asked.

Athenne shook her head, and Bhathric and Eclih exchanged a look, their expressions perturbed and tense. Eclih, especially, seemed disconcerted.

"This post is vacant," he declared after a short silence. "Who is the priest of Ghora?"

"Couldn't say. We ought to check the officer's stead, see if she's there." Bhathric assumed the village's paladin was a she, as most field officers were.

What has happened here? No village priest, no residents. At least, none they had encountered. At some point, the people of Ghora had awoken to a service led by their attendant guardian. They prayed, sang in chorus, bathed each other in the blessings of the Mother. Then they were gone, priest's cottage and hovels left bare, the hearths cold, the world outside, still as the dead. What would the three of them find if they scoured the entire region, extending feelers in all directions, in search of anyone or anything?

Back atop Shah, Athenne started up the path behind her comrades, their heads dipping in the white dark. The night's air swung lifeless around them like a body dangling at the end of a noose, cold enough to show their breath. Another dwelling, similar to the priest's cottage, resided not far away.

"Here," said Bhathric.

At the front of the building, adjacent the door, a plaque shone from beneath a thin veil of snow.

Bhathric hopped off her mount. "We can't let our Athenne have all the heroics."

Eclih's face twisted with displeasure, but he kept quiet.

Bhathric brushed the sign, sweeping it down to the polished surface and shaking her hand off to the side, flinging melting ice and water. The beams of the moons almost certainly exaggerated the plaque's clarity. Bolts seating it to the wall gleamed a clean silver. Someone had replaced it recently.

"*Field Officer—Mirea Athelys*," read Bhathric, carrying out each syllable. "Hm."

She turned to them. "It's the one." Bhathric drifted a few paces back. "Let us not dither." Without hesitation, she kicked the door. Unlike the priest's abode, no fitful orange light blinked at the bent end of a failing candle. What Athenne perceived from her position—furniture—took the shape of black masses.

The door banged against the inner wall. Bhathric stepped forth, swallowed by the darkness. Eclih and Athenne exchanged an anxious glance, and then she peered to the sky. Except for spots of thin and dense clouds, only faint stars bled through the blackness, too many to count; burning balls of gas, according to the natural philosophers. Their simple, silent beauty would have mesmerized her any other time.

"Quiet as the crypt," she heard Bhathric say. The light poured over Bhathric as she materialized from the house's shadowed embrace. "Someone was here not long ago, but there's nothing now. No arms, no badge."

"Any sign of struggle?" Athenne asked.

Bhathric raised her hands at her sides. "Nothing."

No hint abandoned, same as the priest's cottage.

"We should turn back. We ought to inform Aitrix of this. The Church could be aware of our movements and evacuated the village. We could be riding into a trap." Athenne didn't believe this to be the case, but she could muster no more reasonable an argument in the moment.

Bhathric focused on the officer's bothy. "Not so dull now." She reseated in her saddle.

"Not what I had in mind." Eclih frowned. "Nonetheless, as I stated, we can't afford to lose the time. Whatever this is, we must drive on. We'll deal with what comes when we meet it." Athenne sensed the fear in his voice through his effort to conceal it.

She wanted to survey the remainder of the area, but withheld the desire. If it were anything similar to what they had already witnessed, there would be more of the same. Nothing. Scouring the village and outer forest would cost them hours of time and valuable energy. In that, she agreed with Eclih.

They rode over a hill and down a northwest angled track,

passing by clusters of hovels, littered among field ploughs and stables. Revealed by the skylights, they glimpsed the neighborhoods in their distant vacancy.

"Even the animals have evanesced," Athenne said. Full troughs for pigs and sacks of feed for cows, chickens, and horses were visible from the roadside, yet no creatures stirred. Only the woeful silhouettes of deserted homes, idle apparatuses, and empty pens greeted them. Ghora was a burial ground without markers, underlaid by an insidiousness like the whispers of a fatal secret.

She shuddered.

"The more we ought to depart with haste." Eclih faced forward, paralyzed at the back of his horse.

A tangible constraint had come over Bhathric with the mood. She no longer dissented or nudged.

Athenne did not want to push or upset him further. He had humored them enough to wait as they examined two dwellings, and so she would leave their investigation at that. As much as she desired to overturn each rock within a mile every way in hunt for answers, she concurred, both with Eclih's spoken and unspoken censure. Whatever had done this, if it had been a thing, would not be something they could handle as they were.

Still, we might regret not turning back when we had this chance.

CHAPTER VIII: FALLING

Garron

He dreamt of blood. An ichor which threatened to swallow the world. A deluge that overcame forests and cities. A sea that would engulf him whole and drag the planes with it. The ichor was a horror, a force of nature that swept away all in its path. It was monstrous. Nothing could stop or slow it. The Mother would weep to see Her beautiful Earth, consumed by its dark red embrace.

It had been less than a day, but the prior evening waned as a distant memory. Months, he had survived during his weeks in Aros. He wondered whether Epaphael—mutant god of destiny, time, and damnation—had cursed and given him a dozen days to suffer for every one that others felt. Might death take pity on him, come sooner? He hoped.

If only it were so.

He stirred, drenched in a soup of sweat. He rose most days around this hour, no matter the time that he had slept, chained to force of habit. In what may have been a lifetime ago, he had spent mornings in prayer to cleanse himself for the callings to come. This dawn, he awoke to no such righteous fervor, and instead remained motionless in his bed, deliberating. Why not? No place offered him safety anymore.

As he had expected in the wake of his capture by the inquisitors, a knock came upon his bedchamber door. It must be Archbishop Delacroix. The solidity of the upright slab of shaped wood hindered his sight, but his confidence sustained. She alone had visited him in his weeks there, save the stray deacon, machine, or sadistic creature of the Overrealm, bent on his ruination.

"Father Latimer." Her voice sounded reserved yet insistent. "Garron, we must speak now that you've returned." She had taken to using his first name on occasion since their initial encounter in his chamber, after cruel fate had absorbed him in its raging tempest and cast apart the edifice of his resolve. Whether the informality meant to endear her to him or lure him into a false security played through his mind.

She evidently believed that he had already awoken. Priests commonly rose early in the mornings for prayer, and he had lived that life to its fullest for most of his manhood. Indeed, he had awoken, but this morning, he would not come as beckoned. He wanted to lie, and rest, and wait. He wanted to enjoy silence, to sink into his cushioned bed, a sheet over his face, and be without need or want or duty.

He could not have it.

Delacroix addressed him again.

"Garron," she said, in an even, sympathetic tone. "I have reflected long on what has happened and what must come next. I understand that your experience has been harrowing. The Martials informed me of the state in which they found you. Will you allow me a moment?"

Near the end of her appeal, her voice collected a palpable worry. He knew her likely concern, for the ideation had plagued him. She suspected he would not answer, that she may push the door open to find his rigid body hanged from a fixture or crumpled in a pool of blood. Consideration of the possibility would be well placed. Anyone in his condition would have thought on it, might have acted. But Garron was a fool. A fool who wanted to die, yet hoped that life would improve so that he may carry on.

"Father?"

Rising fear shaded her voice. If he had the energy, he might have moved then. Her compassion ran deep, but so did her composure. He found himself fascinated to hear her apprehensive and frightened, if only in slight. Did his interest signify that a force had touched him for the worse? He ought not take pleasure in any such thing, and yet he had, for a breath. It proved a shift, something which he could not consider without a confliction so fearsome it brought him pain and crisis. He had to drag his thoughts elsewhere.

"Aye," he responded finally, in an effort to correct himself.

"Might I enter?"

Hauling his legs over the side of his bed, his hairy-knuckled toes splayed and groped for the polished stone ground. His movement had slowed since the months prior, before the attack. He felt more aged too. Perhaps the stress had withered him. He had to be careful. The cuts and bruises across his forearms had turned purple, near black. Another marker of his development.

Each day, he sat like this in small instances, reflecting on what he had become. He beheld himself in the water of his washbasin. How eldered he grew presented plainly. His face wilted. The color of distressed leather overtook his skin, rough and rugged, lined and wrinkled. The hairs from the top of his head to his neck greyed to white. These ordeals had cut up the vestiges of his youth in a most horrid fashion.

When he passed away, what would remain of him, beyond the stain he left on others? Those he served as guardian in the Vale of Erlan had perished. The last person upon whom he had inflicted himself, in his final sight of her, had been a writhing mass of blood, tears, and terror on her floor.

Delacroix worried sensibly, and she knew so little.

Another knock came at the door.

"Aye," he said, lost for a moment in an undeserved self-pity.

Archbishop Delacroix entered. "I am glad to see you well." She offered a pleasant half-smile, her account of his wellbeing a generosity, in itself. Yet he knew that she meant it. He heard the lingering tone of concern underlying her words.

His head dipped in reply.

"May I?" She signaled toward his lonesome chair.

He shook his head once more.

She walked to the chair, grabbed it by its back, and positioned it a few feet from his bedside. Sitting down across from him, as she had each visit, she crossed her legs and folded her hands in her lap, ever formal, even in welcoming company. Her eyes moved over him, studying, as if to acknowledge the truth of his current state. He supposed she had not seen him since before his uninvited parting.

"To imagine you, lying upon the ground in the cold dark, feeling the awful torments exacted on you—to think of it as the wish of this thing to harm you, as you worked so well to recover."

Her jaw knotted at the sides as she clenched her teeth. "We underestimated our foe. That was my error."

Garron stared off into the distance.

She had wanted to keep him safe, but the Ennead, including Delacroix, had not regarded the events of the Vale with due seriousness. "There are many kinds of evil," he said, almost in reflex. "Evil that lurks and preys, steals away the innocent—evil that devours flesh and kills. Then there are evils that torment the mind. They have neither kindness nor want beyond their ends. They walk among us, unseen." He swallowed. "These are the ones that frighten me most." His insides, already crawling with unease, contracted with dejection. "I fear the longer I am tortured, the nearer I come to being evil myself."

"Garron—"

"*You do not understand!*" The ire rose. "*I was flung beyond this city by no more than the creature's touch! It came unhindered through your wards!*"

Aramanth did not react to his outburst. "What did you feel?"

"Forgive me, Archbishop." A long pause trailed. "Terrified, beyond myself, but drawn. Nay, further than that. The Beast had taken hold of me, gripped my very mind."

"What does she wish of you?"

"It calls me. It calls my spirit for its own."

"Garron," her tone bordered on reproachful, "you have been a servant of the Church for decades—"

"I know not whether I have the will to endure."

"If this Beast, as you call it, has elected to assail you, then it assails the Church. You must not surrender. Do you recognize the important of this moment, of your struggle? You must endure."

"If I cannot?"

"To capitulate would be to forsake your duty to the Mother."

"Duty?" he replied, the word dripping with a red indignation. "Most of my life, I have labored in Her service. I have bled with Her daughters. I have sacrificed with Her sons." His voice trembled. "In Her service, I have met the wrath of a god. I have endured against this creature a suffering as no woman or man before." His quaking speech had erupted into another yell. "What have I to show? *Speak it!*" His sitting had turned to standing. As the rage climaxed and subsided, he became crestfallen. Returning to his place at the edge of his bed, he averted his gaze. He could not meet the Archbishop's eyes, which never shied throughout his tirade.

"Father." Archbishop Delacroix reverted to his formal title. "I have respected you, so I ask that you respect me. I understand that you have borne a great hardship, that you are not well. Nevertheless, I must insist that you conduct yourself with cordiality and reserve, otherwise I shall discontinue this meeting." Each word she uttered carried a stern refusal to engage in fruitless bickering, or to worsen his troubled anger with reciprocation.

He made himself remember to whom he spoke.

Aramanth Delacroix.

Archbishop of the Ennead.

One of the finest minds in the world.

She represented more than a superior or colleague. A friendship had developed between them. She did not treat him with cold civility or callous indifference. In the face of his ingratitude and misguided anger, resentment, alienation, she recognized that the pain and brutalities and terrors he had witnessed and felt gave birth to these, and she knew but a sliver of the sum. Intent, she had listened to him at length, to the many fine details of gruesome scenes, the intricacies of anguish upon anguish, which in their aftershock he could do no more than imply with quavering lip and tear-welled eyes. Aramanth had provided him solace without hesitation, with an innate indulgence. He committed yet another terrible act in neglecting to treat her with such consideration in kind.

"What are you feeling now?" she asked.

"The ache is real. My suffering is real. This creature, the Beast, is real." Still in a state of imbalance, he recalled the events of the Vale, and the night before, the struggle with the woman, the look in her eye. Fear, pain, dying. So far, he had treated her as a nameless, nondescript object by which to measure his torment and grief. *Yet she is a person in the world.* He needed to find a way to remedy his actions against her. *It happened.* Her hurt existed as truly as his, not merely in his delirious mind. *She matters as much as you—her complexity, depth, strength, agony.* He must remember to carry her with him so long as he lived.

"So these are, Garron." The succor came to Aramanth with ease, his transgressions already dismissed. Her trustworthiness carried little doubt. He need only gaze into her eyes to know.

"Whatever this being is," she continued, "we ought not underrate it further. It plagues you for its own whims. If this entity possesses the strength to penetrate the magics of the Priory, then we shall ward your mind itself. There shall be no tinkering in that head of yours. If every member of the Ennead must lend their power to this spell, so be it. As you are a guardian of the All-Mother's flock and a priest of the Church, so too are you Her son. None may bring harm to Her children."

Garron's chin shook. "By Her grace, Archbishop."

"In the meantime, as we prepare, I'll send someone to keep you company." She rose and turned toward the door. "I must be off to attend to other matters, regrettably."

"Someone?" he asked.

"I'll let her introduce herself." The corner of her mouth turned up. "Lie and rest, if you like."

"Aye." He lay back, tired, his eyelids heavy.

"It shan't be long," she added. "We'll return for you this day."

She left.

The door shut behind her with a decisive thump.

As he lay, he cleared his mind and pushed away frightful memories and contemplations. He calmed himself, forced an internal serenity. The erratic pulsing of his heartbeats slowed and caught a rhythm. He thought of nothing, relaxing against the cool but warming surface of his mattress. A light sleep befell him for a time, yet he remained aware of his surroundings. Then a knock came upon his door, unanticipated this soon.

Already? He wanted to rise, cross the room, and unbar his door, but he remained comatose. His fingers and toes tingled. The prickle crept up his limbs until it met at his center and crawled into his head like reaching tendrils. His eyes would not open. He felt as though he were falling in place, or sinking. His attention concentrated on the banging at the door, as if time stood still around him save that ceaseless thudding. It grew louder as he kept frozen. The door rattled and groaned, until the pounding raised so loud it shook his back, jaw, and teeth.

A silence fell like lightning.

Chatter arose without.

His door burst open, clattering against the stone wall. Suited inquisitors filled his room. "Garron Latimer," a woman said, her voice booming. "You are hereby charged with the murder of—" The words became inaudible.

Sitting up, his uncovered eyes strained against the light. He could not hear the name.

Hands wrapped beneath his arms, dragging him from his bed.

"Murder?" he murmured, struggling against gauntlet-clad fingers. "I've—I've killed no one." He had come into waking and found himself walking, or rather, two paladins pulled him to his feet, the pair who had returned him to the Priory that night at the river. "Where is Archbishop Delacroix? I have killed no one."

"She awaits you in the Ennead's chamber," the inquisitor to his right said. "She called the trial herself."

"There must be some mistake. I've killed no one!"

Within minutes, they had entered the Ennead's council space, to the well before them. A dim, foreboding greyness hued the room. Seven of the nine sat at the end of the chamber behind their elegant table, expressionless atop their elevated dais. He looked down to find that he wore heavy iron shackles upon his wrists and ankles, and prisoner's clothing upon his body, though he did not recall anyone constraining or stripping and redressing him.

"Look ahead. Do not to communicate unless spoken to," ordered an inquisitor.

On the wall behind the panel hung a painting of Breiman Umbra, his gaze as cold and piercing as in the flesh. Garron did not remember having seen that portrait in the past.

Archbishop Sangrey reordered papers in her hands, glancing

up, eyes anchored on him. "Father Garron Latimer." The monotony of her words carried greater authority than he had heard in any voice. "You are charged in violation of Matrian Law with the felonious killing of—" Again, he failed to perceive the name. He strained to hear it, the words muffled to him, as though he listened through a damp filter.

Another pitch swelled, a dense ringing in his head.

"Of whom?" he asked, out of breath. Dripping with sweat, his body weakened, as if his strength escaped with the moisture through his skin. He swayed on his feet.

"Your sentence is to be death by hanging," Sangrey finished.

The inquisitors seized him at the shoulders and elbows. His lips parted to scream, to object, but no sound escaped. A black bag slipped over his head, depriving him of sight.

"Archbishop Delacroix." He found his voice. "Aramanth—" They muzzled him. Tears escaped from his eyes as the inquisitors jerked him backward. The flesh of his lips had merged, rendering him unable to speak.

"You must pay for what you did," he heard Aramanth proclaim. An apathy underpinned her words. No gentleness, no concern, only contempt.

The floor disappeared beneath him, and with it, his weight. A whining, whirring sonority manifested, enough to burst the drums of one's ears, if he had any. His body had vanished again. The sound, muted and piercing in unity. He spasmed and spiraled in darkness, a formless mass. The noise came from inside him, in front of and over him, accompanied by a woman's voice, rising in volume through the morass of competing disharmonies. Its tone held a tender urgency. *Help me!* He was as a blind mute. *Help me!*

"Father!"

The quaking grew with volume of the voice.

"Father, wake up!"

He heard screaming. A man's. A familiar timbre. He sat up, trembling. Light made his eyes squint. A young deacon stood at his side. He found himself in his room, on his bed, soaked through his robes with sweat.

"You were having a terror." Her hand moved from his shoulder.

His heart hammered. He brushed back dripping locks of grey, white, and black hair with his fingers. The deacon placed a cup of some dark, misting drink on his night table.

"Tea, Father, whenever you like."

She sat on the chair where Aramanth had resided not long ago, or what he assumed had not been long ago. The sun shone through his window from outside, so he had not slept much, unless the next day had come.

"How long did I rest?"

"Not long. A duration enough to have a terror, unfortunately."

He brought the cup to his lips, sniffed of it, swirling the contents in their container for a moment before taking a sip. The heat of it spread through his mouth, traveled down his throat, and warmed his chest and stomach. He imbibed again, at length this time, washing the taste of sleep from his tongue. The strong tea refreshed him, and alleviated his thirst. When he finished the drink, he sat it aside.

"Thank you," he said.

The deacon smiled.

"What is your name?"

"Sister Amun Halleck," she answered.

He recognized her, the Ennead's Scribe Officiate.

At his deposition, she had taken the record.

"You are the Scribe Officiate?"

"An alternate to Sister Viessa Birieth, who is at present ill." Her head turned, revealing her profile. She had about her a scarce handsomeness, appearing to be of her early twenties. Lean of countenance, she had a pointed chin and nose beneath hair the color of oiled bronze, tied back, fading into the shadow of the grey hood of her robes. Her eyes were even and almond-shaped. As her face rotated back toward him, gaze level to his, her irises shone a reddish-orange.

"Fair folk?" he asked. It was apparent, for the elves alone had eyes that color. He was half-awake and not rearmed in full of his cognitive functions.

She gave a light laugh. "Indeed, Father, half."

"If I may inquire." He diverted the conversation from his silly question. "For what purpose has Archbishop Delacroix sent you? I assume 'twas she."

"'Twas, Father—"

"Call me Garron," he interjected, waving a hand. It made little difference for the time. So long as he had to remain in the Priory, he could not perform his obligations.

"—Garron." She adjusted. "She requested I keep you company until such time as the Ennead has prepared your warding spell." A pause. "I suppose you've a tendency for melting into the air."

He chuckled. It had been a while since he had laughed. "Aye." He could not find reason to disapprove and invited the visit. Perhaps her presence would aid in keeping him safe. If not, someone would be there to observe if he vanished against his will. "What's your specialty, if you don't mind my asking?" She had beads at her wrist, with one charm attached, a small silver sphere with a ring around the middle, the issue of a first-degree deacon. Not as green as seekers and students, but past her starting year.

"The art of materialism with a concentration in healing spells," she replied. "I hope to find station in a hall of the dying beyond the Priory when I reach my third rank." She referred to the final tier of deacon, third-degree. First-degree deacons practiced their specialty in a supervised setting, and often worked under the archbishops and bishops. Second-degree deacons supervised first-degree deacons and labored part-time beyond the Priory. Third-degree deacons oversaw any of those below them and tended to take full-time employ outside the Priory, in halls of the dying as healers, or in other locations wherein their specialties might be of value. For every degree, the deacons received another silver charm, ending at three.

"Magnanimous work," he said. "Though, grim."

Halls of the dying were no place for the weak of stomach or faint of heart. There, healers would tend to the sickest, sufferers of diseases which consumed their bodies, malignancies, and other terrible illnesses. Many were beyond saving, and the rest could only have their ailments and disorders managed.

"Verily, but I feel it as my calling."

"Have you been to a house?" he asked.

"I would like to."

"We may be given leave when the warding spell is done. Would you enjoy a visit then?"

"'Twould be sound learning." Her eyes flitted to the door and back to him. She eased closer, her head tilted down a touch. "I'd like to confide in you, if we might share in confidence?"

A streak of fear tore through him in a flash.

Not again.

He imagined her as the Beast in disguise.

His heart skipped a beat.

She appeared to observe his visceral reaction and leaned away. "I wanted to ask, between us," she went on, still at a whisper. "Do you believe the restrictions on the Aether provided the opportunity for this—these events? Do you think the weakening of common magics has allowed the underkinds to bring about their power?"

He had considered it. Yet in this place, and particularly if magic warded his room, they could not discuss such notions in the open. "Sister," he replied in near silence, "you mustn't speak of such." He gestured toward the door. "Such ideas could be met with ill-regard." Even so, it was a possibility worth considering. If it had been the case, it was further conceivable that the Church was blind to its own harms and the potentialities it had unleashed.

"Whence do you hail?" He had detected an accent in her enunciations, foreign to Imperials. He knew the answer, but wanted to let her tell him herself.

"Reneris," she said. "Thralkeld."

"A splendid place." Grand elven architecture exalted Thralkeld, unique among the kingdoms. The city served as home to the largest elven population in Imios, far denser than the proportion of elves in the Empire. "I heard it in your words." Her face expressed wonder. His cultured ears discerned foreign elocution without much trouble.

"I thought I'd lost my accent," she challenged him, a grin playing about her lips. However, the play fleeted. Her expression fell somber. "I must tell you, word of the attack on your village has flown. They are calling it the Erlan Massacre."

"The common body?"

"And others."

He had suspected as much. "I reckon it must have a name." *Ominous as that one is.*

"There's more." She returned to her forward posture. Her legs overlapped, hidden beneath layers of grey robe, with an elbow rested on her knee. A high collar framed her defined jaw, a personalization to her attire, uncharacteristic of deacons. How had she received permission to have her standard issue customized? "I overhead inquisitors in the yard discussing that communication with other sites near the Empire's edges have fallen. Imports and exports diminish. Supply loads leaving the major cities for rural farmers and graziers are, but a few, stalled. Even fewer arrive. Chevaliers have been dispatched to investigate."

Is the Undeath spreading?

This was not welcome news, but the truth did not depend on whether he welcomed it. If left unremedied, this would cause discontent from Aros to the underlands in the south and the Grove to the east. Starvation would flourish like overflowing weeds without caravans of stock departing from and arriving at the cities in a regular pace. Starvation meant unrest. Unrest meant rebellion. Rebellion meant military action. Military action meant mass death. Wars began this way, and governments, kingdoms, and societies collapsed.

The ichor that swallows the world.

Then again, there would be no starvation in the south if there were none to starve. The Undeath did not leave warm bodies wanting for sustenance. It left houses standing hollow.

A gentle knock interrupted their discussion.

"Aye," he called out. "You may enter."

In the opening stood Aramanth, alone.

"Have you gotten better acquainted?"

Sister Halleck nodded with a smile and he followed, eyes traveling from her to Aramanth.

"A fine deacon," he said, "and enviable company."

Aramanth's cheeks dimpled and she held out her hand. "The warding spell is prepared."

He breathed a sigh of relief as the words met his ears, running fingers over the scraggles of his beard.

"Amun, might you be so kind as to give Father Latimer his shaving razor before the ritual?"

"Oh!" The deacon fished about in the lining of her robes. "My apologies, Father."

Sister Halleck had resumed the use of his honorific in the presence of Aramanth. He understood.

Not long after, the deacon produced from her garments a straight razor for him, and rose. "Thank you for allowing me your time." She bowed and he tilted his head in response.

As Sister Halleck started out, she looked back. "I hope to meet again." She disappeared down the hall, leaving Aramanth as a solitary figure outside his bedchamber.

"If you'll follow me once you're finished," Aramanth directed in her soothing mezzo, indicating in the general direction of the Ennead's council chamber. "We anticipate your arrival."

He gave her a gesture of accord, and so she turned and left as Sister Halleck had, closing the door to his room before she did so. Sauntering away, her footsteps receded.

When he entered his washroom, he discovered that clothes awaited him, no doubt laid out by a machine given the faultless folding at the seams and creases. Dark grey robes and black boots of polished leather, nicer than any he'd had in the Vale. His washbasin centered the counter, filled already with steaming water. The water must have arrived not long before Sister Halleck woke him.

Wonders abound.

He thinned his beard with scissors first, then applied a layer of shaving soap to his face, which he had found along with a brush and a towel next to the basin, each neat in space and uniform. To avoid cutting himself, he shaved with care. The rough agedness of his skin provided the benefit of being more resistant to self-mutilation than it had been in his youth.

His hands dipped into the water, now milky with soap and pleasantly warm, and splashed it against his face and beard, washing away excess hair and lather. He wiped the remnants of his shave from his jaw and lips, dabbing to dry himself. In the looking glass reflected the person he had known. He felt better, and appeared less like a madman.

Not wishing to keep the Ennead in delay, he resolved to complete shaving his body when he returned, unless his dream, or terror, came to fruition. If they apprehended him and threw him in a dungeon or hanged him as a murderer in the city square, whether he finished his grooming wouldn't matter.

Another idle fantasy of a myriad, increasingly macabre in

nature. They had become frequent, every manner of deranged ideation, creeping into his head like insects through a window's crack. He expended great effort to bat them away, but the thoughts persisted. Such ideas had never occurred to him before all this. Before the massacre. Before *it* touched him. Before his crime.

It will not always be so. The Ennead will mend my troubled mind.

Convinced, he dressed himself and set off.

CHAPTER IX: MATRON

Athenne

Wordless, she walked. A river ran with vengeful ferocity to her left. Rain cascaded in lonely trickles. A hugging mist held in suspension, rolling over her, evading as she approached.

In the distance, a figure.

Features swimming out of the fog were diminutive and soft, a child's. Round faced with green eyes, wrinkled and squinted, a hand shielding her brow.

The girl screamed. A shriek burst forth, expanded, as if a seal had dislodged in the pit of the girl's spirit. Athenne kept walking and observed her clearer, changed in a blink. She looked pale and black about the lips, rotten, purple and green at the neck, her temples incurved, with gnaw marks near her chin and nose. Her eyes were glassy as a doll's, clouded and recessed. The girl threw herself back into the river, and Athenne, as though moved by another power, dove in after her. Water swirled, dark and boundless, tasting bitter. A mass formed below Athenne, its details indiscernible. She sank with rising quickness.

Athenne rotated in the water and swam up for the air, but

something snatched her by the wrist and dragged her toward the bottom. Her lungs blazed. She struggled to hold her breath, thrashing against the water as it drew her in, hungry, vicious, and cold. What pulled was invisible. No light shone there, only the flowing, enveloping void. She ached at the back of the legs, the neck, the arms, with the strain of resistance, her limbs stiffening in the chill. Her eyes stretched wide and stung.

No! I didn't mean it! Please, I didn't mean it!

"Eclih!"

A calamity exploded beyond the waters, something external to seeing and touching and hearing. Through the surface, light broke in varied hues of silver, orange, red, and blue. Athenne heard a shuffling and howling, muted and muddied by the bubbling and gushing in and out of her ears.

This is not real. You are not here.

In the evening, after they left Ghora and set up camp, Athenne stirred at a commotion and screaming. Half-asleep, she propped herself on her elbows and peered around, discomposed from her night terror and groggy from her rest and unrest. As the forest developed, she saw two objects in the distance, fading away.

"Athenne!" Bhathric called, at a gallop on horseback, tailing the furthest object. "They've taken Eclih!"

They were gone.

Athenne scrambled to her feet and followed on an agitated Shah, both of them unprepared for such a hard ride. She had already packed most of her belongings, but left her sleeping mat at their makeshift clearing. They all had abandoned their mats, in fact. Pursuant, fearful, frenzied, fatigued, raw at the hands and thighs, she caught up enough to see Bhathric. The sight did not assuage her discomfort.

Bhathric looked back. "Knights of Faith!"

Knights of Faith? Athenne had heard tales. The Order without Order, they called themselves. A thorn in the spine of the Church. A testament to their mental god, Vekshia, the Matron of Hope and Despair. This did not bode well for the three of them, if these were true members of the Orderless.

They were Acolytes, higher servants of the gods. Rather than being direct creations of their Matron, as other Acolytes were under their respective celestials, the Knights of Faith were mortals who had sworn themselves to Vekshia for a share of her goodwill and strength. Their mastery of her favored magic granted them immense power, too monumental a challenge under Matrian wards for her and Bhathric and Eclih, even as a joined force. The wards did not restrict the Knights the same as others, for they drew upon an outer authority.

Bhathric stopped at the fore of a building.

Athenne came around her side.

"A Matronian temple?" Bhathric sounded surprised.

Wet stone formed a windowless structure, streaked with black moss, lichen, and dead vines from its square base to its conic apex. Bare greenery and misting, black pools encased in rock surrounded it. As they approached, slurping mud, clay, and decaying vegetation clung like quicksand to the hooves of their horses.

Bhathric dismounted. "We'll have to leave them outside."

They secured their steeds to a nearby bush.

Few had witnessed these phantom temples, which disappeared from one place and reappeared in another, seemingly at random. A phrase etched atop the doors of this structure made it clear to whom it belonged:

All know She who walks beneath the Crown of Two Spirits
Matron of the Order without Order

"Wait," Athenne said. "Should we rush in?"

Temples of Vekshia were not places of worship as most temples, or spaces for mortals not of Matronian persuasions to wander. She had read of them; illusory mazes where the senses deceived their source. Those who intruded without the Matron's fondness were subject to her whims.

They reached the entrance, a tall, rectangular mouth housed in a wall in the likeness of a woman's face, perhaps an homage to the Patron of None herself.

The doors of this mouth, like teeth parting, split down their seam, disappearing into the walls at either side. No light guided their way within, only a black hole and the slightest sight of a descending staircase, narrower than one could wish. Something about it tugged at Athenne, beckoned her forth.

"We haven't the luxury of wise reluctance," Bhathric replied. "Eclih is here. We cannot leave him."

Athenne would not deny Bhathric this, could not demand that they desert her partner. If the Knights had brought Eclih to this temple, Vekshia had surely willed it so.

Inside, the cold crippled them. They meandered through corridors, aromas of honeysuckle and other sickly-sweet scents concentrated in oily air, no doubt with intent. Athenne abhorred the odor, so thick she could taste it.

A toxic wind from further in ripped at the dust and filth that coated the ground and walls and their skin and clothes, shredded through the cavernous bowels of the temple, which seemed to plunge perpetually into the Earth. The air gripped, searching, seeking, as though looking for anything in motion, anything alive. It found them, and cut them to their bones. They huddled together, tried to see, fought to draw breath without pulling in the frost that threatened to shatter their lungs.

Athenne choked as the rush tore the air from her throat and filled her mouth and nostrils. She turned her head to inhale, a shallow gasp. The wind stifled Bhathric as well. She gazed at Athenne through half-shut, teary eyes.

With embattled motion, Bhathric indicated toward the ground. Dropping to the floor on their hands and knees, they ducked beneath the spiteful gust. Their heads low to keep debris from their faces, they crawled, fingers clawing at the begrimed surface, until the roaring ceased and the temperature of the room and its light changed.

They had come into an antechamber. A blue haze filtered down from wide vents at the peak of the temple. The stone of the space glittered with what looked to be a merger of shale, marble, kimberlite, quartzite, and diamond, amalgamated into a deviant, impenetrable skin. On walls tilted out at the ceiling and in at the floor, they found three doors, not counting the hallway by which they had entered.

Shadows of indeterminate origin passed through the rocks, swaying and shaking at the margin of view. From the dark corners came a hum. The tone arose at one side then moved to the next. Each after another, singing a low-pitched tune. A soft twittering and droning chatter bounced through them in rotation. The discordance whirled and wound upward until it became as a raging storm of no distinct quality.

They covered their ears.

As soon as it had come, the disharmony fell silent. The tonal shift jarred Athenne's ears so that they popped, as though she had climbed to the crest of a cloud-touched mountain.

With the quiet, they relaxed.

At the center of this chamber rested a tome wrapped in leather of an ashy hue like moth's powder. The middle of the cover, bordered by black vines, depicted a woman. Pupilless eyes sat shaded in low-lidded sockets. From her temples splayed six spikes. An ovular black jewel split her forehead. On the sides of her skull were four horns, shaped as those of a ram. Around her horns, she had dark hair with banded braids to both shoulders.

Vekshia.

"How does the magic of this temple sustain within the wards?" Bhathric said now that they could hear and communicate again. With heedful footfalls, she proceeded toward the altar.

Standing around four feet tall, intricate carvings converged at a focal point on the structure's front: the seven-sided Matron Star. The ends of the star represented the three features of hope: love, friendship, and peace, the three facets of despair: disease, famine, and war, and these features in sum: death, the ultimate source of hope and despair.

In most temples, altars served as a home for rituals, sacrifices or gifts to gods, but in a temple of Vekshia, they were places of offering from the Matron to the lost.

"We're in Vekshia's domain. These temples must derive their

energy from her. The Ennead has no grasp beyond the walls." Athenne was not certain of this, but considered it a safe conjecture. "The Knights of Faith could have killed us already." She examined one of the doors. "Vekshia must have wanted us here."

Bhathric opened the book, cracked around its corners. Within, a black wooden display and a bronze key nestled in a socket. Below the key, a verse, which Bhathric read aloud:

"Be ye, the bird
Be I, the wing
Fly here, to west
Whence there, we sing"

She glanced around. "Which way is west?"

"I think, this door," Athenne said, pointing to their left.

Bhathric removed the key from the tome and closed it. Fitting the key into a latch, she rotated it until the lock disengaged with an audible *thump*. Metallic clicks followed as iron bolts inside the wall retracted and mechanisms churned. The key dissolved in her fingers. She looked back and shrugged.

Athenne returned the shrug.

With a grunt, Bhathric pulled the door open by its drop handle.

They entered a long passageway, dozens of feet tall and as narrow as the stairs by which they had arrived. Down the stone tunnel, they observed sparse torches in symmetrical rows, burning with dim, white flames. The path wound and sloped upward and downward, its air growing warmer and less still by the step.

Relief flooded Athenne as the roof above them ended following what had seemed like miles. They emerged to fresh air and sunlight. The way they had come had disappeared. Bricked rock stood in its place.

Bhathric ran her palm over the coarse exterior of the wall that blocked their way back, her eyes inspecting the area around them. "Have you seen this before?" They were in an alley, a different world compared to where they had been. The gloomy ambiance that had pervaded their weeks had lifted. Cool, but not cold, the weather afforded their senses a welcome reprieve. Puddles dappled slick cobbles at every side.

Is this real?

The crooked lane tapered beyond its midpoint such that the two of them could not walk abreast. As they exited the dead-end street, they found themselves in a city. High curtain walls, dense and colossal, towered in the distance. A familiar building rose into view. Familiar, that is, in that Athenne had seen renderings of it in art during her youth. The Grand Priory, peeking over the rooftops from far away.

"*Aros*," she blurted out, "*the Imperial City*."

Without warning, night fell in unnatural fashion, attended by a low hum and awful din. The sun blurred and warped as it dove behind the walls and then the world. The skies darkened to a pitch like coal. A coldness blanketed the air, their breath visible in streaming vapors.

The four sisters rolled overhead, burrowed within a backdrop of clouds and stars. As if budged by the gods themselves, they moved at a rapid pace, uncanny in their path. Starlight bled together from each of its sources like fire spreading across an oil sea. Beholding the frenzy brought her nausea.

Their eyes searched about nervously before coming to a rest

on one another. The air churned, blowing and whipping their hair and garments in circles, freezing and thick with a scent akin to burning copper and firewood. Perception overwhelmed Athenne, inundated her with too much at once.

From her periphery, she caught sight of a man. He appeared as a single point of higher motion in a lake of inanimate buildings. She made off toward him and Bhathric followed.

"Mysr?" Athenne's voice went unacknowledged.

They were at his back. He stumbled over stones down a steep decline and collapsed to one knee. "Mother—Mother, please—" His voice trailed off to repetitious muttering.

"Look at the robes," she said to Bhathric. "A priest."

The man knelt, his wrists, ankles, and neck frail, atrophied. His hands rested on the uneven road, hide raw, scraped, busted at the knuckles, split at the fingertips and frames of the nails. Blood and dirt smeared the skin exposed from their position. A layer of filth cloaked his attire, torn at the edges and porous and thin in other places. She sat on her haunches to his right, watching, working to distinguish his overwrought pleading, or praying.

What has happened to you?

As if picking at her mind again, Bhathric echoed her contemplations. "Vekshia shows us this?" She faced the opposite direction with her hands on her hips.

Tilting her head to the side, Athenne assessed the man. "Aye." In observance, she lost sense of the world around them. "Must be." He had the hunched posture of one starved and beaten. Grey, white, and black peppered his hair and beard. Pink with irritation, his dull eyes watered. His tanned skin peeled, as it would if one had been under the sun's watchful leer at length. The vision enraptured her, caused her back to stiffen.

She leaned forward, striving to hear him.

"What's he saying?"

"I can't—" Athenne answered. "He's saying." Her eyes shut. "The ichor." No matter how close she moved, she could not hear him well. "*The ichor that—swallows the world.*"

His voice faded away, as if in response.

"*Athenne*," she heard Bhathric say.

Her eyes opened.

Daylight had unfurled around them once more.

They had transported somewhere else, if they were anywhere at all. An expanse of sea thundered to the west, the storm impelling smoke from boats and steam from groaning apparatuses against a wharf's walls and through open warehouses at their rear. Some few waves and an effervescent crown arched and strained to grasp the peak. Some fewer succeeded and capped the low parapet that fenced the wall, descending from view soon after. Inside the bay were calmer waters, turquoise and like glass, barely disrupted.

It was a waking imagining of a dream. A hallucination made real. The ground, air, sense of being so familiar and so foreign; an iridescent world of twirling particles and false noise, of flowers blossoming and unblossoming in broken pretense. Even the silences between the sounds felt contrived.

Without warning, the barricading wall burst. Savage ocean rushed in and drowned the rocky shore, rubble strewing wide. The water which funneled through formed a channel, seeping into every crack and crevice of the inner stone ground, eroding the material at its finest level, grating away loose bricks.

The surge started to run pink, a terrible color, until it ran dark with that terrible color. As swift as the water had risen, it drew back out. First feet and then yards, then into a distance indistinct to her eyes. The abandoned sand where the water had been almost glistened as the light touched it from above.

She wanted to flee, but could not. Bhathric stood juxtaposed, unflinching. A sour smell of corrupted flesh and brimstone trampled them with a tangible solidity, leaving her skin greasy and damp.

The fountains of the world broke apart and a great red death sprang forth. The wave gained and bloated, miles high; a wall, speeding, swelling, screaming, a malicious froth foaming between its snarling lips.

They needed to retreat, yet they hung under its path. Light rain caught them first, then the flood. It came in aweing fury, as though dragging with it the whole of the ocean.

When Athenne's eyes separated in the wake of the deluge, she was dry, and had returned uninjured to the foremost chamber of the temple. Verglas and rime covered the room in white and clear patches with veins and webs from thinner to thicker layers, explosions in the frost. There were dangling stalactites as slender as their fingers and as big as their arms, coiled and bent upward at their ends to points in anomalous perfection. Despite the glaze of frozen water, a dense heat swelled in the space, like liquid air, too warm for freezing.

"*What's this to do with Eclih or us?*" Bhathric cried to stone walls and ceiling, to the shuddering stillness in every angle, to this place as it held its breath, waiting to exhale and shuffle them off to another spectacle.

It was not real. What you saw was not real. Even as the sea had imbibed them, brutal and battering, she tried to remind herself. No matter her mental measuring and preparation, her hands shivered. The illusions were taxing.

The tome's cover flipped over, revealing a fresh key and a second poem. Bhathric did not read this one aloud, but plucked the key from its holster and slammed the book shut. A spray of dust erupted into the air.

"We must abide her will," Athenne said.

"If only our *All-Mother* was as enterprising. Why must we endure these false sights?"

"Gohheia has not forced us here. We—"

"Yet we *are* here, Athenne. You, Eclih, me. Are we not Her children? Does a mother cease to love one child because they defy her others, even when these others subjugate them, abuse them, deny them her favor?" Athenne's comment had vexed her. "*The Ennead sought to have me murdered!*"

"So they did," Athenne deflected with a gentle tone, steering the conversation toward their present circumstance. "The two spirits, hope and despair."

"What of them?" Bhathric permitted the diversion, to Athenne's relief.

"Vekshia is not a wicked god, but an agent of chaos. They say she does not lie, insofar as the showing of truths through untruths is not a falsehood, yet still a trick. Her aspects are hope and despair. She is a source for each—perhaps, *the* source. If she has summoned us to witness these visions, it must be for a purpose. We ought not to jump to conclusions as to the nature of this reason—her design."

"Are the gods bound to their aspects or the cause of them? Did the aspects precede them before Gohheia bequeathed their stewardship?" Bhathric moved closer. "I'm not the theologian you are."

Athenne detected no derision in Bhathric's remark.

"What does it mean?" Bhathric continued. "Is Vekshia chained as a machine to act by one predisposition, alone, infinitely? If we have the capacity for a shift of heart or mind, why not she?"

"I cannot say."

The key rose to level with Bhathric's face, in the delicate clasp of her index finger and thumb. "I care not whether she spins lies or weaves truths. I want Eclih returned, unharmed." She pivoted toward the door across from their last. "Nothing shall hinder me."

CHAPTER X: ENIGMA

Garron

"Relax, Father Latimer," said Archbishop Sangrey. "The sculptors of perversion shall be exiled this day."

Waiting, he quivered, and attempted to collect himself, his focus on the individual directly in front of him. *Camille Sangrey. Studious, clever, somber, a beacon of power and control.* An exemplar of one of the three pillars of the Matrian Truth as a pure embodiment of order. Despite having worked long in her service, Garron did not know her intimately, but he knew a great deal *of* her, and had learned even more in his present stay at the Priory. If Umbra served as the mouth of the Ennead, Sangrey and Aramanth represented the mind.

Archbishop Sangrey had been born the daughter of a wealthy, doting mother, Magus Ailuin Sangrey, once head of the Academy of Metaphysics. Atypical of women in Imperial society, who as a standard took many partners over their lifetimes, Ailuin Sangrey held singular in her affections. A consequence of growing up in Reneris.

The elder Sangrey involved herself further in a civil union with a man named Errendon, who had by tradition assumed her surname as her wer, the lone man ever permitted into her coupling den after her flowering rite at year twenty. While most Imperial men, including fathers, resided with their mothers and aided in raising children in their matrilineal home, Errendon Sangrey had lived with his wif and raised his own daughter, Camille, beside her.

This deviant nesting and androphilic progressivism had rendered Camille's mother a subject of ridicule, in spite of her station and talents. Later, this derision shifted to Camille. Many presumed that the daughter Sangrey's particular personality and intense desire to govern everyone around her were a product of her unusual rearing.

From Camille's youth, Errendon Sangrey had raised his daughter with the notion that order, as macro, as meso, as micro, epitomized the apex tenet of Matrianism, from which altruism and progress flowed as a natural result. In his rare role, Camille's father had instilled in her an idiosyncratic industriousness, even in a society organized around industriousness. Yet this influence by her father, or her mother's affection for menkind, or a man, had not inculcated in Camille the same measure of progressive fervor. Camille did not champion men's exaltation, though she had not objected in public to Archbishop Breiman Umbra's appointment as Vicar of Gohheia.

A number of ages had Sangrey been a member of the Matrian Church, silencing those who had mocked her and her mother, and many ages had she and Aramanth labored to perfect the merger of their combined gifts. Between them connected a confidence of brilliance.

Along with Archmagister Estatha Khraemine, who had

assisted more as an architect than a builder, their united effort had produced one of the most intricate acts of magecraft in history, with the efficacy to subdue the Aether across the entirety of the Sacred Empire. Nowhere else throughout the continent of Imios had anyone achieved a feat comparable to the modern system of Imperial wards. Not since the days of the Andesite. Not in the golden sands of Abbisad to the northwest, the karst-laden hills of Beihan to the southwest, the grim mountains of Xarakas to the southeast, or the treacherous Renerin tundra to the northeast. Great minds abound, but none so accomplished.

The true power of the present Ennead lay with the depth of Aetherian knowledge possessed in Aramanth Delacroix, unrivaled by but a few, and the pathological diligence of Camille Sangrey. Through their principal works and the aid of their fellow members and the Order of Magisters, they had, as their ancestors, tamed the essence bestowed by the All-Mother. Not in defiance of Her, but to ensure an orderly employment of Her worldly blessing. So long in the past had the Aether without regulation resulted in chaos and destruction, bringing about disadvantage and suffering which threatened the existence of the Mother's true kingdom in the underrealm. This cause, at its root, claimed the heart of their objectives.

Garron understood this, beneath his conflict over their current circumstance; their ethics, their honor, their purpose. Yet worry plagued him. He had left his room at ease, but doubt had infiltrated him along his way to the Ennead's council space. The longer he had to reflect, the fuller with it his mind became.

His last several weeks had brought him such uncertainty and distress, not what he considered irrational ideation. If it were, of course, he could not know. Even as he stood in the chamber of the Ennead, the safest of any location on Earth, he vacillated between an assured hopefulness and irregular despair.

Aramanth and Sangrey helmed the ceremony, as he had anticipated. In the interim, their words flowing, what had occurred, and what might come next, enveloped his mind. If anyone could spare him, it would be then and there.

The nine archbishops surrounded him and chanted, their hands adjoined. They incanted in deep whispers, eerie when he held his eyes closed. Every word resonated in perfection, cut like quality jewels. He looked at them, their faces radiant in the glow of the caster circle at his feet. Their collective gaze concentrated on him, as subject and object. His mind felt clearer than it had been since before the massacre, more so by each passing syllable.

The running of time had slowed to his perception, for he resided within a sphere of mental magic within material magic within metaphysical magic. Their words distorted in pitch and frequency and reverberated and slurred. Disorienting, their movements blurred, drifted, and smeared. Light outside the sphere sifted through in colorful prisms, wavering and rippling as a distant image in the rising heat of deep summer. The air around him cooled and bore no odor, with enough static to set his hair prickling on end.

Not long after the ritual had commenced, it finished. The heaviness he had so long felt in his chest had dissipated. He inhaled deeply. The weight carrying on his mind had flown away as dust departed by the breeze. He could not move for most of the procedure, but had since recovered his usual wits and autonomy.

"How do you feel, Father Latimer?" Archbishop Mallum asked as the effect lifted.

"My well-being, as grave a concern as it has been, is right as the Mother, Your Reverency. My mind's regained clarity. My body has banished its torture. I am glad of your service."

The members of the Ennead returned to their places behind the council table, leaving him standing in the well.

"Father," said Aramanth, "we have deliberated at length." She sat next to last seat on the right. "Confining you to the Priory as we did may have been a mistake. The creature passed through the wards, which we have nonetheless reinforced, without breaking them. Restraining you to this place might have contributed to your mental deterioration, and therefore, to your mental susceptibility." She leaned forward on the table. "We may come to regret this decision, but we would like you to take time to yourself beyond these walls. Leave here, visit the city at your pleasure. We only recommend that you return by nightfall, to be accounted for."

Aramanth glanced to her left. "'Twas Archbishop Mallum who first made the suggestion." She smiled at her. "If it goes awry, we know to whom we'll pass the blame."

Garron's eyebrows raised. After the state in which the inquisitors had found him, he did not expect the Ennead to grant him leave of the Priory for some time. On the one hand, it frightened him to think of himself strolling about the Imperial City, knowing that the Beast lurked in the vast beyond. On the other hand, he longed for any sight not of the stone walls and floors within this labyrinthine edifice, lovely as it looked.

"Thank you, Your Reverencies."

Aramanth spoke again, her voice gentle, as always. "I shall ask Sister Halleck to accompany you, as she has requested further audience with you. You are protected such that I don't believe this entity remains a threat."

One can but pray.

"If, of course, you've no objection," she added.

"I've no objection, Your Reverency."

"You're dismissed, Father." Mallum's light brown eyes glittered. She wore a costume of teal and purple this day. "Be well. Inform us at once if you've any troubles."

Garron thanked them and departed, his eyes glassy with tears at the sensation that inched over him. So long had an anguish strangled and crippled his spirit, caused an aching in his throat and chest. So long had he suffered terrors and wept and endured vile ideations. These were gone. He felt reborn.

He did not hear Sister Halleck as she approached.

"Father?"

"Sister Halleck." They met near the exit of the main vestibule, amidst cleaning machines which went about their usual duties, humming and chittering, brushing, sweeping, wiping. "I've been given leave of our Grand Priory. I'm off to the Aros Athenaeum. You're more than welcome to escort me." Why had they chosen this deacon, in particular, to follow him? She seemed amicable enough, at least.

"Gladly." The corners of her mouth curled into a fond smile, revealing even, pearly teeth, the whitest he might ever have observed, save perhaps Archbishop Sangrey's. Care of health in Aros had always been excellent. Further south, care existed in fair quality, but less so.

Manicured hedges, twice his height, bordered the path at the fore of the Priory. Outside of these were towering oak trees aligned in rows about fifteen feet apart from one another. Sister Halleck's slender features slipped in and out of the light as the branches overhead broke the sun's rays. A pleasantness permeated the day, cool instead of frigid, the clouds above, thin and scattered against a pale azure canvas.

The aptly-titled street, Commerce Lane, opened at the edge of Crescent Plaza, a large market named for its zoning arrangement similar to a crescent moon. Merchants of all stripes stood at their vendor stations, framing the road at the right and left. Women, men, and children filled the space, conversing, shouting, laughing, browsing, buying. As Garron and Sister Halleck approached, most made way, on occasion acknowledging them by their titles. Many had probably learned his in gossip.

"Father," a man said with a courteous tilt of the head.

"Sister," a woman murmured, stepping aside.

The pair returned polite gestures as they continued forth.

Merchants selling fine wares littered the market, along with inquisitors, keeping the peace by their presence. There were tables and racks displaying dresses of fabrics in multi-hued variations, garments from jerkins to trousers, leather and metal accessories, jewelry including earrings, bangles, and amulets, encrusted with precious stones. Around these were farmers and graziers at their goods carts and tables.

"Melons, apples, oranges, and pears! Best anywhere this side of the Black Canal!" called a man.

A woman near the end of one row sold brined beef ribs, spiced slabs of pork, and live chickens, which clucked and cawed from cages at her right, marching in circles around their wire enclosures.

Garron and Sister Halleck emerged on the other side of the Crescent and turned down Ash Route. There were a few more merchants strewn about here. Shortly, timber and stone houses with wooden rooftops slipped in, standing two or three stories high, shadowing the walking paths below.

The Aros Athenaeum rose into view.

"How long have you been in the Empire?" he asked.

"We moved to Kordyr in my youth. Family of middling standing, if you wonder."

He had not, yet. "Your parents?" Not dead, he hoped.

"Still in Kordyr. My father resides with his mother to aid in the care of his sisters. Mother lives comfortably and works as a writer in the showhouse."

"An interesting profession."

"She wished that I would follow in her footsteps and write. I had little interest in the art. My passion lay with theology and service to the Mother."

"I suppose there's an irony in your becoming the Scribe Officiate alternate." He chuckled.

"Indeed," she said, a smile dimpling her face. "What of your parents, if I may ask?"

"Long gone. Father passed of a malignancy in the liver when I was fourteen-yeared. My mother went soon after I made my priesthood and became guardian of Erlan." The name of the village rolled over his tongue like a foul taste. "Mother fell prey to what the healers call drowned lung during the winter. Persistent fever, pain in the side, shortness of breath, a gurgling cough. That sort. Didn't take it long to subdue her."

"I'm sorry for your loss, Father."

"She lived her life well."

They began their ascent of the hall's stairs, which led up to the front doors of the circular structure, its façade shielded by eight marble pillars. A stone and glass dome capped the building as a helm, many feet tall, with a statue at its peak in the likeness of Aros, the First Woman.

The steps themselves, stone laid high and wide, were a daunting climb for one as eldered as Garron. Sister Halleck experienced no similar difficulty, and kept pace in a considerate manner. Youth still blessed her, after all, and elves were known for their natural athleticism.

"If I may," he said, "have you any notion why they've asked you to accompany me? Not that I object."

"Archbishops Mallum and Delacroix believe I have a gift, though I'm not quite sure in what." They came to the top of the stairway. "I'm interested in materialism. That's all I know."

"We may hone our craft, but ultimately, we're each limited to what is lent us, I'm afraid."

"I suppose it so."

They entered the grand main floor of the hall, passing the young man at the front desk, who had the stature of a leaning weed. He greeted them as they walked by with a grin, his black eyes crinkled at the corners. "Welcome to the Hall of Knowledge of the First Woman and Undermother," he said.

The open center of the structure exposed the rounded ceiling, which depicted across its curvature the All-Mother in Vreosiqar, Her golden plane in the Overrealm. Lit lanterns hung from columns above guidon banners of crimson, adorned on their fronts with the Overcross in white. Between windows around the walls, sculptures of archbishops and imperial sovereigns of the past gazed down to the black and white marble floor.

"If I may ask a question," Sister Halleck said.

"Certainly."

Her orange-red eyes traced the shelves as they walked toward the back. Symmetrical beneath her pointed nose, her mouth remained at a semi-regular smile. "What are we doing here?"

He studied her countenance, the subtleties of her expression, then spoke forthright with her. "I seek texts beyond the *Blest Writ* which discuss Vor-Kaal and the Patron of the Undead, as well as necromancy. Reanimation, in particular." He had concluded her trustworthy, but kept his voice quiet.

"Have not such texts been banned by the Vicar?"

"Abbessa Alamanor's *Obsidian Manual* and her other works," he corrected, gentle and precise. He turned toward a nonfiction section ranging from A to J. "There are more."

"Do you not agree these works are heretical?"

"We may not always concur with the assessments of our betters, Sister. I serve the Mother first." He came to a shelf and searched from one spine to another, across codices bound in leather, reads in paperback, written by hand and printed, of conditions new, hardly used, and worn. "The Vicar decrees what is willed right by the Ennead, yet my circumstance, as so, means that I require knowledge of heretical matters. Alamanor's work represents a seminal text of a theological subdiscipline." He put a finger to his lips. "If the Vicar believes her a proponent of necromancy rather than an objective narrator, so be it. I'll seek my learning elsewhere."

"May I assist you in finding anything?" The desk attendant had appeared behind them.

"I know what I seek," Garron said.

The man smiled and left without another word.

After a few minutes of sifting through texts, Garron slipped a finger over the top of one of the books and pulled it out, loosening filth in a small cloud with it. "*Tales of the Blackened Yonder.*" He held the book up for Sister Halleck to observe. "By Xiressa Venlee, a magus in her time."

"Have you read this?"

"Heard of it. By the grime, no one else has read it in a while." He blew on the cover, sending up a puff of dust. "These are the things they don't teach in the institutes or the Priory."

"It says, *A Collection of Folklore and Myths on the Land of the Dead,*" Sister Halleck said. "What good is a book of falsehoods and fables for getting at truths?"

He strode toward the back of the hall, past rows of stone tables and white chairs wrapped in red leather and ornamented with carvings and rubies. "We're looking for kernels of truth among half-truths and tall tales." A statue of Aros, handsome and graceful, stood at the farthest end of the room.

"You mean, confirmation of your experiences?"

Garron stopped and gazed at her, his lips taut and downturned. "Aye, confirmation of my experiences." He seated himself at one of the tables, opening the book.

"Forgive me, Father Latimer." She sat across from him. "I meant no offense."

"I took no offense, Sister. Call me Garron."

"All right, Garron. Call me Amun."

He chuckled through his nose. "All right, Amun."

A particular passage caught his eye. He read its contents aloud: "'*Following a great struggle between humans which resulted in the loss of thousands of lives, Korvaras came to the world. From those many slain, he created Vor-Kaal, and imbued her with his power. She is obedient to her Master and will not hesitate to carry out any command given to her.*'" Garron paused, his eyes moving ahead. His next words carried greater emphasis: "'*Vor-Kaal has the ability to raise the dead as well as steal the spirits of the living. Referred to as the Keeper of Death in ancient writings, few have witnessed her physical body, which the Rotter's Tome states bears resemblance to a mortal woman with black horns as those of a ram. Some claim that she comes in the night to draw spirits from their sleeping hosts, leaving the bodies to decompose or, if she wills it, to walk as empty shells.*'"

"*The Rotter's Tome?*" Amun said.

"The Mythosian version of the *Blest Writ.*"

A woman with horns as those of a ram. He sat back in his chair.

"She raises the dead and steals spirits." Amun sounded excited. "This confirms it."

Garron ran a hand over his beard. "It makes no mention of any instance in which this has occurred. I've neither heard nor read any credible stories which speak of such events."

"You saw it, firsthand."

How could anyone know this unless it has occurred before?

Amun echoed his considerations in a whisper: "Could the Church have concealed a previous attack?"

He scanned the room and saw no one. "With just cause, if they have."

"Do you think the Ennead knows?"

"Couldn't say. We best not speculate."

Amun wallowed in her seat. "Perhaps a harvester disguised itself as Vor-Kaal?"

"Theologians claim harvesters are mindless creatures, a force of nature. They lack the necessary cognizance to perform mimicry or sophisticated trickery."

He let his mind wander through a mental index of likelihoods. A few minutes passed before Amun pulled him back to the present. He had not heard what she said.

"It could have been"—he rubbed his chin—"a necromancer."

"A necromancer?"

"Not the mortal practitioner as those of Mythos. A higher being in service of Korvaras, from Eophianon itself." He grew pensive. "Archbishop Delacroix reckoned no mortal necromancer could've accomplished what I experienced within the wards. She may be right. A true necromancer, however, could have."

Amun looked at him and down at the book. "What could it mean?" Her voice had lost its enthusiasm.

"Couldn't say," he answered in earnest. *Nothing desirable.*

Garron stood. "Amun, will you allow me time alone?"

"I am meant to stay with you."

"Fear not." He tapped a finger at his temple. "I'm protected."

"As you will." She sounded more conciliatory than cheerful. "Thank you for allowing me to accompany you."

With a bow, she left.

Garron returned the book and departed the Athenaeum by the light of a late midday sun. As he navigated back to the Crescent, he found a roadside boarding stable. There, he rented a horse for a few hours with coin given to him by the Ennead as a stipend for his needs. He rode out in robes, not ideal wear for a saddle.

Despite having only made annual visits to Aros since his appointment as guardian of Erlan, he had lived there beforehand for ages and knew the layout of the capital and broader countryside well. He knew the maps of the Empire and Imios beyond too, having studied them at length during his tenure in the underlands. Witnessing locations in the flesh presented an altogether different experience than reading descriptions of them or seeing them drawn from the memory of another on parchment, but the maps had portrayed the land with decent accuracy.

The further he ventured from the market district into the neighborhoods and the lines of stone and wooden houses, the calmer the world became. Energies and noises of the excited activity and movement of the city gave way to the chirping of birds, the rush of the wind, the scurrying of forest creatures. Houses grew sparser. Streets, road signs, and businesses became rolling flint hills, their grass spotted green, brown, and yellow with winter's touch. The road beneath the hooves of his horse shifted from cobbles to soil and rock.

He traced his journey from the night of the incident, when the Beast had flung him beyond the city walls, leaving him to traverse the distance on foot. With trees at every side, in differing shades of oak, pine, and cedar, he proceeded west. His surroundings looked more familiar the further he rode. He had arrived nowhere close to Outmore Loch, which meant he had not traveled as far as he had surmised. A couple hours passed, and the Mother's Eye descended lower to the horizon, but not out of sight. He still had time.

Finally, the house floated into view. The unassuming home where he had committed his terrible wrong. A light emanated beyond the front window, that oil lamp.

He had hurt her.

She and he alone knew, for he had been too much a coward to confess before Aramanth or the others of the Ennead. He considered knocking on the door, offering her the remaining gold on him, but he did not.

Any knock, even the faintest and kindest, would likely be loud and unexpected in her present state, if she suffered as one likely would, enduring a harm as she had. *The inquisitors should hunt down anyone who would cause another such pain.* He did not want to dwell on this for fear he might jeopardize the work of the archbishops on his mind, but he must find a way to right his offense, in any fashion possible, if any prospect existed.

The woman emerged from her home and sped off on foot, not spying him. Her hooded cloak of dark green snapped in the wind as she rounded the bend down the road and vanished out of sight like a specter into the evening.

He would not forget, and no matter the external compulsion he had been under, he would not forgive himself. The woman persisted as a measure of his former agony and affliction. He would not, *could not,* let her go unremembered. In any manner, he would find a way to help her, without traumatizing her anew by the view of him, if she might recognize his face and regress in her mind's eye to that night.

Turning on his horse, he set off down the lane. His gaze did not leave the woman's lonely abode until it faded too far to observe without straining. He made his way back east, toward the capital and the Priory, every step of his mount a conscious stride into the future.

CHAPTER XI: PRIEST

Athenne

In the distance, they heard dissonant music. The sound hung in the air like a bird in flight.

Having exited through the door to the right of the chamber, they beheld a twisting hedgerow, larger than either of them. The hedges cast shadows over the path. Light peaked over the crowns of the vegetation from an array of unknown sources. A cool, moist murkiness rippled against her skin. Small particles of water suspended throughout the air in clusters, only moving as they passed, as if repelled by their presence. The pull of the world and the flow of time did not maintain normal function here.

Following twenty or thirty feet, they came to a crossing. At their right, a route faded into mist. To their left, another led into fog. Every direction looked the same.

"Which way?" Bhathric said.

Athenne went right, and Bhathric accompanied.

They walked. And walked. They had been walking for a while, perhaps miles. A grey void with no beginning or end stretched off into the white gulf in either direction.

"In my girlhood." Athenne needed a distraction. "I used to

wander the Hinterlands of Reneris for hours, sometimes with nothing more than pauper's boots on." She chuckled. "Nearly lost my toes to the frost once."

Bhathric smiled. "I'm sure that pleased your mother."

"I thought she would punish me when I returned and saw her waiting. She embraced me instead. Called me a foolish child. Said to never do something so daft again. She was a good woman."

"What happened to her?"

The question set Athenne into a sentimental longing. "Taken by the pox. Healers couldn't save her. I lived with my aunt for a time after that. Kind person, well-natured. No interest in being a mother. It wasn't her fault. She did the best she could."

"I'm sorry. That must have been difficult."

"I had a fair childhood." Athenne pulled her hand through the stems of the hedges. "I would live it again, if I could." To be free, to run, jump, play, to swim through quick rivers, to climb trees and slick rocks until her fingers and face went numb from the cold. She studied the bushes in a half-absent way. "In Orilon, there's a hedge maze within the gardens at the base of the Mother Sentinel. Titan Spring. Similar to this, though with cobbles of granite, basalt, limestone. When you're a child, the rows rise so high. Higher than you'd ever expect to reach. My mother and I used to walk the maze together. She'd tell me stories, sing to me."

"I suppose you trained for this." Bhathric gave an inward laugh.

The corner of Athenne's mouth lifted.

Bhathric untied the waterskin from her waist and drank of its contents, extending it to Athenne.

Athenne's lips split and cracked. The water tasted as sweet as red wine pouring down her throat, and nearly choked her. When she finished swigging, she returned the pouch and Bhathric re-strung it at her side.

"I know you didn't trust us," Bhathric said with an apologetic tone. "You still aren't convinced." Her fingers brushed long black hair from her face. Their eyes met. The pair of them walked slower, as if on a stroll. "No matter what transpires, you are my true friend, so long as I live."

Athenne couldn't recall the last time someone other than Uldyr had spoken to her so. She had never forgotten her life before Uldyr. The world outside Reneris, where choices overwhelmed like so many pleading poor, terrified her. She had no one to which she could turn, until he came along.

"Yes," Athenne replied, after an interval. "And I, you."

As the minutes passed and the sameness as far as her vision carried did not abate, discontent rose in Athenne. It took all of her will not to turn back. The dissonant music grew louder, as if in response to her fluctuating emotions, bouncing between the hedges. It sounded as every instrument Athenne had ever heard, and none of them; a foreboding droning, filled with sorrowful tones and nervous, piercing harmonics. In the next measure, the noises were joyful and soothing, then flipped once more.

Nausea overcame her.

The sound. Second after second, rising and moving through them, unwavering and steady, panning from side to side. The noise would drive one mad at length. She put her hands over her ears. Bhathric did the same.

"Mental illusion!" Bhathric yelled. "It's not real!"

Vekshia was a mental god.

Such sorcery conformed to her nature.

For what purpose, Athenne did not know.

Perhaps, bare amusement.

Athenne did not recall collapsing to the ground, but as she opened her eyes, she found Bhathric drawing her to her feet. Bhathric's strength exceeded her appearance.

"Don't succumb, sister. We will leave this place, together."

Sister.

Athenne's heart fluttered. She regained her balance, grasping the shrubbery as she fought illness.

"Can you walk?" Bhathric placed a hand on her shoulder. "You look pallid."

"It's the music." Athenne's words were thick with the saliva in her mouth, swept up by the sick sensation at the back of her throat. "It's making me ill."

"If Eclih were here," Bhathric murmured.

"It's nothing. I'll endure."

Emptiness filled the path ahead, except the fog and endless straightness. Ever so many feet and yards, Athenne expected a turn. Any turn. Right, left. A curve. A trick. A dead end. None came. Perpetual nothingness unsettled her more than hindrances might have. The soil and rock beneath them shifted into white sand the further they traversed. *What is Vekshia's play?* After an hour or more, she heard singing in the distance, an elegant, musical reverberation, echoing as sound might through a cave.

"When I arise, when I arise
I'll see thy face
When I arise, into thy light

Monsters and martyrs, their Matron is mine
Death into death, nestled somewhere in time
O' Matron, O' Matron, no warnings or signs
Judgment in judgment, despair and despair
Hope and god arrive, hope and god arrive
When I arise, when I arise
Swift are the works of the Matron, on high
Seven in seven, the number of life
When I arise, when I arise"

A clearing materialized from the fog, which diminished with their footfalls beyond the hedgerows. Air that had been dead came alive in jerks and fits, lifting their hair and clothes and dropping them in repetition. The rush grew, cooling the dampness against Athenne's skin and turning it to ice.

The broad face of a mountain claimed the opposite edge of the clearing, a rocky structure that disappeared into the sky and glittered with crystal fragments. At the sides of the area, open water, blanketed by the silver veil of the omnipresent haze. A light shone overhead, perhaps the sun, but heatless. In the center of the space, the figure of a woman took shape.

"*When I arise*," she sang. "*When I arise*."

Her tune faded as they neared. She stood atop a platform, a round structure of stone, roughly a foot tall, ornamented with the Matron's septagram in black.

"Who are you?" Athenne asked.

"I am the siren, Ennaletes." Her honeyed voice sent a tingling through Athenne's scalp, ears, and neck, akin to fingers tracing the surface of her flesh.

Athenne shuddered and rolled her shoulders. "Are demons not the children of Isanot?"

"I have chosen another. Here, I attend the Patron of None. My sisters of the ocean sing seafarers to shipwreck. I guide those in need of answers, the despairing and the hopeful, each."

"We must go back," Bhathric rasped.

"If it were the Matron's will that you should die, we would already have killed you, Bhathric Ezeis. The two of you are selected for another purpose."

Bhathric walked around to the creature's side. "Dispense with the cryptic riddles. *How* are we selected? For *what?*"

Silver eyes in deep sockets flickered in the muted light, the siren's flesh so pale it had an ethereal glow. "You happen to be here, so your selection happens to be." The ends of her mouth bent up, revealing fangs. "All things that are, are—all things that do are random to each other, where the best interest of everyone cannot be fulfilled. Fate is the craft of the hand."

Bhathric's anger flared. "Tell us why we are here," she growled. "*Where is Eclih?*"

The creature locked focus with Bhathric, her high cheekbones and sharp features accentuated by an outline of blonde hair. "You are in the right place at the right time. Nothing more, nothing less." She turned toward them. "Follow the path the Matron has forged for you. If you do, Eclih Phredran shall be returned."

The siren's hand raised, wrist hanging limp. "*Away.*"

At a sweep of the demon's arm, a cyclone erupted; a swirling vapor which locked her from their field of vision. The cover as dense as a fortress wall rose from the ground and closed around them, until the moisture coated Athenne's face, mouth, and eyes.

It churned rapidly at first, but weakened. When it came to a halt, it diffused and revealed to them the fork they had been at previously. Except, the rightmost path had become another hedge wall, leaving their first way and the way that had formerly been left.

"I grow weary." Bhathric stormed off down the remaining unexplored pathway. Shimmering drops of water, catching the light, drifted away as she passed. Athenne strode after her.

Their footsteps scraped and crunched against the gravel and wet pebbles. Shadows shifted, and the rocky track melted into cobbled street. They had surfaced in a city, nearer countryside, or so it looked.

"*Where, now?* Do you recognize this place?"

"Anger will not avail us, Bhathric. We'll be finished when we've seen what she wants us to see." Athenne squinted through the darkness. In the distance, yards away, a man stood. He cast a spindly shadow, much like a spider, splitting the road asunder. Athenne marched against him, past a number of empty homes.

He mumbled to himself, too low to make out, even in range.

"It's him," Athenne called to Bhathric over her shoulder.

The priest became frantic, yelled, swiped at the air.

Athenne backed away.

"Can he see us?" Bhathric slipped behind him.

The man continued in his terror. He walked in rigid paces toward a house across the street with a light in its window. Soon, he had entered and vanished. When they crept up to the door, the living quarter went dark. Athenne peered within, perception dulled by the pitch.

A wailing exploded inside, guttural and piercing. Rushing noises arose, followed by a violent clatter. They entered and ran to the bedchamber. The man had positioned himself on top of a woman, his fingers clutching her throat. Athenne reached out for him, but her hand passed through his back like a specter. She tore her arm away and stumbled in reverse.

"We can do nothing," she said.

Bhathric left the room. "What is the purpose of showing us this?" She fled from the home as quickly as they had come. Athenne lingered a breath longer. The woman's face reddened and the veins around her temples bulged as the man squeezed her neck. Tears rolled down her cheeks and she sputtered.

"Enough!" Athenne withdrew as well. "I've seen enough!"

The world faded out, from the corners of her vision to the center, like falling asleep. Athenne blinked, and her surroundings returned. She stood in the antechamber, as did Bhathric.

Rolling silence hung over them, except the hum that rebounded from wall to wall, as it had since they arrived, less audible at present. A reflective sullenness masked Bhathric's face, and her hands trembled. They examined the tome on the altar in the center of the room with mutual unease, neither uttering a word for some time.

"Well." Bhathric broke the hush. "One more, I presume."

One more key, for one more door.

"Eclih is on the other side," she added with determination, as if it should be indisputable.

CHAPTER XII: EVOCATION

Garron

Garron leaned back in his chair. *What has caused this Undeath, and what is its aim?* His notions varied as to its ends. *Was the creature truly Vor-Kaal? It must not have been.* No joy befell him by the revelation, either way.

Whether the being had been the highest servant of Korvaras or a lesser one, the result remained unchanged. People died, and terror spread. News came in bursts to the capital, worsening with every report. The great death could expand all the way north to Aros, and further.

Even with this, he could not feel hopeless, not since the Ennead's warding spell. He had become industrious again, heartier by the day. Meeting with deacons, he talked to them of their journeys and lived experiences. Sitting in the Priory's hall of knowledge, he read, took notes, pieced together intimations from the texts. He preferred obscurer readings, few as they were. The Church had curated the hall's contents to avoid literature deemed subversive or heretical.

If the Church was right, and in the right, why must they limit access to knowledge and opposing perspectives? The feud of contrasting views, after all, had forged progress: a central tenet of Matrianism.

"Unraveled the mystery?" said a voice as he perused Elas Orimalor's *Aspects of the Celestia*, a work discussing the Overrealm and the individual planes of each of the Celestial Nine.

Garron turned to see Archbishop Mallum.

"May I?" She gestured to the seat across from him.

"Certainly, Archbishop."

"You'll not find the answers you seek here," she said. "If the truths we yearn for were in these clever words, bardic treatises, philosophical disputations, we would have uncovered it. Archbishop Sangrey maintains an itemized list of every book in this room, mad as that sounds. We would all be reading the work if it were present."

The sum in view, he suspected she was right.

"Not that I lack faith in you. You are a wise man, beyond dispute. Much wiser than the rest of us to this. When you disappeared, I knew we had erred, that we had not been well enough on our guard. The failure is inexcusable. I hope you find it in your heart to forgive us."

"Already forgiven, Archbishop. I was there, and even I was not prepared for what came."

"If we had understood, it might not have been so wretched. We have seen since. Now we are ever on the defensive. In the conjecture that the trouble will persist, and we expect it shall, we consider it an existential threat. Not solely to the underlands, but to the Empire. This is our All-Mother's true home, Father, as you well know. If we fail, if this horror that creeps across the Earth prevails and consumes us all, then we have failed Her. There is no graver a wrong. We shall not be let off mercifully."

He had never heard Archbishop Mallum so zealous over any matter, though he felt glad of her earnest consideration. Sound of mind and learned of thinking, she lived unrivaled in her adherence to the three pillars, even by Aramanth, Sangrey, or the Vicar, Breiman Umbra.

A woman of integrity, the Clergy and common body alike adored Holle Mallum. She represented in her quotidian character an unpolluted embodiment of the three virtues of the Matrian religion. Altruistic and kind, she gave for the sake of others; a paragon of order, and of progress, she had driven the force behind the inclusion of men in the greater ranks of the Church. Yet in spite of her rationality and consistency, one respect limited her reasoning: prejudicial thinking in favor of the Church. She would not consider its faults objectively, beyond what had already made itself apparent, such as in Garron's case.

That the Church must act elevated beyond controversy. He hoped the Ennead had a plan, a way to limit the loss of life. Regardless of whether they had a strategy, he may have to consider possibilities that no one else would. He would need to discuss such ideas further with Amun, who shared a like-minded sentiment to him, or at least the curiosity and skepticism of youthfulness. Her suggestions at the Athenaeum, similar to his own passive thinking, had influenced the direction of his recent considerations.

Every stride toward the truth necessary from this point forward will require careful guidance. I must restrain myself to gentle urgings and subtle encouragements toward particular ends.

He wanted to propose the possibilities that he and Amun had

concocted to Archbishop Mallum, but did not. She dedicated herself as well to the Church as to her integrity and the All-Mother, even when they might conflict in ways unknown to her. There would be no convincing her, yet.

"I must take my leave, Father. We have little time." The archbishop rose. "The peace within this great structure does not extend to all those under our protection. For every moment we spend idle, they suffer. Their suffering is the Mother's suffering, and so our suffering too."

He closed his book. "As so." None knew that better than he.

With a shake of her head, Mallum exited the room.

Invariably, he had considered the Priory a safe place. Not for himself, for he had no concern of that currently; he could perish, face exile for undermining the laws that bound followers of Matrianism to certain conduct. Not directly for members of the common body, either, who could not enter the Priory or walk upon its grounds, save the times when the Imperial Sovereign or the Ennead used it to address the people. What held him most firmly to the Church was the belief that at its heart existed the best interest of those within its domain, beyond these walls.

As he doddered toward Nihil, that endless sleep, he should be well away from such concerns, the hugging tendrils of things that might threaten his sense of the future.

What more could happen to an eldered priest who had given his life in service of Gohheia and his mortal sisters and brothers? He had endured many torments and trials, and emerged with his resolve intact. His conviction in the righteousness and rightness of the blessed All-Mother, that was.

Until what others had called the Erlan Massacre, in which he had suffered a central role, his devotion to the Matrian Church had persisted without question or self-scrutiny. He had done away with such doubts of the spirit over a decade ago, when his service under Archbishop Sangrey ended and his guardianship of the Vale began.

Dusk and dawn, hour to hour, day by day, the struggling of his aged muscles and the soreness in his frail bones, none of these worried him anymore. The suffering of another concerned him now, that woman from the countryside. One speck of pollution in her mind, beyond the cleansing of the most skilled mentalists, could inflict torment on her until her final hour, force her to relive his attack over and over. *I must do something.*

Earlier that morning, he had awoken to the whirring of a machine as it polished the floor of his bedchamber. As the day progressed, as in any, he slinked more immediately to the time when fate would have its say with him. The Nothing or Eophianon. From this breath until his final exhalation, he would have no alternative but to face the predestined, to take what chance and fate permitted. A single stain on the spirit, for an eternity in the Land of the Dead, reliving his worst moments up to his death, without relief or loss of sense.

Perhaps she and I share a reality—a pain that I have brought her.

Garron stepped out into the cloistered gardens.

Warmth seized the day, odd for winter, and fair-weather cumuli bespattered the welkin. Peace hung in the yard like a gliding falcon. From the residence halls, deacons came and went.

Aros persisted as a major center of herbal and medicine sources, and the deacons tended them, usually those of the first-degree. Through material magic, they kept the garden producing in spite of the weather, sun or frost. They had even grown fruits, the ripest of which sometimes fell to the ground if not harvested soon enough.

Aramanth appeared at his elbow. "Walk with me, Garron."

A silence fell over the deacons at the far side of the yard in the Archbishop's presence.

The two of them walked until they came to the edge of the garden, where fewer were in earshot.

"Aros," she began, "is the sacred flower of a holy nation, a servant of which I am proud to be. When I started here as a girl, as a deacon, I sought the direction of the decent women who served before me, before this Ennead. Through their guidance and altruism, I learned to share in a great love. In their stead, I learned to forge an Empire for a new era: strong, virtuous, sculpted in the Mother's vision, born of Her gift.

"Through us, the common body enjoys a standard of life unseen, inconceivable, in any recording of the past. Farmers and graziers, who we subsidize, provide us food. The people enjoy the convenience of our aqueducts. Inquisitors, priests, such as yourself, and vicereines bring peace and prosperity once threatened by war and the avaricious and lawless, protecting the common woman and man in thoughtful employ.

"You have personified each pillar of the Mother's Truth. Order, progress, altruism. If needed, you would have died for the people of Erlan. You suffered, fought for them, for your place with us. I laud you, as do we all."

Garron said nothing, only tilted his head to one side and listened. A smile crept through his lips. Shortly, he returned his expression to its stillness. Then he gazed toward her.

She stopped. "Please, do not give up on us." A genuineness infused her words.

What had been the catalyst for this imploring?

Aramanth was the same candid, sharp-witted, commanding woman she had always been. He had hoped he might have an opportunity to speak to her soon. However, the time had not yet arrived to convey his worries.

"We have dispatched a company of chevaliers along with bishops to the underlands to investigate the goings-on there. 'Tis the concern of Archbishop Umbra that Mythos may have a hand in these affairs. We expect that the company's journey will be swift. When they return, they are to report their findings. In consideration of your own revealings, their orders are not to engage with anyone or anything."

"Wise," he replied.

"'Twould seem, from what we can ascertain in scrying, that the village of Ghora has fallen. Whatever works here is a great power. Archbishop Sangrey and I cannot penetrate the area. Our magic is disrupted." She smiled with one corner of her mouth. "To keep you informed, not to worry you." Her eyes scanned him from head to toe, as if evaluating. "How are you faring?"

"Well." He returned the grin. "The Beast has not resurfaced. Nothing whispers its miseries. My mood has lifted. I'm grateful for the reprieve."

He felt well overall, but troubled. Better than before, without question. Yet in his quiet moments of reflection, the nature of his agitation returned to him. The events of Erlan and those after did not plague him alone.

It was *her*.

Thoughts of the woman and what he had done to her burrowed into his mind like a hound digging in search of its lost bone. *The time between now and the incident could not have healed her*. More for her would be necessary. He could not reverse the wrong himself. It would be incumbent on another to aid in what he must avoid.

It did not cast him into a despair comparable to his former manner of affliction, but he longed to declare the misdeed to Aramanth, to confess the harm he had caused, compelled or not. Yet to do so would be to admit a crime among the worst. He could not elude justice forever. His wrongdoing would not pass into memory without response, something which would unknot his present tranquility and force him to answer for her pain, as he deserved.

"If anything should happen," Aramanth interrupted his pondering, "please, let me know. Do not delay. I told you that they shall not have you, and I meant it."

"As you say it, Archbishop."

With a look part commiserating and part fondness, she left.

He stood alone in the garden once more.

Eschewing thoughts of darker things, he remained in high spirits, ready as ever to enjoy the beautiful day. He might seek out Amun. To him, she had become something of a confidant. For her, he had become something of a mentor. He felt that he could confide in Aramanth or Archbishop Mallum, but a difference of disposition existed in Amun. A sort of free-mindedness that even Aramanth, in her kindness, intelligence, and wisdom, did not share.

His steps returned him to the Priory, that grand edifice of

soaring arches and flying buttresses of white stone, unlike any other substance on Earth. Abbisad had its spires and minarets, Reneris had its pyramids, Xarakas owned the most lavish of Gohheia's shrines, and yet the Grand Priory rose above them all. He ascended steps, first to the innards of the Priory, and wandered down the halls until he had by happenstance collected Amun.

They climbed further to his well-warded space in the side wing off the central vestibule. *The Ennead must not be listening to me here.* He could not bring himself to suspect Aramanth of allowing such invasions of his privacy and trust since they had shielded his mind.

"Mythos?" Amun's curiosity overflowed as she sat across from him in his bedchamber.

"We could have snuffed them out. The threat of destruction once loomed over the followers of the schismatic groups. I presume they do not discuss it much in your lessons."

"Not as you do," she said.

"During the Century's War, blasphemers, false prophets, and those practicing the magics of the heathen gods were to be gathered and executed. Another folly of the Andesite."

"Why didn't they?"

"An inability. Lack of resources. The Empire had won and lost the war with Abbisad. Then came the revolutions. The Andesite had no time to hunt down religious dissidents in their own state, let alone elsewhere. Cults became too many, and the cultists, too widespread."

"What reason would Mythos have for killing so?"

"We do not always act in accordance with the balance, neither us nor them. We abhor their god, they detest ours. 'Tis a deep and fierce contempt, in my view, rooted in a misunderstanding of the delicate equilibrium of the Celestia, persistent well from the early days of the *Blest Writ*, when Aros and Ankhev walked the Earth.

"Every cult believes their god serves the highest calling, has the fairest nature. For some, such as the druids of Sitix, this comes easier. Their god is simple, gentle. His aspect is in everything around us, nature itself. His Incarnation guides the lost and forlorn in his forests. The minions of Vekshia see her as the agent of all change—that everything is born from someone's hope or despair. In this, they may be right." He paused. "If Archbishop Umbra is correct, that Mythos is behind these acts, we shall see greater hatred, horror, and bloodshed before the end of it."

"What can we do?"

"Nothing, as yet, except prepare for the worst."

Without Amun, Garron may have resided in intellectual solitude. It could be her in exclusion who shared his concerns. "It might be our task to convince the archbishops and magisters to act against what they view as the Empire's interest, what the Vicar and Archmagister believe right, what the Andesite before us believed right. We must open our minds to learning truths not for the comfort of this institution."

A decisiveness swept over Amun's face. "I am with you," she said, "whatever the task."

"I suspect I shall need you."

For one day, we may be the only ones left.

CHAPTER XIII: ORDER

Athenne

This is the last door. Eclih has to be here.

A serpentine tunnel lay before them. This time, the pathway presented no illusion. It manifested neither outside nor elsewhere. Nothing more than dark stone walls, floor, and ceiling filled the space. Poor light from unknown sources illuminated the halls, as if through invisible torches, lanterns, or candles, perhaps the only evident magic or trickery. They walked forward, eyes searching for a door, to the sides, ahead, above. As in the last path, exhausting in its twisting course, there came nothing.

The longer they ambled down the passageway, the wider the hall grew, and the taller. After miles, they came to a towering iron door. On the outside of the door, inches from its face, protruded the Matron Star.

Athenne laid a hand against the metal.

It shuddered.

She backed away, until she stood next to Bhathric.

The door opened, sliding into the floor by a groaning mechanism within, dirt and dust spilling down from the ceiling. Upon entering, they arrived at the fore of a long chamber. Pillars at both sides of them faded into the darkness overhead, wrapped in stone vines like veins with sculpted leaves.

At the far end of the chamber stood a massive altar. A face like the one at the front of the temple decorated the wall behind the platform. In the center of the floor, another seven-sided star, filled with a crimson color and outlined in white. An orange light, hazy and blinking, wavered in the space, once more from imperceptible sources.

Athenne's heart pounded. They waited and listened. A kind of electricity hovered in the air, static enough that it prickled on her skin and caused the hair of her arms to stand on edge.

They strode forth, passing pillars and statues of armored women and men. *Knights of Faith.*

Each step they took sounded louder than the ones before in the empty room, filled with a spectral stillness. Tension clutched her, as though someone or something may accost them at any moment. She felt the many pupilless eyes of the sculptures on them. There were phantasms in this place, shadows dancing in her periphery, stirring and receding as she jerked her head to catch them; tricks of the mind, either from the columns, the statues, the deviant light, or all of these.

When they reached the end of the path between the posts, the center of the room at the septagram and the altar lit up. The sculpted face appeared larger than it had from afar, so colossal Athenne had to tilt back to see its peak. Standing atop the star were three armored figures, not there before.

Eclih knelt at their feet, his head drooped. They had bound his hands behind his back.

Black, interlocking plates over mail and jackets, embossed with the Matron Star at the center of the breast, protected the Knights. The resemblance of a woman, likely Vekshia, adorned the face guards of their one-horned helms. Athenne had never beheld such immaculate armor, not even among the Renerin High Guard and Alterforce.

"Eclih!" Bhathric sprinted in his direction.

"Don't come any nearer," Eclih called, not looking at them.

She halted. "Eclih, what have they done to you?"

"Bhathric Ezeis," said the soft voice of a woman, one of the Knights, "keep your wits, and no harm shall come to this one. The Matron has need of you"—she pointed past Bhathric—"and her."

Athenne moved closer. "What does your Matron want?"

"They took me to ensure you would come," Eclih said instead. "Since our departure from Ghora, they've been watching. They brought us here because they wanted you to see. The man in the visions, a priest of the Matrian Church. A guardian in the underlands. Undeath touches him. He has not long to live. They say a miserable demise awaits him. He is a sick man." He paused a moment, slender shoulders slumped. "The Church has replaced their lunar tears. Ours no longer work. We won't be able to gain access to the Priory without their new ones, not even with Aitrix's help. The priest has the beads we require."

"How is it they came upon this information when Aitrix did not?" Bhathric shifted another step forward.

"Aitrix Kravae is no god. The Matron has informed us so." The voice of the Knight sounded different somehow. "We desire as the Matron does to aid your Saints in defying the Church."

"Why not undertake and fulfill the mission yourselves, if you know so much?"

"We may act but so far. Our place is to guide."

Athenne stood abreast of Bhathric. "Why does Vekshia have any interest in this? Why help us?"

"Because."

This interval carried longer.

The Knight tapped the tip of her blade against the stone floor twice, the contact emitting a whistling resonance.

"She can."

A force flung Athenne to the outside of the temple. She spilled onto the ground, landing hard on her back. The Knight had expelled Bhathric and Eclih along with her. She felt glad of the moonlight and night sky. Relief, warm and sweeping and dizzying, swathed her.

Bhathric lurched to her feet and staggered over to Eclih, falling to her knees at his side. "Eclih," she whispered. She unraveled the bindings at his wrists and he rolled over onto his back. "Are you harmed?"

He swept back his long blonde hair. "I am well."

"I'm afraid we've lost your horse." Athenne sat up.

The temple has vanished.

"It's only a horse," Eclih said.

Eclih and Bhathric embraced and shared a kiss.

Athenne averted her gaze after a time.

Bhathric uncorked her waterskin and allowed Eclih to drink of it, which he did, in deep gulps. Her hands moved under his arms when he had finished and helped him to his feet.

They untied their horses. Bhathric attached a riding cushion to the back of her saddle from her satchel. Eclih would have to ride pillion until they found another horse. Common for men.

"As much as I've enjoyed this secondary venture," Eclih said from horseback, "I'm not interested in a fast. We ought to find a campground, fetch something to eat."

"We've yet to reach the Black Canal," Bhathric reminded them. "We'll need to make haste if we want to arrive anywhere near schedule. The others are surely ahead of us."

Athenne chewed her lip. "We need to turn back."

"Turn back?" Eclih repositioned the sword at his hip. "To Aitrix's fury—"

"Aitrix is no fool, is she?" Athenne said. "We must tell her what we've seen, here and in Ghora. These events are of consequence to our mission. If she's unable to see the need to inform her, she isn't worthy of leading the Saints. The others will wait until they've had their signal."

"On second thought, Athenne is right." Bhathric's grey eyes gleamed in the starlight, her expression and tone stern. "There's no value in fighting to maintain our time if we die before we get there, or if whatever it is that interests the Knights of Faith and steals away entire villages is elsewhere. This is an extraordinary circumstance. Our comrades may already have perished."

"One village, that we know," Eclih corrected.

"More importantly," Athenne said, "if what they say is true, we'll require new lunar tear beads to infiltrate the Grand Priory, which means finding members of the Clergy outside of it. We don't know where that priest is."

Eclih's face looked contemplative, but motionless as stone. "So be it." He sighed. "Doubtless, you two utter truths." He placed his hands on Bhathric's hips. "Before anything else, I want to eat. I may fall out shortly."

"We're not taking the same path back," Bhathric said. "I can't bear to see it again."

Eclih nodded. "It's best to avoid major thoroughfares. Anything that might split another village. We'll take the ruts through the tall timbers."

This delay would cost them weeks of travel. For the better, Athenne hoped. Their situation had altered such that she no longer felt confident in their trajectory, or less so than she already had. There would be so little traffic on the backwood routes that they were certain to avoid prying eyes. Then again, there had been no others to contend with since they left Uldyr, aside from the Knights.

Uldyr.

Would they find him alive?

"We ought to check Uldyr on the way," she said.

"Certainly," Bhathric answered. "If he's well enough, we'll bring him with us."

Eclih laughed. "The man will be a pillar of steel."

If only I could be as certain. Athenne would feel better with Uldyr at her side. Eclih and Bhathric were fine companions, but he endured as her first and dearest. She had come to find solace in his presence. Without him, that assuredness had evaporated like water set to a boil.

The roads they found on their journey were more treacherous than those prior. They encountered detours from barely-beaten trails to paths nary beaten at all, forcing them to battle foliage and branches and brush. The woodland around them seemed peaceful enough, still too peaceful for her liking, but better than too full. There were inclines and declines, winding streams and jagged rock sides, which on one occasion required them to pursue a track hundreds of yards around before they found a pass. They stopped at another point to attach feedbags to their overworked horses. The time to establish a camp had yet to arrive.

After a number of miles and hours, they ventured into a share of the Fausse Woods which few had seen. Clearings ceased, trails, paths, roads, and markers ended. Their horses trotted through damp weald and muck. She grew worn of the scenery in permanent repeat. *You must push forward. This venture has scarcely begun.*

Her stomach gurgled.

They had reserves with them, goods to stave off hunger for a time; rye and wheat bread, sun-dried fruits including raisins, apples, pears, and nuts and legumes, some raw, others salted or roasted. Despite that, Athenne weakened. A dull ache throbbed in her head at the right temple and around her eyes.

As if born of the air, a white rabbit with stubby ears appeared from behind a tree, its nose twitching as it sniffed at the ground. An adult male. Enough to feed their meager cohort.

"Look," Athenne whispered to the others.

This could be their sole opportunity at a decent meal for miles.

They stopped.

"By Sitix's blessing." Eclih lowered himself from Bhathric's horse. A silver knife with a black handle emerged from his belt, squeezed between his fingers in a pinch grip. "No one move." He eased toward the hare, drawing back the blade, trying not to spook it. The creature turned its side to them as if to give him a better target. He threw the knife, catching it in the neck. It let out a squeal, fell over, and spasmed. After a few final jerks of its legs, it came to a rest.

Bhathric applauded. "Well done, dear."

He gave a bow, sauntering over to the defeated critter and retrieving his blade. "With the eye of an eagle, I suppose," he jested. "Let's find a place and start a fire."

They continued until they stumbled upon a clear patch of land adjacent to a narrow river, at the base of a cliffside, which jutted out at the top over the spot and receded at the base.

Eclih skinned and prepared the rabbit while Bhathric gathered kindling, returning with logs, twigs, and pine needles. Snow and rain had soaked half the fodder she had collected. They spent a while working to catch a spark in any of it.

With the hare ready—flayed, beheaded, gutted—they skewered it on a metal rod, encasing their modest flame in a fire ring of riverside rocks, their meal in a delicate balance over the heat.

"Well." Eclih sat down with a grunt on one side of the fire. "We neglected to double back and retrieve our other supplies. It'll be cool earth for us this night."

Bhathric dropped next to him, crossing her legs. "I've one more mat in my saddle-bag. Anyone can have it. I don't mind. I've slept on worse."

"Athenne." Eclih set his focus on her through the fire as she lowered opposite them with veiled effort. Fatigue burdened her, but she refused to let it show, not when Eclih and Bhathric had rebounded so quickly after such a physical and emotional ordeal. "You have it. We'll huddle for warmth. It wouldn't be fair to leave you out."

"I couldn't. You two take it."

"Eclih is right," Bhathric said. "I insist. Have it."

Athenne smiled through sealed lips. "Fine, fine. If I must."

"We'll refill our skins and water the horses." Bhathric shook the last drops of liquid from her pouch onto her outstretched tongue, which had turned white in its center. "I could use a bath, but I fear I'd catch my death."

Eclih adjusted the rabbit over the flame to keep the grill even. The hind legs had charred already. "I'd enjoy a wash, but we can't risk a fever out here. We'd have no way to help you. We're still far from the Keep."

"Don't you know healing?" Bhathric asked Athenne.

"I can cure minor wounds, not deep illness or injuries like Uldyr had. Otherwise, he'd be here with us."

"What else've you studied, if I may?" Eclih turned the skewer over on the fire to help the flame get at the back of the rabbit, the underside already browned.

"Theology, combat philosophy, primarily. I'm ignorant of a great deal. I wouldn't consider myself a theologian."

Bhathric grinned. "Combat philosophy?" Her pitch climbed higher than usual. She rested her chin on her palm, braced at the elbow by her knee. "How well can you fight?"

"More theory than practice," Athenne said. "I can watch a fight, name the motions, predict what one or the other might do. If it'd been me the daggerhand attacked, I would've perished." *I may have died if Uldyr had not bested the mercenary*, she reminded herself. Not that she had forgotten.

"An Abbisan dancer is no easy foe." Eclih tugged a sliver of meat from their roast and slipped it into his mouth. "I could eat my weight in this."

Bhathric took a portion as well, tossing it to Athenne. She had another for herself. “One trained in Abbisad and in Forgebrand, presumably. It’s no wonder he gave Uldyr such trouble.” She dropped the charred meat into her mouth and chewed. “They say the leader of Forgebrand is a diavora.”

“Diavora?” Athenne had heard of Forgebrand, but less about their leader. Few outside the highest ranks of the mercenary company had met or seen him, to her knowledge.

“The last of an ancient kind, born of Old Earth magic. Half-dragon, half-human. Strong as ten men. Hard to kill as an indervorg.” Bhathric gathered a cloak around her. “They’re immune to most magic, but they don’t suppress it by their presence as true dragons do.”

“I’m surprised you haven’t heard of them, given the concentration of hessants in Reneris.” Eclih pulled a bit of tendon out of his teeth. “Before the Primal Era, they say the diavora hunted the forestkinds to near extinction. The elves and druids came against them and wiped most of them out. Whispers claim more exist, hiding in the northeast mountains or the Forests of the Other Spirits. None besides Ikkath are confirmed, if he is.”

That name rang familiar. “Ikkath the Mad?”

“Aye.” Eclih tore another bite from the rabbit. “Nearly done.” He slid the chunk between his lips. “Dual-wielder of the Xarakan tradition. If he’s as fearsome as they say, I can see why the best work for him.”

Bhathric chuckled. “They’re never as fearsome as they say.”

“How did you come to meet Uldyr?” Eclih said. It occurred to Athenne that neither Eclih nor Bhathric had thus far asked about the origin of their kinship. "I've never seen him take to someone with such warmth."

A heat spread from Athenne's nose to her ears and chest. "It's not that sort of thing."

"Not starry-eyed?" Bhathric said with a measured softness.

"That night in the church served as my induction into the Saints, if I've had one. Uldyr has been a mentor to me. We were companions on the road from Reneris to the underlands of the Empire."

"Did he tell you much of himself?" Eclih rolled a log in the pit with a poker from his satchel. The fire crackled and sent embers flying. "He's never been much of a talker. You may know more of him than we do, save Aitrix."

Aitrix. "Our personal conversations have been few, despite how long we've journeyed. The first time he spoke of his life before was the day the daggerhand attacked." *What should she know that I don't?* "Still, I consider him a true friend." *She probably does know things I don't, with how he speaks of her—in admiration.*

"Whatever the case," Bhathric said, "Uldyr is a good man."

Athenne looked down. "Beyond contention."

A hush fell around them for a time, like the mist of a spring shower, clinging grey to the air and their skin. Finally, Eclih asked the inevitable question: "Why did you join us?"

Athenne's eyes shifted up, aimed at him first and Bhathric after. Their expressions were curious, relaxed. *Why did you join?* "I suppose." Her gaze lowered once more. "I suppose I needed purpose. Uldyr told me that I could help the Imperial people, that I would be useful. My learning had led me nowhere. I saw a world deserving of better, and awareness of it possessed me, yet I sat idle, doing nothing. The Saints have afforded me an opportunity. So, here I am." She shrugged, unfolded her legs, and leaned back on her arms with her palms to the ground. "You?"

Eclih glanced over at Bhathric for an instant, then back to Athenne. The ends of his mouth spread into a closed smile. "Much the same." His tone drifted from light to sympathetic.

When the meat cooked brown and black, front to rear and top to bottom, they removed the skewer from over the flames and divided it. To a few of her bites, Athenne added various nuts from her pouch. She had flesh of the legs and abdomen, sweet and tender, seared through. A trail of clear liquid escaped the corner of her lips and she brushed it away with the back of her hand. Never had she tasted anything so delicious. Every mouthful mollified the rumbling demon in her belly, until at last she had licked the creature's bones clean.

Athenne washed her hands off in the river.

Eclih took the rabbit to discard it and clean the skewer.

"Mayhap we should sleep in rotation," Bhathric said as she lay down next to the fire. "No one can get the drop on us if one of us is awake. Not as easily, anyway."

Eclih slipped the meat skewer into the saddle-bag of Bhathric's horse. "As the former abductee, I concur." The upward quirk of his lips indicated the return of his jovial disposition. Athenne felt glad of it. "I'll take first watch."

"You've endured a great deal. Both of you. Now you've given me the only mat." Athenne tossed a stone into the water. "Sleep. I'll keep watch until near light, then catch a few hours to dawn."

"You're certain?" Bhathric rested her head on her bent arm.

Eclih lay down behind her, likely too tired to object.

"Yes," Athenne said. "Sleep."

Not long after, the pair had drifted off, their breathing regular. In her rest, Bhathric's mouth had lifted slightly into a dreamsmile, her expression peaceful.

Athenne tended their fire on occasion and sat on her mat near the water's edge.

The moons and the thin line of the rings reflected brightly in the black current. Fireflies frolicked over the river, fluttering and floating like tiny stars pulled from the sky. They were a foreboding, an omen of misfortune or ill fate. Totems of Kismet, set apart from the kinds of Sitix by their hypnotic mutant light.

That night, she thought of Ghora, of what they had seen in the temple. That flood.

The ichor that swallows the world.

It must be significant if Vekshia had shown it to them.

In her imagining, Athenne stood in the midst of it. Watching, helpless. The wave, miles high, roared toward them, drew them into its deathly red maw and consumed them living. She maintained doubts, but if Vekshia wished to aid in their success, then an importance attended their business, nasty as it was.

A pleased stomach, the warmth of the fire, and the tranquil night conspired to make her drowsy.

I must not fall asleep.

She removed her boots, rolled up her trousers, and draped her legs into the water. The water felt cold, too much so. She would not leave her legs submerged long, but enough of a duration to wake her up. Bhathric's satchel had a cloth in it with which she could dry herself.

When Athenne finished risking her limbs to frostbite and

had dried herself, she lay covered at the bank on her loaned mat. She longed to observe the stars performing their dance with the moons and the rings before the clouds enveloped them. Camping marked the best and worst part of travel.

The days and evenings were more pleasant when no one suffered capture, of course.

At its finest, travel permitted a time for one to appreciate the meekest of things. The murmur of running water, the trees crying in the wind. On most nights, a symphony of animals would sing their melodies throughout the woods, as far as one could hear. No such music had played since prior to their arrival at Ghora.

Their dinner hare had been the first animal to cross their path in some time, except the horses, and now the fireflies. The three of them were short on supplies, but if they rationed, they could make it to Aitrix at the Blasted Keep, situated as far south as one could travel through the sprawling Fausse Woods, at the cusp of Imperial territory.

Athenne turned over to her side, head on the ground, and listened to the sound of the water as it pulsed through on its course, reflecting like a looking glass in the light from above.

Something is coming.

She hoped they would be ready when it did.

CHAPTER XIV: DECLINE

Garron

"State your names for the record," Archbishop Sangrey said as she looked up from the papers in front of her. "Abbisan first, Xarakan second."

Garron watched from the side of the room. Next to him sat Scribe Officiate Amun Halleck, poised to transcribe every word of the inquisition.

"I am Kocia Arellano." The woman on the left spoke with an alveolar trill, her bronze skin glowing in the light of the council chamber's braziers.

The girl on the right named herself next: "Valhrenna Thrall." Her defiant brown eyes raked Sangrey with icy disdain, her pointed chin tilted up.

"From where do you hail? Same order."

"Khor Dohaid, Abbisad."

"Xarakei, capital of the Xarakan Republic."

"You are each members of the death cult, Mythos, devoted to the worship of the God of Death, Korvaras. You practice forbidden arts, including necromancy and plague sorcery. Do you confirm my accounting of these facts?"

"Aye," they replied one after the other.

Sangrey gestured toward the Abbisan woman. "You are a priest of Mythos, are you not?"

"Aye."

"And"—she indicated to the girl—"you are a witch?"

The girl nodded.

"Speak for the record," Sangrey ordered.

The girl held her tongue.

An inquisitor behind the Xarakan struck her across the thigh with the baton in her hand. "*Speak.*"

"Aye," the girl said in an insouciant tone, seemingly determined not to whimper or express pain.

"How is it that a Xarakan national came to reside near the Imperial city of Imbredon? To our knowledge, Imperatrix Diomira has maintained the strict national border of the Xarakan Republic, as her foremothers. None may enter or leave. So, how did you?"

The girl glanced at the Abbisan, who shook her head once as if to give her permission.

"Look not at her," Archbishop Umbra commanded. "Answer."

"I was smuggled out," the Xarakan girl said.

Sangrey leaned on the support of her chair. "By whom?"

"The one with me."

"How did our inquisitors identify you as members of Mythos?"

Her arms shackled at her front, the Abbisan tugged down the center of her tunic, revealing a tattoo at the top of her chest. "Our members have tattoos of eight hands joined at the wrists behind a skull, within ringed circles denoting our rank by their number."

"Most peculiar." Archbishop Mortem's blue eyes, colder than

any frost, aimed squarely at the Mythosian priest. "Your kind are typically more content to die than divulge."

Sangrey went on. "Seven ages ago, a number of Mythos cultists came into the city during Idoss, to Crescent Plaza. There, they unleashed plague spells. Flesh-eating flies, locusts, hail, boils, skin-consuming disease. Do you recall this event?"

"Aye," said the Abbisan. "The Night of Thirteen."

"Do you recall that, subsequent to this, affiliation with Mythos became punishable by death?"

"Oh, I recall."

Three-hundred citizens died in that attack. Curses afflicted livestock for weeks near the capital, rotted them from the inside out. The hailstorm destroyed hundreds of homes. To Garron's knowledge, no executions of Mythos reapers had occurred since that day. Most reapers were more careful than these two had been.

"How were you captured?"

Brow knitted, the Abbisan's eyes flickered between Archbishop Sangrey and the inquisitors at the edges of the room. "Don't you already know?"

The inquisitor who had struck the Xarakan earlier hit the Abbisan in the same place at the back of the thigh. "*Answer*," she barked. The Abbisan flinched, her jaw visibly tightening.

"We were lodged at the Hall of Marquis north of Imbredon. Valhrenna left her wrist uncovered. The inn's guard recognized her tattoo and sent word to your paladins. They rounded us up and brought us here."

"Priest of Mythos. I'll do you the small honor of employing your title, illegitimate though 'tis." Sangrey was in a more amiable mood than usual. "Are you aware of the happenings in the underlands?"

"Happenings?" The woman sounded curious. "I could not say."

"Residents of the villages of Erlan and Ghora, along with those of smaller holdings, have vanished. Father Latimer, the man there, was guardian in the Vale." She motioned at Garron. "An Undeath spreads across our southern territory. Bodies fall and rise again. One such reanimate claimed to be Vor-Kaal herself."

The Abbisan laughed. "I'm afraid I'm of no help."

"In time, you may reconsider," said Umbra, with a tone that brooked no contention. "You might wonder why we have been willing to entertain you." His humorless frown did not relent. "You shall have two weeks to confess what you know. If you offer valuable information, we'll permit you to live out your days as prisoners here in the capital. Provide nothing, and we'll hang you in the square."

At last, the faces of the women betrayed expressions beyond apathy and resistance.

The lips and hands of the girl, in particular, shook.

"Gaze not so long," Umbra continued. "Mythos cultists yearn for death, I've heard. You ought to be grateful to meet your Master sooner. If we were a less civilized people, I'd have you whipped through the streets. Consider it fortuitous that you have any alternative." He turned his attention to the inquisitors behind the women. "We've no further use of them at present."

The inquisitors seized the women, yanked them around, and marched them out of the chamber. There were a number of cells deep beneath the Priory for distinctive prisoners, no doubt the destination of these two.

Archbishop Mallum indicated to Amun Halleck that her record-keeping had found its need for the day. Amun gathered her equipment and exited by the same doors the women and inquisitors had gone through.

"They know more than they admit," said Archbishop Crane.

"Of course." Sangrey snuffed out a candle at her left. "And they'll inform on none of it."

Umbra moved to exit the chamber. "'Tis of little consequence. They shall die, no matter." The Vicar disappeared around the corner and the other members of the Ennead started to filter out.

Aramanth approached Garron as he rose from his seat. "Garron, I have matters to discuss with you." She spoke in a low voice. "I'll be over momentarily."

"Certainly, Archbishop."

Not long after he had returned to his chamber, a light knock came upon the door. Aramanth stood without, her hands in their habit folded at her front. He turned to allow her passage inside.

"How are you?" she asked. He appreciated that his well-being remained of concern to her. "Are you well?"

"Better."

"Are you wanting of anything?"

He sat on the edge of his bed. "I have all I need."

She closed the door behind her and took a seat at his bedside. "We'll move to the business at hand, then. I'm sure you've better uses of your time than further tediums."

He gave a thin smile. "I've much time."

"Since we dispatched the company two weeks ago, there has been no word from the chevaliers or the bishops. We suspect them dead, but we cannot confirm it. We remain unable to scry in the region." She crossed her legs. "Scouts have reported no trace of life beyond Abela and Arkala, save animals in the Arnlan Forest south of Imbredon. We've ordered that they venture no deeper. We expect that Ostland has succumbed as well." A grim expression befell her. "We are considering evacuating the territories past the Black Canal."

There were tens of thousands of Imperial citizens living south of the Black Canal. "Would not that cause great hardship in the north?" Not even Aros had the resources or space for an influx of refugees on such a grand scale.

"How long will the common body tolerate these events and our inaction before they rise up in blame of us? If everyone beyond this city vanishes into the air, as those of the Vale and Ghora, what have we left? The Empire is a sum of its parts. Without those constituting the share of its portions, we are a city, not a kingdom. The wars may be long over, but opportunism never ceases. When our rival nations sense weakness, they'll strike."

Garron gave her a long look, reflecting on what he might say. "Archbishop." His throat narrowed. "Could it be that the restrictions on the Aether are contributing to this havoc? Our people endure limitation, but those whose magic is born of the favor of the other gods are not so inhibited. The reapers conjure their plagues. Druids continue their forest rituals. Many still practice their craft."

Aramanth stared at him, unblinking. The softness that so often pervaded her features, as much a part of them as the bone that comprised them, no longer presented. "Nay." She did not sound certain. "Warding began in the days of the Andesite, and nothing of the kind has ever transpired. Favored or not, the wards lessen all magic within the boundaries of our country, to the exclusion of our own. Even at their strongest, the high priests of Mythos could neither steal away whole villages nor compel you within the walls of the Priory. Whatever works here rises beyond the purview of the intent of our wards." She was surely not certain. This was conjecture.

"As so, Archbishop." The exchange dissatisfied him, but he did not wish to press the issue further for the time. Cultivating a flicker of doubt, he hoped, might suffice.

Greaved footsteps approached from down the hall. A heavy tap came on the door. It was Garron's chamber, but Aramanth had called the meeting. He glanced to her and she signaled that he should answer.

"You may enter."

The door opened and an inquisitor appeared. "Archbishop," she addressed them. "Father."

"What is it?" Aramanth asked.

"Apologies for the intrusion. One of the prisoners has requested a meeting. The Abbisan."

"Are we in the market of appeasing every whim of terrorists?" Aramanth spoke as if the idea of such a request, itself, was an insult. "The answer is nay."

"She suggested that she has information which may be of value, Your Reverency."

Aramanth sat a while, silent. "Very well." She sighed. "Let's see what she has to say."

With the inquisitor at the helm of their trio, they walked from Garron's room through the Priory, descending further into the structure. They came to a door at the end of a hall. The inquisitor swiped her badge over a rune adjacent to the door. An Overcross on the face of the rune glowed white and the door turned inward, revealing a looping stairwell, which they took down. The air felt dense and stifling, more so the lower they went.

Neither the moons nor the sun touched here. The walls featured no windows. Sparse torches across the corners gifted the space its sole illumination. Most of the cells were empty, but as they came to the barred cage at the back of a row, their prisoner moved into view, sat with her wrists and ankles bound by iron shackles. The other prisoner fell nowhere in sight.

They must have her elsewhere.

"I am Archbishop Delacroix. This is Father Latimer," Aramanth announced as they stopped outside the container. The Abbisan's head pivoted toward them with a rigid motion, like a pin turning in a rusted hinge. "If you have something of interest to present, this is your moment."

"I've heard you may be reasoned with." The woman's voice sounded hoarse. "I needed him here because he's seen what so few have." She swallowed. "I've nothing to tell you that'd save my life, but I wanted to ask something of you." Her chin trembled. She expended great effort to contain the waver of her words and the quaking of her knees. "Spare Valhrenna. She is young and foolish. She has harmed no one." A tear glided down her cheek. If not for the faint light of a torch several feet away, it would not have been visible against her dark skin. "Please."

Aramanth's face bore no expression, her mouth tight. Her response came swift: "You have chosen to labor in the service of Korvaras, the God of Death. Not as a force of nature, but as a figure in defiance of the All-Mother. Your execution will be an honor, a consequence of your choosing, which your fellow reapers have nary extended their victims." She paused as though to allow the words to sink in, or to await a response.

The woman looked away, toward the darkest side of her prison.

"On the day of your execution," Aramanth went on, "you'll be gathered for transport to the city square, in prisoner's garb. The Vicar will detail your identities and pronounce your crimes before the common body. Nooses shall be secured around your necks. You will drop beneath the platform at the end of your ropes, until dead. Afterward, your bodies shall be collected and incinerated."

Their confined Abbisan expressed no pleasure or relief. Her profile readjusted to view, gaze fastened to the floor. She clenched her teeth and her jaw bulged. A shuddering exhalation expelled through her nostrils. "*I have not killed anyone*," she snapped.

The tension in the air shifted.

"*She has not killed anyone*." The woman ran a trembling hand through her mid-length black hair, her head rested against the palm, her bangs interlaced in her fingers. "How can divergence of opinion warrant death? We have nothing to do with what is happening in the south."

"You affiliate yourselves with a known terrorist outfit. This is not a matter of benign, passive ideas. Every reaper is a potential murderer, for to be a reaper is to endorse death and those practices from which it results." Aramanth's voice rose like embers. "You'll find no sympathy here."

Is this justice?

"However, what you say may be true." Aramanth neared the bars. "If your companion renounces Mythos and submits to deprogramming, she might live. Your fate shall remain the same, unless you confess."

"I have nothing to admit," the woman replied without hesitation. She shifted her gaze to Aramanth. "Let me speak to her before you make this offer. A moment is all I ask."

Aramanth shook her head. "She must accept the bargain without secondary persuasion."

Mythos worshiped a heathen god, practiced foul arts prohibited under Matrian Law. Reapers had previously attempted to commit mass murder, succeeding on occasion. Even so, he pitied the Abbisan and the teen-yeared girl. He did not believe they had a hand in what he had experienced, or any killings.

There was nothing more to say. Sorrowful of expression, the Abbisan turned away, and they left.

These dungeons were dirtier than the rest of the Priory, but superior to most prisons elsewhere. The machines made rare trips below, careful as they cleaned to maintain an arm's reach from any of the cells.

Not long after he and Aramanth departed the first captive, they were proximal to the second. She lay on the cold stone floor with her temple propped against the wall. A redness rimmed her lids, as though she had recently wept. When she heard them approach, her brown eyes opened, aimed downward, blonde locks hanging over the right side of her face in thin strands. Brow furrowed, her nostrils flared.

"What've you come for?" she hissed. "To rough me like your guards?" She raised her arm, revealing finger-shaped bruises down the back and side.

Aramanth folded her hands at her waist, the corner of her

mouth peaked, her eyebrows lowered. "Not so." She sounded indifferent. "Tell me, how might your high priests treat me, were I the captive, they the captors?"

The Xarakan's glare rolled up. "You'd already be dead." Her lips pursed. "We hold no prisoners."

Aramanth glanced at Garron, then looked back to the girl. "You are seventeen-yeared, are you not?"

"I am."

"Rather young to hang, wouldn't you agree?"

"I'm not hanging myself."

"Ah, but you are. You've done this wholly to yourself."

"Justify my murder as you like."

"You've such potential and strength," Aramanth told her. "Such a fierce will." She bent down on her haunches as though to meet the girl closer to eye level.

"Say what you mean, *Archbishop*." The girl made the last word a prodding barb.

"I have an offer for you. One you ought to consider well. You may thank your partner for it." Aramanth's words rang with a cordial tinge. "Renounce Mythos. Submit to deprogramming—"

"Deprogramming?" The girl laughed in her face. "You mean, wash my memories of Mythos?"

"—and live another day," Aramanth concluded.

"Do you take me for a fool?"

"The alternative is hanging along with your friend."

"You'll be a murderer after that day. My blood shall forever stain your spirit."

Aramanth rose. "Pity."

The girl stood up. "*Pity*," she mocked.

"We'll allow you a night to—"

Before Aramanth could finish, the girl spat in her face.

Aramanth removed a small cloth from a fold in her robes and wiped the thick strands of spittle from her lips and cheek. Her gaze affixed on the eyes of the girl, who looked as though she would lunge as a mountain cat might on unsuspecting prey if not for the bars between them. "You've thrown your life away," Aramanth said, without inflection, pivoting toward the exit.

Even with what the Xarakan had done, Garron felt regret on her behalf. He wanted to ask the girl to reconsider so that he might work to convince Aramanth to forgive her transgressions. Yet her expression and demeanor told him that the girl would not bend. She moved to the corner of her cell, her back to him, and sat on the floor, her head leaned once more against the wall.

Not since he came to the capital had Garron witnessed this side of Aramanth. He did not disapprove entirely, but a share of him inclined to dissent. As vicious as reapers of Mythos had been in the past, and despite the danger presented by their ideology, summary execution as a response to mere membership represented far too astringent a punishment. Nothing in the *Blest Writ* decreed that those who praised the other gods or received their favor must die. If it were so, this would by necessity apply to peaceful sects as well, including most of the Druids of Sitix, the Monks of Vysyn, or even the Rationalists of Lahrael.

If this consequence could not extend to all, then it surely could not serve as a foundation for such punishment. And they had no evidence that these women had participated in the Undeath, or that they had killed anyone at any point. Nonetheless, the optimal moment to assert such objections had not arrived. The events beyond the Priory embattled the whole of the Church. No assemblies went without tension. The archbishops, including those not appointed to the Ennead, withdrew increasingly from public interaction.

He returned to his chamber and read of Scripture, for he could not escape his growing consternation.

In the beginning, Gohheia arose in this plane, and created the Overrealm and the underrealm, and brought forth the waters and the winds. At Her touch, life bloomed all over the world. Gohheia saw all, and saw that it was good.

In over fifty ages of life, Garron had found such strength and fortitude in the lines of this sacred text. The words did not leave him. He tightened his grip on the book. Their situation grew more dreadful by the day.

The ichor that swallows the world.

Even with the wards on his mind, these words haunted him.

She bid humanity to be fruitful and faithful, and returned to Her throne above.

Are we faithful to Her?

So long had he believed in the verses of the *Writ*. The leather-wrapped book, once pages, once only words, embodied the seminal text of seminal texts. His world mother had taught him of the All-Mother's Truth in his boyhood. He had recited Scripture each day before his morning meal and each night before bed. When worry overcame him in the past, he had often spoken the words as a means of centering himself.

More call to worry arose on this day than ever before.

Garron stood not merely as a citizen of the Empire. He fought as a warrior of the Mother. The archbishops, too, were soldiers in Her army. In many respects, their concerns and measures made sense to him. As a matter of maintaining the pillar of order, severe punishment of deviant factions and a demand of adherence to the one true religion were reasonable practices. Mythos cultists sought to establish Korvaras as the apex god, King of the Celestia. In their fanatical worship of death, their ends would give birth to a cynical, bleak world. Tolerance for their perspectives meant an endless struggle between irreconcilable beliefs.

He had never met any reapers prior to that day, and yet he found himself swept up in the imminent executions of a pair. The Ennead, which he now served in a direct manner, had taken an approach that he agreed with as theory, but anguished over as practice.

These women, one a girl and the other near to, had once been children, just as he. They ate, drank, sang, laughed, cried, slept, and wept, just as he. Flesh and blood, nuanced beings and spirits. However astray, however estranged, they were daughters of Gohheia, as all human women and girls. *If the Mother looked on in our presence when the nooses drop, would She laud us, or condemn us?*

Though Garron had always been a faithful follower of the teachings of the *Writ*, and a loyal servant of the Church, his world mother had taught him a valuable lesson: when something feels wrong, reconsider it. When the reapers stretched at the neck, their faces vacated of life, their eyes glossed and empty, his timidity would become contrition. If he could not stand for their sake before the time came, there would be no second chance.

Despite that the prayers of humanity reached Her well and often, She felt lonely, and so She called upon Her other gods, and granted each an aspect of creation, for which She tasked them to govern and care.

If Gohheia had bestowed upon the other eight of the Celestial Nine their aspects of creation, as the *Writ* stated, how could it be punishable by death for one to appreciate their governance of any given aspect? Of course, this gratitude ought not to entail worship of any god before Gohheia, but he abhorred the wretched duality.

Garron remained in his chamber for much of the evening. A machine came around dusk with his supper, roasted chicken and potatoes. His stomach cursed him for it after he ate.

Renewed fretting, for a new cause, left him unsettled. Less disturbed than he had been prior to the warding; a more natural anxiety. Not even the magic of the Ennead kept him from being human.

The girl, Valhrenna Thrall, did not realize the gravity of her circumstance. *Only the young and the mad do not fear death.* Even those of the Matrian Truth often agonized over their mortality on their deathbeds.

When the Mother's Eye sank behind the hills and the four sisters of the night made their presence known, he fancied a stroll through the Priory gardens. A beauty came over the yard, and a comfortable warmth for this time of the age. Leafy and leafless branches, boughs, constricting vines, the few blooms which remained, swayed in the breeze. The glow of the sisters on the stone and foliage produced an otherworldly air.

He walked until he came to a tree where flowers grew. Stopping, he reflected, watched, and listened to its song as the world moved through its arms, shoving them to and fro.

"You are afflicted, Father." The voice of a man materialized behind him. "Marked by death."

A shadowed figure melted into sight, adorned in unembellished black robes and a mask with a long, pointed nose. Round covers of glass obscured his eyes. Garron had seen such attire before, in houses of the dying. Healers filled the extended beak of the mask with dried flowers, herbs, and spices to stave off the stench of disease and rot, but generally did not keep these covers on beyond their duty.

"Do I know you?"

The unfamiliar man wore the lunar tear charm of a magister.

"Nay, Father," the man answered. "You see what others cannot. Yours is a world of darkness and visions beyond seeing. Ages of authority and status have left the archbishops sightless in one eye. The reach of Eophianon creeps long, and the wealth of each spirit is as deep as the oceans to the Patron of the Undead. Those who cannot perceive the coming storm live in another sort of darkness. You, who bore witness to the red tide, exist in another sort of light. In the Vale, you observed but a sliver. A beast that was one is many. The God of Death will have his due."

Garron stared at him. If another deception befell him, another infiltration, he hoped to meet his end right then. "Forgive me." His legs weakened and trembled, heart thumping against his sternum. The tips of his fingers and the back of his neck tingled. "I'm afraid I don't understand."

"You shall." Unhurried, the magister turned to walk away. "The Blackened Yonder awaits."

CHAPTER XV: MACHINATIONS

Athenne

"We care not what you have or haven't done," the woman mercenary had said. "It's nothin' personal."

In the veil of night, they had traveled, hunted. Mercenaries from the Forgebrand Company had come for them, clamoring for the rewards on their heads, to add them to their lengthy list of felled bounties.

Their new assailants, a woman and a man, were more cautious than the man who had called himself the Red. Athenne scarcely heard the crackle of twigs and crunch of leaves in their approach.

The pair talked of fortune, the detached nature of their work. They refused to confess their hirers, but she knew.

Each one of them knew.

The woman daggerhand and Bhathric had tussled for a while, with fists at first. A sneer across his dark, scarred face, the man traveling with the woman watched, his green eyes twinkling in the pale moonlight.

Both drew knives, and the woman cut Bhathric across her forearms and neck, took the advantage. Eclih intervened before a killing blow, striking the woman across the bridge of her nose with a rock. Bhathric drove a knife into her throat repeatedly, until it resembled a heap of raw meat on a butcher's floor.

Before the woman's companion had time to descend on Bhathric in retaliation, Eclih met him in a bind. They scrapped. Eclih narrowly eluded a number of strokes that would have been fatal. Bhathric and Athenne joined the fray, utilizing what methods they could. The daggerhand fought, skilled and powerful, but not enough to best the three of them. Eclih drove his edge into the man's underarm and withdrew. The mercenary dropped to one knee.

"You'll never be free," he laughed through ground teeth. "We'll hunt you until the bounty is paid."

The three of them recovered their horses and rode into the distance as the man screamed at their backs. They would treat the wounds they had suffered elsewhere, out of earshot of the ravings of a killer a shade from death. His voice grew more strained as they advanced and eventually became a far-off, guttural calling. When it had gone, lost in the silence of the world, they stopped to clean and bandage their injuries, most superficial. Bhathric had endured the worst harm for her stubbornness in demanding single combat.

"They shall feel my wrath for what's been done to you." Eclih sounded surer than he ever had to Athenne, who finished Bhathric's wrappings.

Bhathric smiled at him and placed a hand on his cheek, her back against a tree. "I have no doubt." Their lips met, but only briefly. Eclih aided her in standing. They had little time to delay.

Aitrix would expect them to arrive in Aros soon for their

share of the mission. Their return would suspend by weeks the other dispatched Saints, who undoubtedly awaited their signal, likely to Aitrix's shock or irritation, or both. Fortunately, their allies understood that complications could arise, hence the command to wait for a sign.

Athenne had surprised herself in the melee. In her younger years, she had studied combat philosophy, the arts of battle and war, under Aeyana Thelles of Orilon. Thelles fought with the grace of a dancer and the ferocity of a true warrior. In turn, Athenne had learned to understand a dancer's grace and a warrior's ferocity, but not well enough to perform the elegant pirouettes or to match the sophisticated cues.

She became more concerned with comprehending battle and war than practicing it. This had served her well as a spectator of Uldyr's fight with the mercenary weeks prior. Had the man set his blade on her, however, she would have returned to the dirt in a knowing mass; at the least, fully cognizant of her shortcomings.

Eclih and Bhathric were more skilled than Athenne in sword fighting. Bhathric lacked the experience of an Abbisan dancer or Xarakan dualist, but she held her own. Eclih, on the other hand, clashed with a trained dexterity and quickness. He stood tall and slender, with a fair reach, swift feet, and keen eyes. They did not seem to delight in battle or express contentment in killing, but they would fight if they must.

Athenne's long-ago instructor, Aeyana Thelles, epitomized another sort of person. She spoke often of the pleasures of winning and derived unnerving joy from violence. Had Thelles been mortal at all? Was she some changing, shifting thing meant to deceive her students in their waking hours as a dream might? Athenne could not say, and had never learned, for her teacher had vanished soon after the end of their lessons. Thelles looked to be of no importance anymore, beyond the knowledge she had imparted, boundless in effect.

On the road, since Athenne had met Uldyr, she had come to appreciate simple living, the lifestyle of their ancestors during the days of hunter-gatherers and the Sightless Era, before Ankhev and Aros came to the world and spread Gohheia's will unto mortals. Before empires rose from the ashes of tribes and chieftesses and chiefs, the Old Earth, seldom remembered in the present, and even less frequently discussed.

Aros had seen with the eyes of the All-Mother, the stories said. Her living conduit.

"She shed the tears of the Mother for the pain of Her daughters, and embraced them with her warmth," Athenne's world mother had told her. "A mother's eye holds so much, but love for her children, it holds most."

They passed an apple tree on their way to the Blasted Keep. Their journey north did not seem as barren as the trip back, but it had been weeks. Apple season came when the northern winds brought the warmth of spring, Fevarios to Arrilios, and lasted through the heat of summer, ending near the month of Lerenios. The first small flower buds sprouted around the end of spring. Here, however, well into Vysyn's winter, this tree bore fruit. Tainted offerings, black and withered on their branches, falling to the ground to collapse and mold.

This peculiar growth had occurred near the forests and rivers of the Fausse Woods, through which they had trekked not long before. The decay demonstrated an unnatural event. Beyond, similar trees littered the weald, and each looked the same. What had been a place of beauty and splendor, even where deprived, had shied and atrophied by the touch of something foul. *This must connect to the events of Ghora.* These visions had lingered in Athenne's dreams and imaginings since the day they departed the village.

Not long after, they arrived at Uldyr's house, a lone ship of life in an ocean of dead and dying things. Clouds obscured the stars that had earlier speckled the sky. A light rain fell. At least there was that, wind and rain. For all the natural forces and things of the land that had fled or washed out, to taunt or discourage them, a faint drizzle and a gentle gust comforted her.

They dismounted, tying their horses to the posts outside. Athenne adjusted her robes, dark grey and black as they had been for so long. They each needed a bath, and Uldyr's facilities might be their last opportunity for days or weeks. She tapped on his door with a playful rhythm. They waited, breathless.

Had he survived his injuries?

The door opened, and there he stood.

Athenne threw herself to him, arms wrapped around his neck.

He took her about the waist and nearly crushed her ribs.

A heat permeated her face and tears welled in her eyes.

"Why do you weep?" he chuckled.

She wiped her cheeks. "You're alive!"

"You lot are thinner and rougher than last I saw." Uldyr grinned wider than he had on every occasion since they had met combined. "The world too."

"You're still a lumbering beast," Eclih called as he came up.

"Less so than last we witnessed." They shook at the wrists and exchanged a pat on the back.

Bhathric hugged Uldyr, though not with the intensity Athenne had. "We were needful of you on the road." She flashed a half-smile. "Many a near-death."

Uldyr motioned for them to enter. "I must ask." His tone grew serious. "What brings you back?"

The road-worn trio exchanged a look.

"It's quite a tale," Athenne said.

Uldyr poured the three of them drinks in clay cups. His toxic homemade brew, vicious enough to skin paint from wood. "We've apparently the time." He sat them around his table.

Over two hours, they informed Uldyr in turn of the events that had transpired since they left him weeks ago. How they had camped, the sight of Ghora, Eclih's abduction. They described the Matronian temple, the visions, the man that Vekshia had shown them. Bhathric and Athenne spoke of the woman the priest had attacked, how the Knights of Faith had instructed them to proceed. Uldyr listened, his expression ranging from somber to grim. They talked of the second attack from Forgebrand.

By the time they had finished, the four of them had drunk two or three cups of Uldyr's poison apiece. The drink had defiled them, but not divorced them of their reason.

"We thought it best to return to Aitrix," Athenne concluded. "It seemed foolish to carry on."

Uldyr reflected for a short period, eyes downcast. "You made the right decision, I reckon."

When these words had finished, and they had shared their information, Athenne and Uldyr headed off together for a moment alone. A gladness that Uldyr had lived spread through her, an excitement to end the strain of wondering whether he had survived his skirmish. Yet the cheerfulness did not last, and soon gave way to numbness. She had experienced this detachment in increasing increments since that first day in the sanctuary, and it swelled exponentially.

Narrowly aware of the present, she walked with Uldyr from his house toward the woods, into the sea of trees. She remained within herself, in fear, and what she had internalized; the things they had seen, the bodies and the unnatural elements, the raging stillness that had threatened them from every angle. Each tree that passed, or bush, or patch of flowers, clovers, and weeds, seemed alien to her, or unreal.

She felt both there and away.

Behind her, Uldyr hiked quietly. For weeks, she had desired to be with him, to know that he had endured, and yet she could not speak. He had heard their story, must sympathize with her. Did he wonder about her mental and emotional state? She did not feel well, but she did not wish to betray it.

A deep breath filled her lungs and escaped as a staggered sigh.

They approached a stream, which climbed upward, and down and up and down. The trees became fewer and the hills more numerous. They walked a steepening path, wordless, until at last they came to the top of a ridge.

She halted and he stopped at her side.

"Athenne." His voice sounded subdued.

She had nearly forgotten how he towered since the last time she stood next to him, the top of her head barely to his shoulder. From their place, she gazed down to a peaceful meadow. The more she looked, the better she felt, but only slightly. This would be a fleeting instant, and perhaps their final one alone, in peace.

"When this is over," she said, her words faint. An ache spread in the back of her throat. She verged on weeping, but held it in. "Will we finally be happy?"

Facing him, she found him inspecting her. She couldn't read his expression, even as their eyes connected. He looked, but did not seem to see, or perhaps tried not to.

In that moment, she became aware of the duality of his character. Uldyr, her true friend, and Uldyr, the soldier of Aitrix Kravae. She couldn't tell which eyes gazed back.

"We will," he answered, as if there could be no doubt.

Her focus returned to the meadow.

Expanding past the rolling horizon, the forest went on and on. The world fell more silent in that instant than it had been when they first came to the top of the hill. Their breeze had left them. No birds sang. Few insects buzzed. It felt less unnatural than further north, but choked her the same.

The crushing tranquility persisted. A scent of sweet flowers carried through the air when, at last, the wind graced them once more. Far off, smoke rose from the treetops, probably the product of a campfire.

"I missed you." The strange tension that had grown between them dissipated in a flash. With it escaped some of the stress in her chest, though not enough.

"And I, you," he said. "Our struggle shall soon end." He paused. "I want you to be happy. Yet you are not. My desire was not to cause you misery. I wish you to live free and well." His hand fell on her shoulder. "If you can be brave, all will be as it should, for us and everyone else. There is no better life than to live freely."

She chewed her lip. "Then I'll be brave." Her cheeks simmered.

To live freely as we call it, or as Aitrix calls it?

I must not think about this now. Not now.

His arm lowered. "I suppose we ought to get back, lest we keep the others waiting."

It would be a long walk for her, as she went, deeper in reflection. Indeed, as they marched, even with the generosity of fewer inclines, the return felt far lengthier and more taxing than the arrival. The certainty of her spoken words had not yet made its way to her heart.

At Uldyr's house, Bhathric and Eclih idled by their horses.

"Let's be off," Uldyr said.

Without much postponement, and neglecting an owed wash, they departed. They ventured through woodland paths, orchards, and passages that tore mountains in two. Athenne had traveled this way with Uldyr what seemed ages ago. The stillness that had infected everything north of there, to Ghora and beyond, crept southward.

When darkness came, they would set up camp and eat of the rations Uldyr had supplied from his home. The further south they ventured, the more the eerie quiet relented, until at last, birds chanted from the branches and flew in the sky and other woodland creatures scampered. Hearing the world alive brought an odd relief. She had missed it, like admiring the face of a friend one had not seen since childhood.

Yet they had not escaped the spreading darkness entirely. On the last morning of their journey back to Aitrix, grey shrouded the sky; behind it, the Mother's Eye, a filtered orange glare. The air felt heavy and damp, ridden with a noxious haze that the powerful winds did not dispel. Her nostrils burned.

The Blasted Keep rose into view. Walls of granite connected four thin, square towers. The south tower, ruined in an explosion many decades prior, lent the Keep its name. Across these walls sat sparse windows in serpentine rows. Tens of ages ago, when the Keep belonged to a noble, artillery and archers had crewed the walls, atop overhanging crenellations. A wooden gate with defensive holes for loosing arrows centered the face of the Keep's perimeter, accessible by a stone bridge.

"Who comes?" called a voice from above.

Eclih's hand rose. "Saints. Eclih Phredran, Bhathric Ezeis, Uldyr Friala, and Athenne Zedd."

"We do not recognize the name, Athenne Zedd."

"She's new," Uldyr said. "Aitrix knows her."

A delay.

The doors shuddered as a pulley contraption within drew them open. Riding into the walls on horseback, the four dismounted near a stable. Other Saints resided here, the first she'd observed outside of her companions. They greeted Eclih, Bhathric, and Uldyr immediately, while Athenne received eyes of suspicion or uncertainty before less eager salutations. Foreign leers considered her, analyzed every feature from head to toe.

Collected, the four strode across the outer yard until they came upon the main hall, which looked to have at one time been a throne room of sorts. The entrance stood open.

"Forgive us, Aitrix, for this impropriety," Eclih said as they made their way toward her.

At the end of the hall, Aitrix stood with her back to them, gazing up at a statue several times her size, no doubt in the likeness of Aros in this part of the country. Cascading light from clerestory windows threw over her a brilliant whiteness and gave her an almost ethereal aura.

Aitrix turned around. "Why are you here?" Her voice carried a similar unearthly quality.

"We experienced a number of difficulties." Bhathric's pitch touched an uncharacteristic height.

Athenne disliked the tint of fear in Bhathric's words.

Aitrix examined them without any suggestion of fondness. "Kamia caught traces of your ventures, though little precise. She lacks your ability, Eclih." Her red eyes outlined their wounds, and scars. "You were assailed?"

"A daggerhand of Forgebrand attacked Uldyr," Eclih said. "Later, we encountered Knights of Faith and two more mercenaries. We were able to overtake them."

"What did the Knights want of you?"

As they had to Uldyr, they explained what had transpired on the night of Eclih's capture. They recounted the visions, the message of Vekshia and her Acolytes. Aitrix's porcelain features remained unmoved by their testimony, though she did not seem unconvinced. Last, they spoke of Ghora, the vanishing of the people, the village priest and field officer, and of the barren, empty wilderness, too lifeless even for winter.

When they had finished, Aitrix turned to look up at the statue again. Eventually, her lips parted with an audible click. "Our mission is our own," she said, as if countering an opposing claim. "We'll not be instruments of Vekshia and the games her servants play. Whatever their intentions, if their objectives align with ours, it is not our concern. Ignore the Knights. You'll depart immediately. Other agents will follow in two hours, so as not to draw needless attention. I'm certain those already there shall await your signal, as instructed."

"What of Ghora?"

"Bandits. Metaphysicians. Difficult to say. If we are aware of it, so too should the Church be. This may prove auspicious for us. We'll use their distraction to our advantage."

"If I may," Athenne said, the first time she had spoken since they arrived. "Vekshia is called a force of chaos, but not of deceit. She fuels action to create reaction." She paused, perhaps due to hesitation or uncertainty, but pressed on. "If we must procure these new lunar tears, would it not be wise to pursue the priest? All of this will have been for nothing if we are unable to enter when we arrive. We may die for a cause lost before it started."

Aitrix stared at her. For a time, the only sound among them was their quiet breathing. "I have reconsidered. I shall accompany you on your return."

"Do you think that wise?" Eclih said. "You're the kin of one of the most celebrated mages to ever live."

Bhathric stepped forward. "The Church disseminated portraits of your like when they declared us terrorists. Even the least learned of the common body might recognize you. Your life is of great value. Any informer would make herself rich to the grave for alerting the inquisitors to your presence."

"You're also elven," Athenne added, to everyone's surprise, including her own. "Fair folk are few outside of Reneris. You'd draw some attention even if you weren't famous."

"If three days after you departed, the mercenaries of Forgebrand gathered around you and demanded your lives, as ordained by their employers, most likely the Ennead, I would know too late," Aitrix said. "The growing threat to our enterprise is adamant and ever-hostile. We cannot afford any miscommunication."

Relief and anxiety at the prospect of Aitrix accompanying them on their return dueled within Athenne. Despite the danger that her reputation and visibility brought, Aitrix soared as one of the most powerful mages in the underrealm, and she was their leader. She never dispensed with her formality or this managerial quality. The tension of her supervision would be tangible in every deed they carried out once they left.

"What of the priest?" Athenne asked again. Aitrix had assigned her the task of disabling the source ward beneath the Priory. For her, this signified a matter of central import.

"I was remiss." Aitrix's face grew reflective as she appeared to weigh the choices and information they had provided. "We'd be fools to trust the Knights of Faith, yet the Church replacing their lunar tears does not drip of falsehood. If it is so that the Ennead has disabled the function of the former beads, we shall take part in that. They say death magic touches the man and he has not long to live. You affirm that he has participated in violence against others." She pressed a finger to her painted lips. "When we are nearer the Imperial City, we'll scry and unveil his location through your memories of those visions. We'll take what we need of him when we arrive."

They had made the decision.

Athenne reeled inside with the finality of it.

Soon would mark the end of who she had been; the close of

a woman, once among the cherished daughters of Gohheia; the child her world mother had loved, who loved her back. When the priest perished, decayed, and turned to dust, so too would her spirit. Recollection of him would keep with her, as would every other face unto which her actions, directly and indirectly, brought death. Athenne could do little, except hope that once her light extinguished in this plane, it would remain so, and not reignite in Eophianon.

She had become a sedate minion of this faction, carrying out what they decreed, doing what they asked without outward rejection or question or expressions of reluctance. She had not always been this compliant, but she had killed the fiercer version of herself. That day in the Matrian church, in the sight of Aitrix, Eclih, and Bhathric, and with her lies for Uldyr, she had died. Every version of herself would perish in time that did not object to bloodshed and killing in the name of the Saints' cause.

There may be a lesson for her to learn in this, something in her lived experience which would benefit others. Athenne could not say, and would leave it to those who came after them to decide. She had inherited the mind of Aitrix. Her longings and needs were hers, and theirs. There were moments of her, recurrences of her innocent self and good nature. She wanted to turn away, to be somewhere else.

The longer Athenne stayed, the further she descended, and the more this cause consumed her and replaced her with itself. She had long ago bid farewell to her former destiny, her foolish hopes, old loves, the decency her mother had breathed into her, the compassion for the guiltless, the adoration of simplicity in the domain of the Father Earth. Each of these faded by the hour and second.

She increasingly trusted those around her, and lost confidence in the All-Mother from whom she once sought guidance. For the ways the Saints and the Matrian Church were alike, they could not occupy the same space. Neither in harmony nor in discord. One must surmount the other, such that one could not exist. *Only the wretched, the sick, and the feeble require the relief of hopefulness.* She could no longer hope, but think, know, and choose.

Nothing remained to say. Athenne stood there, saying nothing. A feeble tinge of guilt arose in her, despite that she worked so hard to convince herself. In a fashion, she would be responsible for this priest's death, a man whom she had never met or known. The day crept nearer in which such reservations, doubts, concerns, and contemplations would be of no further value. She must either rid herself of them, or flee.

It's too late to flee, you fool. That hour has fallen away.

"Individuals of small minds and great means have taken a hold on this country that we shall not easily undo," Aitrix said as they departed the Keep. "Not unless those who can fight are willing to do so for those who cannot."

Aitrix led their direction and path, allowing them no other way. They found themselves retaking their former route, in a more linear journey than the circuitous directions they had pursued in their return south. The sun seemed brighter with Aitrix at their side. For that, Athenne felt grateful.

Other Saints she did not know, whom no one had introduced, plodded on at the tail of their small host, swaddled in silence. They were to diverge from the main party later, but with the same destination and secondary objectives in Aros. Aitrix believed that a group larger than five would draw too much attention, particularly with her involved, and their noteworthy arms. Athenne agreed.

Uldyr had withdrawn like a turtle in its shell since their arrival at the Keep and subsequent departure. She ruminated over the time they had spent together before this, when she had walked as a Saint in name but not in practice, and had heard of Aitrix but never known her in the flesh.

Does he long for that time as I do?

They had shared a happiness, in budding acquaintance and friend love. Love, it had been, and remained. She had never told him of her love. With so many words, she had, but never in those, and never had he spoken the same. Yet she had felt it, and gleaned it from his grey gaze and the nuances of his expressions and voice.

Perhaps she would say it, sometime before they died.

CHAPTER XVI: PARTING

Garron

The flames of the hearth wilted, the cinders smoldering, the ashes falling into decay. A crackle flared and shot up a burst of sparks like the innards of a machine, whirring and grinding metal on metal. Fragranced wood, imported from the Grove to the east, scented the slender tendrils of smoke rising into the fire shaft.

In the council chamber, aglow with flamelight, a silence had overtaken like the seal of a crypt. Such a quiet that they could hear the low hum of a machine as it glided over the rough stone ground down the corridor. Some gazed at the floor, some at the fire, some to the windows and the night sky. The members of the Ennead were there, and the Grand Provost, leader of the Silver Knights, and the Imperial Sovereign. Garron presented as one of the lowest ranking individuals among them. He had become a fixture at these high meetings.

At the edge of the space, he sat in his usual chair beneath a draped Imperial flag. He wore his traditional priest's robes, grey and black, with lunar tears at his wrist. The room cooled and overheated him at once, hot at his front and chilled at his back. As the hearth died out, the atmosphere remained intense and scorching. If he had moved a fraction nearer to the others around him, he feared his garb would singe.

The Grand Provost, Thalla Aenor, moved from her place against the council table to the well. One hand relaxed at her side, the other hung on the pommel of her longsword. She stood as one of the best fighters in the world, trained in the arts and styles of the four nations of Imios. This day, she wore her shimmering plate armor, far more ornate than the standard issue of lesser paladins, no doubt forged specially for her by the most skilled metallurgists in Aros. Brown hair and brown skin, markers of Abbisan descent, peeked through her ceremonial helm.

"Weeks, it has been. Our knight lieutenant and two companies have not returned. This is no longer a matter of minimal response." Aenor focused on Archbishop Umbra, the Imperial Sovereign, the rest of the Ennead. "Emperor, members of the Ennead, I need not tell you. Silver Knights perish. Servants of the Clergy die. Innocents of the common body disappear in droves, as smoke from that hearth into the air. We must act. Do more."

"I am in accord," called the Emperor, Helies Kallata IV, from across the room. Garron had scarcely seen the Emperor before this day. A man near forty-yeared, with blue eyes, dark hair, and a pale but otherwise unremarkable face. Helies IV, like the imperial sovereigns preceding him, owed his position entirely to the Ennead. "Discontent grows. If left untreated, it festers. We stand at the precipice of rebellion."

"Time and events are against us." Archbishop Zaria Tornaeu's green eyes were like small looking glasses reflecting the light of the fires in the dim room, housed in dark sockets and framed by dyed auburn hair. Her analyzing visage lingered on the rest for a few seconds. "Many fear for their safety in this city. Rumors of the tortures of Father Garron Latimer"—she looked to him—"have leaked into common imagination." The high and low knew Tornaeu as a woman of the people, spending much of her time among the common body beyond the walls of the Priory. "They lie in their beds and eat their meals in terror of a threat we have hidden from and kept our tongues on. By the mercy of the All-Mother, the Undeath has not yet beset Aros. I say to you, it will not last. This malady shall soon pass the Black Canal. When it does, we'll be at peril's gate."

"We ought to send a full regiment," Archbishop Mortem suggested. "I'll attend the venture, if need be."

Tornaeu concurred. "I second this proposal, and I shall accompany. We must move if we expect to overcome this."

"Have you any objections?" the Emperor asked of the Grand Provost.

She strummed the hilt of her blade. "This is reasonable. Knight Captain Bashek shall join the host." She paused, as if to think. "If you come upon the body of the knight lieutenant or any others, please recover them, as you are able."

The meeting adjourned for later planning and preparation. Garron would not be in the field, so he disengaged, until the arrangements became a garbled noise in the background.

For weeks, terrors had plagued him in waking and in sleep. He had existed so long in a fog of pain and fatigue that subsumed all his other emotions, until the Ennead and their powerful artistry freed him from his burden. His first instinct since the warding ritual had been to pray.

Crying, screaming, cursing the Mother, he had tried these, and regretted them. Prayer was all that it took. The Mother did not torment him. Their god endured, ever-impressive. Grace, strength, power, She bore these, and more. To curse his loving god would have been cruel, and no matter the Beast's abuses, he would not be cruel.

Tried not to be cruel.

But you have been.

No matter what he was, or was not, he had inflicted cruelties on another. The woman's eyes that night, like a deer's as a wolf moves in for the killing strike. He saw the woman more than he thought of Erlan. Where warding had swept the Beast's empty stare away, the panic of the woman's gaze did not abate.

The memory of his crime had become as much a part of his person as heat to flame.

"Father," said a voice at his back. "Garron."

Sister Amun Halleck. He had hoped to see her this morning.

A modest smile broke across his face. "Amun."

"How are you feeling?"

Everyone expressed curiosity these weeks.

"I'm well." They had little time before the events of the day were to proceed. He looked around. "Are you familiar with a magister who wears black robes and a mask of plagues?"

"That's unusual garb. I am not. Why do you ask?"

Amun had eyes for everything and everyone. He detected no nefarious intent in her, but inquisitiveness. *This will set her on him.* "He came to me with a prognosis of sorts."

"A prognosis?"

"He believes that I am touched by death." Garron would not mince words, for if it were so, he had information which he needed to convey. "That I am not to recover."

"He could not know it."

"The Ennead's warding has deflected my external torment, but my trouble festers beneath the surface."

"Garron." Her eyes widened. "What do you mean?"

Before he replied, bells rang, a medley of iron on iron from afar. They knew what it represented.

Deacons poured out from the residence halls at the far end of the garden. All those within the Priory and much of the rest of the Imperial City would soon assemble at the public square, before the statues of Aros the First Woman and Ankhev the White, which threatened to touch the sky. Excited voices would drone like buzzing wasps.

He and Amun followed the throng.

"Trust in Gohheia." A material spell of projection amplified the Vicar's commanding speech. Upon the square's elevated stage stood Umbra, Sangrey, Aramanth, and a number of inquisitors. Behind them, gallows decorated with two nooses. At the end of these ropes, the Mythos reapers, Kocia Arellano of Abbisad, and Valhrenna Thrall of Xarakas.

"Trust not in the conceits of the self, but in our blessed All-Mother. If these who come before us had done so, they might have lived as you shall live the morrow. They have subsisted in abomination. This day, they die to make amends. For what little they can, those who turn from the *Blest Writ* of the All-Mother to stand in the fond sight of the wayward gods shall meet the same fate a thousand times, and more. May the Mother be merciful and gentle as they take their leave of this world." He raised a hand as his piercing gaze scanned the crowd.

Archbishop Umbra indicated to the Abbisan first, who stood with no betrayal of fear upon her face. "Have you any last words? Speak them shortly, and we shall pray for you."

She looked at the Vicar and smiled. "Good people are always so sure they're right."

The Xarakan to her left did not fare as well.

Her arms and chin quivered, eyes fixed on the dreary sky.

Garron and Amun moved nearer to the front of the crowd, wading through the people who had converged by the hundreds around the platform which played host to the day's spectacle.

"And you?" the Vicar requested of the Xarakan.

Her bloodshot gaze fluttered toward him, then down to the rabble. "I—" Her voice trembled. Could she manage the words? "I die this day for a difference of belief. Seventeen-yeared, you have stolen my life. Each of you who stands and watches and says and does nothing murders me." The girl pursed her lips as her face quaked harder, her breathing staggered. Shortly, her focus realigned upward. "*Get on with it.*"

The Vicar continued, unfazed. "Let this deed serve as a warning to all those who would kneel in reverence of the heathen gods, who would participate in malevolent ventures against the children of Gohheia and Her sacred kingdom: you cannot escape the Mother's justice, for we are Her arm, and our reach is boundless."

With a gesture to the executioner by Umbra, the women dropped, and the slack of their nooses snapped taut. The vision felt surreal, the air thick and harsh. As they sputtered and clawed at their throats, their limbs twitching and thrashing, the hanging became a festivity. Garron peered around him, at the clamor, the cheers, the commotion, enthralled faces, mesmerized and writhing in vicious waves of foul elation. He could stomach no more.

He placed a hand on Amun's shoulder. "Let's be off."

She looked entranced, but in a different manner, and did not hesitate to accept his proposal. They departed the assembly without a second glance.

Garron wished to visit a house of the dying with her, as they had discussed. A number of blocks from the square, they came upon one. Only those with lunar tears could enter without explicit permission, for wards restricted the houses as a measure of quarantine and to preserve the safety of resident deacons and patients. A deacon of the third-degree greeted them with an address by titles on their way in.

"Sister Halleck has never visited a house," he explained.

"Very well," said the resident deacon. "Proceed with care and keep a wise distance."

Garron offered a bow. "Thank you."

On the outside, the house appeared warm and modest. Rock and wood in large and small blocks and beams comprised the building's exterior. Within, polished stone made up the walls, floors, and ceiling. Marble columns supported an upper section, and hanging lamps lit the ground level. Signs meant to remind caregivers of their duties and colorful mosaics of religious scenes ornamented the space, simple but elegant.

As they walked through the antechamber of the building into the lower care floor, Amun's eyes seemed to meet everything with curiosity and sympathy. He wanted to speak to her of particular subjects while he had this opportunity, matters which drove deeper than flesh, to ills of the mind.

"Unlike these, there are those whose frailty is a sham. They come for grief and pity, use of our charity and disabuse us of our compassion, in time." He slowed his walking. "We mustn't let them, however. They suffer another malady, less observed, less known, a disease of the mind which the brightest of healers struggle to understand, or outright deny." He gave her a somber look, but with a hint of geniality. "I am so afflicted, beyond external influence. Scholars of our internal processes shall strive to the end of our days for comprehension of this sickness. We are complex by Her design beyond our wildest inklings."

Amun admired the room. In this house of the dying, so many harbored varied illnesses, from babes to the eldest. They passed by a woman who clutched at her chest; pallid, frail, perspiring, white at the lips save dry bits of blood, pink around the eyes. Her brown gaze fixed to the ceiling between rattling, wheezing coughing fits, as if disinterested with her fate. She seemed accepting, ready to transcend her human vessel.

"Consumption, the healers call it," Garron said to Amun, who had stopped at the end of the woman's bed. "They believe it spreads between us, borne in the air. The sick suffer pain of the chest, gradual emaciation, fatigue, fever, night sweats, the coughing of blood. No remedy as of yet, neither by conventional medicine nor through materialism, but the best minds in the world work at it."

"Dreadful, Father. We can do so little."

"For the incurable, we aid in different manners. We clean their waste pans, prepare their meals, change their bedding, comfort them. For one dying, the simplest of pleasantries that we of good health take for granted can be powerful. Some will be bitter, rightly angered when their bodies betray them. They'll demand we make a dying form whole again. A cruel existence. We can do so much of wonder. Manipulate time, conjure fire, influence the mind. Yet we cannot cure a woman's diseased lungs or excise a malignance in the brain.

"Many of these people have none to care for them beyond our halls, compounding their pain. For those whom we can, we restore life. We endow them with the rest of their time. On occasion, we do what we believed we could not. Many whose illnesses are beyond us feel accursed. Low, as the creatures that scurry along the ground. 'Tis our duty to bring a different wholeness to this lot, to show them that our blessed Mother has not cursed or forgotten them. She is here through us and outside of us. Inside of them and with them, She lives."

"Do you feel it so?" Amun said at a near whisper.

He smiled. "I must, for I remain."

They strolled about the house for half an hour or so. There were beds sorted by age and gender, segregated by illness. They passed women, men, girls, and boys with diseases of the flesh that ate at their skin and caused it to peel and blister. Others endured sicknesses that tore at them from within. Some patients received curative treatment, while those too far along got palliative care, kindnesses in their dying. Deacons read stories to them, talked with them, made them grin and laugh, fed them.

Garron and Amun returned to the woman suffering from consumption. She had not moved. Amun walked to her bedside, a foot away. Garron stepped beside her. The sick woman's eyes held a glazed, distant look.

"How are you feeling, Mys?" Amun asked her.

The woman coughed. "I'm dying. Ye?"

Amun sat in the chair nearby. Garron remained standing.

"Mys, what is your name?" Amun took the woman's hand, pale and near skin and bone.

"Katya Irrelin."

"I am Sister Amun Halleck. This is Father Garron Latimer."

Katya coughed with her lips closed, sounding more like she had cleared her throat. "Ah." She motioned to sit up with effort, pushing back on her elbows. "Nice to meet ye." A jagged breath drew in through her nose.

Amun glanced at Garron and back to the woman. "Do they treat you well here?"

"They do. The Church provides for us."

"Sister Halleck, I don't think Mys Irrelin may want to expend her energy answering questions. Mys, would you like us to leave you be and let you rest?"

"Nay, Father." The woman waved her hand. "I'll die whether I talk or lie quiet. Might as well have the company. Questions don't bother me none."

Amun tilted her head toward Garron and then refocused her attention on Katya. "If I may ask, did you hear anything of the events taking place in the square?"

"I did. The sisters speak low but we still hear. The dead tell no secrets. They might as well not bother."

Some dead.

His eyes meandered between the pair of them. What was Amun's objective? Had he not been there, the house would not have permitted Amun to speak to the woman, let alone allowed her inside. He shot a look over his shoulder. The deacon at the entrance observed them from her station.

Amun leaned closer to Katya. "What do you think of it?"

"I reckon," she answered, with a delay as if to collect her thoughts, or to stave off wheezing, "that it's a service to the Mother. Our Church has kept us safe. The Empire prospers under its rule. Reapers are malice made flesh." She coughed once with her face turned away from them. "Send them to their Master."

"Do you find that most people you know hold the same view? Please, be true."

The woman chuckled. "Why lie? I'm soon dead." She readjusted on her elbows with a wince. "Some ages're better than others, but ye do us well. The Vicar is a good man. Ye bring honor to the All-Mother and Her kingdom, sound living to the people. Can't say I've much to complain on."

"How do you feel about the restrictions on the Aether?"

Katya shifted her gaze to her body, a slight mound beneath layers of blanket. "Most don't use magic what's affected. I never had a talent for it." She swallowed. "If Mythos had their fashion, they'd destroy everything. Loot the Palace, burn the city. No'n ye'll find wants to work in service of heathen gods."

Amun smiled. "That's good to hear."

Silence filled the air like smoke. The woman lay back down, evidently no longer of the strength to keep herself propped up. She closed her eyes and rested her arm on her forehead, which shone with a glossy layer of perspiration. Her hair looked damp. She appeared worse than she had when they approached, as if the blood had drained from her face. Garron feared their exchange had been too much for her.

"We ought to depart." He hoped Amun would concur.

Amun bowed her head. "Indeed, of course." She pressed her lips to the back of the woman's hand. "Mys Katya, it has been a pleasure speaking with you. Thank you kindly for your time."

The woman grinned. "Will ye return, Sister?"

"One day."

"She still has much to learn," Garron added.

Amun's cheeks dimpled. "Indeed, I do."

"If I live so long, see ye, then."

Garron considered the experience instructive enough and did not wish to burden the woman further, despite her willingness to converse. They left and took another stroll about the city.

Houses and other buildings watched them pass, as did those settled within. In neat rows, block after block, the glassy eyes were endless. He felt over-present, as though they witnessed his naked thoughts.

"Amun," he said after a silence. He could not look at her as he pondered this. "I must speak to you of something while I still have the time to do so."

He sensed her focus on him, evaluating. "What troubles you?"

"There was a woman—" His voice trailed off. He sighed. "There is a woman beyond the walls. I have written the address." Removing a slip of paper from his robes, he extended it to her. "She has suffered a great deal. I wish for someone to attend to her and take stock of her well-being." He gathered the courage to return Amun's gaze.

Her pale red eyes, well-defined by long black lashes on top and bottom, danced across his features with a drawing of the brow. "I understand." She looked ahead again, and he did the same.

They had made it to the entrance of the Priory, the gate of the long hedges, outlined by rows of trees. “If you would remain here,” he said. “I’ve personal work to see to.”

“Certainly.” She stared toward the square, her face reflective. “Be well.” With that, she walked through the gate, between the rows, and into the Priory.

All right.

I must be off.

He felt compelled to go.

The city sprawled, empty to the horizon, as if the citizenry had moved aside for him. This day, the tired clomp of his boots against the cobbles echoed, reverberating across the faces of the surrounding edifices and vacant nothingness. When he started his trek, the vision in parts coalesced. That famous, living landscape. The Imperial City, Aros. Mighty capital of the prime nation of Gohheia on Earth. Ancient, magnificent, powerful.

A girl skipped by, likely no older than eight. She wore a teal and white dress from nape to knee. Her dark cheeks dimpled and her brown eyes squinted as she went.

He returned an amiable half-smile.

After a duration, the world enraptured him at every angle, as though he had become one with each stone and sign and the drab, beclouded sky. Every step, identical to those he had traversed previously on this path. Each misshapen and misaligned stone, irregular and rough underneath his feet, almost regular to him now.

The trip he had made in the opposite way once flew to him. That day’s dejection, half as potent, reawakened. How many times had he gone this direction? The ventures melded like molten steel. His worries of the past, the present, and the future ran together like fluid, until nothing but the moment and the sentiment persisted. That instant, the walk, each aged inhalation, every conscious blink, each weighted step. He felt it once more, a pressure in his palms; a latent, hostile tingle, bubbling to the exterior, the phantom of a surface long untouched, but forever sullying his hands. His warded contentment had eased away.

There had been a time when he felt happier, when he thought only about the service of Gohheia. He had resided with, loved, and consoled the high and the low, wherever they came from, whomever they were, no matter their worship or their crimes, misdeeds, or deviations. He had fed and washed the feet of the wicked and the good. Why did it have to be him?

Why?

A torment he could not understand.

Why?

The thought had become banal.

Must it have taken from another, as well?

Afternoon crept into evening and the sun made its gentle descent, the rings and stars growing brighter. He plodded, step after step, to the house, outside the walls of the city, shy of the deep country; the home of the woman, as much a feature of his terrors and dreams as the Beast or the horrors of Erlan. He had come alone to this place a number of times since the Ennead permitted him leave of the Priory's grounds.

As he stood across the road from her simple abode, a dull light flickered within. He felt as overwhelmed as he had on that initial day, when he'd witnessed it for the first time. In quiet instances, he forgot he had been there, but never her face. It repeated in him, a perennial wheel of recollection in which every rolling inch contained her. He did not hold all of the blame for what had happened, yet there could be no one else on Earth responsible. What befell him, and her, stretched beyond the aching, arching fingers of justice and truth and fairness.

The weather had altered from the Priory to that isolated road off the larger thoroughfare. With each beat of his heart, a grave oppression coursed through him, like that of the sky and air this evening, now cloaked in soupy black and grey thunderheads, tears of the Mother showering down from on high to the Earth. He heard Her voice, the voice of his one true Creator. Her song about that which lived inside him intoned, hummed hymns of that which could have saved him, and which had kept him from destruction for as long as it could.

He came upon the name of the gods in his mind: Gohheia, Epaphael, Asdamos, Vekshia, Lahrael, Isanot, Sitix, Vysyn, Korvaras. The First Gods. The Celestial Nine. The stewards of so many aspects of existence; creation, destruction, being; time, destiny, damnation; dimensions, space; hope, despair; reason, wisdom, greed; love, hate, passion; nature, calamity, matter; energy, fire, winter; death and life. He appreciated at last that these existed in union, that all contained each. They were within every person, and beyond them, as more than they could know. Forever, these truths, above mortal ken, condemned them to long for apprehension.

The enemy and the friend were one, as part of a cycle, as he had been his own ally and adversary in life, from childhood to that present. He had discovered hope in misery and misery in hope in these last few weeks, too fully lived. Beyond his reach, he had sought a kingdom of Gohheia during this life in which to love and rejoice. He felt it deep. For the torment and suffering, for the wrongs and cruelties, for the sacrifice, this place, the underrealm, would be the nearest thing to Her kingdom that he would ever know.

An odd sensation sparked through him, and soon another.

His light faded.

The world went black.

CHAPTER XVII: LOSS

Athenne

Under the failing light of that day, the woodlands stretched without edge, in barren hues of grey and brown. There were rocks ten times their size and thin, gurgling streams. Though Athenne loved the Father Earth and appreciated his beauty, she longed to be free of endless wilderness. They had already crossed the Black Canal, and were west of the village of Soignan and the Grove, as best she knew. Between forests, fields rose and fell, harvested and cleared.

There had been a number of frosts these last weeks, the occasional flurry of snow or rain, but no cold as fearsome as in Ghora or their initial endeavor. With Aitrix at their side, the forebodings of the world had receded, shying into the shadows.

Beside the path, there were lesser creatures again, more so the further north they went, and more plant life. The air smelled cleaner, no longer reeking of sulfur or hinting of death from far off. Birds chirped, lower critters skittered, climbed, and grazed. The livelier ambiance brought her a shade of joy, in contrast to her earlier tones and moods. It had been so long without these facets of nature that she had forgotten how full the world could be. Well behind them, beyond the Canal to the south, there existed nothing but desolation, save Arkala and Abela a few miles from the river, which had looked untouched from a distance. To be rid of that gloom made her glad.

"Yield," called Aitrix from the head of the party. They halted. Aitrix dismounted and pulled her horse to the side of the road beneath an oak tree whose base dwarfed the half-elf.

"Why are we stopped?" Bhathric asked.

"If we are to find this priest once we arrive in Aros, I'll need to see your memories. The visions. You, and Athenne. Any further north and the source ward may be too powerful." Aitrix removed her riding gloves, crafted of brown leather and lined with animal fur. "Come."

Athenne and Bhathric descended from their horses and approached. Aitrix held out her hands, palms up, and placed them against their faces on opposite sides. Her skin felt warm and soft.

"Close your eyes."

Aitrix shut her eyes and so did they.

A painless prickling spread from where the hand touched Athenne's cheek through her face, similar to the sensation of a sleeping limb. The tingle dispersed until it ran across her entire skull. She did not want to think too much, else she may render the task more arduous for Aitrix. Mental spells were difficult and delicate, particularly when the wards of the Church already hampered the caster, and when the art represented the shallowest part of the mage's well, as mentalism did in the case of Aitrix.

"Clear your minds," Aitrix said.

Athenne felt Aitrix had been talking to her, but she imagined Bhathric also clouded with thoughts. This thinking about thinking likely made the problem worse. She worked to push all reflections from her mind.

Minutes went by in gripping hiatus, and at last, Aitrix retracted her arms. The prickling subsided.

"Eclih." Aitrix gestured toward him, then knelt and drew a caster circle in the soil. "I had hoped that I could save us the trouble and do it alone, but it appears not." Insight spells were among the most difficult incantations to perform in mentalism, surpassed only by compelled hallucinations and psychic driving.

After she finished outlining the symbol, Aitrix pressed her palms to it and whispered a low vocalization. Her marks in the soil filled with a white glow like hot metal poured into a foundry. The radiance continued as she withdrew and stood, and Eclih took his place in the circle, channeling a share of Aitrix's essence. He began the same procedure that Aitrix had attempted, with his palms on both their faces.

The prickling returned, stronger this time. An ugly, unpleasant sensation, as though someone tickled her skull from the inside. The longer it went on, the more she wanted it to end.

After a few moments of discomfort, Eclih's hands dropped to his sides and the sensation abated.

Athenne ruffled her hair and massaged her scalp.

"I've identified the man's signature," he said.

Aitrix approached him. "Show me."

The two of them clasped hands and shut their eyes.

"Is he marked?" Bhathric rubbed the side of her head.

"It would appear," Aitrix replied as she and Eclih released their hold. She walked over to her horse and ran a hand along its mane. "Something has marked him, but it doesn't matter, not to us. All we require are his lunar tears." Her gaze flickered to Athenne. "You're prepared?"

Athenne's ears rumbled. "I am." She had little choice. No further discussion of the matter would change that. Her objective, recited to her again and again, shone with blinding clarity.

Aitrix handed her a folded piece of paper. Athenne opened it to find a detailed map of the Priory. "We created this over a long period through scrying," Aitrix said, as if still in Athenne's mind. "You are to place the bombs and flee. If you are not able to flee—" She paused. "We will make well of your sacrifice."

She expected Athenne to be willing to die for their cause.

Athenne knew this already. She had claimed that she would be eager, that her life belonged to them. With Uldyr, to Aitrix that night in the church, to Bhathric and Eclih on the road, she had said it. She had told everyone, all the while remaining conflicted in her heart. *What a fool, I am.* She resigned herself to her fate. As her world mother had said in her girlhood: *we must live our choices.*

Portions of this scheme seemed hobbled together at the last minute, but considering the obstacles they faced, no other way made itself apparent. Deacons from which to take beads were difficult to access, either in the Priory or beyond. The Knights of Faith believed this priest to be their best chance, and they directly communed with a god.

Undoubtedly, too many people frequented the Priory for more than one or two people to attempt to make their way to the underlevels, so she understood why she must skulk alone. Save an army to march against the capital and defeat the chevaliers, they had no choice but to operate covertly. If any measure existed by which to reason the Ennead into a non-violent compromise, she wished that they had found it. But there had been none. The day to act had arrived, their first and last chance to succeed.

"We understand our roles?" Aitrix asked of everyone.

They returned unanimous agreement.

Uldyr would accompany Aitrix in her share of the mission, whatever that may be. She had not informed them of their part, and they would not ask. Athenne trusted Uldyr above all the others. She must.

"I'll protect you as best I can." Bhathric placed her hand on Athenne's cheek. "Make it out."

Eclih scried. This proximal to the source, even one with his gift would strain for farsight. They watched and waited, each dressed in a hooded cloak, billowing behind them as the wind rose and fell. The world held motionless for a time, as if the things beyond them had ceased to exist in a fleeting instant.

Eclih's voice dragged Athenne back to reality. "The priest is northwest of the Grand Priory, somewhere near a road off a major thoroughfare. Black Pass, I believe."

"To our fortune," Aitrix said as she received the vision from Eclih. She charmed a small mechanical compass, one used for seafaring or woodland excursions, and handed it to Bhathric. "North shall guide the way."

Aitrix enchanted another for Athenne and extended it. "To lead you to the source."

Their leader was a woman of wonders. Without her, this mission, in its entirety, would not be possible. Only Aitrix could imbue a caster circle with enough essence to amplify someone else's powers this near to the capital. The rest of them could hardly manage anything above minor magic within Imperial territory. Even Eclih, with his psychic gifts, required her aid to read their memories and to scry.

What would Aitrix be like, in all her might, if they prevailed?

"That guidance spell has a life of four hours," Aitrix said. "Let us not linger in waste."

What will she do once she has her power back?

Athenne had scarcely considered what might become of the Saints when they had completed this venture. What would be their mission if they undid the wards or toppled the Church? Would they replace the government of the Empire and establish their own? She and Uldyr had not discussed this beyond vague abstractions. Every conversation, plan, action, foreseen deed, and outcome had centered on the liberation of the Aether.

The depths Athenne treaded consumed her. Knowledgeable as she was, she had never found a passion for fighting. Her mind spun in circles with fear and uncertainty. *I must do this if I wish to survive.* She had spent so long with these people. They were her friends, except Aitrix, and glaring their deed in the face, fanatics.

Athenne had become strange, alien to herself. Her part in this purpose, this design, had stolen her agency. She had allowed it, offered her wrists for shackling, even when her mind resisted.

She felt pathetic, ashamed, that she had gone so far and maintained misgivings. No matter the consistency with which she worked to subdue and eschew them, her reservations stayed. In most cases, they were in the back of her mind, but when it came time for action, they rose to the surface like oil on water.

Not long after their stop, the party had remounted their steeds and pressed ahead.

The city walls rose in the distance, crowned by overhanging parapets with visible embrasures below. Many ages ago, these walls, houses, and towers of stone were forest and field, a place where hunter-gatherer tribes lived and roamed. Then Ankhev the White, the great dragon and Incarnation of Gohheia, came to the Earth to aid humanity in building the All-Mother's sacred kingdom in the underrealm, through Her want and will.

So it was that the Imperial Palace, Iron Court, Grand Priory, and the other architectural wonders of the capital ascended, facets of the greatest civilization to ever exist. In the wake of the Century's War, which brought about the independence of the kingdom of Abbisad, and the revolutions, which gave life to the sovereignty of Beihan, Reneris, and Xarakas, the Sacred Empire remained the pinnacle state. The richest, the grandest, the most powerful, the largest, both in actual claimed and staked territory and in population by count.

The Imperial Palace, home of the Emperor, protected the city. Athenne recognized it from drawings she had seen in books as a child. It stood before Aros's main gate, for the Imperial Sovereign was not merely a ruler in name, but a guardian; the representative of humankind's protector, Gohheia. Silvery stone and smooth marble comprised the structure, akin to other prime constructions within the city's walls, she had read.

Caravans came in and out of the central gate, transporting supplies to and from, past the Palace and down the main road, which split around it on both sides. Travelers moved in either direction on single-rider mounts, on aetherlight-fueled and horse-drawn carriages and wagons, and on foot, some dragging carts and others pushing barrows. She observed an airship floating outside the city walls to the east, nearly scraping the peaks of the trees. They would enter with the throngs, undetected in the traffic, their hoods pulled over their heads and tied at the fronts. Aitrix, in particular, needed concealment.

Elves were rare in the Imperial City. They could not risk anyone recognizing her. Matrian decree had deemed her a terrorist leader, attached infamy to her already-known name. Per the wording from the proclamation of the Church's Vicar, Breiman Umbra, Aitrix was a *dangerous, heretical apostate.* She seemed to take pleasure in that designation.

They discontinued communication as they progressed by the guards of the front passage. Athenne tried to appear nonchalant, as though she belonged. It did not require such effort. Only a person who knew they were up to suspect doings would worry about seeming suspicious.

Uldyr broke the silence some yards inside. "We've blundered," he whispered. "Black Pass is west, before Outmore Loch. Bhathric and Eclih need to leave, if the man's still there."

Eclih rotated toward Bhathric and she nodded. They diverged from the party. Athenne redirected in kind. She must travel with them to retrieve the lunar tears she needed.

I have to keep my focus.

A palpable anxiety hung over their group.

Aitrix eyed them sideways, her expression unamused.

"Remember," Bhathric explained to Athenne in a muted voice, "keep your distance while we take care of the priest. Once you have the beads, head for the Priory."

Athenne repeated a notion to herself, to motivate and stave off the fear: *I shall be brave. I must not dither. They will not infringe upon our natural prerogative, endowed by our god. We cannot be refused or denied. They have no authority.* She thought it with such intensity that her lips mouthed the words. *They have no right.*

"I understand." She sighed through her nose.

A drizzle fell. Houses succumbed to fields and forest and became scarcer. The thoroughfare phased from stone to a lesser mixture of rock and dirt. They came upon a sign, its letters faded by weather and the sun, which marked a road as Black Pass. Athenne grew more anxious the further they went. The place felt foreign and familiar, for she had been there, but not there, exactly. Their surroundings were different, but the few residences and the ground, flowing under the hooves of their horses like water beneath a boat, were the same. From the back of the line, she could not see Bhathric's reaction, but assumed that she recalled it too.

Patches of grass and cloves bordered their sides, interspersed with lit lamps, shrubs, tall trees whose leaves had fallen and withered long ago, and abandoned handcarts, new and old.

To one shoulder of the path stood a great oak. She stared at it as they passed. It had probably been there for hundreds of ages, its roots dug deep into the soil like sinking fingers, its branches swaying with the wind. For a moment, Athenne imagined herself hanged from that tree, members of the city gazing upon her, drawn to the spectacle. Such a space would become a symbol for what could happen to those who deviated from accepted belief; heretics, infidels, apostates. She may soon become one of a few martyrs for the causes of religious and civil liberty, and a reminder of the strong arm of the Church.

Athenne recalled a calm winter's day when she was six-yeared.

That morning, she had stood at the cusp of a field behind her home, in her woolen mittens, breeches, coat, and hat, woven by her mother. To her child's eyes, the field rolled out vast, boundless. A simple beauty and delicacy accompanied it. It was her first memory of spending a day in the snow. She had played until her nose and cheeks turned pink.

A joy and sadness attended that recollection; a love of the moment, of the glowing flood of white as the sunlight that shone through the clouds reflected off the icy landscape. She could have been anything and anyone, almost anywhere. Instead, she had chosen to fill her heart and mind with someone else's justice, aims, and reckoning, until she had emptied of herself and been replaced with them.

Athenne's world mother, if she lived this day, would not know her. She would be a stranger to the young woman who rode to observe the murder of a man she'd never met. Her mother would be unfamiliar to the daughter who had forsaken all her lessons and guidance for the needs of a fanatic and her pursuits. If their eyes had tangled, her mother would not know who looked back at her, as Athenne no longer knew.

She felt well outside of herself, a passenger in her skin. *Is this happening?* Would she awake at any moment, a child again, or in Orilon, or on the road with Uldyr before they had arrived at that cursed church, when she could have turned and run? *Live your choices*, her mother had always said. That was her common refrain, and one at which Athenne had sometimes rolled her eyes and snorted in her youth.

Next, she recalled one of their nights at camp and rest, as she had gazed through the fire watching Bhathric and Eclih sleep. A sea of stars had hung overheard with the bright line of the three rings. Leaves floated against this dark ocean, dried, gnarled, apt to fall. A cluster of airships had glided with the silence of creeping insects overhead, cloth sails billowing in the wind as aetherlight propelled their wooden hulls and decks. Their windows fluttered a hazy orange, signifying others within. This had made Athenne's longing greater. She had pretended for a moment that she drifted up there, safe above the treetops, sipping sweet drinks and dining and laughing.

These musings embarrassed her. More of the same. More fear, doubt, weakness, self-pity. *Disgusting.* She never relucted regarding the Saints or their mission until her time to act arose. When others imperiled their lives, she had her concerns, but never so much as in her moments of risk. *You are committed. You live and die with them. If they have lost their way, so have you.*

Step by step, trot by trot, a distant figure faded into view, near a single home across from a wooded cluster of trees and bushes. They drew off to the shadowed edge of the road, into the brush, creeping, stalking, watching. It was the man from the vision, the priest. Healthier in the flesh, he stood motionless as he had when they saw him in the temple, mouth agape a sliver, eyes fixed on the house across the way, the home where he had attacked the woman.

She and Bhathric exchanged a look. Bhathric turned to Eclih, shaking her head to signify that they had discovered the proper individual. The truth of it swam heavy in the rainy air.

Has he come for her again?

Bhathric gestured for Athenne to move into the tree line, so they could take him down without him seeing them first. She did so, and pulled her horse with her.

Bhathric and Eclih did not hesitate. When they collapsed on him, the man did not pivot to look. His first reaction, a jolt and groan, as Eclih drove a knife into his back. Bhathric came swiftly at the other side of him and ran a blade into his neck. With an arm wrapped around the priest's throat, they dragged him from the damp road into the trees. By the time they laid him at Athenne's feet, he was dead.

She stared at his face, his almost grey hair and beard. *Another monster who preyed on women.* A gladness they had found him, that Vekshia had selected him to show, expanded inside her. Deprived of this target, they would have had to find someone else, without due consideration for justice.

"How will you dispose of him?" she asked Bhathric and Eclih.

Eclih removed the lunar tears from the priest's arm and gave them to Athenne. "We'll head deeper into the forest and burn him when the shower quits, scatter the ashes. Won't take long."

Athenne tucked the beads in the lining of her robes. "Won't the smoke draw attention?"

"We've aetherlight for a clear burn." Bhathric removed a glass container from the satchel on her horse, wrapped in animal hide. She withdrew a leather carrying bag and tossed it to Athenne. Inside were the black powder bombs enhanced with aetherlight that the Saints, Aitrix in chief, had made. Enough to destroy the ward, and more. "You're to line these around the source ward. When you're done, you'll have roughly five minutes to escape the building before Aitrix detonates them. The explosion may cause a partial collapse." Bhathric embraced her, and Athenne reciprocated with her free hand.

With the bombs tucked into Shah's satchel, she proceeded

back toward the Priory, the burst faltering to a mist. If anyone stopped and searched her, it would be the end. She would have no means of explaining why she possessed these items.

Upon reentering the city walls, to the exclusion of the paladins near the front entrance and the occasional citizen and patrolling officer, the neighborhoods were empty. In the distance, she heard a commotion.

Though she needed to shy away from interaction, Athenne felt compelled to ask a man walking by about the disturbance. "Excuse me, Mysr," she said.

He stopped and faced her halfway. "Hm?"

"I am not common to the city, could you tell me what's over there?" She pointed toward the noise. It sounded as though someone gave a speech.

He squinted in the direction she had indicated. "Mhm." He rubbed his shaggy beard, a mix of brown, grey, blonde, and red. "The Vicar hanged two Mythos reapers this morning. Couple of women. Hundreds showed at first. Now half the city's there."

"What was their crime?"

The man's scarred brow furrowed. "They was Mythos reapers."

"Ah, of course." She needed to discontinue this conversation. "Thank you kindly."

"Mhm," he replied as he turned and strolled away.

This settled one concern for her. The Church would permit no dissent or deviation. If they caught her, if they captured any of the Saints, they would execute them. The Church considered the Saints a radical faction in a similar vein to Mythos. If two women hanged for no more than their affiliation, as the man had implied, what would happen to a group of declared terrorists plotting to obliterate the source ward and a segment of one of the most sacred buildings in the world? Fortune would shine if the inquisitors did not flay, tear, and whip them in the streets.

Distress rising like a boiling spring, she continued forth. If she retreated or delayed, she might risk the apprehension of all of them without meeting their primary objective. Total failure and death would be the worst outcome. She did not wish to perish for nothing. *Enough, you coward.*

The compass Aitrix had bestowed as her guide, a grand edifice at last blurred into perspective; a towering structure of white stone with soaring arches and flying buttresses, as described. She breathed deep and exhaled.

This is my time.

CHAPTER XVIII: BEYOND

Amun

"Did you see his assailants?" asked Mallum.

The Ennead had convened for Amun, excluding Archbishops Umbra, Sangrey, and Delacroix, who were at the square. Braziers burned in the chamber, for the light of the day waned. A morass of emotions swirled.

Amun squeezed the cuffs of her sleeves anxiously. "Two hooded riders. Brown and grey cloaks. I did not witness their faces, Your Reverency."

"Retaliation from the fools of Mythos, perhaps." Archbishop Morena Hart weaved a strand of dyed magenta hair between her fingers. "He ought not've been so far from the Priory on a day such as this." Her sky-blue eyes affixed on Amun. "Neither should've you." She spoke as though rebuking the sea for wetting her.

Amun set her gaze to the floor.

"It matters not. 'Tis done." Archbishop Crane's tone sounded flat rather than scolding. "The task at hand is to decide how we wish to address the incident."

"We must send word," Mallum said. "The reapers move upon us. Inform Grand Provost Aenor of these incidents, have her triple the inquisitors' presence in the city. We need them patrolling the streets, and we require a squad sent to Black Pass to survey the area." She addressed Amun directly. "Sister."

"Your Reverency?"

"Remain within the Priory, until the city is safe. We're soon to recall the rest of the first-degrees."

"As you will, Your Reverency. May I go?"

"You may," said Mallum. "Rest."

With a bow, Amun exited. The hall beyond the chamber stretched long and solemn, lit by lanterns, glimmering against black marble. Pillars from the floor to the ceiling bordered the passage, the stone between engraved. She walked to the end of the hall and turned, continuing to a point where no one would see her around yet another corner. With her back against the wall, she slid to the floor.

Her eyes held shut, she strove to rationalize what had transpired. She exhaled with deliberate force and drew in again. Sighing relieved the pressure in her chest, weighing on her heart. The truth lingered beyond her. How many minutes had passed, she did not know, though her back and rear ached. She did not care.

"This is all so—ridiculous," she whispered to no one.

Too begrieved to rest, the sordid fate of Garron had affected her. Her red eyes blinked through tears. She sniffled and wiped them away. Visions of that ghastly scene filled her head. *He did not deserve to die that way, alone.* She despised this place, these tragedies, this war, if it were such. Whatever it was, she detested it. She wanted it to end. No more blood, no more death, no more tears, sorrow, and pain.

Had Garron found peace? He deserved rest after what he had endured from the Vale of Erlan to the Priory, including the creature that had tormented him, the one he had called the Beast.

Soon, the Ennead would dispatch more soldiers, for the last had not returned. Their attention divided between the underlands and opportunistic murder within the city. Mythos or not, even the reapers, as deluded as they were, would suffer if the Undeath took hold of the territory north of the Black Canal.

They must know that.

If the Empire fell and the spreading death continued, or even if it stopped at Aros, there would be chaos throughout Imios. The continent would fall into a state of war again, until one nation claimed the region and vanquished whatever resided there. Or perhaps the Undeath would swallow them all.

"Aye, 'tis a nuisance," Amun heard someone say from around the corner. She froze. *I ought to move, make myself known.* But she did not. She listened.

"What of Forgebrand?" The second voice sounded like it belonged to Archbishop Crane.

The first voice spoke again, louder. "They've yet to thwart them." *Archbishop Hart.*

"Perhaps they are more resourceful than we anticipated, these *Saints.*" The derision with which the second voice spoke the last word seemed uncharacteristic of Archbishop Crane, but Amun's thoughts went elsewhere.

Forgebrand?

"The Vicar is unhappy with their performance."

Turning down another hall before her own, the two continued. Their words trailed off. She could no longer hear them.

Minutes later, Archbishop Delacroix rounded the bend in the opposite direction.

Amun stood. "Archbishop."

Archbishop Delacroix stopped promptly and looked back. "Sister Halleck."

"May I have a word?"

The Archbishop eyed her with a curious expression. "I have little time, but I suppose so." She pivoted and carried on down the hall. "This way."

Delacroix had gone into her private chamber, and Amun had followed, peering into the shadowy room, illuminated by less than half a dozen candles.

"You may enter."

Amun stepped inside, closed the door, and leaned back against the smooth slab of wood. She recognized that she must be direct. *Who can I trust?* Garron had been her closest confidant. Before him, she had kept but a small assortment of friendly acquaintances. None so dear. She swallowed. "I overheard Archbishops Crane and Hart in the hall." Her fingers laced, bending at the knuckles.

The corner of the Archbishop's mouth curled up. "What did Archbishops Crane and Hart have to say?"

"They said—" She bit her tongue. *No, I must.* "They seemed to imply that the Church, the Vicar in specific, hired the Forgebrand Company to deal with people calling themselves the Saints." It took all she could muster to maintain eye contact. Archbishop Delacroix's expression did not change. "I find it difficult to fathom that the Church would rely on the aid of daggerhands."

Delacroix raised a silver goblet from the table at her side, embellished with floral patterns, carved with a thin-tipped tool by a skilled hand. She brought the cup to her painted red lips, sipped from its contents, and returned it to its place. Moving from her seat, she made her way toward the window across the room.

Amun longed to melt through the door and flee.

"Aye," she answered, after what had seemed like an hour of unbearable pressure. Every syllable that followed carried a tangible certainty. "We have relied upon them for ages."

"Archbishop, how could we?" Amun's face grew hot. "How can we call ourselves righteous and true to the Word of the All-Mother if we consort with these kinds? They are killers."

"Hiring mercenaries to carry out activities deemed unseemly for the paladins, or a waste of their time, is a noble alternative. I have entertained your inquiries, but I must remind you: this is not your place."

"With respect, Archbishop, we've hanged two women in the square for the simple act of affiliating themselves with Mythos." Amun would not back down, panic rattling in her stomach. "If that is not an unseemly deed—"

"Sister Halleck," Delacroix interrupted, "affiliation with Mythos is a direct rejection of Gohheia. All that She is, all that She represents. Us. The Saints that you referred to are the Saints of Aetheria, led by the great niece of the Archmage Besogos, Aitrix Kravae. They are a different matter."

The Saints of Aetheria. Amun had not made the connection through the shorthand. The Vicar had declared them a terrorist faction not long ago. "We've hired Forgebrand to kill them?"

The Archbishop's eyes lowered. "The Saints of Aetheria are

responsible for the death of Father Latimer. They have plotted in opposition to us for some time. We captured two of their agents on their way back from the Black Pass, returning from murdering Garron. The slaying which you witnessed."

A sensation swept through her. Grief, shock, sorrow. Amun's bottom lip shivered and her ears rumbled with the tension in her jaw. "You mean—" Her words dropped off.

"Aye." Delacroix seemed to predict her question. "The killing bore no relation to the hanging, as best we can tell. Mythos had no hand in it. These Saints, as they call themselves, have been mobilizing against us since Kravae formed the group and vowed to destroy this institution. We've had an eye on them. This day, they made their move. They act as we speak, ignorant of our knowing, 'twould appear."

Amun needed a moment to draw together and reclaim her composure. Absorbing the words like an infection, they left her hollow. She wished she could have intervened to save Garron. But she could have done nothing. Not against these outlaws. They would have slaughtered them alike.

The Archbishop made her way back to her table and chair for another drink. "Aitrix has always had a flare for the grandiose." She looked at Amun. "Deluded ambition."

"Do you know Kravae?"

"Vicariously. I observed her on a few occasions when she was teen-yeared, sitting alone in the gardens, gazing into the air with a dull expression." A quiet exhalation of amusement escaped the Archbishop's nostrils. "Ages ago, I made regular visits to the institutes of erudition across the capital. Aitrix was a pupil at Anukara's Institute of the Material Arts. Her preceptor was

Magus Mia Kreighton, a fine materialist. Naturally, as the prodigious great niece of Besogos, everyone took an interest in her. Aitrix had a starlit future."

"What happened?"

"Magus Kreighton described her as a virtuoso, deeply connected with the Aether. She has a natural capacity which, for many, no amount of training could surpass. They believed that she may be an energist, the first in generations. Eventually, however, her limitations became undeniable."

"Forgive me, Archbishop," Amun said, her forehead creasing. "I know little of energists."

"Of course." A pause. "There have been but a few casters throughout the ages who were powerful in all three of the Aetherian arts, who could perform spells without incantations. Certain philosophers say these mages, energists, derive their power from a source known as Infitialis Res, an energy which comes from Asdamos's portal in the sky. Not even Besogos, for his talent and knowledge, was an energist."

"Do you believe this?"

"I can't say that I do, but I can't dismiss it."

The admission surprised Amun.

"While favor gifted Aitrix in materialism and metaphysics, like myself, mentalism was her frailty. She could neither influence the mind nor shield her own. This limitation consumed her." The Archbishop smoothed the lap of her robes. "Aitrix suffers from what the magi refer to as aetheromania. She is gripped by magic, shattering her ceiling, deepening her well, unlocking the mystery of energia. Yet there is no secret. Energia cannot be learned. One is an energist, or not. Aetherian limits are inherent to the individual, insurmountable. Aitrix refuses to accept these realities, and has let them manifest a rage within her that I suspect she carries still.

"Her frailty became clear when she nearly killed another student during demonstrations. The task was to ward their minds against psychic influence, and to influence their partner. Aitrix could do neither. Her opposite had an innate gift in the art. Aitrix lost consciousness during the challenge. When she awoke, she demanded a duel in materialism. Her partner accepted and suffered severe injury. Magus Kreighton subdued Aitrix by force. She admitted to me later that she did not do so with ease."

"Terrible," Amun replied.

"The school allowed Aitrix to remain for a time, due to her name and innate talent. She was Aitrix Besogos then. Even as a girl, she conducted herself with a feigned composure and grace. I saw her true self. She veils it well." Her tone became grey. "She would kill us all, if she could." The Archbishop stood. "Aitrix was expelled shortly after, at my suggestion. She went on to form her organization, pledging, I suppose, to have her vengeance against those she feels so wronged her." Her expression fell stolid. "Aitrix Kravae is a mad dog, escaped from its leash."

A thought, unrelated, nagged at Amun. "Archbishop."

"Hm?"

"Do you think Father Latimer has gone to Nihil, or the Blackened Yonder?"

"That's difficult to say. If his overarching life course determined his placement, I would imagine, the Nothing. Yet we know little of exactly what dictates one's destination outside of adherence to the three pillars."

Amun looked down.

Delacroix gave a wan smile. "We can only hope."

"If I may take my leave, Archbishop?" Her eyes glassed.

"You may."

Amun opened the door.

"Sister Halleck," Delacroix said before she could leave.

She turned, a lone tear rolling down her cheek.

Delacroix approached her and wiped it away with her thumb. "Dwell not." Her words were soft. "Do not succumb. You have a starlit future too. I want to see what you become."

Amun inhaled through her nose. "Thank you, Archbishop."

Various halls and chambers separated the base level of the Priory, above the underlevels. Even one who spent significant time there could easily find herself turned around.

Amun came to the bottom of a staircase on the right side of the main vestibule. She was uncertain what she ought to do. What had become of Garron's chamber? Had they locked it? Did they guard it? Had they already assigned it to someone else? A stream swept her mind away. She walked across the vestibule to the steps which led up to the area where Garron had stayed, for no other reason than to see.

At the top of the great winding staircase, on which her footfalls resonated with an unusual loudness, she found Garron's door, as she had a few times. *The door that was his.*

She breathed deep.

With a gentleness as if Garron might be standing on the other side, she entered and closed the door behind her. A room, well-lit and warm, organized and clean, came into view.

Garron had been an orderly and hygienic man, but this was

the work of machines. They had already been there at some point to strip any trace of him from the space, except a ceramic cup on the bedside table.

She crossed the room and peaked around, entering the wash-chamber and returning to sit on the bed. Beaming light filtered through the window at her back, which she viewed with clouded eyes. A dismal ambiance encumbered this place, though it was little more than an empty room. Not even Garron's. She longed to hear a word, a sigh, a shuffle of feet. Nothing of him lingered in the world anymore, save the memory and his shell.

The remembrance of life. A hope of the living. The return of a spirit to its existence as before birth in Nihil. These were a normal part of existence, the want to meet the end soon and well, to find that lasting calm. Had Garron found peace? For all their lessons as members of the Church, they knew so little, even those who had devoted their lives to theology.

Matters of earning salvation and the line between upholding the three pillars and deeds of wrong and bad blurred; whether one would go to Nihil, or Eophianon, if they enacted wrong or bad in order to support the pillars. Order gained and maintained through cruelty, taking to give, forging progress through violence, they did not know which outweighed the others or how the hateful tendrils of wicked influence may taint the spirit.

She recalled their initial meeting there. Garron had been a man of fine moral character and gentle heart. She felt dazed. Masking her face with her hands, she fell back against the mattress. She thought to pray, but instead trembled with heartache. Her tears slid in a wealth and ran along her jaw like drops of rain.

There was neither grace nor dignity in it, though she restrained each sob as best she could. The image of the violence inflicted on him lingered in her head, would not clear. Nothing comforted it away. The scene remained powerful enough that she felt as if she had never left that place, Black Pass. It continued through her mind in permanent repeat.

From their first encounter, after she had listened to and transcribed the horrors of his suffering in Erlan, she had known him. But that alone had not satisfied her curiosity. A need to understand more of the man who had endured such a great deal and lived to tell it had grabbed her. She had asked Delacroix if she could meet him, and the Archbishop had agreed. Her stranger's curiosity became a comrade's emotion, which had since earlier in that day turned to a mourner's lament. He had asked her if he might venture out alone, and she had followed. She did not regret trailing him without his knowledge, but she had not anticipated such awfulness. Such a rancid, sinister affair.

When she stood to leave his former chamber, she bumped the bedside table and knocked the cup that Garron had used onto the floor. She gazed down at it with an absent discomfort, then knelt. A machine came unhurried through the door, buzzing in their common whispers, as she scooped the ceramic shards into her palm.

"I have it," she said as she finished, not looking up.

The machine departed without further chatter.

On her feet, she could not endure in this chamber. She did not believe that she would come again, where she had known her truest friend, as briefly as they had known each other. Garron was wise and critical in his thought, not prone to fanciful musing or fanatical recollection. It would be her duty in his absence to carry his skeptical inquiry; to fight and to know, it could be that he did not die for naught.

No matter the cost, she would uncover the truth.

CHAPTER XIX: SLITHER

Athenne

There was no one in sight. Athenne had crossed the Priory's garden and made her way through its cloisters into a hall. Aitrix's ensorcelled compass served as her guide. Doors shuddered open, closed, and echoed through the building's labyrinthine passages. Every sound not of her own breathing or footfalls needled her with fresh terror. In her head writhed the dread of hearing a voice or seeing another face.

Without warning, she came upon a machine as it turned a corner and moved in the opposite direction. She nearly crashed into the wall at her right as she ran to get out of its field of view. The stony maze rang with a dreadful quiet as the machine disappeared around yet another bend.

She crept, as silent and gradual as trepidation allowed, halting on occasion to listen for signs that someone had noticed or tailed her. At one juncture, she heard a noise like steps and made herself flat in an alcove. Her heart punched against her sternum and in her head, pumping through jagged, ripping splinters of ice. Horrifying visions churned into her mind with every beat. Try as she did, she could not shake the distress, for this place had trapped her in its merciless claws, where pleas of pain and remorse would not avail.

Not a silhouette passed. No machine rolled by. Had there been someone, unless deprived of sight or hearing, they would have spotted her. A joy that she had not lost the task replaced her shaken terror. Peering out from the recess, she admired the shining marble against flickering torch light, appreciating the featurelessness that came into view. She continued to the right, in haste to where the compass drove her.

On more than one occasion, she walked down a hall to find that it led nowhere or that a room fell at the end, but not the one she sought. At last, she met the close of a passage distinct from the others. The door here looked heavy, and rather than handled or latched by some conventional apparatus, it sat adjacent a rune, embedded in the wall to its side. Engraved on this rune, the Imperial Overcross. Her ensorcelled compass indicated that the direction she must venture lay ahead.

Athenne felt the cool wooden face of the door and found no hole for a key. *How do I enter?*

As she reflected on how she came to be here in the first place, she removed the lunar tears from the folds of her robes and ran them across the door. Nothing. Next, she pressed the beads against the rune aside the door. The rune pulsed once and the door shivered.

She threw the door open forcefully, as though she expected someone to be standing on the other side. Nothing appeared, save steps descending into a dark pool. Her mouth soured with fermenting fear. *I must go down, black and baleful as it is.* She could not miss her opportunity. *This leads to the underlevels and the ward.*

It must. Should she turn back and fail the mission for all of them, she would have nowhere to go, no friend or ally in the Saints or the Matrian Church. *Intent is as much a crime as doing.*

An explosion of presence interrupted her ruminations.

She distinguished the words as she spun around.

Inquisitors.

"You there!" a paladin woman called. "What are you doing?" The inquisitor's eyes moved from Athenne's face to her hand, where she held the beads.

Athenne ran down the winding stairway, and the inquisitors followed. Near the bottom, she fell, crashing hands and forearms first onto ungiving floor. She sprung to her feet before the pain came, and ran with confusion through the cells, broken into rows, horizontal and vertical. Two inquisitors pursued her. The commotion must have alerted others, however, because the greave-clad peril at her back grew from a few to many.

At her periphery, to the path between the cells on her right, stood three inquisitors. She froze, moved to retreat, only to discover two more paladins. To her left, she saw the corner of the space; blank, dark rock. She backed away from her hunters, like a cornered animal, her eyes darting.

The inquisitors surrounded her, scowling, hands on the hilts of their weapons.

"What have you in the bag?"

Athenne clutched the strap of her satchel. She had but one choice. "Bombs," she answered, as though the fact were more a threat than a statement of it. "I'll detonate them before you can kill me. Back away!"

The inquisitors withdrew a few paces.

"Be not afraid." A robed woman appeared, and walked from behind the paladins, who had divided for her. "I am Archbishop Aramanth Delacroix. My conjecture is that you are a member of the Saints of Aetheria." She folded her hands in front of her waist and smiled. "Am I correct?"

What is this?

The woman's lips parted with a click. "We've taken your friends, Eclih Phredran and Bhathric Ezeis. The lady Bhathric did not submit as gladly as her companion." She moved closer. "You caught us at a most inopportune moment." Extracting their blades a few inches, the paladins revealed glaring silver steel, radiant in the haze of distant torches. "A chance of fortune for you." The dull space half lit her sharply-angled face. "Had your friends not been so careless in murdering one of our priests, you may well have been successful. Alas, nowhere near the capital is aetherlight employed to my ignorance." Another step forward. "Drop that and surrender." She gestured toward the bag Athenne clutched, white-knuckled. "They're now disabled here."

Athenne's face juddered, her lips shivering as one might in the cold. "I do not fear death," she said, and lied. "If you wish me to surrender, it shall be by force. I would rather take my leave of this world than kneel for you. I would rather perish in bravery than live as a coward in one of these cells."

"So be it." The woman indicated with her left hand.

Before Athenne had time to react, the paladins moved in. One seized the bag in her grip, jerking it so roughly from her hands that her shoulders and elbows ached and her wrist popped. Another swept her at the backs of her knees and shoved her down, subduing her hands behind her and laying her prone.

As Athenne's cheek met the ground, a thunderous rumble erupted overhead. The ceiling quaked and groaned, raining dust and debris. Delacroix's neck craned as she looked up.

"Take her to the council chamber," Delacroix told one of the paladins. She walked with haste in the direction of the steps Athenne had earlier tumbled over.

The inquisitors dragged Athenne to her feet and made her walk, forcing her up the steps and down the hall. At the end of a passage, the space opened into a grand room with various doors at either side, multiple climbing levels with guard walls and dead hanging lanterns. In the center of the chamber, illuminated by the low light that peeked through its windows, a familiar figure slid into view.

Athenne's escorting paladins froze and squeezed her arms tighter, thumbs digging in.

"That's her," one whispered to another. "Aitrix Kravae."

"It is." Aitrix's red eyes shifted toward them and seemed to evaluate Athenne. "It's alright that you've failed," she said, with a tone of odd comforting, breathy and light in pitch. "I shall not."

"Aitrix Kravae." Aramanth Delacroix stood at a distance from Aitrix in the hall. She lifted her hand to inform the paladins that they need not advance as they came into the space. "To what do we owe this visit?"

Eyes to the floor in front of her, Aitrix's expression remained an untouched canvas. "Ambition." She raised her arms. With their rise, the lanterns on the walls flickered to life and revealed the corpses of deacons that Aitrix had slain, at least a dozen. Their blood pooled around her, screaming in the flames.

"I see you've unmasked your truest self," Delacroix said with a cool musicality, either composed or pretending to be. "That ugly, malformed creature which scurries around your sordid heart. The shame of this will hang at your neck like a thousand chains."

"When the blood of your deacons and priests and bishops has drowned this city from here to the countryside, perhaps I'll feel an ounce of shame, and half of what you should. We shall bear the weight together on that day."

"You cannot cast in this place beyond these minor feats, but I can." Delacroix did not dignify her gibes. "Stand down or perish. I'll kill you if I must, to protect those in my service. Your destiny lies with you to make."

Aitrix's hands swirled, tilting at the wrists with the grace of one who had honed her power over many ages, symmetry in every arch and curve. Fingers came together and parted, sculpting patterns in the air. "I cannot be controlled." Her voice reverberated across the room, echoed like sound in a cave, an uncharacteristic waver and wrathfulness underlying each breath.

Athenne had never seen this rage.

She glanced to Delacroix. A tinge of uncertainty flashed in her face. Though Delacroix was one of the strongest mages in the Empire, perhaps in the world, she knew little of the depths of Aitrix's power. None of them knew, not even the members of the Saints, for she so rarely demonstrated her capacity.

"What is my destiny?" Aitrix's voice sparked with anger. "To strike with impunity." A glow enveloped her as the spell she signed took shape, generating a low squealing that trilled in Athenne's ears. "To wield the Aether at my whim." Aitrix stepped toward Delacroix, her brow furrowed, her red eyes smoldering. "To serve not the middling minds of this craven institution, but to live by my own will." The end of her words became a roar. A pillar of fire rose up from the ground behind her, as if from the throat of the god Vysyn himself. Their faces lit as the orange of the flames made the walls and banisters glow like lightning. The spell spat embers in every direction until all the torches of the hall burned, and swam and wavered in the air as though an extension of Aitrix herself.

Delacroix began a conjuration of her own. As she did, two other women emerged on her end of the room. Archbishops, by their manner of dress, similar to Delacroix.

"You have been gifted a great power." With her hands, Delacroix worked material magic which sliced at the pillar of fire through invisible bursts, fighting to snuff it out, causing the flames to jerk and quiver. "You could have made for yourself a profound future."

Aitrix's blaze rose higher and arced in Delacroix's direction, tentacles of fire licking and groping at the floor, spewing cinder. Athenne squinted against the light.

"You have failed to seize it," Delacroix concluded.

The other two who had entered signed.

Aitrix moved toward Delacroix, the flaring cyclone rolling with her, maintaining the dull shriek in the air caused by the strained magic. The archbishops jabbed at the spell from every side, battering, beating, and reducing it only for it to ripple to life anew as Aitrix held her hand seal.

"I grew up differently, alone in my head." Each of Aitrix's words bit and dripped with fury and contempt. "I opposed the mistakes of those who thought themselves my betters, to be censured and ignored."

The flames twisted over the ground, scorching through the bodies of fallen deacons and reducing them to ash. "Nearly everyone offends me, but there are those who will not or cannot learn, who are proud and blatant of their flaws and defects. They cluster together so that they may thrive, not see life otherwise, be free of scrutiny, waste time and resources. The livelihood of any group is a threat to any other not above it, wherefore the world is finite."

Swirling fire leapt at Delacroix, but she deflected it.

"You long for a compromise that ends in your favor, that does not require me to kill every last one of you. Yet compromise cannot be the solution, for the world is compromise. The solution must be to kill off every one of you. Your deaths shall relieve the burden on the well-minded and ensure the liberty of the Aether, so that those such as myself may forge the fates that we desire."

Aitrix stopped and elevated her arms at her sides. "Someone of middling brains may not understand my feud, but if you destroy moths, ants, vermin, and other offensive, detrimental intruders, then you already stand like-minded, and there is nothing left to discuss!" She drew her arms back and directed them forward. The pillar of flame behind her came up from the floor and drove toward Delacroix in the air, as a serpent gliding through water.

Fire divided around Delacroix, whirling and fluttering. The Archbishop vocalized. Orange and red flames flickered in rainbowed shades. A screech so loud came that Athenne worried her ears might bleed. Aitrix vocalized in kind, in an effort to sustain her spell against Delacroix's interference.

Aitrix had overestimated herself, and it seemed the

archbishops had allowed her to. As quickly as her pillar of fire had manifested, a force squeezed and dispelled it with a fading whimper. Cinders of purple, blue, and green rained down and flew up. In union, the archbishops conjured a material compulsion which lifted Aitrix from the ground.

Athenne suffered to breathe or move. Her lungs burned. The room froze, as though the archbishops had suspended it too. Delacroix declined her hand, conducting the incantation, setting the space into motion again.

Aitrix fell. The force knocked the wind from her. She wheezed and sputtered in short, labored breaths. Her back and neck arched, fingers and hands twisted beside her head, legs tense and shaking. She groaned and strained to roll over, subdued by the magic of the archbishops.

"*Athenne!*" Aitrix snarled as she managed the air, red gaze set firmly on her, two drops like boiling blood in milky face, framed in shadowed angles. "*Athenne! Kill them!*" She gasped at the ends of her words, in a hoarse, guttural tempest. "*What are you waiting for, you stupid bitch! Do it, now!*"

"I—" Athenne stammered, paralyzed, entranced.

"*Bhathric!*" Aitrix failed to push herself up. "*Eclih!*" She growled and exerted until her face flushed.

Aitrix did not call out for Uldyr.

"It seems we've deprived her of her senses," remarked one of the archbishops, hinting pity.

The archbishops closed in, as did the paladins.

"This is she, laid bare." Delacroix looked to Athenne. "You may try to kill us as she commands, if you like."

Fingers tightened around Athenne's upper arms.

They had lost their cause.

The archbishops head defeated Aitrix.

In the wake of that display, Athenne could no longer follow the Saints. Uldyr, if he lived, would have to respect her wish. He had explained to her, as had Bhathric, Aitrix's life and the source of her convictions. Understandable as her hurt and anger were, Aitrix could not be her leader. Not after this.

Delacroix approached, and Athenne kept her eyes down.

"Exploitative and audacious, as Kravae has always been, striking when we were otherwise preoccupied. Fellow members of your Saints, as you call yourselves, have slaughtered dozens of Imperial citizens, not merely deacons. Women, men, children, butchered in the streets—murdered as a distraction." Delacroix's pointer and thumb cupped Athenne's chin and brought her head up. Their gazes linked. "Many of your comrades shall perish shortly. You and the rest of greater import will be brought to our chamber so that we may decide on your fates."

Behind Delacroix, inquisitors constrained Aitrix, with far more care and precaution than they had assigned to Athenne. They banded Aitrix's arms behind her back from the wrists to the shoulder blades, with the palms of her hands faced apart. A muzzle caged her mouth. She did not struggle or resist.

The inquisitors took Athenne with haste. She beheld the bloodied faces and garb of the deacons on the ground, some indiscernible from the gashes about them, more vicious than any animal's markings. The flames had scorched others beyond recognition, a burning magic that turned flesh to ash on contact, but did not feel hot through the air.

Athenne had gazed into the black heart of a monster. It awed her, rendered her speechless. Her silence maintained as her agony rose. She fixed her eyes on the empty space between the paladins walking in front of her as they made their way down a torchlit hall, wishing to no avail that she could liquify and reappear somewhere else. In the past, in the woodlands, even in Ghora. The present concerned her less than the series of occasions and events which had preceded and attended it.

In her mind, Athenne saw herself, younger and smiling, walking through a meadow, peering to a blue, sun-kissed sky. Her hand raised in the air to play at the clouds, well out of reach. All who had known her, her world mother, her instructors, her childhood friends, would be as astounded by her current predicament and insensibility to the obviousness of her impending fate as Athenne was to find herself there, even after months of gathering, planning, traveling, reinforcing, and doing. Such a powerful dejection accompanied these musings that she could no longer weep. She had died in the truest sense, save her lingering pulse and shallow, aching breaths.

When they arrived at the chamber, which Athenne presumed to be the Ennead council room, Eclih, Bhathric, and Uldyr met her sight. Her insides fluttered. At least they were still alive. *He* had lived. If the four of them must die, that they would do so together provided her with a feeble solace. As Bhathric had promised, they had not forced Athenne to kill anyone. The rest of them had done the slaying for her. She was their greatest failure.

The inquisitors pushed them to their knees before nine archbishops, who stood behind a table and gazed upon the woebegone bunch with ominous expressions. One man at their center, eight women at his sides. The man's stare pierced as two needles.

Athenne could not look up as they examined and dissected her, shattered her. With the four in their row, Aitrix the most restrained, the inquisitors in the chamber lined up at their backs.

"Fiends," the man began.

The Vicar. Breiman Umbra.

He uttered with authority, and admonishment: "How dare you come into this city, kill our people?" His voice grew louder and nearer every few words as he walked around the table.

"Beasts. Witches. Warlocks. 'Tis all the same. The four of you have chosen this wayward thing as your helm." Umbra signaled toward Aitrix. "She has led you to the precipice of a great fall."

"Their members have taken the lives of many this day," said another voice. A woman. "Innocents dashed about the cobbles with their throats cut." An interval passed. Even the silence disapproved. "They should be lucky not to spend the rest of their miserable lives tortured in the cells."

"We would be quite alike then," Bhathric said.

Athenne's head rose as the woman stormed around the table, grabbed Bhathric by the collar, and jerked her to her feet. The woman's grey eyes watered. "My name is Archbishop Aris Crane. I want you to know that." Her chin quivered as she struggled to speak. Hair like fire fluttered around her face. "My daughter." Crane's face stopped inches from Bhathric's, close enough that Bhathric was sure to feel the drops of spittle that bounded from the archbishop's lips. "You killed my daughter in the street, seven-yeared. She was innocent. *You murdered her!*"

"Aris—" Delacroix attempted, but Bhathric interrupted her.

"I did not kill your daughter." Bhathric looked at the woman in her eyes. "Neither did I witness her departure."

"You brought this on us!" Crane drew her arm back and struck Bhathric across the face. "You killed her the same as the one who swung the blade!"

"Enough," said Umbra softly.

The archbishop released Bhathric and backed away.

An inquisitor returned Bhathric to her knees.

Crane retook her position behind the table, wiping the edges of her eyes with her thumbs.

"I ought to permit her." Umbra's stare moved from Bhathric through the rest of them. "I ought to license the loved ones of each innocent murdered this day to punish you as they see fit, short of death. Dying would be too much a kindness, too simple and forgiving." A slight and terrifying pleasure sparked across the Vicar's face. "There is another solution for you, one to which we have already agreed."

CHAPTER XX: ACCORD

Amun

As the alternate Scribe Officiate, now the primary for practical purposes, Amun had observed many of the Ennead's actions and important discussions. She had been in their company so long, especially the Archbishop Delacroix, that she had formed a unique perspective on their dealings, though she kept it quiet.

The Ennead had at first believed the members of the Saints of Aetheria to be Mythos reapers, until the two whom Amun had reported for the murder of Garron confessed their affiliation after their apprehension. They did not reserve themselves in their admissions, but were bold and proud. One had exhibited pride, anyway.

In the chamber well, they had assembled five individuals.

"Before we continue, state your names and nations of origin for the record." Archbishop Sangrey gestured toward Amun, exposing her by the acknowledgment. The poppy-red glare of the one in the center aimed at her. *Aitrix Kravae, half-elven.* "From left to right," Sangrey added.

The largest captive began: "I am Uldyr Friala, a citizen of Beihan, but not Beihanese."

"Obviously." Archbishop Mortem rolled her eyes.

"Athenne Zedd, Reneris." The woman's voice sank so low that Amun scarcely distinguished the words.

Then spoke their leader, ungagged: "Aitrix Kravae."

"*Formerly*," Delacroix interjected, her elbow rested on the table, her chin on her hand, "*Aitrix Besogos*, after her great uncle and his sister and their mother before them."

"Bhathric Ezeis." This woman, the most defiant of the captured, save Kravae. She struck down one inquisitor in a melee and nearly slew another before capitulating.

The last one sighed. "Eclih Phredran." Amun had to examine the man with care, for she thought him elven at first. His green eyes and round ears betrayed his humanity.

"You are charged in collective complicity with terrorism, murder in the first-degree, heresy, blasphemy, and apostasy. You have aimed to strike fear into the hearts of the Imperial common body, to turn them against the Church. You have murdered, not only members of this sacred order, but innocent members of the citizenry. You have participated in heresy, the spreading of doubt for the ends of promoting disorder and regression. You have practiced blasphemy, in open disdain of the All-Mother, for the ends of promoting disorder. You have participated in apostasy in each of these acts, and in particular, in your sedition and defection, and in the abandonment of your duties as children of Gohheia to maintain an inborn loyalty to Her." Archbishop Sangrey paused and clasped her hands on the table in front of her. "Your leader will speak as representative for you. How do you plead?"

Kravae's head rose and met her gaze. "Guilty." Her voice

carried without fluctuation. "Although, fair folk are the children of Epaphael, so I've only half the duty."

Amun stifled a chuckle through her nose.

"Do you know how we uncovered your plot, captured your underlings?" Sangrey said.

"Couldn't fathom."

"Our new issue of lunar tears, which you were evidently aware differed from their predecessors, are attached in permanence to the essence signature of their owner. This did not tell us the exact location of where you murdered our priest, as their accuracy decreases the further from this building that they are. They do, however, inform us whether the wearer is the intended user, and whether the user is alive or dead."

"We were monitoring your victim. That is how we knew that he had perished around Black Pass." Delacroix's eyes moved from Kravae to the one called Athenne. "That is how we were so quickly enlightened that his issued beads had re-entered the Priory after his death."

Kravae's lids flared in mockery. "Fascinating."

"This is a serious matter," the Vicar said, not one for fooling. "Whether you planned your attack so or not, and we suspect not after detailing the thinness of its conception, you have surely noted that we executed two Mythosian reapers in the square." In the introductions, he had moved to his seat. Now he stood and came around the table once more. "Their immediate crimes were far less severe than your own, that we can prove. We had other suspicions, but on its face, their guilt lay in the lesser share of yours—heresy, blasphemy, apostasy. All manners of sacrilege born in submission to their death god." He halted in front of

Kravae. "We hanged them by their necks until they were dead. I would like to do the same to you." His face remained without a flicker of emotion. "However, in this circumstance, as I stated earlier, executing you is not in our interest."

The group of captives remained quiet, even Kravae. Her eyes did not waver from those of the Vicar. If a look alone could strike one dead, he would have fallen.

"There is a great Undeath sweeping the south. We suspect some relation between the event and Mythos. Those we have sent to investigate the issue have not fared well. Yet we cannot rest on the matter. Due to a secondary condition, rather than submit you to summary execution, we are willing to broker a deal."

The Vicar indicated toward Archbishop Crane. "Some of our members were by reason and right in objection. But through the wisdom of Archbishop Delacroix, we have come to recognize that you may aid us with your talents, and mitigate the risk to our own." His gaze returned to Kravae. "Loath as we are to allow you to carry on, your gift is undeniable. If not for the cleverness of this council, you may well have bested us."

Kravae was impatient. "Arrive at a conclusion, if you will."

A thin-lipped smile came across the Vicar's face, unnatural among his grim features. "Aid us in handling this Undeath, and you shall not hang. You and your ilk, this cabal of heathen dissidents, such as you are, will live. Far more than you deserve, we shall not only spare your lives, but we shall submit you to no more than five ages imprisonment in the cellars beneath the Priory. When you have served your sentences, we shall expel each of you from Imperial territory for all time, and any direct descendants after you. You shall neither return nor interfere with Imperial life in any manner, remote or proximal, foreign or domestic."

The five exchanged glances.

This deal sounded undeniably charitable.

"Allow us to reiterate your misdeeds," Delacroix added. "Terrorism, murder, heresy, blasphemy, apostasy. We could have added further acts to the litany, but these were the grandest offenses. Two young women hanged before the common body for less than three of these. If not for your gifts, if not for this singular opportunity to redeem yourselves by assisting us in saving tens of thousands of lives, you would be hanging now." Uncharacteristic indignation tinted her voice. "Aitrix Kravae, you have sullied the good name of your ancestry. You are a blight on all that your great uncle accomplished. 'Twas not without a measure of disappointment that I suggested your expulsion from the academy so many ages ago. I had thought to give you a modicum of benefit this day. Then I witnessed you standing there among the slain in the hall." She stood and walked around the table. Her hand pulled Kravae's head up by the chin as she stopped in front of her. "*Look at me when I speak to you.*"

Kravae's expression seemed morose and indifferent at once. It was difficult to tell how she felt about the words. "Speak, then." She pulled her face back and the Archbishop released it.

"You had such potential. Look what you've done with it." Delacroix motioned to the line. "You've thrown your life away, and the lives of these people. That is, unless you accept this offer, which is, indeed, more than you deserve. Let your comrades live, so that they might overcome the misfortune of knowing you."

The fair-faced fair folk dropped her head for an instant, stared at the ground, then raised it. "We accept your offer." She appeared to reflect on the choice. After a few seconds, the pensiveness left her face and she spoke again. "If I may offer one suggestion, it is possible that your restrictions on the Aether have empowered the minions of Korvaras. Your wards have certainly not exalted your people to the end of their self-defense."

As Garron and I conjectured.

The archbishops returned to their places behind the table.

Delacroix responded: "Others have offered similar surmisals, but we have found no proof. As the prime source, any restriction applied to the All-Mother's favor should affect the rest. Furthermore, the feats enacted in the underlands have exceeded what even a powerful mortal necromancer could accomplish in the reported durations."

"Unless," Kravae objected, "the favor proportioned and administered between the gods is equal."

The Vicar ground his teeth. "Hold your tongue."

"Disregard possibilities defiant your beliefs, it matters not." Aitrix concentrated on Archbishop Delacroix. "What do you suspect is the cause, if not this?"

"A true necromancer," Delacroix said.

"Which has purported to be Vor-Kaal herself." Archbishop Mallum turned a folded sheet of paper on the table beside her. "Of course, we've dismissed this notion."

Kravae's eyes flickered. "In either case, if what you say is a fact, we are certain to perish."

"You have a deep understanding of the Aether. None of us

deny that." Umbra gestured to his fellow archbishops. "Your understanding of the Mother's favor, on the other hand, is—what were the words she used?" He looked to Aramanth. "For the minds of this *craven* institution?"

"Middling minds, I believe."

"Ah, aye. *Middling*."

That may have been the first bit of humor Amun had observed from the Vicar.

"Not long ago," Mortem said, "Archbishop Tornaeu and I ventured south. The Undeath overran us. A horde. If it were Vor-Kaal, we might expect her to steal away spirits, to raise a few dead for her own ends, but not to reanimate an army. If her objective was to kill us all, she could do so without the mass. This is why we suspect the magic to be the work of a necromancer, claiming itself in falsehood as Vor-Kaal."

The half-elf's brow creased. "To what end?"

Archbishop Tornaeu answered: "To spread substantial fear, as the wicked gods do."

"We reckon the next major target will be the city of Imbredon," Delacroix said. "As such, we shall lift most of the restrictions on your abilities, the five of you, with lunar tears, but you won't be able to cast traveling spells. If you attempt to defect, we shall destroy the beads and inhibit your capacity to access the Aether. In that event, we may abandon you to die by the Undeath, or the inquisitors shall execute you without delay." Her voice sounded stern but kind. "Adhere to the terms of our agreement. Do not betray us. This is your warning."

As powerful as Kravae was, their use of lunar tears was complicated magic. Only the most knowledgeable mages could craft such spells or undo them. Kravae wielded the strength, but not the learning, to interfere.

"A regiment of paladins and a knight captain, as well as Archbishops Sangrey, Dred, Hart, and Mallum, shall accompany you in this venture." The Vicar tapped the table with his pointer. "This common body must see that we are willing to risk our lives for them, and the Empire."

Kravae frowned. "Not your life?"

"*Insolent beast*," Archbishop Crane said. "Not long ago, you were willing to murder everyone in this room if it meant you would have your power again."

"All Saints would die for our cause. Liberating the Aether is a pursuit of the utmost good."

The woman called Bhathric agreed: "We are. I would."

"You shall depart on the morn," Umbra concluded, indicating that the meeting had adjourned. He and the others exited, save Delacroix. None acknowledged her lingering.

On the table, the Archbishop's hands folded.

"Are we dismissed?" Kravae asked, in a tone of desire.

"I wanted to take a moment to speak to you in front of your underlings." Delacroix glanced at Amun. "I'd like you to remain, Sister Halleck, but discontinue the record."

"Instead of further moralizing, be open and be done with us. You believe you know me so well."

The Archbishop smiled. "You, I understand—"

"You could not know what life is like," Kravae interrupted at the outset, "to be apart from every group, to find everyone of every calling and background to be beneath you, and beset with lack-witted trash, scum, and crooks. How nearly every statement, every day, by everyone, drives me mad. How I am the only person in the world who knows what is wrong with it." Her voice amplified. "What makes me better than any charlatan of your order is that I can explain in specific what one has done wrong, where this one is even the standard of common sense or custom if only by fiat, but not self-scrutiny."

"You talk of crooks, yet you extol freedom as a virtue."

"Freedom is for the good. Your control of the Aether is an oppression of that good."

"The antithesis of order is freedom." Archbishop Delacroix shifted in her seat. "Is there good and bad? Are there good folk and bad folk? That is, do they regularly embody good and bad deeds? Then there shall always be something or someone to oppress. Freedom is for the trash, scum, and crooks, as you so eloquently described them. Freedom is to be free to be, do, say, think, make, and believe wrong. A lack of freedom is what distinguishes us from lower animals and the hunter-gatherers of the Sightless Era. There is no freedom in ethics and morals, only our three pillars—which you, in your wrath, have no respect for, despite that they have been to your benefit, even this day."

"I do not respect the pillars of your society or its rights because you base none of them on truth-accounting. Social liars like you go unpunished for your deceits, yet you do endless harm by forcing everyone into the impressions of your inept and uninspired heads and hands. No one can show the truth if everyone with the most might and say has the least ability or yearning to hear and understand. Reasoned words and deeds from someone better, who the same reason cannot erase, should destroy false and cowardly beliefs such as yours. If necessary, we must resort to weapons, violence, destruction, and war. Wrath is a natural tool for that end."

Delacroix had allowed her tirade, perhaps so she might demonstrate Kravae's temperament to her followers. *We argue not for our opponent, but the observer*, she had once told Amun. "You are a killer, Aitrix Kravae. Not a martyr, not a prophet, not a savior. A killer. Nothing more, and nothing less."

"You also kill. You murder and command murder. You lie of me, know it, and have abhorred me in your envy since our first encounter. You are responsible for all of the hardships that have befallen me. In your conceit and cruelty, you call me mad, tell others that I don't comprehend social norms, cues, figures, intents. I do understand them. I comprehend many to be wrong. I understand many to hide, defend, and promote flaws. You are one person who speaks as though yours is the absolute authority. You are not so wise as you think."

Aitrix stood. The inquisitors in the chamber permitted her movement at the Archbishop's signal. "Your kind of mediocre liar is one facet of society I seek to get rid of," the half-elf went on. "Everything I do is for a better world. I do not grovel to get ahead. I do not repeat the mistakes of others. These goals and means are like your own, but because I am here and you are there, I am the monster, and you, the saint."

The Archbishop had an expression of mild amusement. "Such a paroxysm of umbrage and grief. Poor you, hm? Mistreated, given no compassion in her plight."

"So, my soul throes—so, what? If you or others are too foolish to understand justice, it is needful for me to correct you. The cause of my beliefs is a mind with compassion for everything that meets its ken. Compassion does not mean that one should accept or allow what is deeply wrong, which not everyone could wit."

"You needn't tell me this." Delacroix rose from her chair. "I have humored you. I thought that you may have grown beyond this petulant hubris, but I was mistaken. We must focus on what is more important now. A darkness comes for us, and threatens to swallow us all."

"*The ichor that swallows the world*," the one called Athenne said.

The Archbishop's face flashed a measure of genuine surprise. "Where did you hear that?"

This intrigued Amun.

"A Matronian temple. Vekshia showed us a number of visions, including of the priest we killed. In one image, he uttered this. Then Bhathric and I witnessed it, ourselves. A red flood."

Delacroix admired a window of the chamber. "When you face the Undeath, our mounted chevaliers shall strike first. There are likely to be mountains of the dead when this is through. Fear may overtake you. If you wish to live, you must remain steadfast, fight as though each breath could be your dying rattle. Engage in song or prayer, or forsake these. If you fall, you might become another element of the Undeath. Many have perished or vanished in the underlands—innocent women, children, and men." A sigh escaped her lips and she stared at Kravae. "I know you care little for them, for all your rhetoric of freeing the Aether for the good of the common woman and man. Let us disabuse ourselves of any pleasantries and fables. Stand with mortalkind against this unyielding viciousness, this churning, hateful wickedness. You face a wretched demise, but at least you may find redemption."

"My contempt for you is without bound. Nevertheless, we shall do as we are able." Kravae looked down the row of her allies on each side. "For those I've brought to this."

Before the Archbishop had a chance to reply, a figure emerged by the entrance of the chamber. "Apologies for my intrusion." Black robes and a mask of plagues shrouded the man.

Is this the one Garron described? It must be.

"Magister Adra Erin," Delacroix greeted him, crossing her legs. "What may I do for you?"

He titled at the waist. "Word of your endeavor travels. I wondered if I might accompany, witness this Undeath." His voice sounded gruff yet strangely sweet. It made Amun uncomfortable.

"They depart on the morn."

"I know."

He left.

"Take these to the cellars until the morrow." The Archbishop gestured toward their prisoners.

Inquisitors removed the five Saints from the chamber.

Delacroix and Amun sat alone.

"Archbishop," Amun said.

"Hm?"

"Forgive me, but I recall you mentioning that you had not met Kravae. She stated that you had envied her since your first encounter. What did she mean?"

"I said that I did not know her and that I had seen her." Delacroix seemed agitated by her implication. "We met on an occasion or two and did not exchange words at length."

"I see." Amun decided it best not to bother her further.

"If that is all, Sister, you are dismissed."

Amun bowed where the magister had stood.

As she emerged into the hall, a cold gloom of bent shadows received her. Every torch was out. The Priory always appeared darker than when had Garron lived, at least to her.

She must know what they encountered in the underlands.

For Garron, Amun would follow the host in cover, without the Ennead's knowledge.

First, under the assumption that it was safe, she returned to the Black Pass, to the house Garron had named on the paper he gave her. The home stood opposite where he had been when the Saints killed him.

She knocked on the front door.

A woman answered, revealing a few inches of herself.

"Can I help you?" she said.

"Hello, Mys. I am Sister Amun Halleck."

"What do you want?"

"Might I come in?"

The woman shifted from foot to foot. "You are alone?"

"Indeed." Amun peered around.

Seconds more passed, until at last the woman opened the door. Her house was simple and clean inside. She gestured for Amun to take a chair at her table.

"Tea?"

"No, thank you." Amun sat down.

The woman poured tea and then came over and sank into a seat, steam rising from the contents of her cup. "What brings you here, Sister?" She blew over her drink.

"An incident transpired outside of your home earlier. I wanted to check on your well-being."

"I saw the inquisitors arrest two people."

"They did. Members of a terrorist organization."

Something shook in the woman's eyes. "Why?"

"Nothing to do with you." Amun tried to sound reassuring. "What is your name?"

"Demetria Victoire."

"You grew up here?" *What am I doing?*

"In the city. My mother moved to Laorta when I took my womanhood. I came to the countryside."

"Work?"

"I attend the Braxany Institute of Magic."

"What's your concentration, if I may ask?"

"Mentalism, I think," Demetria said with a wan smile. "I'm not able to cast much due to the warding, so my learning is largely theoretical. On the campus, I can spell like most others, of course."

"Does that bother you?"

"I still enjoy it. I'm not sure I would be any good even without the wards." She paused. "Why have you truly come, Sister? Not to ask a stranger questions about herself for an incident that had nothing to do with her."

Amun shook her head. "We had a report that something terrible has befallen you, perhaps a crime."

The woman's features hardened.

"We needn't discuss it if you don't wish—"

"Nay," the woman protested. "We may." She drank her tea, and waited. When she sat the cup down, the shimmer of her russet eyes and the intermittent tremble of her chin evidenced her grief. "I long to sleep, to leave, to be here without the fear. Never waking would be nice. A wipe of my memory." She bit her lip. "Anything to rid me of this, the ugly thoughts and whispers. He remains forever in my mind."

"Can you tell me what he looked like? The inquisitors ought to know." Amun placed a hand on Demetria's wrist. "You needn't make a formal statement. I'll take care of it."

Demetria's gaze moved across her own.

Is she analyzing me for trust?

"I often ask myself," Demetria said, "what am I still doing here? Why do I carry on? It was not as bad as what some have suffered—no violence of the sex. Yet I fight the man every day. His wild blue eyes have burned into my lids. The sound of him never leaves. His grey hair. His hatred. What wrong did I do? Why did he choose me?" Anger, fear, and mourning laced her voice.

"I had never seen him before that day. If he had seen me, I did not know. We met that one night, fought that one night, not knowing one another. I did not know why. Now I see him everywhere. I am chained. I am no longer who I was, cannot be again. I feel his hands around my throat in every breath. He is out there, still. Perhaps he has moved on, forgotten me. Found another. Perhaps he's waiting to return."

"He's dead," Amun whispered.

"Dead? How do you know?"

"He died recently." The words almost stuck in her throat. "I know it. You are safe."

"Are you certain?" A tear trickled down Demetria's cheek.

"Sure as the Mother is right. Go out, enjoy your life." Amun stood. “If you would like to return with me to the Priory for any sort of evaluation and care, you may.”

“Nay, thank you. I am well here. As well as one can be.”

“If you change your mind, ask the inquisitors for me.”

Demetria thanked her again, and she set off. A light breeze buffeted her as she walked, and thought. *He would not have done this on purpose. It was the compulsion of that thing.*

She stopped and stared to the sky.

He would not.

CHAPTER XXI: IMBREDON

Athenne

The archbishops, knight captain, chevaliers, and the Magister Adra Erin were steadfast in their belief that, this time, the endeavor would be a triumph. Their host made its way southwest from Aros, toward the city of Imbredon, with little outward recognition of the discomfort of this affair.

Athenne sat atop her horse, apathetic to the world. The chevaliers had taken Shah, and would not give her back. She felt disquieted by the strangeness of the steed beneath her.

The sun had set, its haze creeping beneath the Earth's edge. In the distance waited their destination, a bleak and endless terrain. The emptiness darkened the further they rode. Taxing as it became, they rarely halted, and fed their horses and themselves as they went. On occasion, they had made camp, but only for half a night at a time. The Imperials kept the five of them apart. Prisoners as they were, their guards did not permit them to speak, but otherwise treated them with mildness and dignity.

Do they blame me?

Do Bhathric and Eclih and Uldyr despise me?

She had failed, the prime catastrophe of the mission, captured like a scurrying rat in the cellars. The inquisitors had surrounded her, exterminators cornering frantic vermin. No doubt, Aitrix viewed her as such, by the words of her diatribe in the Ennead's chamber. She had followed this vicious madwoman into the belly of darkness, and in the process, abandoned herself. Yet she had known deep in her heart that they were likely to fail. The construction of the plan had not been sturdy. Aitrix had probably wanted her to perish.

"How much farther, Knight Captain?" asked the woman called Mallum on an evening long into their travel, a number of days and nights which had carried them many miles.

"Approximately seven miles, Archbishop." Knight Captain Helotta Bashek's decorated plate armor gleamed so silver and clear that it looked almost white.

Athenne did not speak a word.

None of the paladins or archbishops had thus far acknowledged the Saints directly.

Uldyr, Bhathric, Eclih, and even Aitrix, had been silent as the tomb for the duration of the journey.

Bhathric kept sending Athenne glances, as if she wanted to speak to her, but dared not.

The mane of Aitrix's horse had absorbed the half-elf's gaze for most of the trip. Uldyr admired the horizon, stone-faced. Eclih looked around rarely, but otherwise expressed no obvious emotion beyond boredom.

"We're all our own heroes." The archbishop named Sangrey peered at them over her shoulder while riding one evening. "Though 'tis trite to say, no one thinks themselves the villains of their life, but there is such a thing as good and such a thing as bad. Whether something or someone does against one's liking defines what is bad, and what is wrong is whether something or someone does against one's will. Unless, of course, these should occur in the name of good, in retribution of what is bad and what is wrong. Do you see?"

"We are bad and wrong, you are good and right," Aitrix replied for herself and the rest of the Saints. "We are the villains. You are the heroes. All well, all tedious."

"You think yourself the hero, after you murdered so many innocents?" Mallum said.

"I've done no bad or wrong that your lot haven't. Killing in the name of my cause is no different than slaying for yours, except you claim your All-Mother as an ultimate authority in your support. Should I have asked you politely to undo your warding of the Aether? Would you have agreed to reverse your mistakes?" Perturbation befell Aitrix again. "Peacefulness does nothing to help the many who suffer at the Aether's limitation—those who submit from the teachings of their youth and can't tell the difference between right and wrong, or know only one of either. I could complain of your abuses toward me, your efforts to butcher my friends by hire of the Forgebrand Company, murderous, raping, thieving daggerhands. There should be no rule or law which prohibits pointing out the errors of others, or which disallows religious dissent. Access to the Aether is a natural right, and its restriction is a mistake. The only ones who disagree are those who prefer making such mistakes."

"*Enough*," Sangrey ordered.

"Strike me down, then. What I say is the bare truth. There is no justification for disallowing someone to point out the fault of others. How I behave is needed to deal with the many lies, fabrications, myths, delusions, obstacles, timewasters, obfuscators, and charlatans that stay and run in any large group of people, here and everywhere else in the world. Forbidding dissent, where true and required to discourage someone willfully wrong, hurts and hinders all of us—the very nature of truth. You justify arresting and threatening me with death for doing what you have done by your might and station, not by rightness and fact. I do not offend unless I have been offended, more. You call me mad because I am sensitive to what people say and do, when others are not. You think I've made a mistake, when it is you who made the mistake, and I know better."

Sangrey scoffed. "Your self-importance is without bound."

"I am self-important." Aitrix did not relent. "I can't and mustn't let people be wrong. I can't and mustn't let people do and say whatever they want or like by virtue of their birth and happenstance success or power. There are more important truths, rights, and needs than those of which you few have thought."

The archbishop they called Bardot Dred broke in: "We have allowed your deluded ramble." Her large grey eyes, like the gaze of a mad insect, fixed on Aitrix, as sharp as daggers in their shelter of black hair and dark skin. "Be quiet now, or the chevaliers will quiet you."

Knight Captain Bashek changed the subject. "We're not headed directly to Imbredon, keep in mind. We're on to the territory between Erlan, Ghora, and Imbredon. For the inclusion of you," she addressed the Saints, "'tis our hope that, if a horde of reanimates marches on the city, we can intercept it."

A horde of reanimates.

They were off to fight an army of the dead, and Athenne, along with Aitrix and the others, would be fodder. Either their abilities would allow them to assist the cause to victory—Aitrix, in particular—or they would die. Athenne expected the archbishops and the knight captain had an escape plan for themselves.

In the distance, a glowing light appeared, wavering in oranges and reds, rolling from the horizon.

"Imbredon burns," Bashek said.

Stillness crept over the air, silencing the world in every direction. The temperature dropped. A heaving, consuming darkness blotted out the stars and moons above.

Fog enveloped them.

A hiss and dull ringing writhed in flight.

The knight captain raised her lance. She called in a voice more commanding than any Athenne had heard: "Draw, sisters and brothers! The Undeath comes to claim and keep! If many of us die, let us be enough, not to fail our Mother's quest! If we should live, the fewer, the greater the spoils of glory!"

Those behind them cheered, a unified roar.

The drummer's march and flaghands at the rear of the host began their chant and song, to drown out the hissing and wicked whispers of the Undeath. Their thunderous beat, thump by thump, swelled with such intensity that even Athenne's resolve increased by every rhythmic burst. The show of the march and the drums became as a mighty storm upon the ground and swept up their morale.

Bashek glanced back. "Be vigilant!"

A sinister wind blew through them, ruffling Athenne's brown hair around her face.

As she wiped it away, a sea of screams arose.

The fire that had flowed in her turned to ice. Their approach halted. Thousands of paladins shrieked in horrific chorus and then were soundless, flanked by an invisible enemy, until the drumming ceased as well.

Those at the rear seemed gone, swallowed by the frigid fog, so thick she could hardly see. The dark power had not taken the cavalry before them yet, and their horses panicked. They ran in every direction, frantic and nearly throwing Athenne from her mount as they brushed by, jerking her to and fro.

"We are in an ambush!" she heard the knight captain shout.

The omnidirectional hissing grew louder, as did the ringing in her ears. Another thundering ascended, feet at a run. Many. In the mist, the voices of Bhathric, Aitrix, and others were casting. A material shielding spell, she thought. Athenne incanted, hoping to aid in the conjuration. Her voice wavered.

Before they completed the spell, the sound of reanimates came upon them. The fog lifted. She accounted for all of the archbishops, her friends, the knight captain, but not the magister. None of them knew where to look. There were remaining paladins, but what attacked their lot had slain many of them or pulled them into the mist. Athenne drew the shortsword the Ennead had outfitted her with.

"Do you know how to use that?" a chevalier on horseback at her right asked, rotating and alert.

"In theory."

A power unseen jerked the paladin from her saddle into the white wall behind her.

Athenne's horse reared back, startled, but she managed to hold on and quiet it.

I am going to die.

Their group fell toward Imbredon until Athenne's eyes rolled skyward to find them within the city, at the edge. The smog had almost dissipated. Around twenty chevaliers remained. On one side of their group were reanimates by the dozens or hundreds, twitching and hissing in eerie concurrence, as if a single creature in a mass. At their other side, a droning pitch climbed until she had to cover her ears.

They turned to behold the silhouette of a man, or being, near black against a backdrop of burning city, fires licking and billowing in every direction.

"A necromancer," Aitrix said.

The necromancer did not speak, but cast without incanting or signing, at the raise of its hand. A blue ribbon of fire tore through the air, squealing as it ripped past her, so close she felt its heat. Athenne could not see where it had gone, for its light caused her to cover her face, but she knew before she saw.

Bhathric screamed a terrible scream, one only a terrible loss could haul from the throat. Eclih fell from his horse. Bhathric had descended from her mount to catch him, and she did. She held him in her arms as a parent cuddled a newborn babe. Tears streamed down her face as she clutched his head to her chest.

She laid him gently on the ground and stood, turning toward the necromancer. Her blade drawn from its sheath, she began in the creature's direction. Uldyr brought his steed into her path.

"Bhathric!" he called.

"*I must!*" Her voice sounded thick.

The sequence felt as a dream to Athenne, as though she had drifted from her body and watched the events unfold around her.

Her eyes ambled across the faces of the few remaining. Horror, confusion, shock, dismay, anger; an array of emotions so varied, and so much the same. Odd detachment embodied her own feeling.

Her sight rested on Aitrix, who appeared bewildered.

The world moved as if slowed by an unnatural energy.

"We are going to die here," Aitrix said. "We cannot defeat a necromancer." Before any of them had time to react, Aitrix signed a relocation spell and vanished, in defiance of the limitations of her lunar tears, which burst into rays of showering orange light as she disappeared, sprinkling to the ground as smoldering embers from a hearth. She had abandoned them. Betrayed them.

The necromancer released a noise like a thousand voices.

Athenne felt nauseated.

Reanimates swarmed them, and the chevaliers fought with great urgency, as did the rest of them. In the lingering fog and night, Athenne could hardly make out who clashed for which side, for the felled paladins from their host reanimated almost as quickly as they dropped. Those left alive stormed over the field in a furious current.

As the chevaliers came across the cobblestones of Imbredon, the reanimates scattered them like clouds of disturbed dust. Feet from Athenne, one reanimate drew back a poleaxe, and with precision, struck a paladin between her helm, mail, and cuirass. The power of the weapon's cleave swept her head from her shoulders. Her body crumpled to the ground.

Athenne gasped. The reanimate clamored in its animalistic howl, driven toward her at a run until Sangrey destroyed it with a bolt of fire. Their eyes crossed, and Sangrey pivoted away.

The chevaliers perished one after another.

Uldyr came around to her. "I shall not let you die." He raised his steel and slashed at any reanimates that neared. With damage to their brains, the risen seemed to lose their strength. Bits and gruesome chunks of skull and meaty innards, rotten and fresh, sprayed around them.

The horde of reanimates backed away again and circled them, facing in at every angle.

They were in the eye of it; a ghastly, hateful tempest.

"What do we do?" Bhathric asked.

With a few more sweeping blows and stabbing thrusts, the reanimates overcame the last of the living paladins. Not long after they fell, they raised anew, and joined in the surrounding rows.

Uldyr turned to her. "Athenne—"

Out of the darkness hurled a javelin. The tip of it burst through Uldyr's face, drenching Athenne in his blood, teeth, and flesh. Exiting through his mouth, tongue split asunder, the point pulled him toward the ground.

As Uldyr plunged from his saddle, Athenne did not scream as Bhathric had when Eclih struck the stones. She hardly moved or breathed. The world around her dissolved for that moment, however long it lasted.

She did not wrench her face from his body, lying prone in undignified death. Terror struck, numbed, arrested her. She felt voided. A sound escaped her lips, some noise like a whimper.

This is not real.

A javelin flew past her head, so close it ripped the edges of her hair, but she did not react.

Bhathric took her face in her hands and spoke, a muffled blur of slurring words she did not comprehend.

Athenne had lost her horse, but when? She did not know.

She did not weep, though tears fell from her eyes and rolled over Bhathric's fingers.

Bhathric pulled her nearer. "*Athenne!*" she heard her say. Athenne strained to listen, with all of her concentration, striving for clarity in the swirling chaos. "*We have to fight, Athenne!*" Bhathric cried.

Athenne felt herself falling, but Bhathric kept her upright. She wanted to draw away and let the horde devour her. Uldyr had died, her truest friend. She could not go on without him. A crippling lament and fatigue gripped her. Her life had no further purpose. She had surrendered it long ago.

Bhathric released her. "She's no use!"

The archbishops looked from Bhathric to Athenne.

Athenne watched the mass, who did not approach, but continued spinning around them. She looked to the necromancer, who stood beyond the circling figures. Its puppets.

Why does it wait?

Why does it not kill us now?

A light erupted.

Athenne masked her face in reflex.

Mallum had unleashed a powerful spell and annihilated many of the reanimates, dispersing portions of their bodies in bloody shreds and tattered chunks. The pungency singed Athenne's nostrils.

Dred cast a barrier around them next. "This will not hold for long!" Expanding, the shimmering dome of white energy, pure

Aether made visible, turned a few of the ensorcelled corpses to ash in violent, shrieking explosions.

"We must retreat." Sangrey indicated for them to draw toward the center of the barrier.

Athenne and Bhathric made their way, regarding Uldyr and Eclih with a sense of finality.

Bhathric no doubt reeled as she did, but managed to handle it with greater strength.

They admired one another, Bhathric's eyes glistening in the soft light of the sphere, Athenne's face deadpan and undoubtedly pale. She was surprised she had not yet collapsed.

Will they take us with them, or leave us to die?

She imagined the archbishops would depart without them. Their shield would fall. The reanimates would converge, rip them apart. They would perish, and after, travel to Eophianon for their bout of eternal torment, or be reborn as a share of the Undeath; this carrying, malevolent force like a wave.

The ichor that swallows the world.

Sangrey incanted, her eyes half shut.

The air and sky, the world around Athenne, had become foreign. Her beating heart, she felt, and yet it did not seem as hers. She clutched her chest, heavy with severance, separation, isolation. With the dread of abandonment, she scanned the glowing eyes of the dead, burning like stars against the darkness. Nothing to hope for remained but the swiftest release.

Our Mother shall have no place for me. That is my fate.

If Athenne had any spirit left, it expired in her that instant. She had erred, in all that she had done. Tired of embracing, reflecting, thinking of the past, she drowned in the misery of it. *Mother, please take me. Pull me from this wicked shell. I am feeble, weak, rancid to the core. My heart collapses. Take me, or throw me away!*

Sangrey's spell erupted, and she lost all sight, only for light to rush in soon after.

They were elsewhere, a place open to the air. Hundreds of seats surrounded a central dais. Behind the platform sat a throne with a desk in front of it, numerous candlesticks at its sides. Even in her daze and stupor, she recognized this location, though she had never seen it herself. They had arrived at the Iron Court in the Imperial Palace.

Still half-absent, she examined the area. All four of the archbishops had survived, as had the knight captain and Bhathric. They had left the bodies of Uldyr and Eclih behind.

Athenne turned toward Sangrey, still on her horse. "Why?"

Sangrey wiped blood from her nose. "Why, what?"

"Why save us?" Athenne's voice crept, breathy and frail.

"To have left you to such a miserable fate at the hands of underlings of the God of the Dead would have been a grave injustice against daughters of the All-Mother. Misguided as you are, I am not so cruel."

She wished she had a moment with Uldyr to say farewell. The sole memory at the fore of her mind was the gruesome image of the javelin exploding through his face. He had gone forever. She wandered alone in the world again. A closeness and kinship denied her for most of her life, dissolved in an instant.

Athenne looked away from Sangrey without further acknowledgment. She wanted to weep and grieve and mourn their losses, but she could not. She felt hollowed, ashamed that she had lived, and more so, a broiling hatred for Aitrix, who had ruined her, fractured all of them, and left without a trace.

Aitrix could have taken them with her, yet she had deserted them. A flurry of emotions ripped through Athenne, then dissipated. She fell beyond them, deprived of lasting sensation.

Gazing up to the dark sky, she scoured the moons, the stars, the rings. She imagined herself in a field somewhere, the cool breeze washing over her. Her mind envisioned Uldyr at her side, and Bhathric and Eclih, talking, laughing, reminiscing, away from Aitrix and her machinations and self-interested schemes.

Athenne wished she could feel more. She had thrown away her life, and she had gotten what she deserved. Even so, one feeling, one thought, simmered beneath the surface.

She saw her younger self. Bright, kind, filled with joy. Running through woodlands and streams, at peace with nature, overflowing with potential. Unsullied, unmarked, worthy as any girl had been. Ambitious, loving, hopeful. Gone too soon, before her time. So much lost, so quickly, to lead her to this place.

What could have been.

CHAPTER XXII: OVERCAST

Amun

"Our losses were nontrivial," Archbishop Sangrey said, countenance still sallow after the mass relocation spell. "Over one-thousand chevaliers, felled. The Magister Adra Erin, vanished. Aitrix Kravae, escaped."

The Vicar scoffed. "How did she escape?"

"We underestimated her."

The members of the Ennead sat, considering the air.

Amun kept her eyes down, her quill, paper, and ink readied.

This ought to be the work of machines. Recounting would be well-suited to them.

Unbeknownst to the Ennead, Amun had seen it all. She had traveled on the outskirts of the host, beyond sight, even taking a few times from their supplies. Their capital had been in such a frenzy that no one had noticed her missing. The Ennead had held no official meetings in the chamber.

Exhausted by her journey, she had taken a bath so hot it reddened her skin when she returned.

A muted discussion between the archbishops went on for some time, audible enough for her to hear and transcribe, but not without minor difficulty. She kept quiet as she always had. On a few occasions, the Archbishop Delacroix glanced over at her, causing Amun's chest to tense.

"You ought to have let those women die."

Sangrey waved her hand. "Vicar, you are not in command of this body. You are a voice by elect. I need not explain my decision to you, but if I must, I shall do so simply. If you saw what we have, the monstrous storm which approaches this city, creeps across the land like a plague, you would have saved them." She stood. "These young women, still daughters of our blessed Mother, I remind you, fought valiantly, lost individuals they cared for, and did not attempt to flee. The one, Athenne, did not kill in their attack on the city. They were subordinates to Kravae, and nothing more. We have lost our way if we should hand them over to the God of the Dead."

"I concur with Sangrey," Archbishop Dred interjected, unusual for her. "I would resign my station this instant if we had left another spirit to Korvaras. Our duty is to save and protect, to maintain order and promote progress, not to enact vengeance or cruelty. We've done too much of these, already. The women are outlaws. They have done harm. 'Tis for Gohheia and Kismet to decide their fates in death, not for the Patron of the Dead or his minions to trap them in a state of suspension between. Our foremothers would shudder."

An image rolled in Amun's mind, that legion of horrors, countless as the stars in the sky, torn and tattered, a terror in the night. She had watched from afar, but still too near. They had once been people, like she and they, dressed in jerkins and tunics and trousers, in gowns and mails and plate and thick jackets and pauldrons, boots, and braces. They carried weapons, if they had the limbs for it.

There had been no animals, beyond the churning mass of mortals, human and fair folk alike. A company of jittering, taunting cadavers, all shrieking in the same odious tongue, descended on the host in the mist, death made flesh. They were death. Screaming and cackling and hissing, cloaked in the veil of white that must have been denser the closer one stood, for Amun had perceived more than the Ennead described this day from her high point in the distance. The dead had appeared as if they were always there, waiting.

"Those that they killed, these terrorists, deserve to be avenged." Bitterness shadowed the Vicar's words. "Have we forgotten Father Garron Latimer, the innocent deacons, the child of Archbishop Crane? Kravae fled. They stayed because they could not. There must be retribution, else we confess we were too weak—"

"Vicar," Delacroix interrupted him, "we promised these young women that they would have a sentence of confinement at five ages, half a decade, in the Priory cellars, should they attend the host and face the Undeath. They did so. Two of their allies perished in the battle. Their leader betrayed them and left them to die. If we renege on our word, we invite chaos into our declarations. We shall sustain our end of the deal and uphold order, or have you forgotten that there are *three* pillars in our keep?"

"They knew with whom they consorted when they sided with Aitrix Kravae. Kravae is a dangerous ideologue, a devious craven with little regard for the lives of others, and even less for the will and want of the All-Mother." He turned to Archbishop Crane. "Aris, these fiends murdered your daughter. What say you?"

Amun glanced around the room. *Am I still meant to record?*

Crane looked reflective. "We promised them five ages, and after, they may go free. We swore them and those who descend from them exile in perpetuity. That is enough."

With displeasure, the Vicar succumbed. "All in favor?"

"Aye," they answered together, finalizing the conviction.

As the members of the Ennead filtered out, Delacroix lingered behind. Amun suspected she wanted to speak to her, but she had a question of her own.

"Archbishop, may I have a moment?" she asked.

"You may."

"I would like to visit the women in the cellar."

"For?"

"I want to speak to them of the Mother's Truth."

The Archbishop gave a half-smile. "Ever dutiful. I'll let the inquisitors and others know."

"Thank you, Archbishop."

"My pleasure."

Amun turned to leave, but Delacroix addressed her once more: "Sister Halleck."

She stopped. "Archbishop?"

"It has been a while since I've seen you."

"I was—" Her words trailed off. "I was spending some time at the house of the dying near the Plaza, Archbishop. Forgive me. I know 'tis above my station."

"Curious."

"Archbishop—"

The Archbishop chuckled through her nose. "No matter."

Delacroix surely knew the truth. If the Archbishop could

overlook her transgression, her unauthorized sneaking after the host, Amun would not press further. She bowed graciously and exited the chamber.

The Priory extended as a dark, grey labyrinth. In a haze, Amun felt at once as though she had no idea where she was going and as if she followed the correct path.

Walking, she thought of the great women and men who had erected this grandiose monstrosity. She passed few, machines more than other deacons or inquisitors. A dream, until she came upon the entrance to the cellars.

At the bottom of the stairs, Amun paused between the two guards, who did not address her. Evidently, Delacroix had somehow sent word of her admission already. One of their prisoners came into view as Amun approached, sat against the bars of her compartment not far from the mouth of the space.

The woman saw her, and turned.

"Forgive me, Sister—" Their captive did not appear to know her name, merely her title.

"Amun Halleck, and you are Athenne Zedd."

"Forgive me, Sister Halleck." The woman grasped the bars of her cell. "I am not in a proper frame of mind." Her lids fluttered, the blue orbs beneath them bloodshot, veined in red and glistening pink.

"Your mind pays for your wrongdoing."

"I know." The prisoner called Athenne peered at Amun through tired eyes, ringed in black and purple, likely from lack of restful sleep. "Will She have me?"

"Whom?"

"The Mother."

Amun examined her face at length. Her own coquelicot irises no doubt ominously aglow in the dim torch light. Humans called the elven gaze the *bloodlit stare* for its innate menace.

The question drove the air from Amun's lungs as she contemplated her response. This woman sat helpless. Amun did not wish to confirm her grief, yet she would not lie. "I cannot say," she answered. "You have time, and the opportunity in five ages. Devote your life to embodying the three pillars of the Matrian Truth on Earth, as our Mother in the Celestia, and you may be saved in eternal rest."

In a shallow, defeated way, the woman inhaled.

Amun clasped her hand on the bar. "I pray She may forgive you." She tried to sound reassuring. "Have you ever heard the tale of Athenne the Good?"

"She was an archbishop, Saint Athenne." Their captive's head lifted. "I was named for her."

Amun smiled. "In her later life, she was a woman of profound scholarship. She went about the common body long before any who stand now, expounding the Word of the Mother, Her *Blest Writ*, to the people, young and eldered. It was not in this piety that she upheld the three pillars, but in the devotion of her life to good works. She declared her desires openly, made the knowledge plain and simple, for anyone's understanding.

"Unlike others of her time, she did not delegate the task of spreading Scripture to her lessers, but took it upon herself." Amun withdrew her hand from the woman's. "My point is not that you ought to preach Scripture, but that she is seen as a saint in the present for her devotion to good-doing. Good deeds cannot undo bad, but the bad do not negate the good. While we cannot say for certain what leads us to Nihil, 'tis said that the wayward daughter, lost in a sea of despair and darkness, may find her path to shore, by the Mother's light."

"Did you know the man we killed?" the one called Athenne asked abruptly. "The priest?"

Amun's throat tightened. "I did."

"Well?"

"Well."

"Was he a good man?"

Amun dropped her head once in affirmation.

"We saw him commit a terrible crime against a woman. That's why we chose him for it."

"How?"

"At a Matronian temple. Knights of Faith there informed us that he was sick, marked to die. Where we killed him was around the location of his crime."

"His name was Father Garron Latimer," Amun said. "A creature of Korvaras that he referred to as the Beast cursed him. Under its influence, he committed a crime. I spoke to his victim. He did not harm her of his own want. 'Twas he who asked me to tend to her well-being, if I could."

The woman's eyes darted about. "He was compelled?"

"Father Latimer devoted his life to good-doings." Amun swallowed, staving off tears. "What the Beast forced him to do tormented him so that I suspect he may've taken his own life, if you hadn't murdered him."

Tense silence fell, longer than sorrow alone could occasion.

"I am sorry." Their prisoner broke the unease, her focus to the floor, her voice deep with contrition. "I hope you may forgive me for what I've done."

"Forgiveness is not pardoning, and mine is not the indulgence you ought to seek." Amun pointed upward. "Only the mercy of One matters. None but She may absolve us from our wickedness and relieve us of our wrongs."

"I know," the woman named Athenne replied.

Amun stood from her seat. "I must be off."

"Will you return?"

Their gazes met.

"I suspect not."

"Before you go," the woman said, "I have a confession, if this may be my sole opportunity to speak to anyone with regard for what I have to say." She collected herself in a pause, then went on. "As a girl, I committed a terrible act." Her voice trembled. "I suppose I had no right to judge the priest worth dying." A tear spilled down her cheek. "I grew up in Orilon. I won't trouble you with the details, but I—I killed another girl in anger. At the time, I thought it just for something she had done to me. I did not intend to slay her, only to teach her a lesson. I left her body in a river. No one ever found her."

Amun said nothing.

"I have felt for much of my life since, that I did not deserve—" Her words broke off. She inhaled and exhaled, sniffled, on the verge of weeping. "—I did not deserve the Mother's love."

"Have you told anyone else of this?"

"*Her*," she answered, "in my prayers."

Amun's brow knitted together. "Athenne, our Mother sees the truth of your heart. All of Her children are deserving of Her love, no matter their faults."

Athenne cried and then responded with contrived composure, at a shore of gasping. "I joined the Saints because I felt purposeless and helpless. If I could go back—" She released a quaking exhalation and wiped tears from her cheeks, pulling hair back from her face.

"I believe that you are not a bad person," Amun said.

As if to thank her, Athenne nodded.

Amun would not visit the other woman. Instead, without another word, she walked away, between the cellar rows, and to the staircase. She ascended the steps until she arrived at the hall, closing the door behind her.

There was but one place that she wanted to be.

Outside, nature had allotted this day a dismal atmosphere. A curdling sky of clouds rolled overhead, like the foaming waves of an angry sea, battering against the jagged rocks of a craggy cliff; except, this ocean extended beyond the horizon, beyond seeing and the upward ends of the world.

Where Amun had come, stone pillars and bricks of black and grey stood uniform, encircled by high, elven-wrought iron fencing in the shape of a diamond, with four gates at each side. She walked the rows of new and crumbling mounds of marble and granite, scanning their varied inscriptions and flowering laments. At the northwest corner of the yard, she halted. Gnarled trees surrounded a stone there, singular and fresh in its placement, bathed in the watery light of the Mother's Eye, which hovered behind its veil above, casting timid shadows.

This afternoon, there was no wind, only far-off bells, a ritual of collective mourning for the city in the wake of its recent hardships and defeats. Their noise reverberated against the faces of the trees and the stones, in deep notes of grief and loss. She idled among the bodies of the many loved, somewhere, at some time, who had returned to the Father Earth; their spirits, she hoped, dissolved into their forever peace.

The world stood in suspension, frozen for her and for him, and the rest of them. A calmness attended the moment, and unrest. She had no words to say, but filled with passions and reeling. Uncertainty shadowed what came next, yet whatever the ambiguity, she had found her place of belonging. The Ennead would do as they saw fit. Their Vicar, in particular. She would carry forth, in grief, in fury, in love, toward wisdom, hope, understanding, and a reckoning as none before.

Her eyes danced to a rest on his name. She heard the song of his voice as if he stood there beside her. Her memories would maintain him, that deep reverence and admiration and short-lived kinship. Along with the ages of his life, the runic script of the gravestone read:

The Clergy of Gohheia raised this marker in memory of the good Father Garron Latimer, who served dutifully and well his Church and All-Mother

These delicate instants of remembrance would be their lasting bond. He no longer existed here, not in the tangible sense, but he remained within her, stirring, as did the countless others whom they had lost. His work had made her its creation, rooted deep in her mind, ineluctable and driving.

There was a great deal that they did not know and much more for her to learn and to become. She had resolved, for herself, that their path no longer held true, that they failed to act in the Mother's interest. The Undeath that had risen in the south would come, in time. Whether they could defeat it, she did not know.

Even so, she did not feel frightened. From her hair, she drew a single white lily, and placed it atop his grave. The sun broke through the clouds and fell upon her face, and warmed her to her core. In the distance, the bells continued to ring, persistent and unyielding, as she was, ever more.

Her gaze set on high, she prayed.

The End

*(*To be continued in Book Two: The Ember Reach)*

**Dear Athenne will not return until Book Four: The Vile God.*

APPENDIX

THE NATIONS of IMIOS /ihm-ee-ohss/

The Sacred Empire
—first nation, formally established in Age 1
——capital: Aros
Kingdom of Abbisad /abb-uh-sahd/
—second nation, gained independence in Age 51
——capital: Almiraaya
Republic of Xarakas /zerr-ahk-uss/
—third nation, gained independence in Age 235
——capital: Xarakei
Kingdom of Beihan /bai-hahn/
—fourth nation, gained independence in Age 364
——capital: Jianjing
Kingdom of Reneris /ren-ehr-uss/
—fifth nation, gained independence in Age 440
——capital: Renbourg

NOTABLE LOCATIONS (SACRED EMPIRE)

Aros /ahr-ohss/: the Imperial City, largest city in the Empire
Laorta /laye-orr-tahh/: second largest Imperial city
Kordyr /kohr-deer/: third largest city
Imbredon /imm-bree-dohn/: fourth largest city
Erlan /uhr-lahn/: small southern village
Ghora /gohr-uhh/: another small village in the south
Ostland /ohst-lund/: modest southern village
Arkala /arr-khal-uhh/: village southwest of the Black Canal
Abela /uh-bell-uhh/: majestic village in the east
Soignan /soh-nahn/: modest village in the northeast
Fausse Woods /fowse/: largest Imperial woodlands, bordering Beihan
Arnlan Forest /ahrn-lahn/: second largest forest in the Empire
Ventlan Marsh /vehnt-lahn/: modest swamp in the west
Outmore Loch /owt-mohr lawk/: large lake in the northwest

THE FIRST GODS (CELESTIAL NINE)

Gohheia /goe-hie-uhh/: All-Mother, Mother, Mother God, Queen of the Overrealm
—aspects: Creation, Destruction, and Being
Epaphael /epp-uh-fye-ell/: Otherkind Mater, Malformant, Kismet
—aspects: Time, Destiny, and Damnation
Asdamos /azz-dahm-ohss/: It, He, Lord of the Lost
—aspects: Dimensions and Space
Vekshia /vehk-shie-uhh/: Matron, Patron of None
—aspects: Hope and Despair
Lahrael /lahr-ai-ell/: [no sobriquets]
—aspects: Wisdom and Greed
Isanot /ee-sah-noht/: Abhorrer, Amor, King of the Tower
—aspects: Love, Hate, and Passion
Sitix /see-tiks/: Father Earth, Father Nature, Preserver, Wooded One
—aspects: Nature, Calamity, and Matter
Vysyn /vai-sin/: [no sobriquets]
—aspects: Energy, Fire, and Winter
Korvaras /kohr-vahr-uhss/: Patron of the Undead, God of Death, Lord of the Dead
—aspects: Death and Life

THE MATRIAN CHURCH (THE CLERGY)

Breiman Umbra /bray-muhn umm-bruh/: an Archbishop Premier of the Ennead; the Vicar of Gohheia or Sovereign Father; first man to hold the title

—other members of the Ennead, Archbishop Premiers:

——Aramanth Delacroix /ahr-uh-mahnth dey-lah-croe/

——Camille Sangrey /cam-eel sahn-grae/

——Holle Mallum /hel-lah mal-umm/

——Aris Crane /ahr-iss krane/

——Bardot Dred /bahr-doe drehd/

——Morena Hart /mohr-enn-ah hart/

——Zaria Tornaeu /zahr-ee-ahh tohr-nay-oo/

——Serafina Mortem /sare-ah-phee-nah mohr-tuhm/

Garron Latimer /gare-ohn lah-tih-muhr/: attendant priest of Erlan

—Amun Halleck /ae-muhn hal-ekk/: a first-degree deacon, substitute scribe officiate

The SAINTS of AETHERIA

Aitrix Kravae /ae-uh-triks kruh-vae/: leader of the Saints of Aetheria

Athenne Zedd /ah-theen zehd/

—Uldyr Friala /uhl-deer phree-ahl-uh/

—Bhathric Ezeis /bath-rikk ezz-eez/

—Eclih Phredran /ekk-lee phree-druhn/

OTHER CHARACTERS PRESENTED or NAMED

Abbessa Alamanor /abb-ehs-uhh ahl-uh-mahn-ohr/: heathen chronicler

Adelheid Valiana /add-uhl-haid vall-ee-ahn-nah/: the first Matriarch

Adra Erin /ae-druhh ehr-ihn/: a magister who wears a mask of plagues

Aefethla /ae-feh-thuh-luhh/: vanished young girl of Erlan

Aeyana Thelles /ae-yah-nuh thehl-uhhs/: combat philosophy instructor, of Orilon

Ailuin Sangrey /ae-lew-ihn sahn-grae/: Camille Sangrey's world mother; a former magus, once head of the Academy of Metaphysics

Aliester Haldis /ahl-uh-sturr hahl-dess/: slain Forgebrand mercenary, called The Red

Alina /ahl-ee-naa/: deceased young girl of Erlan

Ankhev /ahn-khehv/: Great Dragon, the White; Incarnation or Second God under Gohheia

Aros /ahr-ohss/: the Undermother and First Woman

Arulan /arr-uhh-lahn/: the Beast

Athos /ahth-ohss/: Uldyr's horse

Barielle /barr-ee-ehl/: young elven girl of Laorta [Special Edition Print]

Besogos /beh-soh-gohs/: the famous Archmage Besogos; also the former surname of Aitrix Kravae

Demetria Victoire /duh-mee-tree-uhh vik-tohr-ee/: citizen of Aros

Diomira /dee-oh-meer-uhh/: the Imperatrix of the Republix of Xarakas

Elas Orimalor /ell-ahs ohr-mah-lohr/: chronicler

Ellia /ehl-ee-uhh/: inquisitor, field officer, of Laorta [Special Edition Print]

Emmelina Avelane /emm-uhh-lee-naa ahv-uh-lain/: slain inquisitor, field officer, of Erlan

Ennaletes /enn-uhh-laye-teez/: a daughter of Isanot, second legion demon; vassal of Vekshia

Errendon Sangrey /ehr-uhn-dunn sahn-grae/: world father of Camille Sangrey

Estatha Khraemine /eh-stah-thuh kraye-mine/: the Archmagister, head of the Theurgy

Fausta Haltan /fows-tuh hahl-tunn/: a doctor, former women's and elven health specialist, general practitioner; present Imperial medical examiner and talk therapist; eldest heir of the family Haltan; daughter of Lady Soras Haltan

Helies Kallata IV /hell-ee-uhss kehl-ah-tuhh/: the Emperor or Imperial Sovereign

Helotta Bashek /hehl-oht-uhh bash-ekk/: chevalier, knight captain

Ikkath /ick-ahth/: leader of Forgebrand; diavora

Janren /jahn-rinn/: inquisitor, field officer, of Laorta [Special Edition Print]

Kamia /kah-mee-uhh/: member of the Saints of Aetheria

Katya Irrelin /kaht-ee-ahh ihr-ell-ahn/: sickly woman in a house of the dying

Kocia Arellano /koh-shie-ah arr-eh-lah-knoh/: an executed Mythosian priest

Lasson /lah-sohn/: a daughter of Isanot, first order angel, current Incarnation or Second God under Isanot

Luscia /lew-shuhh/: a doctor of Laorta, substitute medical examiner [Special Edition Print]

Maxima Ayleth /max-uhh-mah ae-lehth/: a bishop

Mia Kreighton /mee-uhh kraye-tuhn/: a magus or preceptor of Anukara's Institute of the Material Arts

Mirea Athelys /meer-ee-ahh ath-ell-eez/: inquisitor, field officer, of Ghora

Rennera Bhojith /renn-her-uhh boh-jihth/: a writer of historical fiction

Rivana Fausse /rih-vah-nah fowse/: a mage decried as a witch; namesake of the Fausse Woods; also called the White Lotus Witch

Ruhlter /rull-turr/: an imp; Incarnation or Second God under Vekshia

Shah /shaa/: Athenne's horse

Taerem /taye-rem/: a nature spirit; Incarnation or Second God under Sitix

Thalla Aenor /thahl-uhh ae-knohr/: the Grand Provost

Ulraut /uhl-raht/: a mountain beast; Incarnation or Second God under Vysyn

Valhrenna Thrall /vahl-ren-ahh thrahl/: an executed Mythosian witch

Viessa Birieth /vee-ehs-uhh beer-ee-ehth/: a second-degree deacon, scribe officiate

Virya /veer-ee-uhh/: inquisitor, field officer, of Laorta [Special Edition Print]

Vor-Kaal /vohr-khal/: Keeper of Death; Incarnation or Second God under Korvaras

Xiressa Venlee /zeer-ehss-ahh venn-lee/: chronicler

MISCELLANEOUS ITEMS

Anukara /ann-uh-karr-uhh/: Anukara's Institute of the Material Arts, the foremost Institute of Erudition or school of magic in the Sacred Empire, located in Aros

Arrilios /ahr-ill-ee-ohs/: fourth month of the year

Braxany /brax-uhh-nee/: the Braxany Institute of Magic, in Aros

Diavora /dee-ah-vohr-uhh/: half-dragon, half-human beings

Enon /ee-non/: one of the four moons

Eophianon /ee-ohh-fee-ann-uhn/: Korvaras's celestial plane in the Overrealm; also called the Blackened Yonder or the Land of the Dead

Fevarios /fuh-varr-ee-ohs/: second month of the year

Hallion /hal-ee-uhn/: named for Devia Hallion, the materialist scholar who invented Hallion Oats, the enchanted horse feed; also called Scarlet Oats

Hecos /heh-kohs/: another of the four moons

Hessant /hehs-ant/: magical woodland creatures; namesake of the Hessantwood in Reneris

Idoss /eye-dohs/: a historical, religious, sociopolitical festival celebrated across the Sacred Empire, from Protas I to Matrios XXIX of Senterios; established in Age 12 by the first Matriarch, Adelheid Valiana

Indervorg /inn-durr-vorg/: fish-like swamp beasts

Khor Dohaid /kore doh-haed/: fourth largest city of Abbisad

Lerenios /luh-rinn-ee-ohs/: sixth month of the year

Minaris /mehn-arr-uss/: another of the four moons

Nihil /nie-hill/: the grave or eternal sleep; also called the Nothing

Nimphre /nim-free/

Orilon /ohr-ih-lohn/: second largest city of Reneris

Senas /see-nuss/: another of the four moons

Senterios /sin-tare-ee-ohs/: final month of each age

Thralkeld /thrahl-kehld/: third largest city of Reneris, de facto capital city of elves

Vreosiqar /vree-ohh-sih-karr/: Gohheia's celestial plane in the Overrealm; also called the Golden Plane

*Double letters in the appendix represent long or stressed sounds.

ACKNOWLEDGMENTS

If there is any fault with this book, it is due to my own shortcomings as a writer rather than those that I, with great pleasure, am going to recognize here for their contributions to this project since its inception.

Firstly, my editor, *Mark Antiporda*, one of the smartest people I know (we could say *the* smartest, but we don't want to overinflate his ego), has been an indispensable source of clever guidance, critical feedback, and sound judgment over the years. Without his labors and observations, as well as his wide-ranging input on the setting, I may not have had the confidence to release this book at all. He talked me out of a number of bad ideas.

I must also thank early readers of my manuscript:

Catherine Thomas, who provided detailed in-document notes throughout the text, as well as a dedicated file summarizing their thoughts on the work, including its concepts, symbols, representations, and themes.

Mariam Naeem, who sent multiple pages of feedback on my primary and secondary characters and the book's overall plot progression. Her commentary helped contextualize how I depicted numerous elements of the story.

Duffi Jo Clements, who offered extensive replies on the book, particularly regarding the early and middle sections. She aided me in understanding whether I was succeeding or failing in conveying what I intended.

Amelia Littlejohn, who gave me vital positive encouragement and fairly assessed the early chapters.

Sarah Potter, who nearly caused me to redo a large share of the book after her evaluations confirmed some of the analyses of other readers (but everyone talked me out of that, and I adjusted what I had instead).

The significant assistance of those above, along with others who read various excerpts and sections of the manuscript across multiple revisions, not only helped me write and rewrite, but resulted in entirely new scenes and complex alterations of the existing narrative. I hope that I am able to do justice to the individuals who have volunteered their valuable time and energy for the end of aiding me in improving my work.

Thank you, everyone, for all that you have done!

ABOUT THE AUTHOR

J. Gibson is a published researcher in the field of criminal justice with a concentration on gender differences. Holding degrees related to criminology, sociology, and psychology, his primary interest is academia, but he has always had a passion for creative writing and the genres of horror and fantasy, as well as history.

The Planar Lost universe is his effort at merging his interests into something that others might want to read.

jgibsonwrites.com
@PlanarLost

Subscribe to the newsletter at the link above to keep up with releases, discounts, reviews, news, and more.

Remember to leave a review wherever this book is sold!

Made in the USA
Columbia, SC
28 October 2024